BEAR

"A funny, poignant, romantic exploration of mental health and of the way love can help us heal. Katie Shepard has a unique talent for mixing gentle humor, weighty topics, and swoony moments. You will fall in love with Darcy and Teagan on page one, and you will laugh and cry and cheer as they discover themselves and each other. A perfect, dazzling debut."

—Ali Hazelwood, #1 *New York Times* bestselling author of *Bride*

"I didn't even have to play dead, because this book already killed me. Shepard's nuanced wit and vibrant prose sparkle off the page. Readers will go wild for this sexy and heartfelt romance between two unforgettable characters as they help each other make it out of the woods of life."

—Thea Guanzon, *New York Times* bestselling author of
A Monsoon Rising

"Angsty, swoony, sharply written, and full of heart, *Bear with Me Now* is a deeply compassionate romance about finding love in the midst of profound struggles and vulnerabilities [and] discovering the gift of entrusting all of yourself to a worthy someone to love and be loved by in return."

—Chloe Liese, author of *Once Smitten, Twice Shy*

tear up the next. . . . A powerful and sweet love story, sprinkled with hilarious jokes and winks at fandom culture."

—Sarah Hawley, *USA Today* bestselling author of *Princess of Blood*

"A gorgeous, heartwarming look at love and second chances, and an unforgettable story about family (both the ones we're born into and the kinds we make for ourselves). It's full of both laugh-out-loud moments and scenes that made me cry, with the sort of prose you want to savor forever."

—Jenna Levine, *USA Today* bestselling author of *Road Trip with a Vampire*

"The coziness of small-town meets the yearning of second-chance in *No One Does It Like You*. Shepard brilliantly stirs together the comedy of fandom personalities and the creativity of an HGTV show into a swoony love story full of lovable characters."

—Julie Soto, *USA Today* bestselling author of *Rose in Chains*

THE
YOUNGER
GODS

Katie Shepard

ACE
NEW YORK

ACE
Published by Berkley
An imprint of Penguin Random House LLC
1745 Broadway, New York, NY 10019
penguinrandomhouse.com

Book design by Alison Cnockaert

Library of Congress Cataloging-in-Publication Data

Names: Shepard, Katie, author.
Title: The younger gods / Katie Shepard.
Description: First edition. | New York : Ace, 2026.
Identifiers: LCCN 2025008937 (print) | LCCN 2025008938 (ebook) |
ISBN 9780593819166 (trade paperback) | ISBN 9780593819173 (ebook)
Subjects: LCGFT: Fantasy fiction. | Romance fiction. | Novels.
Classification: LCC PS3619.H45425 Y68 2026 (print) | LCC PS3619.H45425 (ebook) |
DDC 813/.6—dc23/eng/20250227
LC record available at https://lccn.loc.gov/2025008937
LC ebook record available at https://lccn.loc.gov/2025008938

First Edition: January 2026

Printed in the United States of America
1st Printing

The authorized representative in the EU for product safety and compliance is
Penguin Random House Ireland, Morrison Chambers, 32 Nassau Street,
Dublin D02 YH68, Ireland, https://eu-contact.penguin.ie.

For my mother, who bought me so many books

58. To Eros

incense—aromatic herbs

I call upon you, great, pure, lovely and sweet Eros,
Winged archer who runs swiftly on a path of fire,
Who plays together with gods and mortal men.

—*The Orphic Hymns*, translation by
Apostolos N. Athanassakis and Benjamin M. Wolkow, 2013

Selected Members of the Pantheon and Their Cults

THE ALLMOTHER—the Mountain. Ultimate ancestor of all immortals. Laws, the Earth. The *mountain-priests*.

DIOPATER—the Skyfather. Weather, agriculture, the nobility. The *sky-priests*.

GENNA—the Peace-Queen, Queen of Heaven. Healing, bureaucracy, fertility. The *peace-priests*.

LIXNEA—the Moon. Creative arts, dreams, secrets. The *moon-priests*.

MARIT—the Waverider. The ocean, fishermen, potters, glass-workers, drunks. The *sea-priests*.

NAPETH—Death. Fire, the Underworld, sacrifice. The *death-priests*.

SMENOS—the Shipwright. Craftsmen, scholars. The *crafter-priests*.

WESHA—the Maiden. Dawn, surgery, childbirth, children. The *maiden-priests*.

WIRREA—the Huntress. Hunting, wild animals. The *hunt-priests*.

1

F OR THREE YEARS, the god of death tried to kill me. Death collapsed the high temple at Ereban, and I crawled alive from the rubble. He massacred every other maiden-priest, and I survived to begin the rebellion against him. I ran faster than the mudslide that crushed the capital last year, and I quenched so many wildfires that my nightmares stank of woodsmoke, and I survived battles and ambushes and assassins and the near destruction of my entire country—and after all that, I nearly died in the stupidest way possible: tripping over my own feet.

In the hills above us, hidden in the lush groves of figs and almonds, death-priests had been singing down their god's fire since dawn to cover the loyalists' advance. As soon as we spotted the attack, the acolytes in the queen's army began singing the same blessing of flame. Setting backfires. At the beginning of the rebellion we sang for rain instead, but we soon learned that Death's fury could consume even the wettest wood, and only starving it of fuel would stop the fire's spread.

Wasn't that ironic? Our strongest weapon against Death was his own blessing. I trained to be a priest of the Maiden for twelve years, but during the rebellion I mostly sang the power of the husband she always despised. I got very good at singing Death's blessing of fire, probably as good as the priests we spent three years fighting.

We had won several battles with the firebreak tactic, and earlier this morning I thought we had trapped the death-priests against the sheer drop to the south where the hills fell into the sea. Over the past hour though, something had shifted. Huge columns of black, oily smoke wheeled up to the sky and arrows began to penetrate our firebreak, sending us diving for cover.

I called a retreat, but I wasn't sure that even half of my band of half-trained acolytes heard it. Smoke started blowing into our faces as the wind changed, and our scramble down the cliffs toward the questionable safety of the beach was nearly blind.

Falling, like everything else, was my fault; I didn't look where I was going. I was thinking about the retreat and whether everyone would make it down the cliffs. I was thinking that I should have warned the queen that an orchard in a dry summer was a bad spot to camp, though I hadn't believed there were enough death-priests left alive to call this kind of firestorm. Last week our queen had said the war was nearly over, and I smiled when Taran put a hand on my lower back and told her he was looking forward to planning our wedding.

In my rush to escape the inferno, I caught my heel between two rocks, and I stumbled and skidded toward the edge of the trail. A lightning bolt of pain shot up my left leg as I flailed for something to stop my slide, hands closing on empty air. The path down the granite cliffs was narrow, and the drop was sixty feet or more, but my feet couldn't find purchase on the dry gravel.

War flattened people. War stole our thoughts and feelings. War frittered away all the righteous fury I started the rebellion with, sealed off terror and regret and anger. When I lost control and nearly went over the edge of the cliff, I was mostly *embarrassed*. How appalling of me to splatter on the ground right in front of

Taran and all the other acolytes! *I'm so sorry, I didn't want you to see me die.*

The noise I made shouldn't have been audible over the sound of exploding trees, but somehow Taran heard it from two paces ahead of me. Before I could be trampled or fall to the narrow strip of beach below, he was there, scooping me up and pulling me against the cliff face.

Perhaps that was why I wasn't more afraid—I knew Taran would catch me.

"You alright, nightingale?" he asked.

"A sprain," I gasped through clenched teeth, clinging to his arms to avoid putting weight on my injured foot, which radiated lances of agony.

The trail was barely wide enough to shuffle down single-file, but Taran didn't hesitate. He dropped a shoulder to lift me against his chest and drape my legs over his forearm. He was very tall, and I was not, but I was occasionally shocked by the strength in his lean body. Clutched to the hard, reassuring plane of his stomach, my descent resumed.

"I can walk—" On one foot, at least. Hop, maybe.

"I've got you," he said.

It seemed impossible that he could carry me and both our packs, even downhill, but he did. I tossed my arms around his neck, seeking his warmth with my cheek. With my eyes closed, I could pretend for a moment that we were both safe. The lurch in my stomach told me we weren't.

When Taran gently set me down on the pebbled beach, I saw our band of former acolytes beginning to regroup. I had known most of them since the day Death began demanding human sacrifice—the day I was supposed to take my vows as one of the Maiden's priests. Their young faces were grim and sooty, but they sighed in relief to see me, even carried in like a small child. I didn't know whether anyone regretted joining me in the disastrous riot that became the rebellion, but as Death hadn't apologized, I hadn't either.

"Did everyone make it?" I panted to Drutalos, a barrel-chested acolyte of the crafter god.

"Not yet," he said anxiously.

Before I could start calling out names, Taran squatted next to me and tried to pull my boot off. I yelped and grabbed for his hand as a fresh bolt of pain burst through me, my vision nearly whiting out when my foot was jostled. It was already beginning to swell.

"Is it broken? You said it was only a sprain," he scolded me.

"Also sprained," I weakly defended myself just to hear the reassuring rumble of Taran's laughter.

The small beach was filling up with soldiers covering our retreat, but I spotted some of my missing acolytes with them. Those who could invoke the curative blessings of Taran's patron goddess were singing their best hasty triage. Taran also hummed under his breath, one melody to open his mind to the extent of the damage to my foot, another to stabilize it. His low, smooth voice barely had to shape the words to send a wave of the Peace-Queen's power through my body and lower the swelling enough to get my boot off. Taran was better at this than anyone else: blessings that took peace-priests a lifetime to master flowed out of him as easy as breathing. I, on the other hand, could barely manage the simplest of those prayers when I was rested and concentrating.

It violated a terrible taboo to invoke the blessings of someone else's patron god, nearly blasphemy. The first time I heard Taran sing one of the Maiden's blessings, I reacted like he'd just desecrated one of her altars. But like so many beliefs that once shaped my world, I'd abandoned that taboo in the interests of survival. I still thought of myself as almost a maiden-priest, but I sang for fire and rain and healing as I needed them. Instead of taking a vow of celibacy, I had Taran's betrothal ring on my finger. Instead of delivering children, I fought to keep Death from sacrificing more.

Sometimes I wished I'd had the chance to know Taran before the war wrote faint sadness into his face, wondered what he'd been like. Peace-priests were sworn to nonviolence, acted as healers and bureaucrats, but Taran also put his knowledge to a very different purpose than he'd probably once intended.

Today, his vivid green eyes were bloodshot enough to turn into chips of glass, and new lines of stress bent his full mouth and thick dark brows, more worrying to me than the line of wildfires at the top of the cliffs.

Taran was unusually beautiful for a man—not just tall and strong, but so remarkably lovely to look at that we all teased him about it. He'd been sleeping on the ground and trudging through the mud like the rest of us, but it touched him less. Exhaustion wouldn't affect his thick eyelashes or the bold lines of his nose and square jaw, but it never even carved shadows into his perfect face. He didn't complain, never faltered, and this wasn't the first time he'd carried someone off a battlefield. But his glance at the cliffs above was worried, and that was different.

"What's wrong?" I whispered. If Taran was worried, the rest of us should probably be gibbering in fear.

"Just realized it's my turn to cook tonight," he said lightly, arranging my unwrapped foot in his lap. I expected him to start healing it, but he cocked his head and went still, his gaze flicking up to the cliffs again. I didn't hear anything new above the roar of the inferno and the calls of the retreating soldiers, nor could I see through the smoke and flame. Taran hesitated though, then stood.

"It's not safe here. We should go farther up the beach."

I opened my mouth to object—we needed to stay close to the injured—but then I did hear something. Yelling.

"Iona! Iona Night-Singer. Where is she?"

Among all the soldiers fleeing down the cliff path was one with the queen's purple standard embroidered along the edge of his tunic.

Taran grabbed for me, but I raised an arm before he could pick me up. I hadn't seen any of the queen's retinue or her small corps of professional soldiers reach the beach yet, and this man looked like a messenger.

The messenger saw my wave and sprinted across the pebbled shore to our group. The rebel acolytes wore nondescript clothing rather than draw fireballs from death-priests, and I was fully covered against cinders and ash, so the queen's man had to duck and peer beneath my hood for my distinctive red hair before he was satisfied that he'd found me.

My broken foot throbbed despite Taran's efforts to stabilize it, but I smoothed my face to reassure the soldier as I took his message.

"We're cut off," he bit out, pointing at the wildfires above. "Half the army. We're trapped between the cliffs and the fire. I was the last one who made it out."

My head jerked up.

"That's impossible," Drutalos objected. "We came in from the west. There was nothing behind us. They can just withdraw the way we came in."

Taran didn't say anything, eyes still on the cliffs. The beach ended in front of us with rock dropping straight into the ocean, and there was only one path down the cliffs, but the army should have been able to retreat to the west.

"It's the fucking god of death himself up there," the messenger said, spit flicking from his lips in his haste. "He's pulling fire out of the Earth. There! On the point."

Every other acolyte had leaned in to listen, and there was a sudden babble of frightened voices.

Death's crimes were the reason for this rebellion, but the last we saw of him was the day he destroyed the temple of all the gods. Death was a coward, one who let his priests and his bestial children fight his battles for him, one who only attacked by surprise. Still, he was also a terrible power, one even the other gods had always appeased rather than opposed.

I followed the line of Taran's gaze and just barely made out a tall figure in golden armor standing on top of the promontory on the opposite side of the trail's terminus. After seeing him in every flame, every funeral, every pang of hunger or hollow cheek, it was almost confusing to see something shaped like a man, though he was as tall as a house, his armor shining like the noonday sun despite the smoke in the air. Death's arms were outstretched as his hands tossed wheeling gusts of fire into the fruit groves.

Taran started shaking his head. Saying *no, keep retreating up the beach*. We'd thought today was just a few loyalists.

This was my fault.

"The queen and half the army are trapped up there," the messenger repeated, eyes wild.

Suddenly I could name it. The breakthrough emotion I felt after numbing myself for months wasn't embarrassment, after all—it was shame. I'd started the rebellion against Death, but how could we defeat a god?

I shouldn't have asked so many people to fight this hopeless war alongside me.

I should have married Taran the day he asked me.

"Everyone, back up the cliff," I said. My words were curiously thick until I realized my teeth were chattering. "Sing the blessing of rain. We'll make a corridor for the army to withdraw."

"What about the god?" one girl asked, her pretty round face pinched and frightened. Hiwa ter Genna. Another acolyte of the Peace-Queen, like Taran. All of sixteen years old.

I licked ash off my lips. Maiden's mercy. I had to send them all back up into that fire, and I didn't know whether I could protect them.

"Taran will heal my foot. And then I'll find out whether the Maiden's blessing of night is stronger than Death's flame," I said, trying to sound like that would be an interesting experiment in theology, rather than suicide. It was the only thing I could think of that might slow Death long enough for the others to escort the army out through the inferno up above. "I'll distract him while you get everyone out to the west."

I turned back to Taran, some tiny part of me hoping he'd thought of a better plan, but he was looking down at my foot, and his face was as pale as mine had to be.

He wrapped a large, strong hand around my ankle, and I waited for him to start the blessing, but he remained silent.

"Taran?" It wasn't like him to freeze.

Everyone looked at him. Waiting for a reprieve.

Instead, he gently tapped my foot with a fingertip.

"The bone is broken here and here," he explained in an oddly distant voice, like we had all the time in the world. "You can't put any weight on it for six weeks or it won't heal right."

"What?" Taran could knit bones with a couple of minutes of chanting. "I can't wait for it to heal. You need to fix it now."

He gave another tiny shake of his head, tangled dark hair falling over his forehead, then stood up and gestured for everyone else to follow. I didn't understand what was happening.

"Like she said," Taran told the others, turning away from me. "Build a corridor until the line of fire breaks. I'll handle Death."

I grunted a rejection and grabbed Hiwa's hand to haul myself to one unsteady foot with her help, balancing between her and Taran. Neither Taran nor I could *handle* Death. We could at most delay him, and I wouldn't risk Taran's life too.

"Hiwa, please," I told the little acolyte, pointing at my ankle.

Taran wasn't the only one who could mend broken bones, just the best at it.

But he stuck out a palm to counter my order.

"*Stop*," he said, his tone harsh and entirely unfamiliar. "You're not going, Iona. You've done enough." My back snapped rigid, and so did the spine of everyone else in earshot. I hadn't heard my name from his lips in years—it was *nightingale, sweetheart, my love*—and I gasped like he'd slapped me.

There was a brief flash of regret on his face, but only for how he'd said it, not that he did.

Starting the first riot against Death was my very thin qualification for leadership, but it was one that had never been challenged before. Taran was the oldest among us, not to mention better at most of the blessings we wielded during the war, but this was the first time he'd ever opposed me in public. The others were as thrown by it as I was, and they weren't sure who to listen to.

"I'll heal it when I get back," he said, softer now. I was shocked again that he thought, after three years, that I couldn't tell when he was lying.

"No. Don't do this," I whispered.

One corner of his mouth pulled to the side in a familiar half smile. I opened my mouth to object again, but he grabbed my chin hard enough to bruise and kissed me with none of his usual finesse, just desperation and a bitter farewell. My lips were chapped and swollen from the fires, making the heat of his mouth more painful than the press of his fingers, and I was crying before his lips left mine.

"You started this war. I'll finish it," he said softly, pressing one more brief kiss to my cheek. His eyes held mine, liquid and intent. "And I'll love you till the stars fall out of the sky."

"I said *no*," I started to babble, throat clenching with horror. I'd contemplated my own death every day, but not even for a second had I allowed myself to imagine Taran's. "Go with everyone else. Keep them safe, I'll go, I'll do it, please, not you—"

Taran still had one hand on my chest, and I'd thought he was holding it over my heart out of sentimentality, but he was actually unknotting my new silk scarf from around my neck. He neatly filched it, then favored me with that shattering half smile again before wrapping the fabric around his own face to ward off the smoke. With his next move, he stole one of the stone knives off my belt, because he wasn't even armed.

His eyes left mine as he turned to Drutalos. "Get her out of here!"

With an apologetic whimper, Drutalos evaded my attempt to block him and grabbed me around the waist. He dragged me over his shoulder and pinned my wrists against his hip with one hand. I heard Taran and the others go as Drutalos began to haul me up the beach, shaking off my ineffective struggles. His shoulder in my gut nearly had me heaving up my breakfast, but I kept fighting to get free, to get back to Taran.

I screamed at Drutalos to let me go, but the treacherous bastard just whined and trudged faster through the sand.

I hadn't even said goodbye. I hadn't even told Taran I loved him.

Drutalos got me perhaps half a mile north before I was under control enough to sing. I was crying so hard that I could barely push the words out, but at least he didn't recognize the melody. I sang three measures of the Maiden's blessing of night, the song that gave me my name, and as soon as her power reached my lips, the other acolyte dropped like a stone, limbs falling slack. We collapsed in a tangle on the beach.

The Maiden's blessing could be dangerous under the best circumstances, so I spent precious seconds to roll him over and check his airway before looking back for Taran. But there was too much smoke. The entire sky was bruise-colored and yellow, and it had already swallowed his figure.

I had never managed any but the simplest of the Peace-Queen's blessings in three years of trying. I could not have sung the blessing to heal my foot even without tears clogging my throat, so I didn't try. Instead I heaved and sobbed my way through a very tricky blessing of the Maiden, modified to direct her power toward myself instead of a patient. I got it on my fourth try: I deadened the nerves from my knee down to my toes, and I stood. My foot held. I would reckon with the damage later, if I lived.

Riding this wave of the Maiden's mercy, I sprinted back down the beach, my breath coming ragged and weak through my chest from the fear and the smoke. Even on a broken foot, I ran as fast as I ever had, eyes fixed on the cliff where Taran had gone. It was so utterly unlikely that we'd both survived so far that I found a childlike faith that if I just ran *as fast as I could*, I'd make it in time, and the Maiden would protect me and Taran both. I was out of the habit of praying with simple words, but I cried the Maiden's sacred names on every breath, begging for speed and strength.

Maiden, I did all this in your name, please help me now.

I wasn't more than halfway to the trailhead before the explosion lifted me off the ground.

Feeling the blast and hearing it were two separate disasters, but they both ended when I hit the sand. Knowing what it meant was the catastrophe that kept rolling through me long after the aftershocks had faded, all the stones had landed in the sea, and my seared lungs had found the air again.

How could a god die? They didn't die like people did, quiet and still. Death was torn screaming out of the world, his form dissolving into spite and destruction, and his ending took half the cliff with him. The Allmother herself mourned her child, and she made the world shake and roil in her grief. I heard later that the earthquake lasted only seconds, but the Maiden's belated mercy took away my memory of the rest of the day.

When the survivors reached the promontory, skin singed and ears still ringing, we found only stone and ash. The queen would have liked a trophy, but there was no shining armor, no crown, and no golden blood on the hillside. Nothing to show for three years of war or to prove that our tormentor was gone forever. Our victory was marked in silence and loss, known only by the absence of our gods and their blessings.

We did eventually find Taran's body. The sea brought it back the next day, still wearing my scarf.

2

Five months later

WHEN THE MAIDEN-PRIESTS taught me to sing, all our great epics started in the middle. When we sang the story of how Wesha, the Maiden, trapped her husband Death in the mortal world, we didn't open with the Great War between Death and the other gods, with battles and fire and lightning.

To most people, that was the important point: a long time ago, all our gods lived among us, but after Wesha shut the Gates between the mortal realm and the divine Summerlands across the sea, only Death remained to demand worship here.

But no. That part had to wait.

We sang first about Wesha walking alone down the Mountain in her white silk wedding gown. Innocent. Doomed. We described the tears on her flawless cheeks. The sharp knives on her golden belt.

We sang about the lonely tower where our goddess was to be imprisoned for eternity, and we made the audience understand the weight of Wesha's sacrifice when she married the greedy monster whose war had nearly reduced the world to ashes.

Eventually, the listener would hear the full tale: how Death broke the ancient laws of the Allmother when he started the Great War, and how Genna, Peace-Queen, broke her youngest daughter's heart when she gave Wesha to Death as the price of peace. How Wesha then locked away Death's power over the Underworld and exiled him from the Summerlands for his crimes. How Death schemed and fumed for centuries, seeking to return. All of it out of order.

When stories have a beginning, people expect an ending, and the maiden-priests wanted listeners to understand that they were part of a story still being told.

I was now the only one left to compose and place the verses about how my rebellion ended the three hundred years of Death's tyranny in the mortal world, but I hadn't sung since Taran died. I knew the story wasn't over, but I wanted my part in it to be.

"Does she have worms?"

I'd forgotten where I was and what I was supposed to be doing when a young woman deposited her baby in my lap, and I jolted in confusion. Multiple times a day I was painfully yanked from the gray fog of my own memories into a world where Taran was dead, but there was still work that I was required to do.

I'd come to the new royal residence to speak with the queen on behalf of the surviving acolytes, but this was the third time I'd come, and we'd been left to cool our heels out in the courtyard with the common petitioners for hours. Nobody had dared approach me before this girl in a homespun smock, even though my white dress and ten-stringed kithara used to be as good as a request to be handed strangers' babies. Hiwa had dressed me like a doll this morning, as she did every morning.

Iona, you must eat something. Iona, you must change your clothes. Iona, you must tell us what we are all to do now.

I was scared by how angry those demands could make me, even when delivered by sweet little Hiwa ter Genna. But if I was dressed like a maiden-priest, I couldn't be angry at this young mother for expecting me to act like one and treat her child. She couldn't know that engaging with the present felt like rubbing raw wool across a fresh burn.

After a sidelong glance to check that the single royal guardsman was out of earshot, I quietly chanted one of Wesha's blessings. The Maiden's power flowed obligingly through me, revealing that the baby was a little anemic but blessedly parasite-free.

"No worms," I told her mother, who didn't look reassured by the news.

"But she sleeps all the time. And when she's awake, she's tired. Should she be so tired?"

The infant had screwed up her pearly pink lips when dumped on my lap as though contemplating a good scream, but she only turned her head and frowned at her mother instead. She should have yelled at being handed to a stranger, and she should also have a lot more plump on her bowed little legs.

I took a closer look at her mother. My age, so this was probably her first baby. Very thin too.

"What's she eating?"

"Pap, porridge. She weaned herself a couple weeks ago."

The baby must have weaned when her mother's milk failed. The whole country was doing poorly, but women often ate last. A simple case to diagnose, but a difficult problem to solve.

"She's malnourished. Needs milk. Donkey or goat is best, cow or sheep if that's all you can get."

The young mother nodded stoically, but her shoulders slumped. Death's greed for sacrifices had thinned all the herds, and the drought had kept them from rebuilding. I might as well tell her to sail across the Sea of Dreams and feed the baby the sweet wine of the gods in the Summerlands.

"Thank you, maiden-priest," she muttered without much gratitude.

I bit the inside of my cheek and quickly dug into the purse at my hip. Before the acolyte seated to my left could object—we'd come to beg money from the queen, not to give it away—I pressed some coins into the young woman's hand.

"Buy a nanny goat. Keep it with a neighbor, so your family doesn't know you have it."

The girl immediately brightened.

"I will, thank you, maiden-priest," she said again, this time with real feeling. "Can you bless me too?"

I automatically opened my mouth to sing the benediction for new mothers, but I stopped before the first note. Not because I was being dramatic about not singing after Taran died. I would have done it for the girl's sake. But the guard had noticed the three of us, and his stare was hard and unfriendly. No god's blessing would be tolerated at the queen's residence.

I still tried to conjure the appropriate look of maidenly serenity before passing the baby back.

"She's beautiful," I said in lieu of the blessing, and the girl seemed satisfied when she bowed and walked to the other side of the petitioners' courtyard.

Tell me, nightingale, do you actually believe all babies are beautiful, or is that just something you say?

No, I'm being polite. I actually think that baby who peed on me needs to focus on his personality.

Good thing our children won't have to worry about that.

I'd promised to bear Taran ten humorless redheaded brats if he tempted fate in that way, but he'd only laughed and said he wanted eleven.

Lost in that memory, I didn't realize I was staring after the sleepy baby and her mother until I felt Hiwa's hand curling into mine to squeeze it hard. My sinuses burned as I tried to keep myself in this time and place.

I could be terribly angry at the little acolyte of Genna sometimes, but she was the only person whose presence I could always tolerate. She never seemed surprised when I cried or didn't cry, ate or didn't eat, argued with the queen or looked out at the sea for hours. She would have been a good peace-priest, if she'd ever finished her training.

Maiden-priests trained to treat the dying as well as the young, and a month after Taran died, I woke Hiwa up in the middle of the night, convinced that I had a growth in my lungs from all the smoke I'd inhaled. I couldn't breathe correctly. Couldn't get enough air. I felt the tumor jabbing into my spine and leeching into my bones, and I knew it would kill me if I didn't teach someone how to cut it out, because everyone else who knew how was dead now.

Hiwa didn't even bother with the blessing that would have disproved it. She just put a hand on my chest and matter-of-factly said, *no, that's grief.*

I might sometimes be furious that Hiwa was forcing me to be here, but at least she never expected me to be anything but sad about it. We sat in understanding silence until a second royal guardsman came out and said that the queen would see us now.

I KNEW AS soon as the guard announced me that the queen would say no. Just *Iona*, not *Iona ter Wesha* or even *Iona Night-Singer*, which the queen had been the first one to call me. The mood at her court had an ugly undercurrent tonight, sullen and hungry, and they looked at me when I limped in like they hoped I'd provide them some amusement, musical or otherwise.

I'd declined several invitations to perform on the kithara here, and I sensed another would not be forthcoming. Not that I'd be missing the hospitality. Cheap pitch torches were already accumulating soot on the beams of the high ceiling and fouling the indoor air, because the queen spent every spare coin on imported grain for her people, and oil for lamps was not in the budget.

I'd been in here before, when the royal residence was still a temple of Genna, Peace-Queen, Taran and Hiwa's patron goddess. The queen had plastered over the erotic frescoes and cut down the sacred fruit trees, and her wooden throne sat where a statue of Genna had once loomed over the sacrificial firepit, but she'd made no other improvements.

From the queen's sour expression, she knew she ruled a country in decline, and her residence was only a symbol of it. This wasn't a temple of Genna when it was constructed—from the high peaked ceiling, I knew it had once been a temple of the Allmother, probably constructed before the Great War three hundred years ago. But hardly anyone worshipped the Allmother even before my rebellion; other temples had offered more tangible blessings, and it was hard to maintain gratitude to the Allmother for giving birth to the gods we no longer saw or for building a paradise across the sea that only a few mortal priests would ever visit.

We stopped building new temples at all once Death came to rule us. We never had enough time or money left after making the sacrifices he demanded. But now that he was gone, there was still nothing to spare, even for the queen.

Despite the mood and the queen's grimace, I tried to talk to her like I used to. I had once thought I was a pretty convincing speaker, because I did, after all, convince her to join me in the rebellion that ended Death's rule over the entire country, but ever since Death fell on the cliffs, she seemed to wish I would disappear.

Well, me too, but I still had people I was responsible for.

Taran was dead, but there was still work that I was required to do.

My proposal tonight was designed to avoid all her previous objections to my plans: I would take the other acolytes with me to the ruins of Ereban, and we'd restore the barracks at the temple of Diopater, which had been the least damaged among all the major structures. The old royal palace there was charred rubble under six feet of mud, and the rest of the population had fled, so we'd be alone. The other acolytes and I would only use the blessings of the gods per the strict instructions of the throne, and we would accept no new students.

It was far from the picture Taran had painted of our future. Once Death relented, he thought all the priests would come back from across the sea, we'd rebuild the ruined temples to the other gods, and we'd be prosperous and peaceful again. Maybe he could have talked the queen into that: all I'd done was convince people to riot and fight and burn, but Taran could charm anyone he ever met, from the queen down to the lowest pot-boy. He would have led with a smile and a compliment and got the queen laughing, while I'd come in with a new limp and resentment.

Taran, this should have been you, not me.

The queen told me no.

When I was done speaking, she sat up in her throne, her winged eyebrows lowered, and made her announcement.

"I cannot allow anything in the shape of a temple to be rebuilt. The gods have left the world to us, Night-Singer. We should leave their blessings to them. Let their names and their prayers be forgotten, as they have forgotten us. I want that to be my legacy."

She wasn't really speaking to me but to the crowd, because not everyone agreed. Some of the nobles here had been religious loyalists who'd fought on Death's side until it looked like we were winning. Some of them still worshipped in secret. Some of them had fled abroad at the start of the rebellion to live in gentler lands with gentler gods, and they were unimpressed when they returned to find our country barren and torn.

The queen would only get angrier if I pointed out that I had acolytes who could sing the blessing of rain for our parched fields or blessings over metal to forge tools to rebuild the ruined cities, or that I myself was the last living person who could treat complicated childbirths or infectious illnesses. But I couldn't make her look weak in front of her court, so I threw myself on her mercy instead.

"I'm only asking for the sake of people who fought in your army for three years. I've sent home everyone who still has family, but that leaves dozens of us who only know temple life. What are we supposed to do?"

My voice wobbled when I spoke. My thoughts rarely marched beyond the next moment anymore, but it finally sunk in as I was standing there that I might truly fail at this too. The queen might be stubborn enough to see her country starve. I might be cursed to live long enough to see the people I'd tried to save brought even lower than they'd been under Death's tyranny.

Taran, you said you'd end this. Why isn't it over yet?

My question made the queen wince. She was barely into middle age when we met, but the murder of her daughter and three years of war had put streaks of white into her plaited dark hair and deep purple shadows beneath her eyes.

"If any of your people are young enough to still need taking care of, they're young enough to take up a new trade. They don't need temples to farm or smith or—can't they just pick up apprenticeships like anyone else? And you . . . you know I want the best for you, Iona."

She paused, pursing her lips in thought, then scanned the crowd of nobles seated at the long plank tables. Her eyes finally came to rest on her cousin, Lord Fentos. Unlike most of the court, he wasn't paying attention to my conversation with the queen, instead looking disconsolately into his goblet of wine.

"Fentos! You were saying last week that one of us would have to remarry soon."

Her statement made little sense to me, but the crowd got there before I did. They fell quiet as their interest was seized; I didn't realize I was the target until I saw Hiwa abortively reach out for me.

Why were we talking about royal marriages? I was just here to ask for enough money to take the surviving acolytes somewhere quiet and out of the way.

I wheezed in helpless panic when I understood.

Lord Fentos suppressed a scowl and craned his neck to look me over at the queen's invitation. Even though his appraisal was more commercial than lascivious—a horse he wasn't certain he wanted to buy, not a woman he wasn't certain he wanted to sleep with—I inhaled with instinctive rejection as his eyes traveled across my unimpressive figure to linger on my straight waist and narrow hips.

I clutched Taran's ring and twisted it on my finger like it might offer me some protection, but a drunken sot to Fentos's right took it upon himself to play matchmaker.

"You could do worse for a bride. The hair's a matter of taste, but she sings, you know—wouldn't that be nice to hear in your house? And her family was probably peasant trash, but Wesha's temple would've educated her, so your children won't bark like dogs."

Fentos rolled his eyes, but he didn't disagree with this assessment of my marriageability.

"How about it, Iona? I'd give you the dowry I planned for Elantia," the queen said grandly, and I should have been overcome with gratitude to be treated like a daughter of the royal house, but instead I made a sound like someone had struck me in the stomach. Nobody seemed to notice that I had started shaking.

How did I stop this? What were the words I could say that would not insult the queen but appropriately convey that I would sooner jump off the highest cliff in the land than marry her cousin? Marry anyone at all? I couldn't make my mind work, and it only got worse.

"Are you still a maiden, maiden-priest? You never took your vows, did you?" Fentos reluctantly asked, and he made an effort to be quiet with his inquiry, but I still flushed hot and crimson, feeling naked despite wearing more clothing than any other woman in the room.

"Fentos! That question at your age, and you a widower," the queen responded for me, with the prim outrage I couldn't muster over the horror of the entire situation. "You remember Taran ab Genna. They were practically married. I'm sure she's as virtuous as any maiden-priest, but you can't expect—"

"And I *don't* expect otherwise, but weren't they betrothed almost two years? With no child? If you're not going to remarry, I need to be sure of an heir."

"I suppose you're right," the queen said after considering it. They both examined me as though my heir-producing potential might be visible through the layers of Wesha's white wool vestments. "What do you think, Iona?"

I wanted to say the most vicious curses I knew. Instead, I made the mistake of turning to Hiwa for help, but her face was all cautious hope rather than anger on my behalf.

My brain wasn't so addled that I couldn't follow her thoughts—she'd been watching me night and day for five months so that I wouldn't do something terrible to myself, all the time worried we'd starve when the queen's generosity ran out, and if I married into the royal family, both problems would be solved.

She probably didn't even think it was a bad match—Fentos might have two decades on me, but he wasn't hideous, and I'd never heard that his first wife had had any complaints.

Wesha married a worse man to bring peace to the world. That had to be why Hiwa thought I would do it. I'd never hesitated to make a single sacrifice for my people, and Hiwa had seen me ready to die for them that day on the beach. I could marry Fentos and at least provide for my friends, have children, perhaps influence the path of my country if he did inherit the throne someday. It made sense.

Taran was dead, after all, and there was still work that I was required to do.

No. No.

I was going to be sick. I was going to be sick all over myself in front of all these people.

With my focus expended on containing the wave of nausea that threatened to turn out my stomach at the image of Fentos standing in Taran's place at a betrothal ceremony, I lost track of my breathing, and a loud sob rattled up through my throat. I gasped for air, and another sob sealed my throat shut.

Someone snickered and was loudly shushed, leaving the ragged noises coming out of my chest as the only sounds in the room. A few people here would remember the day that I staggered into the old palace in Ereban to tell the queen that Death had butchered her only child on his altar. I heard the queen had come to Taran's funeral too, but I'd been even less coherent then and hadn't noticed.

For the first time, a flicker of uncertainty crossed her face. A little recognition of our overlapping mourning.

"Your Taran was a fine young man, Iona, but you weren't even married yet, and—"

I didn't stay to hear the end of that sentence. I ran. My bad foot twisted under me before I could run ten steps, and my hip caught painfully against the table I lurched into, sending wine tumbling into the laps of two minor officials. I couldn't manage an apology, just fled faster, tears blurring my vision.

I managed to lose Hiwa in the turns of the corridors and came out of the former temple not via the petitioners' courtyard but the kitchen midden, which sloped down toward the rocky ocean shoreline. Nobody was nearby—the herb gardens were long dead, and the sacred trees had been chopped down.

I made my way to the gray basalt shoreline and nearly crawled to reach the water. Pulled open the neckline of my dress and splashed seawater on my burning neck and chest. It could soothe my flushed skin but couldn't cool my anger at everyone who expected me to recover from Taran's death, much less my anger at Taran for expecting me to do this without him.

My impulse, always, was to fix things, no matter how drastic the cure was to the illness. Cut out the tumor. Purge the infection. Take my surgical knife and fight the death-priests who were burning down my country. But there was no curing death, not even for the most talented maiden-priest.

As the salt dried tacky on my chest and cheeks, I slumped onto a larger rock to stare out at the sea. If I turned my head to look up the coast, I could barely see the peak of Mount Degom, nearly fifty miles away, where the Allmother had given birth to our gods. Ereban lay in Mount Degom's shadow, where the maiden-priests who raised me had died.

Somewhere across the sea, there was another mountain. Every day I looked out at the sea, wishing I could see it.

When people died, we built funeral boats and launched them to the east. They passed through the Gates that Wesha's eternal prison guarded to reach the sacred Mountain. Our absent gods were up above in the paradise of the Summerlands with their priests, and Taran was down below, in the Underworld. My patron goddess lay between us, no doubt wondering why nobody prayed to her for mercy anymore.

Against my will, I was still here alone, grieving the lack of vows that would have made me a priest or a widow.

I'd spent most of my life wanting to be Wesha's priestess and the rest of it wanting to be Taran's wife, and I'd never get the chance to promise myself to either of them. Both Taran and Wesha were across the sea forever.

For three years, I awoke most nights from the nightmare of Death's flames and the collapsing temple in Ereban, the queen's daughter dying on the altar, the riots, and the massacre of the other maiden-priests. I never expected to recover from it—my entire temple died! That would have been enough to haunt one mortal life, and somehow I endured.

I was not going to live through this. That realization, as strong as a vow, came as the first moment of relief since Taran died. I was not going to finish his work. I was not going to live without him, was not going to marry Lord Fentos or take up a trade or convince the queen to seek the blessings of the gods. I would just refuse to do it.

Neither could I serve Wesha, not anymore. I couldn't be a maiden-priest without my goddess's guidance or her blessings, and I had no idea what she'd want me to do now that her husband was defeated and her temple destroyed.

But there was still something I *could* do.

If everyone I loved was across the sea, I could sail there too. The Maiden had shut the Gates between the Summerlands, the Underworld, and the mortal realm, but if she could shut them, surely she could open them.

If she'd do it for anyone, she'd do it for me.

For three hundred years, the Maiden had locked her husband out of the realms of the gods and the dead, and in return he had killed us, stole from us, and tormented us. Maybe she even owed it to me, to give mine back.

I rubbed the dried salt off my face with the sleeve of my white dress and looked to the ocean horizon.

With my decision, my soul was finally calm.

3

One month later

THE ACOUSTICS OF the lower southeast fish-market were very poor for my last performance. Flat, wide-open, packed-dirt floors swallowed most of the sound I picked out of my kithara, and this particular song had actually been written for the lyre—a gutter instrument, by my teachers' estimation, though perhaps more appropriate to accompany this folk song about a sexually adventurous milkmaid, her well-endowed lover, and a bucket that advanced the rhyme scheme more than the plot—but I amused myself by inventing a complex harmony on the fly, making my sacred instrument sing.

Three tipsy fishermen handled the vocals, the crowd clapped and stomped their feet in accompaniment, and everyone shouted the explicit last lines together.

Not my favorite genre of music, but the tips were better when I took requests.

I couldn't perform Wesha's epics, because there was a guards-man loitering nearby. Death-worship was a capital offense as of the last week, and the queen's guard might not make fine distinctions between *worshipping* and *singing about*. I didn't think a song about how Death's own bride had locked him out of Heaven would win the god any new devotees, but then again, I had often been surprised by the number of people who willingly joined his cult.

There were new songs about the rebellion that I might have legally performed. Some were even about me. But they were very to the point, not composed in the epic style they deserved, and it would have not just kicked at the shattered pieces of my grieving heart but also offended my artistic sensibilities to sing about the tragic events of my life like I was giving directions to the bathhouse. So tonight's musical performance for the lower southeast fish-market by Iona Night-Singer, formerly Iona ter Wesha, was about milkmaids.

As I plucked the last chord of the charming tune, I saw Drutalos's appalled face in the back of the crowd. My heart lifted. I'd been waiting for him to return for weeks, so I bent in a half bow and put my instrument in its case to signal the end of the concert, receiving a round of disappointed clamors for an encore before I handed a wooden bowl into the crowd for tips. People were smiling, but not Drutalos.

"You're playing in the fish-market for coin?"

Hello, Iona, you look well under the circumstances, beautiful instrumental work there. No such luck. When he reached my side, Drutalos hissed at me in a low voice—or what he thought was one. That last big explosion on the beach hit all of us differently, and he couldn't hear well anymore, so he yelled.

"It's an honest living," I said, tilting my face up so he could see my lips.

I positioned my cane and waved off his silent offer of help as I got to my feet. I didn't need the cane to walk the short distance we were going, but my foot stiffened if I sat for a long time, and I stumbled as it complained under my weight.

Damn it, Taran, I thought, more cheerfully than usual, since I hoped I would see him very soon.

Drutalos grabbed my elbow, because everyone now felt entitled to manhandle me, and I shot him an annoyed look until I was free. We both turned toward the harbor, the fresh scent of brine on the breeze almost alluring over the stink of tar and kiln fires from the city's new construction.

Tonight! I could go tonight.

"I can't believe it," my fellow acolyte loudly rumbled, still offended on my behalf. "Bawdy drinking songs for fishermen. Do they know who you are?"

"They know. They're very appreciative. Some of them come see me every night."

Drutalos was a bit of a snob, like many of the acolytes whose temples had drawn from the higher classes.

"The last, best singer of Wesha's temple can't perform somewhere better than this?" he ranted.

I vaguely remembered my birth family selling fruit at a crossroads. I was by no means too good to perform for dockworkers and fishermen.

"It pays pretty well, actually. I'm sure I could make even more in tips if I showed some leg, but, you know, I have my pride."

"Iona. This is ridiculous. You were trained to be a priest of Wesha. Why aren't you delivering babies? Tending to the sick? That would have to pay better."

"It probably would, but the queen won't have it." I made a covert gesture, chopping at my neck. Someone had whispered to me yesterday about an old vocate of the sea god, at a town halfway up the coast from here, caught calling the fish to his nets with Marit's blessings. A mob tore him apart before the queen's justice could do the same. "I hope *you've* been discreet."

Drutalos's deep brown eyes widened in a face the same color. "I meant without the gods' blessings. In an ordinary way. Have you talked to the queen? Since . . . since?"

He was awfully interested in my life choices, and I noted that he had a careful hand over the big pack he carried with him as we made our way to the harbor. He didn't approve of what I'd asked him to do for me.

I halted at the rise over the docks.

"Since she tried to marry me off to her old goat of a cousin, who stared at my chest and asked whether I was a virgin?" I asked, crossing my arms.

My friend immediately clasped his cheeks as though they'd caught fire. Wesha's priesthood was the only celibate order, but Smenos's priests were supposed to be modest and respectable, like the tradespeople who adhered to his cult, and they were easily embarrassed.

"But of course you're a . . . a . . . You were almost a maiden-priest, and you weren't married yet, and—I'm sorry," Drutalos squeaked, eyes going round as he realized that he was only digging himself in deeper with every word.

I would have been sorry too if I'd actually planned to marry Lord Fentos, who had certainly not earned any maidenly chastity on my part. But at least I could say that although I never took my vows to Wesha, I had done nothing that would break them, and maybe that would make Wesha listen to me.

I waved off Drutalos's pity.

"Did you find anything?" I asked, looking at his pack.

He took a tiny step away from me.

"I did, but . . . here? Where should we stay tonight?" He covered his pack with a protective hand and attempted a diversion.

"*We* aren't staying anywhere tonight. Hiwa has all the coin I've been earning, so go see her if you need a room somewhere. I'm going tonight before the tide changes."

A month ago, I'd sent Drutalos to the ruins of the high temple in Ereban. Death destroyed it, and then later it was covered by the mudslide that took out most of the city, but if anyone could excavate Wesha's chapel, I'd thought an acolyte of the crafter god could unearth our former headquarters.

"Tonight? Wait. We were going to talk about it more first."

While he sputtered, I grabbed his pack and looked to see what he'd been able to find. It was heavy with recovered treasures. Several white dresses, slightly dusty. A gold diadem set with pink tourmalines and matching enamel prayer beads. Ritual jewelry and stone knives. Candlesticks and offering platters, sacred scrolls recording Wesha's prayers. It was better than I'd hoped, and I felt my shoulders relaxing. I would not be going in front of my goddess empty-handed to beg for Taran's life.

Oh, look—he'd even found the high priestess's gauze veil, embroidered with a pattern of white stars. She must not have worn it for my ordination, otherwise it would have been incinerated with the priestess herself. I allowed myself one moment of bittersweet tribute, glad to have something of hers when Death had left me little else. The high priestess hadn't been particularly affectionate—all of us followers of Wesha were an unsentimental bunch—but she'd joined me in protesting the sacrifice of the queen's daughter on the day the riots started.

The maiden-priests had taught me to sing, but more importantly, they'd taught me right from wrong.

I took the veil and smoothed it over my bound hair to check it for fit before tucking the ends under my belt. Wearing the *high* priestess's veil was a little presumptuous, but there was nobody else to compete for the title, and I was equal parts vain and self-conscious about my hair. Wesha's priests chose new acolytes based on their musical ability alone, but masses of wavy, ember-red hair were not what anyone expected of a follower of the Maiden. It was too luxurious, almost indecent. A particularly mean old vocate had once threatened to shave it to teach me humility.

Taran had thought my hair was beautiful, and secretly I agreed with him, but my hair didn't match the rest of me. As Lord Fentos had silently noted, my body was not curved in the way men liked, and I had the same ordinary peasant features and wide brown eyes as everyone else in my home village. More than once I had turned around to the disappointment of a stranger who'd been admiring my hair, so it was better if I kept it pinned up and covered.

Attire settled, I looked for the boat I had picked out. It was a pretty little pleasure craft of polished oak and brass fittings, belonging to a noble lady who had sampled foreign wines while everyone I loved died. The boat was built for two, but I had watched her take it out a few times, and I believed I could pilot it myself.

"You don't have to do this," Drutalos said. "We *should* talk about it more. Does Hiwa know you're going tonight?"

I didn't stop walking toward the boat, but I did my best to hear him out.

"Don't tell me you think I should marry Lord Fentos too."

"Why couldn't you get married? If not now, someday? Would Taran want you to mourn him forever?"

That made me laugh. That wasn't the sort of question Taran would have given a straight answer to in the first place.

You can't get married. Won't you be too busy leading thrice-daily lamentations at one of my impressive funerary monuments?

For another thing, it was obvious Taran hadn't thought very hard about what I was going to do without him, which was why I was here in the harbor, ready to sail the Sea of Dreams.

My real objection was that I never planned to get married. I was going to be a priestess in a celibate order and dedicate my life to spreading the Maiden's mercy. I didn't change my mind—I fell in love with Taran. Those were two different things, and I was determined that I would have one life or the other.

"I'm not going to mourn him at all anymore." That had been

completely unsustainable, like trying to breathe underwater. "I'm going to Wesha, and he's going home, with or without me."

I was confident, but Drutalos was not convinced.

"Iona, it feels like this is . . . this is a very complicated way of killing yourself," he said, struggling for words. His voice was getting higher pitched and tighter. "I didn't think you'd go tonight. It's my turn to watch you, and—"

"If I were just going to kill myself, why would I ask you to bring me Wesha's relics?"

"I don't know! But why would you think Wesha would do anything for you?"

I snorted in grim amusement and tossed his words back at him. "Haven't you heard? I'm the best singer alive, the last one of Wesha's temple."

The other acolyte pulled back, stung. He didn't want to fight with me, but his eyes were starting to well up.

I didn't want to spend the time to convince him. Everything in me was yearning to cross the sea, a relentless tug in my chest that pulled at me waking and sleeping. The only relief was in deciding to go.

I firmed my jaw and took Drutalos by the arm.

"The rebellion is over. You can do whatever you want to, but this is all I want. I want Taran back. And you don't need me anymore—"

"Of course we do. Not just the acolytes—the queen does too, even if she doesn't know it yet. Look around! It's winter, but it hasn't rained in months. There was no crop this year, and I heard someone say last week that hardly any children have been born since the rebellion started . . . Iona, you have to do something."

"*You* do it this time. Build them an irrigation system or something, acolyte of Smenos," I said, steeling myself against the guilt for leaving him. I'd given everything I had to the rebellion, and I'd never asked for anything in return. No title, no reward, not a single comfort in three years of war. Taran had promised me a stone house with a plum tree by the front window, but I hadn't even stopped long enough to marry him.

I would have given *my* life for the other acolytes, but Drutalos didn't have the right to ask me for Taran's.

"Couldn't you just . . . just wait? See if you feel better in a few more months. You know Taran wouldn't approve of you sailing off alone," Drutalos sniffled.

I frowned at the darkening horizon. "If Taran wanted to make my decisions for me, he shouldn't have died."

"But he *is* dead. Maybe all the priests who left are dead too. Maybe the gods really are gone." He got a mulish expression on his face, the same one the queen got when I had this argument with her.

In response, I sighed and wiped my palms together. I sang six short, harsh syllables.

Hail Death, who kindles flame.

The trick was in the intonation, but it wasn't hard.

Fire dripped from between my fingers, falling safely on the packed stone of the harbor and sputtering out for lack of fuel.

Drutalos still screeched and jumped back.

"What the hell?" he keened, his breathing turning to panic. I was immediately sorry—I could have chosen a different demonstration. Memories of the war hit all of us differently, and Drutalos was afraid of fire now. For the sake of his dignity, I held back my urge to rub his back as he raggedly pulled himself together, hands over his eyes.

"What if someone saw you?" he demanded when he had himself under control.

"Did *you* see?"

"I saw," he said sullenly. "And so?"

"The gods still answer prayers. Even Death does, and Taran killed him."

Drutalos fell silent, unable to argue that point with Iona Night-Singer.

Wesha was waiting across the sea, I knew it. The sworn priests of every god but Death had boarded ships in the first weeks of the war, called through their vows to flee across the Sea of Dreams. I would be going without an invitation, but I was certain I could find Wesha, and the goddess of mercy might still grant her last priestess one final blessing.

Nobody came to stop us when I boarded the boat I'd decided to steal.

"Do you know how to sail?" Drutalos pointed out when I gingerly situated myself between the oars. The square sail was in a heap at the bottom of the single mast, and I poked at the ropes that might allow me to raise it.

"I'll make the wind blow in the direction I'm going," I said confidently.

"I think there's more to it than that," he said with some doubt, and since his former patron god invented ships, he might be onto something, but I wasn't about to stop and take a few weeks to study sailing.

It wasn't like I was going to a real place, anyway. Wesha's prison wasn't on maps. It wasn't in the mortal world. She would either let me find it or she wouldn't.

"Are you coming back?" Drutalos asked, hands gripping the prow of the boat.

I wouldn't lie to him.

"I don't know. I'll *try*."

He looked very young as he silently begged me to reconsider; he was trying to grow a beard, and that project might be more successful if delayed a year or two. I hoped I'd be back to see it.

When he realized that I would not make more of a promise than I had, he nodded and untied the boat from the dock.

The tide was going out, so I was pulled out to sea before I could even get comfortable with the oars or the tiller. But nonetheless I waved at my friend, who stood on the dock and morosely watched me go.

I drifted out of the harbor, far enough that nobody was likely to notice that I didn't own the boat. An hour's worth of tugging on ropes got the sail into what looked to be the correct configuration. I found a mechanism to lock the oars and set a course east, toward the rising sun.

I whispered a blessing for a small wind and called a breeze to push my tiny boat forward more quickly. The sail filled, and a rush of hope swept through my chest with the sea air. There were several songs about making this voyage, which I sang for good luck.

There had been no storms since the day Skyfather's priests left on this same voyage, and the surface of the water was like glass as the night slipped toward dawn. Sailing was easy, it turned out, if the storm god's arm no longer stretched out to touch the waters. I spent the night looking up at the stars. For the first time since Taran died, it was easy to fall asleep. I didn't have to figure out how to live in a world without him, which was what everyone else had wanted. I just had to make this one voyage.

This serenity persisted through the second night, and the third. On the fourth night, I started to worry. I saw the fins of sea creatures on the horizon and the occasional distant sail, so I knew that I hadn't crossed out of the mortal realm. I was following the sun precisely, but there was no way to tell how far I'd gone. I hadn't thought it would take more than a day. None of the songs made it sound like the Gates were very far away.

On the fifth night, I ran out of food. I hadn't brought a fishing line, and when I tried calling for rain to refill my water jugs, I nearly swamped the boat. I squeezed some water out of my dress to drink, but it was as foul as the ocean from all the dried salt in the fabric. Always, I prayed to the Maiden, who was as silent as ever.

On the tenth night, I ran out of water.

By the next morning, I was comforting myself with the thought that I'd soon see Taran again whether Wesha answered my prayers or not.

4

THE BOAT BOUNCED. I had drifted aimlessly, becalmed, for a couple of days. Yesterday a thick mist had risen up and formed just enough dew to keep me alive, but I'd lost my bearings without a view of the sky.

The sudden lurch roused me to wakefulness, and I shook off my daze to find a seagull perched on the prow of my little boat. It examined me through one red-rimmed eye as though wondering whether it dared hop down and eat my face.

I fumbled for an oar and tepidly jabbed it at the bird.

"Go away," I croaked. "I'm not dead yet."

The seagull took flight in a rustle of affronted feathers, making one circle around the boat before landing back in the same spot. It settled down, seemingly determined to wait for my demise.

The changeless days and salt spray had clouded my mind, but not my instincts. With my swollen eyelids barely cracked, I mumbled the blessing of fire, managing a diffuse ball to cast at the seagull.

The seagull was not the most agile of birds, and I caught its tail with my fire as it tried to dodge. I had half a thought that I might somehow char and eat it, but that thought fizzled with my fire when the bird *spoke*.

"Fuck! Shit!" It swore both surprisingly and uncreatively as it hit the glassy water next to my boat to extinguish its singed feathers. "What was that for?"

Birds didn't swear, unless I was closer to death than I thought, but immortals *did*.

Fuck. Shit.

"Who are you?" I sat up and groped for the surgical knives on my belt. I needed a better weapon for a sea battle than fire, but I chanted a ball of it into my off hand anyway. "What do you want?"

"Stop throwing fireballs and I'll tell you," the immortal yelped before diving again under the water.

I wracked my uncooperative brain for any tales of a god who liked to take the form of a seagull, and what they might do to me. No immortal was likely to be very happy with me, in light of the destruction of the temples, but obviously there were gods and *gods*, and worse and worser ways to die.

The bird popped up, waited to see if I had anything else in my divine armory, and then flapped back to the prow when I didn't try anything else.

"I was just coming to ask where you were going," it grumbled angrily.

"Who are you? Did I somehow pass the Gates of Dawn?" I demanded, hands still poised to attack.

"You ask a lot of questions for someone who tried to kill me straightaway!" the bird said in a voice I tentatively decided was female. "I'm Awi, to answer the first one."

I pressed cracked lips together, wondering whether I ought to engage with the immortal. I didn't recognize Awi's name, but there were famously a thousand of the little gods, some of which had helped mortals before Wesha closed the Gates, and others of which had preyed on them.

"I've never heard of you," I said, hoping to draw her out.

The seagull shrugged her wings in a parody of dismay. "No?

I'll tell you, mortals don't appreciate birds the way they used to. Three hundred years ago, nobody so much as took a shit in the fields unless the birds flew west and did the correct loopty-loops first." The bird's shape blurred, and instead of a seagull, a large raven now perched on my boat, glossy black feathers incongruous in the middle of the featureless ocean. She jabbed her beak at me. "Mortals used to *worship* birds. And now I get screamed at? Fireballs? All this time with only Death for company did not improve your manners."

I tried to lick my lips, but no moisture would come.

"I apologize," I said slowly. "For my bad manners."

"You should," Awi said snippily.

I waited in the hopes that she would say more, but I was a mortal dying of thirst on the open sea, and she was an immortal. I ran out of patience first.

"Where am I? Please tell me."

After eyeing me with some curiosity, she deigned to answer.

"In the Sea of Dreams, obviously. Were you *trying* to go to the Painted Tower? It's just that way."

I tried to follow the point of her beak, but got dizzy when I craned my neck. I was about to pass out from this small interaction.

"I haven't seen a priest come this way in years," the bird added, probing for information. "Didn't they all go up the Mountain three years ago?"

"I'm not going up the Mountain. I'm going to the Underworld."

"Huh. Don't know why you'd be in such a hurry when mortals only get a few decades before making that trip in the traditional way. Just wait a bit longer, and then I'll eat you, and boom you're on your way."

I glared and put my hands together defensively, but the bird kept her attitude of benign interest, watching me through one unblinking eye.

"I'm going alive. I'm a maiden-priest. I'm going to see Wesha first," I insisted.

This at last seemed to impress the bird.

"Business with Wesha? I *thought* you might be one of the rebels, what with the fire. Didn't you burn down all her temples?"

I shook my head. "The rebellion was against Death. Who massacred every other maiden-priest. The temples were—just caught up in the war."

Awi cocked her head skeptically. "So you're a nice priestess? Loyal to Wesha? You're going to the Painted Tower to serve her with modesty and obedience?"

"I have been modest and obedient. I will continue to be modest and obedient, if she'll open the Gates for someone."

"You need a big favor, huh? Who do you want passage for? Another rebel? I see all the dead ones come through. Maybe I know the one you want."

I eyed her distrustfully, but she'd already concluded that I was one of the rebels, and she hadn't tried to kill me yet. I had little to lose.

"Yes. Taran ab Genna," I said slowly.

At his name, she stiffened, and all her feathers flew wide in a puff, turning her into the shape of a dinner platter. More news of the rebellion had reached the Summerlands, then, if she knew his name.

"I see," Awi drawled, slowly regathering her avian composure. She shuffled her feet, red eyes flashing with guile. "I did meet him. Perhaps we could help each other out?"

"What kind of help?" I was instantly even more cautious. She was about to propose a deal, but I was not in a great bargaining position, and all promises made to immortals were unbreakable.

"You want in. I want out. If I vow to help you get to the Painted Tower, on your way back, you help me get out."

"You have wings," I said, hooking a thumb back in the vague direction I'd sailed from. "Why do you need my help?"

"Doesn't work that way. I would fly in circles. Wesha still controls the Gates. I'm stuck, and so are all the other gods."

"Are the gods trying to return now that Death is gone?" I asked, my heart lifting. I could barely think about it, as muddled as my head was, but for a moment I pictured Skyfather himself striding through our dusty, barren fields, trailing rain behind him. The Peace-Queen opening her hands to heal the war casualties. Dozens of fertility spirits coaxing life out of the dead lands. Blessings and plenty, after years of starvation.

Awi fidgeted, her eventual answer to my question inscrutable. "Well, this one is, at least. It's been three hundred years, and I just want to go home. Look, can we make a deal or not?"

It would probably come back to bite me, but I was on my way to plead with a goddess anyway. The little bird was only the second immortal I'd ever met, but she seemed relatively harmless, and I was dying.

"All you want is my help to get to the mortal world, if I can convince Wesha to open the Gates?" I pressed. "And in return, you'll take me to Wesha?"

Awi nodded vigorously, giving me her best reassuring wing flutters.

Well, the odds were rising that I was never coming back, anyway.

"I vow it to you," I said, feeling a novel tightness in my chest as the promise sank into my soul. It was unbreakable now. I'd carry it the rest of my life, whether hours or decades.

"Fantastic," Awi said in response, spreading her wings in victory. She pointed off the bow with her yellow beak. "It's that way."

"I need food and water first," I said, sinking back down and closing my eyes. "Wake me up when you have some."

"What? You expect me to fetch things for you?"

"If you don't want me to die before I get there, yes," I said, covering my discomfort at being indebted to an immortal with bravado. "The deal cuts both ways. Get me something to eat."

It had to have been a long time since Awi was worshipped, if she didn't remember that the gods had no choice but to fulfill their promises too. I heard grumbling and then the slap of webbed feet on the wooden deck of the boat as Awi approached.

When I opened my eyes again, an agitated pelican was peering into my face from only inches away, enormous beak slightly parted.

"Get away from me," I snapped, shoving her back.

"You want food? I ate some fish a while ago," she said, tone spiteful. "Open your mouth, baby bird."

I swatted the pelican as she chortled to herself.

"Never mind. I'll just die," I muttered, thinking that Taran wouldn't blame me for choosing death over regurgitated fish guts.

The pelican heaved a dramatic sigh and shook her wings in dismay. "You're so demanding! Fine. Don't die in the next few minutes."

Awi launched herself into the air, nearly overturning the boat, and I marked her flying off in the same direction she'd previously indicated. I was ironically gratified to see that the bird was telling the truth about which direction the Painted Tower lay in—the epics had taught me that the gods might keep their promises, but they frequently lied, and the way they fulfilled their promises was often worse than betrayal would have been.

WHEN SAILORS APPROACH land, they see the peaks of mountains before they see the shore. But that was not how I first saw Wesha's tower at the intersection of the worlds. Everything emerged all at once from the gray mists: the Mountain crouching over the wide cavern mouth of the Underworld, and to the left of that entrance, the single harbor, and beyond that, the Painted Tower.

I aimed for a shallow beach, barely visible through the wreckage of the ships that crowded the shore. I was restored enough to row my little boat into an open space between two larger ships, but this shore was infamous and terrifying, the boundary between the mortal world and the undying one.

When our rebellion began in earnest, most of the surviving priests boarded boats and sailed here, called by their gods to travel up the Mountain to the Summerlands. By the end of the war, the only people still singing the blessings of the gods had been death-priests, trying to kill us, and my dwindling group of acolytes, trying to keep the queen's army alive. I knew sworn priests could not disobey the commands of their patron gods, but it was hard not to feel like they'd abandoned us—the acolytes who had not yet given our vows. I saw no sign of their retreat now.

Some of the boats in the harbor looked like they had just docked, and some of them were no more than piles of scrap lumber that the sea was slowly reclaiming. As I approached, other boats sailed in without pilots, and their passengers stepped onto the pebbled shore.

The dead.

However they'd looked in life, they now gleamed in the phosphorescent green of foxfire, shuffling like sleepwalkers and clutching a few precious possessions to their chests as tribute for Wesha. They went slowly toward the mouth of the Underworld, heads tilted as though listening to instructions whispered over the roar of the sea behind me. I splayed my palms together with fingers spread, making the sign of the Maiden's star out of lingering superstition.

There were no birds besides Awi, and none of the smell of rot that might be expected from thousands of funeral boats. Somewhere between my world and this shore, the mortal bodies of the dead had vanished, and only their spirits had come here. The dusk-souls were hazy memories of the people they'd been in life, faces flickering between old and young, grieving and serene as they moved inexorably toward the dark mouth of the cave at the end of the beach. It was considered very bad luck to see them in the mortal world: their passing drained the life out of everything they touched, and their presence meant a body had gone untended for days, with no surviving friends or family to launch a funeral boat.

I jumped out as soon as I reached land, forgetting that my left foot wouldn't hold my weight after so many days at sea. I hoped the Maiden wasn't looking out her window just then as her last priestess fell face-first onto the beach. I spat out gravel and Awi honk-laughed at me in her original guise as a seagull.

After I dusted myself off, I walked along the shore, completely ignored by the dusk-souls. I saw pristine skiffs with prayers painted in gold along the hulls and rough rafts made of bound driftwood. Some were loaded with treasure, and some were empty. Despite a few minutes searching, I didn't find Taran's funeral barge, which had been little more than a few boards roped together. All I'd owned to send with him had been my scarf and my love.

I had to wipe my eyes. I hadn't actually expected him to be waiting for me on the shore—I just wished he were.

Put down your hair, nightingale. The Maiden likes pretty things, and you want her to like you.

I didn't need Taran here to conjure his advice. I could even picture the face he'd make, seeing me robed and veiled like the high priestess of Wesha.

Jealous of a goddess, my love? I said back to him, deep in my heart. If I wanted my patron goddess to hear me, better to look the part of her faithful worshipper.

Her home was tall and slender, jutting into the misty sky like a piece of white bone, surrounded by ruined gardens and decaying outbuildings. It was called the Painted Tower after its former condition—the story went that Genna had a beautiful home built for her daughter as a wedding gift, but Death stripped it before his exile across the sea, turning it into a wretched prison. There were soot marks instead of frescoes now, the underlying white marble stained and pitted by the green-black moss of the sea and pierced only by a single window at the very top. The rest were crudely bricked up.

I thought someone might challenge me as I approached, but the beach was quiet and empty, and the front door to the tower was open. I could feel the Maiden's presence though, like an electric charge that lifted the hair on the back of my neck. The tower didn't seem vacant, just . . . quiet. She was here.

"So, what did you bring her?" Awi asked, peering with interest at my full pack.

While my eyes adjusted to the unlit gloom of the interior, I crouched in the foyer of polished rose granite and displayed the slightly dingy golden relics of Ereban for the bird's inspection.

"That's it?" she asked, apparently disappointed. "You know she's got rooms full of that stuff here."

"Well, there's also me. Her last priestess." Surely that had to mean something to her.

"You? What do you do?"

"I sing?"

A resigned sigh escaped her yellow beak. "Really? I guess that's something . . . but you're lucky that Wesha isn't just beautiful but merciful too. I'll wait outside."

She spread her wings as though leaving, but I grabbed her by the back of the neck before she could take flight.

"Oh, no you don't." If the bird goddess had a history with Wesha, I wasn't answering for it alone. "Come in so I can ask for you to be released."

"You don't want to bring me in front of Wesha! She has no respect for the Allmother's laws, and she hates the other gods for trapping her here."

I frowned, having never heard that about the Maiden, but I looked down at the cowl neck of my white wool dress in compromise.

"Can you be a hummingbird? You can hide in here," I said, gesturing at the loose fabric.

Awi made a squawking scoff. "You can't hide anything with your bony tits. Just remember to be precise about what you ask the Maiden for." With that, she launched into the air, out the door, and up out of sight.

She hadn't been great company, but my mood dipped as soon as I was alone again. The tower was an uncomfortable house for my poor goddess—lonely and forbidding, with all the softening touches of a home charred away. No rugs, no wall murals, no cushions on the stone benches. The proportions were not human ones: the ceilings were too high, and the ramp leading up the inside wall was too wide. I found full storerooms overflowing off the central pillar, but no priests to tend them. I'd half hoped there might be someone lingering here who'd escaped Death's massacre at Ereban, but everything was silent.

I climbed all the way to the top, mind numbed by the unrelieved white of the walls. Three floors, four, five, more, my foot aching by the end. The ramp terminated at a room that took up the entirety of the top floor under the slate tiles of the roof. The ceiling soared stories above me, illuminated by the huge window in the opposite wall. But my eyes were drawn inexorably to the goddess on the giant throne built into the structure of the building.

Immortals could take many forms. More or less human, according to their will, and Wesha was supposed to be more. Unique among the Stoneborn, Wesha was half-mortal, the result of one of Genna's many indiscretions with mortal lovers. The songs about Wesha described her as a beautiful girl with olive skin and hair that flowed through all the colors of the sunrise—black at the roots, then fading through gold and rose hues to white at the tips. Her features were supposed to be delicate and sad, her eyes like the sky before dawn. This much was true.

It was her size that threw me: Wesha was a *giant*, perhaps fifty feet tall. Her back was bent to scrape under the ceiling, and her knees were folded to brush the walls. She strained at the confines of the room, far too big to have walked up the ramp behind me. Either she'd taken a different form then, or this tower had been built around her.

She didn't move at all as I entered the room. I couldn't see the rise and fall of her breathing, and her eyes didn't track me, instead gazing fixedly at the distant horizon as though she was a part of the walls of this place too. There was lichen growing in the folds of her ruined wedding gown and an abandoned bird's nest in the crook of her elbow, as though she hadn't budged from this spot since the day she married Death, more than three hundred years ago.

I realized I was staring—and lucky that Wesha hadn't already blasted me for my impertinence in arriving uninvited and goggling at her. I made the deepest genuflection my bad foot would allow, then hurried to pull a bench from along the wall into the center of the room, gritting my teeth at the loud scrape across the tile. She didn't acknowledge me by even a flicker of her starry eyes.

My heart was pounding harder, and my plan seemed much thinner than the day I devised it, but what else could I do now?

I set out the relics I brought with me and sat down with my ten-stringed kithara in my lap. It wasn't something Drutalos had recovered from Ereban; it was my own instrument, made for my hands out of wood, sinew, and horn on the day I was brought into Wesha's service as a small child.

Her presence throbbed in my ears like the silence of the tower, making me more reluctant to begin. I had tuned the instrument down below, and Wesha would surely rather hear me play than babble nervously, but it had been years since I had sung in Wesha's honor and just tried to make it beautiful.

I tried anyway. First, I picked out the notes of the melody the priests used to call us in for morning prayers. When I was sure my fingers weren't trembling and my mouth wasn't dry, I added my voice to it, making an offering of myself to my patron goddess.

I sang Wesha's hymns. I sang the great epics. I sang lullabies and work songs and instructional tales. I chanted the words that Wesha's priests used to deliver babies, to wither cancers, and to ease the dying toward the Underworld. I sang children's songs. I sang the wordless melody that Taran whistled when he was in a good mood. There was no change in the eternal midlight of the Gates of Dawn to mark the passage of time, but hours must have unraveled with the lift of my voice and the ripple of the strings. Without any encouragement, I sang as long as my voice held out and my fingers could still hold a pick. Slowly, slowly, Wesha's head turned. My eyes didn't track the movement, but by the time I was no longer certain my voice could catch the high notes, Wesha was looking at me instead of the horizon. My hands fell still on the strings under the force of her regard, my small and fragile body freezing like a rabbit in this unfriendly place. I had the full attention of one of the Stoneborn.

She spoke in a voice as lovely as copper bells, her words even more jarring for it.

"Well, you've buttered me up sufficiently. What do you want?" Wesha asked.

5

"GODDESS," I CROAKED. "They say you can see all the way to the mortal world from your window. I am Iona ter Wesha, called Iona Night-Singer. Do you know me?"

Wesha watched me unblinking, giving no response either way. But I hadn't answered her question yet.

"I am the only one of your priests left living. I came to ask for a boon." I'd practiced that announcement in my head, but I'd imagined myself with a lot more dignity, not rasping and bedraggled.

There was an ironic twist to Wesha's mouth when she deigned to speak to me again. "You're not one of mine. No matter what you're wearing. I'd know if you owed me your obedience."

"No," I admitted. "But I was in Ereban three years ago to swear my vows when Death massacred your priests."

It was cool in the marble room, and the fog outside obscured the sun, but I sweated at the memory of midsummer. Crowded in with the other acolytes at the rear of the temple, our vestments a riot of varied colors and symbols. All of us nervous to endure the presence of the god of flame, the mood shifting darker as the day dragged on. The sacrificial fire in front of Death's altar had been stoked until it reached the painted ceiling of the temple, and the air was thick with the smell of burning meat as Death demanded *more, again, another, or I'll burn the wheat that grows in the field.* When every animal in the pens had been offered, Death's lion mask had turned toward Elantia's small form where she trembled next to him, and the pinched expression on our high priestess's face had turned to horror. An echo of that panic coursed through me now, making me shudder.

"So, why should I give you a boon?" Wesha asked, tone idle.

"Did you see it? The war? Death scorched the world to ashes before he died, but we won. He's dead. I avenged your priests—and you, goddess."

Wesha shrugged, looking almost uncomfortable. "Is that what mortals say I want now? Revenge? I never told you to go to war."

I bit down hard on the inside of my cheek. She was the goddess of mercy, of course she didn't want revenge. "Death took . . . everything from us. We sacrificed to all the gods for their blessings, but it was never enough for him. People went hungry to put food on his altars. Our country should have been rich, but his priests took more tithes than the queen and the other temples together. And at Ereban, the last sacrifice was the queen's own daughter. She was fourteen, and she went willingly, but . . . I couldn't allow it. I know your forgiveness is infinite, Maiden, but you're also the patron of children. I knew you'd want me to stop it."

I opened my damp eyes wide, imploring her to say I'd been right. If she couldn't abide marrying him, how could I be expected to watch his priests bend a living child over his altar?

"Sounds as though you solved that problem on your own," she replied in a dry tone. "No more sacrifices. No more death-priests. No more priests at all, including mine. You thought I'd be pleased?"

"I—your husband is dead," I stuttered. I would have thought she'd be pleased after three hundred years. "You're free."

"Napeth is one of the Stoneborn. Do you mortals still fear death and worship with fire? Then the Allmother will rebuild him from the stone of the Mountain, and I'll face him on this side of the ocean now. Meanwhile, I'm still *stuck* here." She turned her head as though preparing to stare out her window again, but then, remembering that I was still there, fixed her attention on me once more. "I'm not sure you've improved things at all, mortal girl."

"Death's still . . . he's alive?" I steadied myself. None of us, not even Taran, had spoken of killing him. We'd only imagined stripping his power by defeating his priests and denying him sacrifices—not that there had been any other way to stop the war. At Taran's insistence, we'd sent messengers under a white flag to ask for terms, but none had ever returned.

"Of course he's alive. He's Stoneborn. Though probably unhappy to hear of his demise at the hands of mere mortals," Wesha said, lips curling with some satisfaction at the thought. She picked delicately at the fraying gold embroidery on her wedding gown, expression growing distant. "Anyway. Your boon. Everyone always wants something from me—get on with it, then."

Anxiety made my voice squeaky, but it was hard not to bristle at how put out Wesha sounded at my presence. "Maiden, I have followed your commands since I was six years old, honored you with the working of my entire life. I only beg one favor."

The barn-sized girl rolled her eyes, for all the world like a teenager asked to do her chores.

"I gave my priests every blessing I had to bestow. I call the mortal dead to the Underworld and allow mortal priests to climb the Mountain. I don't know what else you could possibly want."

My breath came faster as I worked myself up to it. The other gods had abandoned us, and Death had tormented us, but surely Wesha, the gentle Maiden of all our stories, the goddess who sacrificed her freedom for peace, would do this one thing for me.

"Please open the Gates of Dawn so that I can bring Taran ab Genna home."

Although she'd been like a statue when I entered her chamber, if anything Wesha went stiller at my request. I wondered how much she'd seen from her window.

"Of all the things you could ask for," she said, rolling the words in her mouth, "you want one man?"

"He—he's the reason we won the war against Death. The one who struck him down. And he said that at the end of it, we would reestablish the temples. Restore the blessings of the gods. Sacrifice to you for easy births and gentle deaths, to Diopater for rain, Genna for peace . . ."

Wesha did not appear convinced, so I spoke more forcefully, getting down on my knees on the floor to implore her. I'd planned this too.

"You entered this prison to stop the war between Death and the Stoneborn. Taran ended Death's rule over the mortal world. Please, I ask you to send him home, but if there has to be a price, I would make the same sacrifice you did and more. If someone has to stay, let it be me instead."

When she answered, her tone was a little tart. "*My* sacrifice? Marrying the terrible lord of the Underworld is a little different from serving the goddess who blessed you, isn't it?" She turned away again, staring out the window for so long that I almost thought she'd dismissed me. But then she glanced back. "Who is Taran to you?"

Somehow, I'd been hoping that question would not come up. The veil and layers of white fabric now felt very awkward, even if my chastity was mostly undiminished.

"Two years ago, during the war, we were betrothed," I said cautiously, hoping that I would not be turned into a pile of dust.

Wesha's dawn-sky eyes went even wider. "You were betrothed to Taran ab Genna? In the usual way?"

What was usual? Maiden-priests didn't traditionally attend betrothal ceremonies, so I had no idea. My ring had been a hastily constructed twist of silver wire and the witnesses had been a ragged collection of teenage combatants, but Hiwa had told us the vows to recite.

"Yes," I said, twisting the band on my left hand. "I didn't have a dowry, of course, but—"

There was a quick shake of Wesha's head. "What did he promise *you*?"

I was certain I was missing the point of her questions. When Wesha's straight, dark brows lowered in consternation, I haltingly recited what I could remember of the words. It wasn't like Taran or I had huge tracts of family farmland to negotiate—we'd just pledged each other all we owned, which in either case would have amounted to what we could carry on our backs.

"But he promised to build me a stone house with a plum tree by the front window," I volunteered, because he'd added that at the end to make me smile.

"A plum tree," she repeated as though incredulous, and I couldn't tell whether she thought Taran had gotten a good bargain for me or a poor one. She stared at my grimy mortal self for a long moment, eyes seeming to take in more than my appearance. At last she tipped her head back and began to laugh.

Loudly.

The sound of her laughter was amazed, nearly hysterical, and it went on and on. I squirmed, not sure what to do. Could she not imagine wanting to be married to anyone? Or was this about my impertinence in asking history's most reluctant bride if I could please have back the man I strayed from her path to marry, as he had unfortunately died in combat with her husband?

Her laughter rang louder and louder until it vibrated through the walls and floor of the white room at the top of her tower. It rattled the molars in my skull and shook me until I could see the seams in the stone and a dark frame around my vision. She didn't sound at all like a person when she laughed—it was like a reaction from the sky or ground, like conversing with a storm. I was about to fall on my face and beg her pardon for my offense, but just as suddenly as the noise had started, it ended.

"Yes, alright," Wesha said. "You can have him."

I had to blink rapidly to confirm her calm smile, not trusting my still-ringing ears.

"I . . . yes?" I said in another inelegant squawk.

Wesha lifted her left hand, examining the shining gold and fire opals of her own wedding ring.

"It's fine with me. Bring Taran here, and I'll let him through the Gates alive and whole."

I nearly choked on my own spit. Where was the bargain? What was I paying for this? Where was the catch?

"I have to find him and bring him here. And then you promise I can have him back . . . just as he was, not a dusk-soul. And"—my vow to Awi tugged at me, and I belatedly remembered my choice of words—"you'll open the Gates to the mortal world, so we can go back."

"I promise by all the gods," she said, picking at a cuticle. "Do you?"

"Yes, I vow it," I gasped immediately. For the second time in a day, the power of a divine oath took hold of me and lurched through my skin, but more potent this time. Tears pricked my eyes and I wavered even on my knees. My soul shifted its tuning to ring with this new purpose.

She had not even asked for anything in return. She could have asked me for anything at all, and I would have promised it. When I remained on my knees, staring mutely up at her, she gave me an upraised eyebrow as if to say, *You're still here?*

"Can you—can you help me find him?" I asked, even though I

knew I was pressing my luck. Maybe this was the catch. I knew very little about the Underworld. Maybe she thought I'd wander for centuries and never find him.

Her expression brightened. "Oh, sure. I will. I'll help you. You'll just have to help me too. I don't have much power left, with all my priests dead. We'll need a sacrifice."

With that, there was a clap of sound as the giantess disappeared. In her place was the same immortal, shrunken down to almost my size. She swung her bare legs at the lip of her enormous seat once, twice, before jumping down and landing lightly on the floor.

I was more cautious than ever when she skipped to where I still knelt. It was even more unnerving at close range, how human-but-not she appeared. I couldn't see the dot of a pupil in her starry eyes or the ends of her long hair where it bled into white light. But she smiled at me, the expression of a seventeen-year-old girl with an exciting secret.

"Up, up," she said, hauling me to my feet before pointing across the room to a pristine altar built into the wall. "You'll find everything you need in the rooms down below. Hurry up, I'll get started."

Wesha clasped her hands together and began to sing the melody that commenced every day's ritual sacrifice in her temple, lovely voice clear and eager.

My stomach tightened in apprehension, but there was nothing I could think to do but comply. It was a very familiar task. I rushed two stories down to one of her storerooms, pulling it apart to look for charcoal, oil, and wine among the heaps of treasure deposited by the recently dead. It didn't take long—whoever had organized this place thought just like the priests who raised me.

Wesha was still singing when I returned to prepare the altar. As she watched, I laid out the components of the ritual—everything except for the sacrifice. I spread the charcoal so that it would burn long and evenly, then set the lamps and wine where the priest would normally stand. I'd done this chore at least three mornings a week as a child. Larger sacrifices like sheep and cows would have been made at Ereban, but women would bring doves and chickens to the little temples in every city to give thanks for an easy birth or a child's quick recovery from illness. A bolt of cloth on a baby's first birthday. Portions of food or wine thereafter. I had never performed the actual sacrifice though—that was reserved for sworn priests.

Wesha finished a verse and beamed at me. "You'll have to light it too. I assume Taran taught you how?"

I had flint and tinder in my pack, but every temple kept a flame kindled from Death's altar at Ereban.

"Should I—Death's blessing of flame?" It felt sacrilegious to pray to her dreadful husband in front of her.

"Yes, get on with it," Wesha said impatiently.

I hesitantly sang that blessing, and the lamps and altar took flame in seconds.

Nodding in satisfaction, the goddess began to sing again. After a moment, I sang along with her, just as I had all my life. We called upon all the gods to witness. We acknowledged their power and the frailty of mortals. I hadn't done this in three years, but it was carved into my very bones. By the end of the song, the altar was blazing in a field of white-hot coals as wide and deep as a marriage bed. Sweat trickled down my back.

I looked fearfully at the goddess, noticing, for the first time, that Wesha's bare feet were dirty and covered in sand. She had to be able to leave the tower to walk the beach, at least. She was very different than I'd thought.

"The altar is ready," I said in a careful voice.

This was as far as I knew how to do. Acolytes didn't touch the sacrifices. Worse—I didn't know what Wesha wanted sacrificed, or to whom. There were no women waiting for us with grass cages full of anxious birds.

Wait. There was one bird nearby, waiting for me to return, and my vows wouldn't let me sacrifice her.

Oh, I was an idiot to think I could conceal anything from Wesha. Was this the price she'd ask me to pay?

The gods liked these little tests with no correct answers. I knew a lot of stories that ended that way—the mortal chose wrong, and then there was one less impertinent priestess in the world after her goddess turned her into a mushroom.

What would I do if Wesha asked me to bring her the bird goddess? I supposed I'd run for the boats, and then I would find out exactly where the bars on Wesha's prison lay.

"Yours? Or Taran's?" she asked, reaching for one of the stone knives on my belt and unsheathing it.

"I've had these for years," I whispered. The style was exclusive to priests of Wesha—made not of metal but hand-chipped rainbow obsidian, passed down through generations of maiden-priests. They were too fragile for ordinary use, but we used them in surgery. A symbol of Wesha's cult as much as the white dress. My legs trembled to bolt at the sight of the blade in her dainty hand.

"What did you bring that is precious to you?" Wesha asked, examining the knife.

I glanced down at the band Taran put on my finger at our betrothal, but she shook her head. "You can keep your ring. What else?"

I looked next at my kithara, and Wesha nodded.

"That will work. Throw it into the fire," she said.

My knees went soggy with relief. The kithara was dear to me, but it was the smallest part of what I would have given for Taran. I had been willing to serve Wesha in this tower for the length of her immortal life—what were a few pieces of wood and gut to that? I retrieved the instrument and brought it to the altar, beginning to feel the lassitude of hope after fear.

I stroked the wood one last time before throwing it in, as Wesha had asked. The cured wood shouldn't even have smoked in an open fire, but it was consumed almost immediately, vanishing as all sacrifices did.

Wesha's lovely voice began to chant again. I didn't recognize this prayer or the melody—I had heard the blessings to honor all the Stoneborn and many of the minor gods, but this one was new to me. The language was archaic and difficult to follow, so my mind hung on the syllables, trying to puzzle them out. To which god had we sacrificed my kithara? Not Wesha.

I paid careful attention to her words and not her hands, so I didn't notice her lifting the knife until it was at my throat. Too late, I understood what the sacrifice was.

The pain as the blade parted my skin and her palm shoved me forward into the coals wiped my mind of all conscious thought, but I was positive I heard Taran's name in her song before everything went black.

6

THERE WAS NO moment of transition. Just the shock and pain, and then I landed on my hands and knees on a stone floor. I immediately pressed my hands to my neck, grabbing for the wound in my throat, because Wesha's knife stroke should have ended my life in a second. But while the fingers of my hand came away bloody, all I felt beneath was unbroken skin. I slid my hands next to my chest, trying to discern whether my heart was still beating. It trembled in a rapid staccato there, fueling my wheezy, panicked breaths. I felt alive. I still felt the weight of my limbs, the chemical taste of fear on the back of my tongue, and the ever-present ache in my foot. More importantly, I could still decide what to do. I had to figure out where I was.

The air was warm and dark, and all I sensed around me were vague shadows until I rasped the blessing of moonlight. When my orientation returned, I was in a windowless stone room crowded with wooden crates and stacked casks of wine.

It didn't look how I expected the Underworld to look. The epics weren't entirely clear, but I expected vast underground caverns in which the dead wandered, dreaming snatches of their past lives and searching for the light said to lie at the end of the infinite maze. But this room could be underground, I supposed.

I scraped myself up off the floor and blotted the blood at my neck. I didn't exactly appreciate the way in which she sent me here, but if this was closer to Taran than the Painted Tower was, I'd chant thanks to Wesha anyway. My kithara was on the ground next to me, and I carefully put it away on a high shelf before examining the crates. They were full of valuables—cloth, jewelry, spices, other temple offerings. But there was nobody here, so I inevitably turned to the room's only door, finding it locked and bolted.

I might have been able to finesse the lock with a hairpin, but after a moment of wracking my memory, I recalled that Taran had once taught us a blessing to open locked doors.

There's a god of thieves? Drutalos had asked Taran as we ransacked the villa of a loyalist noble.

The Allmother made a god for every impulse of the mortal heart, Taran had replied, prying open the latch to the wine cellar. *Certainly one for the urge to drink someone else's wine.*

I was cautious but not particularly worried when I swung the door open into a larger room. The dusk-souls on the beach hadn't bothered with me, so I expected nothing worse in the Underworld.

Like the one I emerged from, the next room was cluttered with cargo, but there were windows high on one wall that revealed a starry night sky, and the chamber was lit by oil lamps in niches along the other walls. At the opposite end of the room, two people were unpacking boxes, taking an inventory of the goods within.

Wait, not *people.*

"Shit," I said, belatedly clapping my hand over my mouth. At the sound of my voice, two robed figures turned their heads in my direction. I froze in place, the instinct of a prey animal.

I never imagined before the war how hard my unconscious mind could work to keep me alive. I never dreamed that my eyes would learn to pick red robes from black in the moonlight or that my mouth could shape the words for fire before one of Death's own priests. But I immediately knew this was worse than death-priests, even though the figures at the end of the room wore the same bronze lion masks and red hoods as death-priests. I knew how humans moved. I knew the shapes of human bones and jaws and hands. I was afraid long before my mind caught up and formed the word for what I saw.

Fallen.

Long ago, when the other gods lived among us, they often dallied with mortals, and those unions produced great heroes and brilliant priests. The royal house had a drop of golden ichor in its bloodline traceable to Skyfather himself, though it was probably not safe to mention this to the queen anymore. After the Great War, when the gods retreated from the mortal world, no more such children were born. With one disgusting exception.

Death was forbidden all other women by his marriage vows to Wesha, but he'd found a stomach-churning loophole. He lay down with snakes and beasts and other loathsome things—and the children that resulted were monsters.

Death's Fallen had killed nearly as many people as his fires had.

"What, what's that?" a monster hissed, scenting the air with a forked tongue. "What is it, a thief in our father's storerooms? Come to steal from the offerings?" Clawed feet jutted beneath a robe that concealed legs bent in the wrong direction.

Its sibling slunk toward where I was backing up, even though there was no exit where I'd come from. There was a door on the other side of the storeroom, but both Fallen were between it and me, and I wasn't fast anymore. The second Fallen looked more human, or at least more mammalian than the first, but its large, reflective golden eyes made my gut clench when they focused on me.

"It is a priestess," this one cooed without slowing its approach. "Someone else's priestess is in our father's palace. A maiden-priest? One we are allowed?"

"I'm not a maiden-priest," I protested, even though I didn't expect my denial to be especially convincing, given that I was dressed like the high priestess of Wesha. I put my hand over the remaining knife on my belt, but there was no chance I'd ever defeat a Fallen in simple combat.

"A mortal girl," the first said, wedge-shaped head tilting back and forth to study me like a snake before it struck. Closer and closer it crept, nails scraping the stone tile. "Smelled her blood, honey and copper."

The second Fallen reached me, and I was glad the darkness of the room hid the full, awful planes of its face below the mask. I bit back a whimper as it seized me by the shoulder and leaned in, smelling my bloody neck with a canine huff of stinking breath.

"Smells like a priest," it said through a mouth that wasn't perfectly shaped for mortal speech. "Smell the vows on it. It reeks of priest vows. Whose priest?"

The first Fallen dropped to its belly on the floor, still flicking its tongue to taste the air. That awful reptilian head neared the hem of my dress as though to dip beneath the fabric of the skirt, and I kicked at it despite its sibling's grip on my arm. It neatly evaded me, teeth gnashing in a serpentine chuckle.

"We will say it was a maiden-priest, even if it belonged to someone else," the first Fallen suggested in a burst of inspiration. It surged up to seize my other arm, and the two began to drag me out into the hall. I took mincing steps in feigned compliance, planning my next move as metallic fear coated the back of my tongue. I didn't know whether they wanted to defile me, kill me, eat me, or perhaps some combination in the worst possible order, but Death's spawn had all the strength of their animal mothers added to that of their immortal father, and struggling would be useless.

As soon as we reached the corridor, I began to sing as quietly as I could, praying in my head to Wesha that they wouldn't recognize the melody. I'd only get one chance for this trick; by the end of the rebellion, Death's people had started to put wax in their ears or bang pots and pans to drown my song out.

It seemed that these Fallen had never heard the story of how Iona Night-Singer destroyed Death's temples, because they didn't make any attempt to shut me up. It took many more verses than it would have for a mortal—they dragged me all the way into a room decorated like the inside of one of Death's temples. These were all the same: murals of fire on the walls, too many braziers, winged golden ornaments at the corners of the bloodstained altar. Before we reached the altar though, I got the entire prayer for sleep out, and the Fallen collapsed in unison to the floor as Wesha shut down their nervous systems.

I wheezed in relief that it had worked, nearly falling along with them, but they wouldn't be out long. I still had one stone knife on my belt, but I wasn't sure where the heart was located on a creature whose mother was some kind of adulterous garden lizard, and I wasn't strong enough to decapitate them. I couldn't risk waking either of them up with a nonlethal stab wound. I ran instead, praying my foot wouldn't betray me again.

The corridor led to stairs, and the stairs led outside. Although it had been midwinter when I took the boat to the Gates, I emerged into a night rich with the scent of summer and snatches of distant song.

In front of me was a garden, lit up as though for a royal party, with lanterns on poles and garlands of flowers strung between them. Faraway music and the conversation of dozens of people drifted across the manicured lawn, but it was the night sky that stopped me at the top of the stairs.

There was moonlight, but no Moon. The world was lit all around the horizon by a silver glow, but the full Moon to light the night so brightly did not hang in the sky. The stars were different too—bigger, brighter, and somehow individual, as though, if my eyesight were slightly better, I might pick out a form and shape behind each light.

This couldn't be the Underworld. This wasn't the mortal world either, not with that sky.

The Summerlands.

I was beyond the Gates of Dawn. In the land of the gods, forbidden to anyone except immortals and their chosen priests—a group that I still did not belong to, no matter what the Fallen thought. Wesha had given the other gods entirely new reasons to want to kill me when she sent me to the Summerlands.

There was a howl of sheer rage from the storerooms below as one of the Fallen woke up. I ducked into the shadows along the wall, running along the side of the building I'd escaped from. I had to get away from the Fallen and the immortals both, somehow escape back to the Gates and explain to my goddess that, no, there must have been some miscommunication, what I actually wanted was to take one dead mortal and go home, no trip to the Summerlands required.

The stone wall ended at the elaborate brass gates to an empty garden. All around me loomed the shapes of ornate villas. Thinking that the Fallen might hesitate to follow me into the residence of some immortal, I sprinted away from the party toward the nearest building, a few hundred yards away. It was a broad, low-slung structure of pale pink marble blocks and flower-capped columns supporting a green slate roof. The imposing front door, decorated with white bursts of datura blossoms and golden stars, was providentially unlocked, so I slipped inside and shut it behind me.

With a closed door at my back, I stopped to catch my breath and rub the tremors out of my foot, which throbbed from the force of my flight. This villa was palatial, its walls covered in bright murals depicting the deeds of Genna and the other Stoneborn, and every floor a gaudy mosaic or padded with silk carpets. A king's ransom in oil lamps turned the halls to midday. Ordinarily, I would have stopped to gape and touch and scoff at the wealth that had been carelessly poured into such luxury, but I took a deep breath and set off in a random direction, panic urging me faster. I'd find a place to hide for a few hours and find my bearings.

Each time I heard voices, I turned a corner or cut through darkened interior rooms. I quickly lost track of which way I'd come in, trying only to keep out of sight.

Eventually, my luck ran out. I spun through a doorway into a small interior courtyard with a decorative fountain and flowering almond trees reaching to the night sky above. There was only one other door, on the opposite wall. As I approached, it opened to emit a waft of humid, wine-scented air and male laughter. Before I could fully turn around and retreat, two men staggered into me, taking all three of us to the ground. We tumbled onto the mossy flagstones like empty bottles.

I tried to scoot away as soon as I landed, but my legs were trapped under a young man who was clearly an immortal—his pink skin gleamed like the inside of a clamshell, and the wet hair that clung to his forehead was the color of seaweed. This godling had landed on his knees, and he made a vaguely disappointed grimace before flopping forward to vomit a bellyful of wine on the lawn. I barely escaped the splash in my scramble to get away, but this backed me right into the drunken god's companion, who'd rolled free on his stomach.

"That was my best wine," this one scolded his heaving friend, but his richly amused voice locked the air in my chest. I stopped trying to get away, slowly turning my head as though if I looked too quickly, this reality would vanish.

The second man propped himself on an elbow and blinked brilliant, familiar green eyes at me.

"Oh. Are you lost, darling?" Taran asked.

7

TARAN WORE THE gaudiest golden cloak I'd ever seen, draped over a floral-patterned silk tunic and equally lurid trousers, but I knew every breath of him. Still kneeling, I lurched to press my hand over his heart, right where his body had been most torn by Death's last attack, but there wasn't even the texture of a scar beneath the fabric. I couldn't see through his shape, and his skin didn't glow with foxfire. He was as solid as the last time I'd touched him.

I'd often thought the Allmother had her most inspired moment when she made him. His sharp cheekbones and the straight blade of his nose might have made his face ascetic if they weren't softened by a full mouth and thick, dark hair that brushed his jaw. His square chin and determined jaw might have suggested arrogance, but few people noticed when disarmed by the dimples in his smile and the dark eyelashes that framed his bright eyes. All of him was as perfect as the day I met him, and all of him was whole.

"Taran?" I whispered his name, fingertips burning from the heat of his body. The chains that had bound my chest since he died loosened, allowing a single gasp of joy to fill my lungs as my hands curled into his tunic. "You're alive?"

After a blink of surprise, his smile widened to match mine—

Until his gaze dipped to the knife buckled over my white dress. At once the open, friendly expression on his face vanished, replaced by three heartbeats of wariness. He shot his eyes at the drunken godling, and I watched the playful mask drop back onto his features before the other man noticed the change.

"What have you got there?" the godling said, wiping his mouth on his shoulder and staggering to his feet.

Taran sat up just as slowly, offering me his palm to pull us both up. I clutched his hand. Warm. Alive. I didn't understand.

"A little lost priestess," Taran said, eyes roaming over my clothing again.

"Yes, but whose? I don't recognize—oh! Is she a maiden-priest?" The immortal's bloodshot gray eyes widened. There was a disorienting, swirling movement to his irises that made my gut shrink. "I didn't think there were any left."

"Why don't you go back to the party?" Taran asked his companion in a disinterested tone, though his gaze didn't leave me. "I'll handle this."

Both his words and tone stiffened my shoulders. *Handle?* There was intensity in his face, but as he examined me, I realized there was not a shred of recognition in it. My blood froze into shards.

He didn't know who I was.

"No, let me see," his companion slurred. He grabbed my chin, turning my face to the side and back. "Wesha doesn't pick them for looks, does she? Hard to tell under the grime."

"Singers," Taran said, casually knocking the immortal's hand away from my face. "Wesha picks singers. Marit, why don't I meet you in a moment by the game boards?"

Marit. I knew that name. Waverider. The god of the open ocean, the unreliable patron of sailors, potters, and drunks. His priests fled the war in the first month.

"Singers! How lovely," Marit told Taran, ignoring Taran's request to depart and shoving him playfully. "Why are you here, little maiden-priest?"

"Wesha sent me here," I said, voice grating in my throat. Taran's expression hardened.

"Really. What does she want from me now?" he asked cautiously.

I didn't have a moment to unpack that, because there was a clatter of clawed feet on the tiles behind me. I spun to see the two Fallen from the storeroom, who'd caught up to me at last. They'd shed their bronze lion masks, but their unnatural meld of immortal and animal was worse than Death's sigil.

They slowed as they entered the courtyard to take in the three of us, but they'd picked up sacrificial knives, and rage twisted their bestial features.

I reached for the knife at my own waist, but Taran neatly grabbed me and hauled me back against the hard length of his body. He pinned my arms to my sides by wrapping me in a mock embrace, chin digging painfully into my scalp. I struggled like a dove in a snare, but I couldn't move his grip at all.

Marit belatedly recognized the arrival of the two Fallen and frowned.

"You were not invited to this party," he chided them, leaning back to his full, considerable height in affront, the effect slightly undercut by his wobbling intoxication. "No Fallen outside of Death's sector! We don't want to see you, let alone smell you."

They did smell terrible, but this would be their least offense. The two Fallen looked at each other, regrouped.

"We just want the priestess," the reptilian one lisped. "Give us the priestess. Maiden-priests belong to our father."

"Let me go," I began to insist again, but Taran slid his hand up to grip my neck in a gesture that was equal parts threatening and protective. I shut up.

"Now, first off, that's no way to speak to Stoneborn," Taran drawled.

Marit snorted agreement.

"Before you speak to us, you bow," Taran added.

The first Fallen, whose ancestry seemed to have involved more fur than scales, snarled and took a step forward. "We do not bow to *you*, Taran ab Genna."

Taran didn't respond, but the arm around my waist slipped until his hand covered the one on my knife.

"I assure you, you do," he said, voice dangerously lazy.

"I could go for some bowing," Marit said, scratching his chin. He burped, then giggled, the noise unsettling. "Do it."

The Fallen looked at him sullenly, but after a moment, they both halfheartedly bobbed their heads.

"That's a shit bow," said Taran.

The reptilian one hissed and took another half step forward, and Taran pulled me back by the same distance. But its sibling made a curt gesture, seeming to think the better of it. They bowed more deeply, animal spines curving like bows, then straightened to fix golden eyes on me again.

"I've had enough. You heard Taran ab Genna. *Kneel* or be knelt," Marit said, but this time there was an echo like thunder, and the chamber filled with the scent of brine, fogging the air and dropping the temperature in seconds. Water out of nowhere rose around my feet, enough to soak my boots.

My breath caught in fear of this casual display of power, but Marit's threat made an impression on the two Fallen. They flopped to the floor, prostrating themselves in the new puddles with performative, splashing obeisance.

Marit watched them grovel for a moment, his expression darkly amused. His power thickened the air, soaking my lungs until they felt overfull. And then just as quickly as his mood had dipped, he was done, smile shifting back to hectic cheer. "Well, alright. Say what you want. Politely."

The reptilian Fallen struggled up to two legs again, brushing his soaking robe with scaled hands. His mouth curled into a yellow-fanged snarl as he formed human speech with obvious difficulty. "She's a priestess of Wesha. See her dress? Wesha's priests are ours, she vowed it. All Stoneborn agreed."

"Hmm," Marit said, appearing to consider this argument. "What do you say, Taran?"

"I'm afraid they're confused," Taran replied. "She's *my* priestess." He turned his cheek so it was pressed against the top of my head. "Easy mistake to make."

"Yours? But—" The furred Fallen stuttered, dumbfounded. "You don't have priests."

"Of course I do," Taran said, voice betraying nothing but amusement. "They're so popular these days, and for good reason. What, do you think I wash my own back?"

The Fallen wrestled with this argument, clearly afraid of Marit but no more able to entertain the idea that I was Taran's *priestess* than I was.

"She is dressed like a maiden-priest," the furry one argued.

"It's a costume party," Taran said sweetly.

Marit snickered with a sound like raindrops. "Well, there you have it! Glad we could clear that up for you. She's Taran's, and you'll have to go gnaw your own arm for dinner. It seems you owe us an apology for wasting our time and spoiling the rugs."

His words were light, but there was a taste in my mouth that lingered, a nearly primeval scent of fear. Instinctive fear of one of the Stoneborn—the greater gods. The Fallen seemed to feel it too.

They wrestled with dueling urges to leap upon us and to collapse back down to the ground, but in the end, they retreated, eyes narrowed on Marit.

"Very sorry, Stoneborn. We did not mean to bother," the furry one said, an apology that very evidently did not include Taran. After a moment, he scraped another deep bow.

"Wonderfully done," Marit warbled, happy with how this had played out. "You *can* teach a dog new tricks, it seems. Now, to the kennels with you. Out. Out, out!"

The Fallen slunk out of the room with their eyes still on us, wet dog scent lingering a few moments more, and then diminishing howls of anger pierced the night to vent their fury at being denied me.

When there was no further sign of their presence, Marit groaned and put a dramatic hand to his forehead. "I wish Napeth would develop better taste in women. For the sake of your pretty décor, if nothing else." Then he giggled at his own joke, still very drunk despite the interlude.

I tried to worm free of Taran's arms, but all he did was spin me around, his attention finally refocusing on my grubby and trembling self. Marit approached too, just as interested.

It was only when I looked at the two of them together that I saw it. I'd never seen it before. It was nothing simple that I could point to like the silky texture of his dark hair or the bright color of his eyes, and it wasn't in the sculpted lines of his face or the strength of his shoulders. It was his presence, a reaction he drew from me. The atavistic recognition of something *other*, something closer to Marit than to me.

Taran's features weren't just inhumanly perfect, they were inhuman.

Immortal.

I didn't hear what Marit said next to him over the rush of blood in my ears, or Taran's reply, but he began towing me back the way he'd come in, arms stiffened to keep me upright when my legs would have given out.

How did I never see it? How did nobody notice? Taran wasn't mortal. I began to shiver like I'd fallen through the ice over a winter pool as we passed through a luxuriously appointed apartment with potted fruit trees and thick rugs. Taran pointed me toward an upholstered divan, but before I could fall on it, Marit cleared his throat.

"You're letting them go after they trespassed in your house and threatened your priestess?" the god asked, hooking a thumb toward the direction in which the Fallen had departed.

Taran paused, effortlessly holding me up with one hand. "I thought I'd be merciful?"

Marit laughed hard, not in a nice way, and there was a matching blink of something dark on Taran's face before he returned the sea god's smile.

"Of course I'm not going to let them go. Just give me a minute." He cast a brief glance down my body before plucking the last stone knife from my belt and tucking it into his waistband. He lifted me again and none-too-gently pushed me through a door in the rear of the large living area.

"Wait here," he said.

I unthinkingly complied for two steps, but turned around to find Taran shutting the door in my face. The lock clicked, and I heard the sound of something heavy being dragged across the floor. Only then realizing that he'd trapped me somewhere, I banged my fists against the wood in protest, but heard footsteps recede in pursuit of the two Fallen, heedless of my shouts. The latch wouldn't move, and even after I sang the lock open, I couldn't shove the door past whatever Taran had put in front of it.

With his immortal strength. *Immortal.*

All options to flee exhausted, I slid down to the floor, shaking.

Everything that had happened since I stole the damn boat crawled up my limbs and congealed into an icy-hot, shivering lump in my throat. Just in time, I grabbed a gold-chased urn from the floor next to me and retched into it, though there was little in my stomach and all I could do was dig my fingernails into the glaze while my gut uselessly convulsed, throbbing in time with my head.

How could I not realize what he was? He'd been too strong. He'd known too much. He'd been too perfect—especially to me.

He'd done this to me on purpose, and my broken heart fell to dust as I realized it.

I never expected to fall in love. It wasn't forbidden to Wesha's acolytes, just impossible for her sworn priests and unlikely during my training, which consisted chiefly of care for pregnant women, infants, and the elderly. Acolytes sometimes left the cult to serve other gods or marry, but those of us who remained considered that a personal failing, and I was always determined not to fail.

When I met Taran, the feeling took me entirely by surprise. I barely knew what to call it. I felt like the first person in the history of the world to ever discover effortless joy in another person, to look for his coming and going like the movement of the Sun and Moon. I treasured the emotion, cradled it to myself, and never thought to say anything to him about it.

We should get married, Taran had announced one morning as we swept up the farm kitchen where a dozen of us had slept in a huddle for warmth the night before. Apropos of nothing. We'd been fighting Death's forces for months, and the main variation in our days was the degree of desperation. At the moment of his unexpected proposal, I'd felt something of the same shock I felt right now, the sense that I'd failed to notice something important when it had been obvious to everyone else. I had also wondered if he might be teasing me. Embarrassment nearly made me run out the door.

Why would we get married? I'd asked him instead. I tried even then to conceal what I felt, though I instantly decided I would never speak to him again if he dared mock the beautiful secret thing I'd carried through a year of war and destruction. I still recalled the exact look on his face, because it colored my every view of the world after. The way he tried to smile at me, heartbreakingly vulnerable when he was so rarely straightforward about anything.

That's what people do when they're in love, isn't it?

I loved a man who didn't exist. I didn't know why the gods had done many of their great and cruel works, and I doubted they felt love the way I understood the meaning of the word, but at a minimum, every moment I had known Taran had been based on a lie.

I wished I could cry, but I just shook. I noted in a distant, clinical way that I was experiencing symptoms of shock and someone should wrap me in a blanket. It would have been a relief to pass out or stop breathing or feel my heart seize in my chest, but time continued to pass, the way it had stubbornly continued after Taran's death, when I had wanted it to end.

After half an hour or so, the unfamiliar ache of inaction prodded me to lift my head.

There was only me. Maybe there had only ever been me. But, as I had noted when I landed in the Summerlands, I could still decide what to do. I would get free if I could.

I was in a room with ornate black-and-white tiles covering the floor and walls and three fountains running from invisible pipes into hip-deep pools for bathing. Carved cedar clothes chests and a stand mirror made up the furniture. The only door was behind me. There were open windows high in the walls, probably too narrow to fit myself through. I jumped for one anyway, pulling myself up with all the strength remaining in my exhausted limbs to look out, and came nose to beak with a startled little owl. Awi.

She fluttered to a perch on the sill as I fell on my rear out of surprise. My reaction time was better than she'd expected when I sprang up to catch her in my trembling hands, and I evaded beak and talons to pull an immediate target for my anger into the room.

"Come here, bird, you're going to answer some questions," I hissed, digging my fingers into dappled brown feathers. Her circular eyes went even wider with betrayal before she shifted, and then I had my hands wrapped around the long, naked neck of an angry, feathered creature the size of an ox, standing on long legs capped with deadly, finger-sized talons. She immediately kicked me in the stomach, and I let go.

I staggered back, trying to get control of myself. Awi might be the least of the immortals in this world, but she could probably throw me through a wall if she put her mind to it.

"Glad to see you're alive!" she snapped.

"Am I?" I asked her. I hadn't been certain. I remembered Wesha cutting my throat and feeding me to the altar.

She only rolled her beady eyes at me.

I touched my throat again, where there was still a clot of dried blood. I was tired and so, so lost. My last surge of energy expiring, I sank to the floor, then to my back. Even the ceiling was tiled. Beautiful abstract shapes in black and white and rose, to match the single wall mural of dawn rising over the Mountain. I'd never seen anything so grand as this bathing chamber, and I'd been to the royal palace and the high temple at Ereban.

"Who is he?" I asked the ceiling.

"Who?"

"Taran."

"You found him already?" Awi asked, sounding pleased.

"Obviously. Who is he?" I demanded again. "You knew his name."

"Taran ab Genna?"

"Yes!" I almost shouted. "Who is he?"

Awi ducked into my field of vision, her strange, shovel-beaked face somehow judgmental. "Everyone knows him. 'Taran, son of Genna.' The bouncing baby bastard Genna foisted on her husband. Her infrequent pride and occasional joy."

"Genna, the Queen of Heaven," I managed.

"Did you not know this?"

"No, I did not know this. Of course I did not *know this*."

"You came all the way here, and you thought he was just some mortal?" This was delivered with even more judgment.

I bared my teeth at her in a useless snarl as my stomach throbbed with another lurch of distress.

"He's . . . he's a god? Or one of the Fallen?"

Awi gave a short laugh. "He's an arrogant little pain in the ass, is what he is. He's got a good streak of mortal blood in his veins, but since he came back to the Summerlands, he's been saying he's one of the Stoneborn."

"*Back* to the Summerlands?" For three hundred years, Wesha had held the Gates closed to immortals. How had he come to the mortal world? Why?

Awi paused as though trying to put her next words delicately. "He got through the Gates three years ago because Wesha's . . . sentimental about him. But Genna's the one that sent him on the errand. Putting the mortal rebellion down."

"Putting it *down*?"

An errand for Genna, who was his mother. Taran had been in the mortal world on an errand for his mother, Genna, the Queen of Heaven, the Peace-Queen. The soot-covered runaway acolyte I'd planned to marry had been on a secret mission for his mother, one of the most powerful Stoneborn—and she wanted my righteous, desperate rebellion against Death, the villain of every single tale of the gods, *put down*?

Awi had to be wrong. I rejected with my entire soul the idea that

Taran had been sent to stop us. If he'd wanted to put the rebellion down, he could have slipped a knife between my ribs in the first week he knew me. We would never have succeeded without his help—he'd taught me half the blessings I knew how to sing, fought with us against Death's priests, the loyalist houses—

"Of course," Awi said, unimpressed. "Of course, put it down! You ungrateful brats stopped sacrificing to the gods who'd blessed you. Turned against the rule of their priests—even killed one of the Stoneborn. What did you think would happen?"

"We stopped sacrificing when Death massacred Wesha's priests and destroyed the high temple at Ereban. What were we supposed to do?"

"Well, Diopater wanted to send a big wave and wipe you off the map," Awi said, swinging one enormous foot in a semicircle. "Start fresh. You're lucky Genna won that argument, sent Taran to bring you in line instead. Didn't do much for his popularity around here that he made an utter hash of the job."

My head sloshed with anguished confusion. I'd spent my childhood on my knees, singing praises to the Stoneborn. The last three years falling into a very different kind of devotion. I still wanted to believe that this was Taran being clever, tricking the gods themselves, and at any moment he'd come back and let me in on it. Putting the rebellion *down*?

"Why doesn't he know who I am?" I asked, voice faint.

Awi shook her head dismissively. "He died, and all his power and all his memories died with him. That's how the Stoneborn are reborn. Made anew by the Allmother from the stone of the Mountain. Brought back to be the god of . . . well, hard to say what he's the patron of. Disappointing his mother, probably."

None of this sounded like Taran. Not the man who knit together the bodies of mortal soldiers, the man who fought and sweated and died with us. Not the man I loved.

I closed my eyes for a moment. Distant music streamed through the windows, but in this room it was quiet. My body clung to the floor like a sack of iron bars. It simply couldn't sustain this level of distress for long. Human hearts gave way under this kind of pain.

This reprieve of lying on the floor and trying not to think about anything didn't last, because soon I heard the scrape of furniture being moved outside the door. Awi dove into the form of a tiny bird and took the shelter in the neck of my dress that she'd previously disdained, and I laboriously pulled myself to a seated position for Taran's return.

8

TARAN HAD LOST his fine cloak and tunic somewhere, but he seemed in a good mood nonetheless, considering the dirt and jagged claw marks that covered him all the way up past his elbows. Marit wasn't with him.

He gave my seat on the floor a curious glance as he went to one of the tiled pools to scrub his arms clean, but he didn't immediately speak.

"Did you kill them?" I asked when the silence began to press on me. "Those two Fallen, I mean."

Without looking at me, Taran tipped his head to the side in a half shrug, like he wasn't totally sure. "Time will tell. But they're not bothering anyone while buried under Genna's rhododendron bushes."

He pulled a towel out of a wooden cabinet and fastidiously dried himself off, wincing in elaborate disappointment when he noticed a spot of blood on his trousers. Sighing, he crossed the room to a clothing chest and rooted through it, eventually taking out a simple pair of linen drawers.

Even though I saw his hands move to the laces at his hips, I was not prepared for him to let everything drop to the floor. I closed my eyes and turned away just in time to avoid seeing more than a flash of muscular thigh. My cheeks heated as I reflexively clapped my hands over my eyes.

Bodies. I'd seen hundreds of bodies, of all shapes and sizes. Sick bodies, healthy bodies, live and dead ones, babies and elderly. I knew in detail how they functioned and how I could fix them. I wasn't precious about nudity.

But Taran had always been precious about *me*.

"I see you have the infamous delicacy of Wesha's priests, at least," he observed, voice dripping with amusement. "Though I might have expected you to wash up when you had the chance."

Was he calling me dirty?

As I hadn't bathed since I'd sailed across an ocean, was thrown onto a burning altar, and was thereafter chased by Fallen through the gardens of the immortals, all *on his account*, I did not look entirely presentable, but he'd previously considered my grooming habits to be not only unobjectionable but the absolute height of sophistication for anyone fighting a civil war. I opened my eyes to glare at him, but he was still dressing, expression challenging as he tied the waistband of his underwear.

"My first impulse upon being locked up was not to take my clothes off." My voice was weaker than I would have liked.

"Don't be afraid. I'm not going to hurt you." He said it easily, but the way he said it bothered me—there was a new assumption in his voice that people *would* be afraid of him. He had the confidence of a warrior, the lazy energy of a predator at rest.

I'd always thought he was just very tall, and lean because of that. But he'd filled out since I last saw him. The heavier muscle along his arms and shoulders matched the length of his legs and gave an impression of size and power to match. He was simply not built along ordinary human proportions—he had to have been starving on our diet of charred rabbit and boiled barley mush to ever look like he was.

"I'm not afraid of you," I retorted, and it might have been more convincing if I'd said it in more than a whisper. He was not convinced, and he gave me a close-mouthed smile to say as much.

Once dressed, he walked out of the room, returning with my stone knife in his hand, the blade chipped and filthy. He squatted in front of me and dangled the knife between finger and thumb.

"So, who were you planning to kill?" he asked, trying the tip of the blade until a shimmering dot of blood formed on the pad of his finger. I didn't think it was a real question until his bright emerald eyes lifted to mine for the answer.

"I didn't come here to kill anyone."

At his look of disbelief, I wrapped my arms around myself tighter. He'd just killed *two* immortals with the attitude of a man doing a mildly unpleasant chore.

"You were carrying a stone knife on your belt. Who was it for?"

"Every maiden-priest carried knives like that," I insisted, but his lower lip remained stiff with skepticism.

"This is going to take forever," he sighed, tilting his head to the right side. "Swear that you aren't lying. Give me your vow."

"What? No." I was so offended by the request that my rejection came out as a snort. He'd lied to me for *three years*.

Taran smiled, the expression not reaching his eyes. "Let me rephrase. You're going to swear that you won't lie to me, or I'll turn you out of this palace. You look like a five-course dinner for any of Death's Fallen still alive in the City."

"You don't mean that," I said, studying his face for tells.

"Try me."

The idea that Taran would ever do anything to risk my life was too unthinkable to stick long in my mind, but his eyes glinted like a metal blade. This wasn't the same man. The man I loved was dead, and if Awi was right, this immortal had been crafted anew by the Allmother. He could be different. He could be terrible, a merciless killer.

"I vow that every word I speak to you will be true," I finally said, wincing at the now-routine twist in my soul as the promise turned irrevocable. The quick flash of his dimples indicated that he'd caught the nuances of my wording—I didn't *have* to tell him anything—but he relaxed.

"I didn't come here to kill anyone," I repeated, and he nodded in satisfaction.

"Do you know what this is?" he asked, gesturing with the knife.

"A surgical blade."

"Did you make it?"

I shook my head. The rainbow obsidian came from a quarry on sacred Mount Degom, but I'd never been.

"If you're not here to murder someone off Wesha's long list of people who have it coming, what are you doing here, then . . . ?" Taran inclined his head inquisitively as his voice trailed off, and I realized he wanted my name.

"Iona," I said after letting the silence stretch too long. I had to introduce myself to him for the second time. I had to tell my betrothed my name. "Iona ter Wesha."

"Iona," he repeated, testing my name in his mouth, though he'd called me *nightingale* from the first time he'd heard me sing. I searched his face for some glimmer of recognition, some faint hint that he'd heard my name before, but his green stare was cool.

"What are you doing here, *Iona*?"

I'd come here for him. But if Awi was right about what he'd been doing in the mortal world, I was lucky he hadn't found it convenient to murder me.

"I didn't mean to come here. I sailed from the mortal world to ask Wesha for a boon."

"A bad idea. The Stoneborn don't do anything for free, Wesha least of all."

"I didn't think she'd do it for free. I was her last priest."

"What did you want, then?"

"I—I wanted my betrothed back. He . . . died a few months ago." My voice cracked when I spoke. It made my vow throb in my chest to speak of him in the third person, but it was just barely acceptable to the nearly sentient force of my promise. I couldn't let Taran know that I knew him, not if he'd gone to quash our rebellion.

Taran lifted one eyebrow, attitude now mildly interested.

"I thought Wesha's priests were celibate?"

Any reply stuck in my throat until I swallowed the shame of it, because yes, in retrospect, it was always ridiculous that I had thought I'd marry him. "I never took my final vows to Wesha. The rebellion broke out, and Death started hunting us. The rest are dead."

"Still doesn't explain what you're doing here. What was Wesha's price for your man?"

I blinked at him, hesitating. I was rapidly reevaluating everything I'd thought I knew about his allegiances. What he cared about. And I only realized now that Wesha hadn't extracted any price from me at all. "You. I promised that I'd bring you to her."

"Me? You vowed that you'd bring me to the Painted Tower?" Taran laughed in a rough bark. He stood and paced a few feet away. There was a brief flash of emotion on his face, quickly suppressed under that mask of bored amusement he now wore. "No wonder you looked so happy to see me."

He wheeled around and crouched back down, closer than before. There was an electric aura to his presence that made my heart pound even while broken. He'd always been strong enough to be dangerous—I'd just never thought before this moment that he might be dangerous to me.

"Did she say what she wanted with me?" he asked, words clipped.

"No. Nothing. She didn't tell me anything. I thought you were mortal," I said, banked anger flaring up again.

He'd lied. He'd lied over and over. To me, to everyone. Maybe he'd secretly undermined us. Maybe nothing was what I'd thought.

"Are you sure there was nothing else?" Taran asked intently.

I shook my head.

"It sounded . . . easy," I said, remembering. "I would have done anything she asked. And all she asked was that I bring you to her. I thought I'd get you from the Underworld, then go home." I bent my head forward, heart twisting painfully.

I should have known better. Like he said, the gods did nothing for free.

His gaze softened in response to my slump, or perhaps it was only that the possibility of violence retreated. After a moment, he stood and put his hands on his hips.

"Iona ter Wesha," he said thoughtfully. "Well, you're not Wesha's anymore. Iona. I suppose I'll put you in the solar for now."

"What?" I was startled out of my moment of deep self-pity.

"I'll bring in some furnishings," he said, gesturing toward another door off the lavish front room. "But you can sleep on the pink couch tonight. Bathe first, please, I don't want dust on the cushions."

"What are you talking about?" I asked, climbing off the ground.

Taran smiled brightly. "It seems you'll be staying. Never had a priest before, but I'll accept Wesha's gift despite the spirit in which it . . . well, *you* were given."

"What?" I protested again.

With a playful, insincere gesture, Taran tapped me on my forehead with one fingertip. "You are Wesha's pretty little trap, darling, one which I will not be falling into. But I'm happy to steal the bait, found my own temple."

With that lack of explanation, he turned and walked out of what I'd determined was his personal bathing chamber, and I had to trail behind him. The air of menace was gone. He was almost cheerful.

"I'm not your priestess! I didn't even know who you were an hour ago."

Taran waved a hand like this was a minor detail. "Better mine than Wesha's. I'll have to think about what your vows will be, but I'm sure they'll be more lenient than hers. And you'll have to be someone's priestess. Trust me, you don't want to look free for the taking."

His tendency to treat every turn of events as a cosmic joke had never annoyed me before this moment. "Then are you saying you won't come with me to the Painted Tower?" I clarified.

"Precisely. I have no interest in seeing Wesha ever again. Which she knows, given the terms we left on. But as you rather unwisely promised that you'll bring me to her, I suppose you'll be following me around for the rest of eternity."

My jaw dropped open at his casual appropriation of my life. "Why would you do that?"

He adroitly stepped around me, expression chiding.

"Don't be ungrateful. It's not like I'm the one who came up with your deal. In fact, you're lucky that I'm being so obliging." He opened another door in the front room to reveal a bedchamber. "We can discuss the terms of your service tomorrow."

"I'm also not *serving you*."

Taran chuckled again, turning to favor me with a knowing smirk that hurt all the more for its familiarity. "You're in quite the tangle, aren't you? Tell me, do mortals make oaths so recklessly because they think they'll only have to abide by them for a few decades before they kick off?"

I growled, anger rising, and stuck out my hand to stop Taran from shutting his bedroom door in my face.

"Why won't you . . ." I began to demand an explanation, but my movement caught Taran's eye.

Faster than I could react, he reached out with both hands. One yanked down the neckline of my dress, and the other darted into it. I was so tired that my first impulse was to object to this assault on my modesty, but he wasn't looking at my meager cleavage. Instead, he glared at the tiny bird trapped in his fist. Awi.

His air of cheerful indifference vanished, and the aura of violence returned.

Awi struggled in his hand as the dangerous dip of his eyelids suggested that he might crush her first and ask questions later.

"Stop!" I grabbed for his arm. "She hasn't done anything!"

I got a look of surprise that I had dared to put hands on him, but his fingers relaxed.

"Who are *you*?" he addressed the bird.

Her beady little eyes bulged over the puff of feathers where he'd squeezed her body. "I—I—it's your auntie Awi. You don't know who I am?" the bird said in a tiny peeping voice, so high in pitch that I could barely perceive it.

"Sure don't," Taran said, not releasing her.

"I know you! I knew you as a baby. I used to slip you honey-cakes when you turned up at your mother's parties without a stitch of clothing to cover your dimpled behind."

"My mother? You can't come up with a better story than that?"

"No, it's true," Awi insisted.

"My mother has all the maternal instincts of the cuckoo, which lays its eggs in other birds' nests. I'm sure I was nowhere near any parties until I was old enough to be decorative."

As Taran's face said that squishing was still on the table, I dug my nails into his arm.

"I can't let you hurt her." I wasn't exactly fond of the goddess, but my vow had my chest in a vise. "She's just trying to return to the mortal world. I promised to help her if she helped me get to Wesha."

Taran scoffed at that, but after a moment, he released the bird. Awi transformed before she hit the floor, returning to her guise as a red-eyed raven. She was stiff and fearful as she shuffled away from Taran, feathers a mess.

"You really have made the most inconvenient vows possible," Taran said to me, hand still hovering over the knife stuck into his belt. "And so *many* of them."

I was beginning to realize that.

He heaved an annoyed sigh and turned back to the bird. "Vow that you won't speak to Wesha about me. Or *I* vow you'll be picking your way down the Mountain in brand-new feathers tomorrow, powerless and forgetful."

Awi hesitated, and Taran took the knife out of his belt, face coldly murderous.

"I promise," Awi yelped, cringing away from him.

I had my hands clasped over my throat, stricken at how easily Taran had threatened the little bird goddess. How easily he'd killed the Fallen. How easily he disposed of me.

Taran had been kind. As gentle as someone fighting a war could be. Whether it had all been a performance or whether that man died on the cliffs to be reborn as someone utterly different, there was nothing for me here now.

I had to get out.

"Just let us go," I whispered. "I made a mistake in coming here. I'm sorry for your trouble tonight, but if you take us to the Painted Tower, we'll both go. Please."

Taran looked at me quizzically as he replaced the knife in his belt.

"Why would I?" he asked me, the line of his mouth cruel in a way I'd never seen before.

What was in it for him? I'd once offered him everything I had.

"Do it as a favor to me. Please. Just let us go."

His laugh was silent this time, but equally mirthless.

"I don't do favors for anyone. Not for you. Certainly not for Wesha. She's the one who taught me the lesson, in fact—though when I woke up on her beach six months ago, skull empty and mouth full of sand, she had some regrets about that." His lips didn't part as he tested the point of a sharp tooth with the tip of his tongue. "So, no. If you want me to take you to the Painted Tower, you'll have to make me an offer. A good one."

"What do you want?" I asked, my heart in my throat.

He considered it, then shrugged. He stuck the knife back in his belt and opened the door to his dark bedroom.

"Nothing comes to mind. But if something does, I'll be sure to tell you immediately."

9

I WOKE UP WHEN a heavy pile of fabric fell over me.

I didn't remember falling asleep on the divan's lurid pink cushions, but I must have. I cried for a little, then I tried to get clean in the baths, and then I cried some more while exploring the other rooms of Taran's overdecorated palace. Then I decided that I was done crying over Taran forever. I didn't trust a single god with that vow, but the lying bastard wasn't worth a single additional tear.

Before sitting down, I had made an inventory of everything that could be used as a weapon, then stashed a few sharp objects where I didn't think he'd find them. Stupid of him, leaving me loose while he slept. He'd been scary and threatening instead of gentle and considerate, and so I, scared and threatened, had started thinking how to thwart him instead of writing mediocre poetry about his beautiful eyes.

Awake again after only a few hours of fitful sleep, I fumbled out from under the wad of silk that had woken me up. My unconscious mind had treated the sound of Taran's breathing as a sign that I was safe and loved, rather than the contrary, and he sat by my feet.

He was still clad in nothing but his underwear and the golden light that streamed through the slits in the shuttered window behind him.

This morning he was using my surgical knife to slice a pomegranate, red juice staining his mouth and dripping down his fingers. His long eyelashes curtained his eyes as he bent to catch another seed in his lips, but I knew he was watching me, probably checking whether I was impressed by the lovely picture he made in gilded silhouette. When he saw that I was awake, he wordlessly offered me a bite of the fruit.

I shook my head and pulled my feet away from his lap as I sat up.

"Good morning, darling," he greeted me, daintily licking a rivulet of juice from his wrist. He was a dark shape with brilliant edges, perfectly carved out of warm muscle. "I thought Wesha's priests were early risers."

Perhaps he'd planned this little display in advance, but I was already familiar with Taran's derision for my sleep habits and the way his hair curled appealingly over his ears before he combed it, and I'd steeled myself against him.

"Not this one."

"Hmm. I'll have to ponder whether I require prayers at dawn. In any event, I found you something to wear." He nodded at the bundle of silk. "Can you make breakfast? And press our clothes?"

I bit the inside of my cheek to keep from saying *no, but if you turn around, I can stab you in the kidney.* I swallowed hard instead. "I'm afraid Wesha's training was scanty on the domestic arts," I said through gritted teeth.

Taran ate another bite of fruit before giving me a skeptical, mildly disappointed frown.

"You don't cook at all?"

"Some. Do you like your barley boiled until it's mushy or until it's *very* mushy?"

I was tiptoeing around my vow of truth. I could have cooked breakfast. I'd just sooner die.

"Then let's talk about what you *can* do for me, little priestess," he said with a laugh. "Remind me of Wesha's blessings. Do you know all of them?"

The engaging expression he made as he said this was a practiced performance, probably lethal to women in other circumstances. I used to melt like spring snow when he made any attempt to be sweet with me, but I was entirely unmoved now.

"If you think you might be pregnant, I can confirm the length of gestation."

He dropped the attempt to charm me but was not deterred.

"You know what nobody ever mentions about Wesha? How *funny* she is." He gave me a sterner look. "Tell me what Wesha's priests do."

"I can deliver babies. Cure many illnesses." I didn't know how evasive I could be. Wesha had been imprisoned for three hundred years. If he didn't know about her more dangerous blessings, I would hold them in reserve while I considered my options.

"That can't be all, if you survived this long," he said, eyes narrowing. "I heard that some of the acolytes left behind during the rebellion began to invoke the blessings of gods besides their own patrons."

"Oh?" I asked as if this was news to me. "Who said that?"

"Death-priests. Complaining that someone had stolen their gift of flame. Do you know that one?"

I pushed his clothes to the floor as though planning to go back to sleep, although my chest tightened at the news of death-priests in the Summerlands. "Would you like me to set you on fire?"

Taran gave me another one of those charming smiles and set his pomegranate and knife down on the table next to him. Then in one smooth motion, he lunged to splay his hands on the cushion under my head and cage me in, nearly nose to nose. I tried to squirm away, but he dropped a leg to the floor to hold me in place. He waited for my panting breath to catch up to my racing heart, which stuttered at his body propped over mine. He was warm and close and more bare than he'd ever been when he touched me.

Maybe I could learn to hate him. He'd always praised me for being a quick learner.

After a moment, Taran sat back enough to let me tilt my head away but gave a pointed tug to my braid where I'd left it down for sleep.

"Right now, you're what we'll call an 'indoor priest.' Keep this up, and we will explore the concept of 'outside priest.'" He nodded at the window, eyes as hard as emeralds where they glittered at me from only inches away.

He thought I'd flinch, like I did last night. But he could only betray everything I believed about him one time, and he'd already done that. Today I knew much more about him than he did me. Even if it was all a lie, or it was all for show, Taran had knelt in the dirt in front of dozens of witnesses and sworn to lay all he owned at my feet. I had seen him on his knees, and I would not be *bullied* by him.

"Here's an offer: you promise to take me to Wesha, and I promise you'll never have to see me again," I retorted.

He pulled up one corner of his mouth to acknowledge the parry, but didn't concede. "Don't you think you've already made too many vows, little priestess?"

It was a draw, as battles went, but my heartbeat didn't slow until he stood up and stalked off to the tiled room in a huff. I got up as soon as he was gone to press my ear against the door, discerning the faint sounds of falling water. He was drawing a bath. I stuck out my tongue in his direction.

"What are you *doing*?" Awi hissed.

I'd entirely forgotten about the little immortal, as distraught as I was, and neither Taran nor I had noticed her in the form of a small owl this morning, perched like a gargoyle on the top of a cabinet.

"Nothing," I said, going to the door of Taran's bedroom and finding it locked. I quickly sang the lock open and let myself in.

Awi fluttered to the ground and followed me in nervous little hops.

"Yes, I can see you're doing *nothing*. Nothing to get us out of here, anyway. Why are you antagonizing him?"

I didn't know what I had expected from Taran's bedroom, but I was disappointed regardless. It was ostentatious, with rose quartz tiles accenting the black-and-white marble, but there was nothing unusual about the large, curtained bed, which was made, the rudimentary cot by the window, which was not, or the gilded closets and chests comprising the rest of the furniture. No weapons, no altars, no cages full of terrified mortal girls. I sighed and opened the first closet.

"I'm antagonizing him because he's the demon who's currently holding us captive in the Summerlands," I said, beginning to systematically rifle through his things.

"And I'm sure it gives you a nice warm feeling in your tummy to be mean to him, but how do you expect to get me free?" Awi demanded.

I found nothing but fancy women's clothes in the first closet and moved on to the next.

I didn't have an answer for Awi. I had asked Taran to let us go and he said no, in a way that suggested that his reasons for not returning to Wesha were related to hers for wanting him there. I didn't know enough yet.

"You could at least try to sweet-talk him into it," the bird said.

A self-effacing laugh bubbled out of my throat.

"If you think I can use my feminine wiles on Taran to make him do what we want, I regret to inform you that I don't have any."

The bird looked me up and down, golden eyes assessing my straight figure.

"Yeah, no kidding," Awi said, and I fruitlessly kicked in her direction before opening another chest of clothes.

It burned though. It made my throat ache. How quickly I'd believed that what someone like Taran wanted was a plain, celibate priestess with ash on her face and not a single thought of romance in her head. I'd been so surprised to fall in love that I didn't stop to question why he wanted me. I was Iona Night-Singer, after all, fighting the very god of death. Taran falling in love with me hadn't seemed any more unlikely.

"You said he wanted to marry you though. Why don't you just do what you did last time? Did you sing? Did you pretend to listen to him while he's talking? Are you good at sex?"

"He didn't want to marry me. He wanted to infiltrate the mortal rebellion," I said, jaw tight.

This chest's dimensions didn't make sense. It had to have a false bottom. I quickly took the blankets out of it and knocked around the edges until I found the catch.

"But regardless of his reasons, he would have had to do it, if you were betrothed," Awi said.

I looked up, startled. Mortal vows—vows between mortals—were only as strong as the people who made them. It hadn't occurred to me yet that Taran's vows had been immortal too.

"Would he? Have had to?"

The bird bobbed her head. "Only death breaks immortal vows."

Why had he bothered to swear betrothal vows? I would have done anything he asked, as besotted as I was.

"Maybe dying and returning to the Summerlands was always his plan," was all I could come up with. Though that was not very flattering either, that someone would rather die than marry me.

"That's stupid. He probably planned for you to die instead."

"Oh. Probably," I agreed, shoulders slumping before I thought harder about it and stiffened.

He hadn't wanted me dead. Not by the end, at least. Even setting aside three years of care—little things that made my throat hurt to think of, times he'd slid his dinner into my bowl or warmed my hands in his—all he'd needed to do on that last day on the beach was nothing, and I'd be dead instead of him.

"Maybe that's what he planned at the beginning, but he changed his mind." My breath caught with the pain of a hopeful thought to interrupt my very satisfying wallow in anger.

Maybe Taran had changed his mind. Maybe he'd started off with the idea that he'd put the rebellion down, turn us back toward the temples, even asked me to marry him to cement his control over the people propelling the uprising, but at some point he . . . stopped.

"Stoneborn don't change their minds," Awi said, unimpressed.

"You said he has mortal blood. And he was a disappointment to Genna," I reminded her, speaking more quickly. "Maybe he realized it wasn't our fault when he got there. We didn't turn against the gods. They abandoned us, and then Death took everything we had. It was Death's fault. Maybe he realized that."

The hope, of course, was that if Taran had changed his mind before, he might do it again. I told myself I was a silly girl who couldn't accept that I'd been in love with an evil beast, but I couldn't let go of the possibility. I liked it more than all the alternative explanations.

"That's the kind of talk that'll get your limbs displayed at different crossroads for blasphemy," Awi said.

I made a face at her, then lifted the bottom of the chest. It was full of stone knives—the same rainbow obsidian as my surgical blades, but much more substantial. The bird goddess whistled in slow appreciation at the jumble.

"Enough stone blades to do in the entire pantheon."

Who are you *planning on killing, Taran?*

I heard bathwater begin to drain next door and hurriedly packed the chest back up before fleeing Taran's bedroom—minus the smallest of his hidden knives, which I tucked away for safekeeping. I grabbed the clothes he'd brought me off the divan and made it to the solar before he returned to the front room.

"Are you ready to go, darling?" he called. "If you want to live till evening, I suggest you change out of Wesha's regalia."

I snarled as I flipped through the options. All were cut for someone taller and much more fond of jeweled embellishments than I was; the pearls on the bodice of a single dress would have paid for the house he'd promised to build me. I picked the one with the highest neckline, deciding that I didn't need to wonder why he owned so much spare women's clothing.

Taran, himself resplendent in a sleeveless tunic that showed off the wide golden armbands around his biceps, was all but tapping his foot when I returned, but he stilled to look me up and down.

"What?" I asked. He couldn't be impressed—the dress was made of fine, sleek ramie, but it covered me from wrists to ankles, and coral pink clashed with my hair and made me look jaundiced. Still, he studied me as though just now realizing that I had physical form.

"If someone asks, say I let you dress yourself today. I don't think Wesha's clothes suit you," he said.

I blinked, looking around the room with some outrage as I realized this dawn-pink-and-gold palace must have been Wesha's before she married Death. He'd threatened to throw me out? I should throw him out! Didn't the Maiden's last priest have a better claim on all this than her estranged younger brother?

Heedless of my frown, Taran opened the door and gestured for me to follow him.

"Time to start earning your keep, little priestess," he announced. "We're late for services."

"What services?"

He favored me with a sunny smile. "Worship services, of course. I'd be very pleased to receive your prayers of gratitude. And I'm particularly fond of hymns, if you can manage those. Feel free to compose on the way there."

I nodded slowly. I already knew the sacred names I'd call him, and I'd compose in the key of B major, for bastard.

TARAN'S LONG LEGS propelled him faster than I could ever keep up with, and my foot ached from the effort. I followed him through the same tiled halls as the night before, teeth gritted and limp increasing until he finally slowed his pace to one I could match. When I stumbled at the first set of steps we came to, Taran wordlessly wrapped my arm around his for balance.

I was too busy minimizing contact between my body and his to notice that we'd stepped outside until the light hit my eyes, and I halted as I got my first look at the City of the Gods.

Wesha's palace stood at the outskirts of a gentle, sloping bowl that contained the hundreds of temples and villas where the immortals dwelled. Our epics described the City as a walled garden, and the flowers were the first thing I saw. Espaliered cherry trees bearing both rosy blossoms and lush fruit separated mounds of hydrangeas and lilacs, without a single brown leaf or wilted petal, flowers of every season perfect together at once. Amidst the emerald lawns, chestnut and oak trees stretched their arms hundreds of feet into the sky.

The buildings were constructed in a single style, with the same tall-columned verandas and grand arched entryways as our oldest mortal temples, but no single one was made out of the same stone as another. Here was one in red granite, here another in golden sandstone, a third in blue-veined marble, as though every quarry in the entire world had given tribute. The infinite dots of color across the landscape were harmonized by the green slate tiles each used on their roofs, and the profusion of columns underneath added to the suggestion that the buildings bloomed out of the soil like the other growing things in this celestial garden.

It was just morning by the color of the sky and the golden glow above the mountains, which came from everywhere and no direction in particular, but I couldn't get my bearings. There was the Mountain in the distance, beyond many other snow-capped peaks. But wasn't that the same shape to my left as well, beyond the parapets of the City? There was barely any shadow, even under my foot when I lifted it from the glinting stone of the path.

"Where is the sun?" I whispered.

"Flying over the mortal world, at this hour," said Taran.

I took a deep breath, trying to steady myself against the overwhelming disorientation of the Heavens.

"You'll get used to it," he added, not unkindly. "All the other priests did."

If I didn't focus on any particular landmark, I might cry from the beauty of it all. If I tried to look more closely at any one tree or palace, I got the dizzying impression that I was seeing a slightly different scene through each eye.

I forgot myself and clutched Taran's arm as he led me toward the center of the City, battered by the overwhelming perfume of the out-of-season flowers and hundreds of colors around me. The paved paths turned into boulevards, and the buildings grew closer together, more than my mind could absorb. Our destination seemed to be the very center of the bowl, a vast arena painted with enormous murals depicting the feats of the Stoneborn, all painted in a single artist's style. The arena was set down into the earth like the navel of the entire world, only one story high at the level of the street but dipping down hundreds of feet to accommodate a crowd of the full thousand little gods and their worshippers.

I saw them in the streets with us: gleaming immortals trailed by priests carrying the trains of their elaborate robes or carrying their gods aloft on ornate palanquins with silk cushions and gilded carry-bars.

"The service is for all the gods?" I asked, eyeing an immortal with the hindquarters of a ram and a long, yellow sash carried by a pair of priests wearing garlands of fragrant hops. There might be thousands of mortals here too, in that case.

Taran nodded. "Genna, with her boundless love of peace—and elaborate dinner parties—has invited the younger gods to come together and renew our vows of friendship."

"The younger gods?"

"I am not the only one to experience some recent . . . challenges with immortality."

I stopped, ignoring Taran's impatience.

"Will Death be there?" I asked.

He stopped too, going very still.

"Why do you ask?"

Because you killed him. Because he killed everyone else.

"Because he died. He died six months ago, in the mortal world. Wesha said he'd been reborn. Here? Is he here?"

Taran's expression relaxed. "He's invited, but nobody's seen him. Possibly he's still crawling down the Mountain, since he hasn't more than a few dozen priests and a handful of Fallen left."

"But he's in the Summerlands? The Stoneborn haven't done anything to contain him? They let the Fallen roam the City and eat people?" My voice grew tighter as I imagined it.

"Technically, it is *Wesha* who lets the Fallen eat you, my precious almost-maiden-priest. Because she promised everything she owned to her husband."

I hadn't been anywhere near Death at Ereban. I'd been all the way in the rear with the other acolytes, shouting and pushing through the crowd as his priests led the young princess to the altar. I'd lived because I didn't make it to the front in time.

Like every time I sent my mind there, I began to feel hot and confined. My throat remembered smoke. My arms remembered the press of other bodies. Too hot, too tight, the ceiling will—

Taran waved a hand in front of my face, drawing me back to the present.

"You're not in any danger. If Napeth was reborn on the Mountain six months ago, he'll be just as powerless and empty-headed as Marit. Stymied by the knots in his trouser laces and the names of his ugly children."

"You don't remember him either," I pushed back, my fingernails cutting into my palms. "Everything he did. In the war. In either war!"

"What should I remember?" Taran asked, lifting an eyebrow.

"He murdered every last maiden-priest. Burned down the high temple. Set fires that scorched half the country. And—and didn't he nearly destroy the Summerlands too, three hundred years ago?" I looked around for evidence of the destruction, but there was no indication that this place had ever known a moment of imperfection.

Was this City so beautiful that nobody could ever imagine it broken again?

"He's *here*, somewhere, with a temple full of Fallen, and—"

Taran exhaled, jaw shifting to the side at my obvious distress. "Look, I'm not going to let anyone hurt you," he said. His tone was low and casual, but he ducked his head to meet my eyes on the same level.

I was touched by this unexpected gallantry, but before I could revise my opinion of him, he broke eye contact and amended his statement: "*If* you behave yourself."

My grimace seemed to seal that point for him, because he took my arm and insistently led me up a paved ramp into the highest tier of the arena. I only had a moment to take in its vast size before Taran jauntily stepped onto the outer ring of risers and tugged me into a large group of mortals: the missing priests.

Hundreds of them, properly attired in a rainbow of hues and milling around with attitudes ranging from boredom to celebration—every priest who'd taken a vow of obedience to a patron god. The wise adults I'd obeyed and respected for my entire life, before the survivors of Ereban abandoned us and fled across the sea after the first riots. They had a refreshment table with juice and glazed cakes, where they were enjoying a leisurely breakfast.

I recognized several faces. Before I could think of how I'd explain myself, I saw one that recognized me: the elegant high priestess of Genna who'd advised the queen until the rebellion began. Taran knew her too.

"Teuta ter Genna," he addressed the buxom woman with a cap of iron-gray curls, whose lovely dark eyes flew wide when they landed on me. Taran put a hand on the small of my back. "Have you met my new priestess before? Of course you have. I'd be very grateful if you'd show her around, then."

Teuta's gaze darted back and forth between me and Taran, but she swallowed and rallied when I couldn't think of anything to say. Here they were. The priests who should have been singing green crops into our fields and life into our starving people. The ones who'd left dozens of half-trained children behind to fight and die in their absence, enjoying eternal life and a pleasant morning at Genna's party.

"Oh . . . welcome, Iona ter Taran," Teuta said hesitantly.

I choked on my own saliva then, so I didn't have the opportunity to protest when Taran gave me a satisfied pat and propelled me toward the high priestess of Genna. He straightened his tunic and strode down toward the pavilion at the center of the arena, pausing only to wink at my dismay at being dropped with the other mortals like a lamb in the communal pasture.

Teuta edged toward me when I didn't move.

"You just got here?" she asked in a voice that didn't carry. "You sailed across the Sea of Dreams?"

"Yesterday," I said flatly. Perhaps they had no choice about leaving us or about not coming back, but they did not look very concerned for the fate of everyone they'd left behind. Smiling and laughing, most of them. Nibbling on spiced orange cake.

Teuta exhaled, considering my stony face. "Is it very bad?"

"As bad as you might have expected after Ereban burned."

"Are there others?"

"A few of us survived, if that's what you mean. Hiwa ter Genna. Some other acolytes. I'm the only one who's here."

Teuta would have already heard what happened to the maiden-priests when she fled.

Ignoring my hard stare, she put what she probably intended to be a comforting hand on my shoulder. "I'm so sorry to hear that. We all worried that—well. That it was as bad as it seemed."

"Why are you still here?" I whispered angrily. "The fighting's been over for six months. The queen thinks you're never coming back."

At my undertone of accusation, Teuta stiffened. "We're still here because a week after the riots started, *someone* burned down Death's temple with all his priests inside. The other Stoneborn were afraid their people might be next. Did the rebellion spare any temples at all?"

Her gaze was forthright, and I froze as I surmised she had a good idea of who had been responsible for the first reprisal attack. She looked away when I didn't admit to it.

"The Stoneborn know very little of the mortal world now. You're safe."

I shrugged her hand off. I already knew that wasn't true, if Death was alive and in the Summerlands. Even if it had been, *safe* was not what *my* temple had considered the most important thing to be.

I stalked away to look down at the center of the arena to see where Taran had gone.

It was mostly empty, with rows upon rows of unfilled risers. The priests were in the farthest ring, and the inner rings were filled with lesser immortals: little garden spirits and river nymphs, mountain gods and hearth gnomes. The Stoneborn were in a silk-covered pavilion at the center, but only four of them.

I recognized the golden semicircle of thrones from the epics, and the seats carved with the sigils of their domains. Most were empty—Wesha's sunrise throne and thankfully the flame-topped chair beside hers, where Death was meant to sit. I felt a little of my fear dissolve at the sight of his empty chair, even though the other side of the semicircle held two shining gods whose glow hurt my eyes.

I was familiar with this trick—Death had used it too, during the midsummer sacrifices—but I couldn't quite suppress my awe at being in the distant presence of Diopater and Genna. I couldn't make out their features or clothing on the two luminous beings, just the suggestion of a thick, gray beard on one and long, golden hair on the other. Their power still buzzed against my skin in the tempo of the lightning that casually arced between Skyfather's massive hands.

The Stoneborn were far enough away that their conversation didn't carry, but Marit was speaking with Genna, wine goblet in hand and a puddle of seawater at his feet. Drunk again, with a large cask of wine abandoned on his wave-capped throne.

None of them looked like Taran, who'd looked like a person, not a power. He had been a person who told bad jokes, a person who hated onions so much that he picked them out of his food—a person who used to rub my temples with his thumbs when I got a headache. The man who claimed to be one of the Stoneborn stood behind Genna's throne, his arms folded behind his back and his posture wary. Her part-mortal bastard didn't get a throne, I supposed.

A priestess in Skyfather's purple cloak stepped out in front of the assembly and lifted her arms to voice the universal call to prayer. Down in the pavilion, the Stoneborn were still idle, and there was some dissent among the priests. *Shouldn't we keep waiting? Is anyone else coming?* But the other priests began to shuffle into rows, and Teuta followed me to the highest row in the rear.

"Does he know?" she whispered to me once the voices of the other priests gave her cover.

"You mean, does he know that I . . ." My voice trailed off when Teuta lifted a cautioning finger to her lips and shot her eyes into the crowd. At the very edge, up in front, one wore a red robe and bronze lion mask. A death-priest.

I held Teuta's gaze and shook my head minutely. No, Taran did not know I'd led the mortal rebellion he'd been sent to put down.

"He knows Wesha sent me here. That's all."

Teuta smiled in relief. "Good. I don't think anyone else will recognize you, dressed like that. Taran won't . . . well, I've never heard of him harming a mortal. Unless they somehow crossed the Peace-Queen, that is."

That was a pretty large *unless*. Genna had, after all, forced her youngest daughter into marriage with Death and sent her son to wipe out the mortal rebels. I considered myself and the Peace-Queen at cross-purposes.

"But he still might murder me the next time I object to one of the Stoneborn slitting a child's throat?" I asked, my whisper growing heated.

"No. The Allmother forbids human sacrifice," Teuta said firmly.

The Allmother was not here. The largest throne in the center of the pavilion was crowned with the symbol of the Mountain, and it sat empty, as it had been for centuries. In the epics, we'd learned that she slept, still recovering from her labors in giving birth to the Stoneborn. She awoke only to erupt in anger when her laws were transgressed. But she hadn't saved us in the long years that Death terrorized the mortal world.

"I'm so glad to hear that," I said bitterly. "Has anyone told Death yet?"

"This is not the place for blasphemy, Iona! And Taran ab Genna is not going to condone human sacrifice. He's the one who saved the rest of Marit's priests, after all." Teuta nodded at the god who was cracking the tiles of the pavilion with every step, seawater flowing in his wake. Genna leaned back to say something to Taran, pointing at the sea god, and Taran waded out from behind the throne.

"What happened to Marit's priests?"

"You see how Marit is . . . like that? After Taran had been gone for a year, trying to stop . . . trying to restore the rule of the temples. When he didn't come back and didn't send word, Skyfather ran out of patience and wanted to send a wave to destroy the rebel cities. Marit wouldn't do it—he was afraid Taran would be drowned too."

"Interesting priorities," I muttered, glaring at the sea god as he reeled drunkenly around the stage, Taran in careful pursuit.

"You have to understand, they can't see the mortal world from here. Wesha won't let them close to the shore. All they knew is that the mortals had turned against their priests and withdrawn their worship. It made them furious, even Marit. But anyway, Skyfather was so angry at Marit for refusing to wipe out the rebels that he tossed him into a well."

I grimaced, thinking of all the ships that had docked with empty nets. The storms that preceded the mudslides that had finally destroyed Ereban. The high priestess stoically continued the story when I remained silent.

"Marit's Stoneborn, so he didn't die, but since it was fresh water, he couldn't escape either. He stayed down there, screaming day and night, until Taran came back and fished his friend out. But Marit had gone as mad as a hornet in a jar after two years in the well. Once he was free, he was beyond reason. He cracked the foundations of his own palace, flooded half the City. When his priests tried to flee . . . most of them drowned."

Down on the stage, Taran had failed to pry the wine goblet away from Marit, and the sea god was drunkenly gesticulating as the water at his feet began to flow faster. Genna and Diopater rose to their feet as the waves lapped at their ankles. Even cloaked by the golden illusion that wrapped their bodies, they appeared unhappy with the situation.

Teuta nodded when Taran put an arm around Marit's shoulders and said something into the sea god's ear.

"That's how Taran killed him. He gave Marit a glass of poisoned wine, then put a stone dagger in his heart. And once the Allmother brought Marit back, he was better. A little. Taran stopped him."

My stomach dropped at the conclusion of Teuta's story, but something in me, not the nicest part, perhaps, but the part that had watched Death's temples burn, said *well, good*. Taran was still there. Some kernel of the person who'd gone to war against a god who'd become a tyrant. I just had to find him.

Satisfied that I was reconciled to my new role when I didn't say anything more, Teuta knelt down with the rest of the priests and began to sing along with the prayers that continued unimpeded by the wet drama below. But I would not be singing any more praises of the Stoneborn who'd wanted to drown us. The ones who'd listened to Marit drowning for two years.

I slipped away as soon as Taran finally lured Marit out of the arena, off to start looking for my way home.

10

THE AIR IN the banquet hall was frigid but shouldn't have been cold enough to keep the snow under my boots from melting. Skyfather's power, even though he was nowhere to be seen. This hall was filled with empty tables set for hundreds, and ice crept up the inside of the blue marble pillars despite the summer weather outside. I'd wandered out of the arena with no particular destination, but when the rest of the City proved vacant, I'd returned to the arena and found this meal set and abandoned in an adjacent palace.

I'd never seen ice sculptures before. The ones decorating the banquet tables all depicted Marit's heroic feats—slaying sea monsters, commanding the waves. The monsters were constructed entirely of fresh seafood, which would have made me giggle if I weren't so battered by the past week's events.

I chafed the gooseflesh under Wesha's pink dress as I heard a familiar step behind me. My heart lurched at everything that was familiar about him. The way he walked. The way he breathed. I wanted so much for him to be alive, to be my Taran, to take my hand and call me his nightingale.

But when he approached, it was to call me by my given name,

so I forced a polite smile to my face instead of turning and wrapping my arms around his waist.

"Here you are. Feeling better?" he asked, taking in my diminished hostility.

"A little."

"Teuta seemed relieved to see you. All the peace-priests will be at this banquet later, if you'd like to come."

I hummed noncommittally. I hadn't quite forgiven the peace-priests for enjoying eternal summer while the world burned.

When I didn't snap at him, Taran relaxed, producing a heavy cloak in a shimmering gray-green and draping it around my shoulders.

"There," he said with satisfaction. "You shouldn't wear pink."

I welcomed the warmth, and he was right, so I didn't stop him from reaching around me to pin it closed.

"You brought this for me?" I asked, surprised. I'd been anything but polite to him so far.

"I thought you might get cold at dinner." His hands still rested lightly on my shoulders after he was done arranging the fabric, gentle and coaxing.

"Thank you. Was it Wesha's too?"

"No, one of Skyfather's concubines left it unattended, and I decided it would look better on you."

I closed my eyes and silently retracted my thanks, refocusing on things that mattered. Getting out of here.

"Where were all the other gods this morning?"

Taran ignored my question and ran his palms lightly over the cloak where it draped my arms. "What did you wear before? Wesha's white? I don't think that would suit you either. How about blue? A different shade than Marit's priests wear, perhaps?"

"Taran. Where do you think Death is?"

He ignored me again, instead lifting one hand to brush the edge of his thumb along the knot of my hair. He used to do the same thing whenever I was near.

"Do you ever wear it down?" he asked, idly winding a fingertip into a stray curl. I shivered as his knuckles brushed the bare skin on the nape of my neck.

"No, never."

"Pity," he said. "I bet it's lovely."

One night Taran had taken all the pins out of my hair and coaxed me into brushing it until I could run a comb through the waves from root to tip. He'd wrapped the ends around his fingers and held on too long, until my light laugh had caught deeper in my stomach, and the look he'd given me had felt like a promise. *Oh, that's what desire means*, I'd thought.

"Would you consider it?" he asked, hand still on my nape.

"If you'll answer my questions, I vow I'll dress however you want," I blurted, trying to resist the tightening of my body at the memory of his hands in my hair.

Taran released me and stepped to my front, one corner of his mouth quirking up.

"You should really stop making so many vows. You are going to have to live with them for a very long time." His smile made my stomach drop. "But alright. I vow it."

I felt a slight chill of foreboding as the new vow wrapped its way through my bones, but his choices of clothing could hardly hurt me. Wasn't it a good bargain?

"Where are the other Stoneborn?"

Taran shrugged. "I don't know." Before I could object, he amended his answer with an air that suggested he was humoring me.

"Some Stoneborn, Skyfather chief among them, would like to re-form the armies of Heaven and march back to the mortal world. Restore the rule of the temples by force." He strolled over to the closest banquet table and took a plate. He smiled at the enormous sea monster, whose claws were formed of steamed crab legs and eyes of mollusk shells. Large prawns on waves of ice stood ready to reinforce it in battle. "The Peace-Queen, on the other hand, thinks that if you're left to your own devices for a few decades, you'll remember that you enjoy rain and flowering plants and her blessings of healing, and come to your senses."

"Marit's in the first group?"

"No, the second. Not that he'd be opposed to a good campaign of conquest. I've just told him that Wesha wouldn't let them through the Gates even if the gods did agree on something for once." Taran surveyed the food, then used tongs to remove some pink slices of fish edged in caviar from the robes of Marit's ice statue.

"But is sending a giant wave to teach us a lesson entirely off the table?" I asked unhappily.

"Yes," Taran said, tone light. "Marit doesn't have the power to manage it anymore." He added prawns to the plate with a dollop of sauce. "Have you ever had these shrimp things? Are they any good? I can't remember."

I ignored his question for a change.

"And Death?"

"Death is not going to come and snatch you in the night, little priestess. As I've told you, I'll keep you far out of his way."

"How can you say that, if you don't know where he is or what he's planning?"

Taran scrunched up his proud face in distaste at my repeated demand for basic information about the god who'd spent three years trying to murder me.

"Why should I keep track of him? If he's back, there's no reason to think he'll do worse than pound on Wesha's door to insist on his marital rights, which is all he's done for centuries. Honestly, they deserve each other."

At my wounded look, Taran rolled his eyes.

"Wesha's well capable of defending herself, likely because she never bothers to defend anyone else. Certainly not you, my darling. So please forgive me if I choose to reserve my protection for those who merit it."

I gnawed on the inside of my lip, wrapping my new cloak more closely around myself. He had undeniably done that, despite his enormous deception. Kept me and the young acolytes safe. Genna hadn't asked him to do that—probably would not even have approved, since he'd been sent to bring us back in line. Perhaps he'd done the best he could under Genna's command.

"Teuta told me what happened with Marit. With his priests," I said tentatively.

"With his priests?"

"How you saved them. Even though you had to kill your friend."

Taran paused before answering. "Yes, I suppose I did."

I was very alert to the caution in his voice, what he wasn't saying.

"Isn't it true? Teuta told me—"

"It's true. I did kill him, though he doesn't remember that half the time."

The little evasion there was obvious to me.

"You mean you didn't try to save the rest of his priests?"

With a little shrug, Taran popped a prawn into his mouth. "It's against the Allmother's laws to interfere with another Stoneborn's priests, so I couldn't have done anything for them even if I'd wanted to. Genna was angry at me for letting Marit out of the well, and I was strongly urged to clean up my mess before he destroyed her palace too."

He said it with total unconcern, but I marked the way he looked away and kept his expression bland.

"You're lying."

All the gods damn him, I'd made him promise to answer my questions, but I hadn't made him promise to answer them *truthfully*.

I was never going to survive this place. I was like a toddler in a foundry, wandering around with arms outstretched. My chagrin must have showed on my face, because Taran almost smiled.

"Am I? Oh fine, you caught me."

If I had to live in this world, with all these merciless gods, I wouldn't reveal it either if I had a soft spot for mortal lives. I clung stubbornly to the hope that Taran had failed to put down the mortal rebellion because of it.

"Why did you kill him?" I asked again. We were alone in the big banquet hall, with echoes muffled by the high coffered ceilings. Maybe he'd tell me the truth.

Taran shrugged uncomfortably.

"The other Stoneborn wanted to put him back in the well." His tone was soft, edged with regret.

It wasn't what I had hoped to hear. I spun around, voice rising with outrage.

"So it was mercy for *him*? Not for the mortal cities that Skyfather wanted Marit to wipe out? Not for Marit's own priests, the ones he killed?"

Taran tilted his jaw. *Yes?*

"I suppose you would have killed him for purer reasons?" he demanded.

"By the time you were standing over your friend with a knife, his priests dead around him, I think nobody had *pure* in sight. Do you know how we prayed that the gods would come and save us from Death? Are any of you better than he is, or was Wesha protecting us from you too when she locked the Gates?"

"Ah. Sounds like you're closer to the 'big wave and start afresh' camp than you think, then," Taran said, mocking me. "No. None of us are any better than the others, and I'm sure there are good reasons to murder us all. Alas, the Allmother is strictly opposed to it."

I stared at my feet. I still had my own boots on, and they looked worn and crude with Wesha's dress.

"I saw Death kill thousands of people, but I had no idea he came from such cruelty," I said, shoulders sinking.

"Cruelty?" Taran asked incredulously. "What do you know about it? All I've done since you arrived uninvited is house you and keep you safe. You haven't suffered any cruelty."

"I didn't want to come here! I just wanted my betrothed back, and if I can't have him, I want to go home."

I knew I sounded childish, but the contempt of the gods I'd spent my life worshipping was grinding down my soul.

Taran looked at me with confusion, like I'd shown poor manners. Teuta, who wouldn't have bowed to the queen, had deferred to him—this was probably the first time a mortal had ever spoken to him harshly.

"Are you used to getting what you want?" he asked.

I pressed my lips together, shook my head. Though when I'd set sail for Wesha's prison, I'd held the naive belief that surely, after everything, the gods owed me *something*.

"No, never."

His expression was faintly pitying. "Me neither."

With that deflating agreement, I stared at the full banquet tables, at this unimaginable plenty set out while people were starving in the mortal world. It wouldn't rot in the Summerlands, not if it sat out for three hundred years, but it had not occurred to any of the gods to simply share their bounty and hope for the mortals to return to worship out of gratitude.

Taran refilled his plate with more food, then pressed it into my hands.

"Here," he said beneficently. "Better take this back to my rooms, if neither of us is going to cook. I'll be minding Marit for the rest of the day."

"Alright," I agreed, dejected. I took the plate from him and turned to go.

My lack of fight seemed to make him frown.

"If you'd like, I'll ask if anyone's seen Napeth," he offered.

"Would it matter to you if he were planning another war?" I asked, voice numb.

"Well, of course not, since I'm not about to tell him he can't have his wife back. I'm just mildly curious on your behalf."

I hadn't really expected him to answer, but then I recalled that he was now obligated to, truthful or not. I halted because, for a moment, it felt like I'd caught him in another lie.

Taran swept by me and brushed a thumb over the lapel of my cloak one more time.

"I think I'll put you in green," he said, making it sound like the conclusion of a long, thoughtful deliberation. He pointed at his face and smirked. "To match my eyes."

11

I T TOOK ME more than an hour to find my way back to Wesha's palace. Without the sun, I had no sense of direction, and the peaks that encircled the City seemed to change with my perspective too. Had I come with the Mountain to my back, or my left?

Nobody confronted me as I wandered through numbingly perfect lawns and gilded colonnades with an open plate of seafood. I saw sky-priests setting up a race course and lawn games, and I gave them a wide berth. It wasn't my idea of heaven, but then again, the only paradise I'd ever imagined for myself was the house with a plum tree that Taran had promised at our betrothal.

Solitude was a novelty, one I couldn't enjoy. I couldn't remember the last time I'd been really alone—not during my training, not during the war, especially not after Taran died.

Maybe the company had helped though. The care of my friends couldn't banish the black beast of grief, but they'd kept it from digging its claws into me. I felt it tear me open when I found a kithara hanging on a peg in Taran's sitting room. He played beautifully, but we'd only had my single instrument, and Taran would laugh and say he'd rather listen to me unless I begged him with my nose pressed into the corner of his jaw and my arms wound around his neck. I had hoped to give him his own for a wedding present.

When my eyes began to water, I sternly told myself that Taran was alive and I could go see him right now if I wanted to, but I couldn't make my heart believe in a Taran that I couldn't hold in my arms.

I took his kithara down instead. It was heavier and more ornate than my own, but it felt natural in my hands when I tuned it and launched into practice scales. I had always thought more easily with something in my hands, but by the time afternoon slipped into night, I hadn't hit upon any better idea than knocking Taran out and dragging him up the Mountain in a sack.

My hands were getting tired when the door flew open hard enough to crack against the opposite wall. I jumped to my feet, but when Taran poked his head into the room, he had high color in his fair cheeks and a smile gracing his lips. I wasn't concerned until I saw he had Marit's arm draped over his shoulders, and the other god had a golden carafe of wine clutched in his fist. By the way they were leaning on each other, they were well into their cups.

"My new priestess. Were you playing?" Taran said fuzzily, seeing me with his kithara. "I don't mind, do continue."

I hesitated as Taran dropped Marit on the divan where I had slept the night before. The sea god's expression was morose, and I was afraid of the scent of wine and salt that followed him into the room, but Taran shut the door and slouched into the chair next to mine with an expectant attitude.

"What? Oh, yes. I like music too," Marit said, blearily trying to focus on me. "I think."

"Please," Taran said after a moment, finally remembering the word. He folded his hands over his stomach and stretched out his long legs, posture relaxing as I hesitantly began to play again. His expression was indulgent, which made me want to throw something at him, but I also remembered Awi's advice to win him over, and my music was all I had to recommend me.

Marit's face crumpled as I picked out the first notes of a simple instrumental ballad, and he loudly choked back a sniffle.

"Did something happen?" I asked Taran without stopping.

"Genna's reception this afternoon was . . . not well attended."

"They all hate me," Marit said.

He looked to me and Taran as though expecting us to contradict him. I wasn't inclined to—it was hard to feel warmly about any god who'd killed his own priests, intentionally or not, much less a god who would consider a tsunami to be a reasonable option in any scenario.

"They don't hate you," Taran said, a beat too late. He covered his sour expression by standing and refilling Marit's carafe from a ceramic cask in the corner. He poured out two more glasses, which I ignored and which Marit refused by drinking from the carafe instead.

"If anyone, they hate Wesha, for putting us in this situation in the first place," Taran added.

Marit tilted the carafe back and drained it. He tried again to focus on me.

"Do I know you?"

"My new priestess," Taran said again.

"I'm not," I said, but I finished the song anyway, thinking hard before my next piece.

If this were an epic, I'd change Taran's heart with my music. There were stories that went like that—I hadn't come up with the idea of playing for Wesha all on my own. Taran would hear me sing, and he'd magically be restored. Hadn't he loved my singing most of anything about me? Couldn't it connect us despite his lies, his death and rebirth, the distance between one of the Stoneborn and the runaway acolyte he'd pretended to be? I started to tell myself that story, even as my wounded spirit told me that nothing was ever that pretty.

Taran had a favorite ballad, a love song, though the lyrics didn't say the word. It was about a garden full of flowers that bloomed month after month, with each verse describing a different blossom. The love was in the subtext: the reason that the unnamed gardener would tend the earth in every season and describe the flowers so sweetly.

Taran used to bring me flowers on the first of the month, even in the dead of winter—Genna's power, used frivolously—and I'd tuck them behind my ear and sing this song, which flattered my vocal range and showed off my ability with a ten-stringed instrument.

At first, I almost thought it worked.

He went still when I began to sing, eyes rounding and focusing on me. Halfway through, he sat up and leaned in, hanging on every note. His intensity gave me hope. Did part of him remember hearing this before? In squalid barns, in freezing army camps? With his head resting against my thigh?

In my garden in spring, the plum trees will bloom, all white and snow do I grow in this season.

While I sang he didn't smile, but a small line appeared between his eyebrows. He could have been hearing some echo in his heart. He could have been realizing there was some rich world of mortal thought and feeling that he'd forgotten.

"That was lovely," Marit said when I was done.

I didn't respond, breath held for Taran's reaction. My heart squeezed when a smile dawned across his face, large enough to make his eyes crinkle and the dimples pop in his cheeks.

My delicate bubble of hope popped at the unmistakably smug cast his grin took on. He leaned back and spread his arms across the back of his chair, biting his lower lip in gratified amazement.

Bastard.

"Taran's lucky to have you. You're very good," Marit put in with evident jealousy.

"Isn't she?" Taran said with satisfaction in every line of his body. He was obviously patting himself on the back for his cleverness in acquiring a talent such as myself.

I resisted the urge to chuck the kithara at his grinning face, instead mentally arranging the rest of my performance around the theme of *men who were sorry they hadn't been nicer to women*, which was a perennially popular genre among certain of Wesha's worshippers.

There was an amused glint in Taran's eye when my next few songs described lonely winter nights and young brides who left over the hill and never returned, but I put my soul into it and made the instrument sing along with me. If he had any heart at all, he'd cry himself to sleep, but he just wrinkled his nose.

"Perhaps something more upbeat next," Taran suggested, flicking his eyes to Marit, whose face showed all the sorrow I was wishing on Taran's head.

A big, wet tear rolled down the sea god's pearly pink cheek.

"I don't have any priests that play music anymore," he explained mournfully. A second tear rolled down his face, so large it splashed onto the floor. "Do you know any sea shanties? I bet I would like a song about the sea."

"I do know a few."

"I wouldn't," Taran warned me, but I'd already started the song.

For a while, the two of them seemed content to listen to the music. My fingers were getting tired, but I found some defiant pride that two gods wanted to hear me play.

Lovers drowned at sea was also a theme I was willing to explore.

Marit flopped to his back on Taran's divan, fingers tapping along with the rhythm. "They don't hate Napeth," he complained, still stewing in his thoughts. "And he nearly destroyed the whole world. If Napeth had a party, I bet they'd all go. But they hate me."

"That's not true," Taran said with a bit of an edge. "They're just afraid you're going to flood someone else's palace."

Tears began freely leaking out of Marit's eyes, plentiful enough to puddle on the floor. I stilled my hands, but Taran gave me a stern look, and I kept playing.

"I didn't mean to," Marit said, voice thick. "I just remember the well."

"Do you remember anything else from before?" I asked curiously, looking from him to Taran.

"No. He can't remember anything." Taran took a swig from his goblet and set it aside. The sharp glance he sent Marit made me think that perhaps Taran was not as drunk as he'd seemed when he entered the room.

"I do!" Marit protested. "I do remember." He choked back a sob, wiping splashes of tears away from his face. "It was dark, and I couldn't feel which way was up."

"You don't remember. You're imagining it. You don't even remember the ocean," Taran insisted.

I noticed with alarm that there was water beginning to puddle on the floor under Marit's couch, with more seeping in under the doors from the other rooms.

"They hate me," Marit repeated, beginning to weep in earnest. He gripped his goblet in his fist and drained it. "When I try to sleep, I can feel it. The walls and the dark."

Taran lifted his feet off the floor and put them on a stool when the first wave, just a few inches high, slid through the room. I stopped and put the kithara aside.

"I think he's had enough," I told Taran when Marit reached for the fluted carafe he'd come in with.

"I can't stop him, he'll just make more," Taran said.

It was true; the carafe in Marit's hand looked full again, even though he'd set it aside almost empty.

"Marit? Can I take that?" I asked in my politest voice, but the sea god clutched it to his chest, face screwing up in fear and dismay. Another wave swept through the room, ankle high and larger than the last. With it came a subtle vibration, a distant sound. I tensed, looking around the room with an eye to disaster management.

"You're afraid of me too," Marit accused me, his mouth crumpling. "You think they should have left me in the well."

"No, of course I don't think that," I said, but the sea god had passed beyond rational conversation. He flopped to his back again and started to wail, big drunken sobs shaking his chest. The floor began to shake with the same tempo.

I had barely noticed Awi all afternoon, sitting as still as a statue on a high shelf, but at this she changed her form to a puffin and took flight toward the baths.

Taran, on the other hand, had done nothing but pull up his feet to stay dry, and he was watching me rather than his dangerous friend as though interested to see what my reaction to Marit would be.

Silently cursing Taran again, I sloshed over to the main door, intending to let the water drain. But when I opened it, water swept into the room, not out. The hallway was entirely flooded, nearly knee-deep with cold, turbulent water, and waves were gathering around the corner.

I spun around—the windows were shuttered, and there was no other door to the outside.

"Do something," I snapped at Taran, and the movement of his shoulders suggested both mild surprise and amusement that I found it natural to shout orders at him.

"What would you like me to do?" he asked with a bright, artificial look of attention on his pretty face.

"I don't know, tell him to stop."

With an indulgent shrug, Taran went to the divan and bent over the wailing immortal. He checked to make sure I was watching, then took the sea god's chin in his hand. He spoke to Marit in a cool, serious voice.

"Hey. Cut it out. You're scaring my priestess."

That only made Marit cry harder. He brushed Taran's hand away and clasped his own palms over his streaming eyes.

"Sober him up, then," I said, beginning to feel a real anticipation of danger. They were immortal, but I wasn't, and I had no confidence Taran would see my death as more than an inconvenience.

"Good idea. How?"

I curled my upper lip at him. "Purge the alcohol from his body, starting with his liver and moving to his gut."

"Does that work?" He sounded curious.

It had worked any of the dozens of times I'd seen a peace-priest cure a hangover.

"It's the blessing of Genna that starts, *Queen of Heaven, may your steps light a path*... the key signature shifts from E to D minor in the second and fourth verses."

Taran paused as if scouring his memory, then shook his head.

"Don't know it." His tone was light even though water was beginning to lift small objects and carry them around the room.

You do, I wanted to cry. But maybe he'd forgotten it, just like he'd forgotten me.

"Why don't you sing it yourself?" he asked, as though hitting upon a good idea.

I remembered the words but felt shaky on the wordless vocalizations—and the liver wasn't an organ I wanted to make any mistakes on. Maybe it wouldn't kill an immortal patient, but Marit could do worse than slowly filling the room with water if I accidentally tortured him. The entire building could come down on our heads.

"Priestess of Wesha," I said, pointing at myself. "Genna's son," I said pointing at him.

Taran stepped onto a low table to escape the rising waters, and I did the same.

"Genna hasn't taught me that one yet. But I heard that Wesha's priests can put a man to sleep," he said, watching me carefully.

"He's the god of the sea, not a farmer with a tumor on his neck. Can't you do anything?"

The waters rose to the point that they began to lap against Marit on the cushions. When the first wave hit him, he keened like a child and tossed his limbs so wide that he tipped into the water. The walls shook violently, making tiles pop off the murals and vases on shelves crash with a ricochet of pottery shards.

Forgetting that Marit was immortal, I lunged for him to haul his face out of the water. He fought me, sputtering, and his elbow in my gut knocked the breath from my lungs. When I collapsed to my knees, my mouth filled with cold seawater before I spat it out and gulped for air.

"Taran!" I cried, and he grabbed Marit by the front of his tunic to get him off me, but this did not stop the rising water.

I wasn't a strong swimmer. Neither was Taran, unless he'd lied about that too.

Marit was screaming now, unintelligible babbling about the dark, the well, the water. I scrambled to get my feet back under me as the water pulled hard at my sodden clothes and the walls vibrated in time with Marit's voice.

The sea god's body flailed as Taran held him up, the cords in his arms straining from the effort.

"Stop it, please, *please*," I yelled. He'd known this would happen. This must have happened before, at some point since Marit was reborn only slightly less mad than the day Taran rescued him from the freshwater well.

"Do you want me to kill him?" Taran's voice held far less panic than the situation deserved.

"What?"

He pulled my stone knife off his belt. Marit was so panicked that he didn't even notice the weapon, instead clawing at Taran's hand on his tunic while the water rose higher and higher.

"Do you want me to kill him again?" Taran repeated, face finally flashing with the anger that must have lurked under that cheerful mask ever since I rebuked him for Marit's dead priests.

"Just stop him from bringing the building down," I said, tears finally rising to my own eyes. I grabbed for the divan as the water rose high enough to knock me off my feet, pulling at my legs like a retreating tide even in the enclosed space. The furniture wasn't buoyant enough to keep me afloat though.

"You want to do it instead?" Taran demanded, dark and bitter.

With a grunt, Taran took a wide step to shove the knife at my hands. I took it to keep him from dropping it in the floodwaters, but once it was tight in my fist, I could imagine using it.

"If you want to do it, I'll hold him," Taran growled at me. "Go on! Here's your chance. Better do it in one blow, but I'm sure you know where the heart is, *maiden-priest.*" The water was nearly to his chin, but he spun Marit so that his chest faced me and looped an arm around the other immortal's neck to bow him backwards.

The water was past my nose, and the room was shaking so badly that I could barely see for the foam splashing in my eyes. The handle of the blade was icy in my fist.

I sobbed once, out of anger more than fear.

"Cover your ears!" I yelled, then gulped a deep breath and sunk until my feet hit the floor. I had to kick up to get my head above water again. When I opened my mouth to sing, my voice was thin and hysterical, totally drowned out by Marit's screams.

How many times would I have to sing this song or die, or worse, sing this song so that someone else died? I learned this blessing to save suffering patients from pain.

> *Blessed Maiden who separates day from night,*
> *dawn-star who opens and closes the eyes of Marit*
> *Waverider, hear my song and bless my voice.*

I didn't know if it would work. But it wasn't in me to kill the weeping god of the sea, who was afraid of water and didn't remember the ocean. A wave hit me and salt water choked my throat, leaving it raw and hoarse as I chanted the words. There was a sense of pressure—not just the cold water pulling me down or the shaking of the building that obscured my voice, but also like heat, pressing against me and through me. Wesha's power, overcoming Marit's.

I didn't even realize it had worked until I could hear my own voice above the crashing of furniture against the walls of the room. Marit had stopped screaming and hung slack in Taran's grip. Slowly, slowly, the waves receded, but I kept singing, repeating the blessing as a chant instead of a melody. My feet touched the ground, and then the floating objects found their rest.

I fell to my knees, exhausted and terrified, as Taran lowered Marit to the floor. He pressed his ear to the sea god's chest and nodded in satisfaction when he heard his breathing.

I could have anesthetized an entire team of oxen for the number of times I'd repeated the chorus. Dropped an army in their tracks. But Marit was just asleep, his expression finally easing from horror.

I ended my song, leaving my panting as the loudest noise in the room. No, I heard Taran's raspy breathing too. There was a tremor in his arms when he shook them out—it must have taken all his strength to hold the other god.

My fingers clenched around the knife before I made them relax.

I met Taran's eyes as I tucked it into my own belt—a wordless threat—instead of returning it.

He squeezed some excess water from his tunic and stepped around Marit's limp form to stand over me. With one graceful hand, he swept his wet hair back from sharp cheekbones, then pulled me to my feet. His expression was practically glowing with affection.

"Thank you, Wesha," he said to the empty air. "She's perfect."

THE FLOOR WAS bone-dry even before Taran laboriously draped Marit's snoring body over his shoulder and hauled him off. I slumped on the divan, dazed, watching as tiles clicked back into place and vases turned themselves upright.

Is that you, Maiden? I gathered my strength and stumbled to the bathing chamber to clean the salt off my skin and hair. Whatever divine protection kept this palace as Wesha had left it did not extend to me.

If you're listening, Maiden, and if it please you, fill Taran ab Genna's boots with scorpions, his underclothes with lice, and his perfect chin with boils, I sincerely prayed to my goddess. But she was as silent as she had ever been.

I unlocked the door to Taran's bedroom and went through the chests of her clothes in search of a nightgown, but after I found a marginally acceptable linen shift with only a little gilt embroidery on the hem, I discovered that I couldn't put it on. My hands shook when I tried to pull it over my head, and my skin burned when I imagined it covering my body. I added gallstones and ingrown toenails to the ailments I wished on Taran and put on a green dress embellished with horridly tacky carnelian starbursts instead. *Green, to match his eyes.*

Taran was imperfectly whistling the melody of Wesha's blessing of night when he came back. He sat down right next to me on the divan, ignoring my stormy lack of welcome, and batted his knee against mine.

His silence was bait, and I was determined not to fall for it, but as he picked up the tail of my braid and ran a fingernail across the ribbon that held it together, I spoke when I couldn't jerk it from his hands.

"Please don't," I said through gritted teeth.

He let go, and I swept it away over the opposite shoulder. Even braided for sleep, my hair hung past my hips, and Taran's prior fascination with it was not something I could tolerate now.

When I still didn't speak, he continued humming. Trying to get the melody right. Good luck—I had been the first of Wesha's priests to master it with less than two decades of practice.

"Where's Marit?" I asked when I couldn't take the sour notes anymore.

"Sleeping it off in the plaza. I left a lamp burning, so he shouldn't panic if he wakes up before morning."

Such tender care, when Taran had pointed a knife at the sea god's heart an hour earlier.

"Would you really have done it if I'd told you to?" I wasn't sure which offense would have been the worst. Would he have killed his friend again? Would he have let me drown?

"Yes," Taran immediately said, unbothered. He crossed his feet in front of him, noticed that the leather of his boots was soaked, and reached down to pull them off.

Liar. He was terrible at lying to me. How had he gotten away with it for three years?

I shoved his shoulder with both palms, hard enough that he should have toppled over. Instead, I was the one knocked back.

"Stop lying to me!" I cried, scrambling to stay on the furniture.

"Then don't ask questions you already know the answer to," Taran said, quirking one eyebrow at my disarray.

"What would you have done, then?"

He smiled at me, his gaze dipping to appreciate the color of my new dress. "I would have broken the window and tossed him out into the yard. This happens at least once a week."

"Oh," I said, now feeling stupid. I could have thought of that. I curled on my side, wishing Marit had left his magical wine carafe behind.

"I have *one* priestess. Everyone would call me extremely careless if I let anything happen to you," Taran added, which he no doubt considered reassuring.

"You don't have me."

His thick, dark eyelashes shaded the brilliance of his eyes as he gave me a slow blink of wordless disagreement. *Keep telling yourself that*, his look said. As my cheeks burned, Taran stretched out an arm along the cushion behind me.

"Anyway, I'd be interested in learning that song." It was very carefully couched so as not to be a request or a command. One more test, to see how I'd react.

"Wesha could teach you better than I could. If you took me to the Painted Tower," I said, but then I regretted the words. I was tired of every sentence being a parry or riposte with him. He used to bring me flowers in winter. He used to ask me for lullabies at the end of the day. Fighting my instinct to give him everything he asked for, fighting my expectation that he would do the same for me—it was exhausting me.

I rubbed my face. "I probably can't," I amended my statement. "I'm not a good teacher, and it took me my entire life to learn."

"We have your entire life. Lifetimes, in fact. Till the end of eternity."

That was how long he was planning to keep me here. No doubt assuming I'd break down and agree to serve him at some point.

"What's so objectionable about being my priestess, anyway?" he asked, laying the charm on thick. "You were willing to be Wesha's, and Wesha's a terrible patron. What would her vows have been?" He began counting on his fingers. "Obedience? Well, if you're afraid of that, I could be more specific. Poverty? Ha! Wesha and I both like nice things, and unlike her, I share. Celibacy?" He tilted his chin, shot me a heated look that made his green eyes sparkle. "Not really my guiding value."

I couldn't manage more than a soft groan in response. "Please. I told you it was a mistake to come here. Let me go home."

He didn't bother to reject me out loud, just looked with renewed interest at the fall of my braid on the green dress.

"I don't know why you're so eager to go back to the mortal world. From what I've heard, it's an awful place. You get a few decades of hard work and then you die. Don't you think it's possible that Wesha wanted something better for her last priest? And your lover too?"

He was trying to be convincing, but I knew it was a load of bullshit. Wesha didn't care about me. Neither did he.

"I could have been very happy in the mortal world, except that Death killed everyone I loved, and now he's *here*," I pointed out, eyes narrowed.

Taran hummed thoughtfully. "What if I proved that you're perfectly safe here, free to enjoy your reward for mortal devotion? Would you teach me that song?" he asked after a moment.

I pulled up my knees and wrapped my arms around them, fuming.

"I'm not making any more bargains with you, Taran ab Genna. You know what I want."

Taran grinned at me, unsurprised. He ran one more finger over the end of my braid, then stood up to go to bed.

"I do," he said. "But as I'm inclined to keep you, you're going to have to think of something else."

I WAITED HALF an hour after Taran went to bed before getting up. Just the waiting had been uncomfortable. Forming the intent to wait gave a sense of unease, one I fought by concentrating on the mnemonics for childhood illnesses. It was a long way to Wesha's tower from the City, and if I had to fight my vow the entire time, it would be a painful one. Putting on my boots made my stomach cramp. Fastening my new cloak gave me a chill like the first day of a flu.

I could do it. I didn't have to think about it. I just had to go. I didn't pack anything else, because packing was planning, and planning was the first step to breaking a vow. I didn't picture the Painted Tower as I took my first step into the hall. Instead, I imagined one of the low buildings at the edge of Genna's sector of the City—a storehouse, or perhaps a barracks. There was no reason I couldn't go there. I'd been farther from Taran earlier today.

My vow wasn't fooled. When I silently closed the door to Taran's rooms, I felt tightness in my chest. I breathed past it, and by concentrating on the names of the muscles that filled my lungs, I was able to keep walking through the interior courtyard and through the entrance hall.

True pain began once I opened the exterior door and looked for the horizon. At each cardinal direction there was a different slope of the Mountain. Wondering which I ought to climb made pain spark in my fingertips and toes, the little nerve endings coming alive as my vow to Wesha was seriously tested.

I tried to bargain with it. Perhaps Taran would come after me, and we'd both end up at the Painted Tower. Perhaps I'd be able to tell Wesha something about him that would show her how to lure him there herself.

My vow wasn't satisfied. I'd promised to bring Taran to Wesha, end of statement, and it wouldn't let me do anything contrary to that promise. The priests sang of vows wrapped around our hearts, and I could feel my heart's rhythm stutter as I tried to run from Taran, but the vow wasn't just in my heart. It was woven into every part of my body and soul, and as I walked faster, trying to outrun it, that fabric pulled and caught.

I tried to think of anything but what I was doing. I thought of my first mentor, Lascius, a sweet man, dead at Ereban, who taught me the rules for a breech labor when I was nine.

If the child is due and the waters haven't broken yet, try to turn it. You'll need all your strength, Iona, don't do it halfway or the mother's pain is wasted.

I nearly stumbled on the steps as pain began to radiate up from my feet into my legs. But I was in pain every day—I could endure pain and keep moving.

For complete breech, we'll try labor for a day. If it doesn't progress, boil your knife and call for a priest of Genna.

When my feet touched the path, I moved more quickly. One foot in front of the other, that was nothing to do with Taran. It was growing more difficult to coordinate my breathing.

For a frank breech, we'll try labor only if the child is a second-born. Otherwise, boil your knife and call for a priest of Genna.

I felt tendons tightening, pulling away from my muscles. My bones ached like I'd fallen from a great height. Another step made pressure rise in my skull like a high fever. The pain made it easier to forget the idea of kneeling before Wesha and asking her to release me from my vow, and it momentarily receded. I tried to run past it. I had to be able to get farther than this.

For a footling breech, boil your knife and call for a priest of Genna. For a transverse lie, boil your knife and call for a priest of Genna. If one can't be found, wash your hands with lye soap and make a last attempt at a turn during labor.

I opened my eyes to orient myself, but looking at the Mountain with the intention of climbing it made every muscle in my body lock up, and I fell. I couldn't even extend my arms to protect myself, but luckily my head struck the lawn, instead of the path. It still rang, but that dizziness was barely perceptible over the agony my vow pulled from every sinew in my body. I imagined myself torn apart into my component atoms as my vow consumed every disobedient part of me. My muscles were separating from my bones; my tendons were twisting until I was afraid they'd snap.

Something leaked from my nose and wet my upper lip. A nosebleed, probably. Though if it was spinal fluid, I wouldn't be hurting much longer.

All I needed to do to end my suffering was imagine that I was going to walk back into Taran's room. All my vows were aligned on that course of action.

But I won't ever have to cut the baby out, Lascius, I'd exclaimed in horror. *I'll just sing the blessing for an easy labor, and Wesha will turn it.*

I was a prideful brat as a child, and I didn't know how Lascius put up with me long enough to pass on half of what he knew—but it had taken me this long to realize he was trying to pass on something else important.

He'd known, like all the priests must have known, that the gods didn't love us. They didn't care for us. They transacted with us, and the price was far too high.

I thought I could sing so well because Wesha had blessed me. I spent my life certain that if I ever called, she'd answer as best she could. Gentle Wesha, the Maiden, who'd sacrificed herself to save the Heavens and the Earth both.

The stories had left out a few facets of her personality, just as much as they'd lied about the nature of the other gods.

Where the Maiden's favor had failed me, my pride remained, and I lay panting on the ground, trying to summon the strength to stand and keep moving toward the Mountain. When my vision remained gray around the edges, I gave up on standing and tried to crawl instead. I would *not* spend eternity in service to a man I'd once loved. I gained an inch. Another. There was a rush of darkness as I lost sight, and fear of blindness finally stilled me.

I didn't lie there very long. Not long enough for dew to chill my skin or the blood on my lip to clot. I heard a door, then the slap of Taran's bare feet on the path as he made his way to my side. I hadn't even made it fifty paces from the building.

I hadn't cried from the pain of trying to break my vow, but I cried at the shame of that. When Taran approached, yawning and sleepy, I tried to curl into a ball, but he squatted next to me and pushed my shoulder to roll me onto my back, which allowed him to briskly pat me down.

"You didn't even steal anything?" he asked, sounding mildly outraged.

I blinked at him through watery eyes. He hadn't bothered to dress and wore only loose linen trousers. He looked very human in the diffuse moonlight, very much like he had when he'd been mine. When I didn't answer, he leaned in. "What was your bribe for Wesha? Your sunny personality? It wouldn't have worked. She was never going to help you."

I could do no more than bare my teeth and pant as he shook his head at my folly, but when he sighed and reached to pick me up, I managed to grit out a single *stop*.

"It's late, Iona," he said, but he didn't touch me as I slowly rolled back to my stomach, then dragged my knees underneath me.

I wiped the blood off my face with the sleeve of Wesha's dress.

If I was going to live, and if I was going to have to live here, at least I wouldn't have to wear it again.

I had to take Taran's hand to get to my feet, but I tried to make it back without more aid. As though I had any dignity left. My knees buckled at the threshold of Wesha's palace, and Taran, who'd been shadowing my slow shuffle, gave up on letting me walk. He scooped me into the same embrace as the day he died, frowning when it made a sob squeak out of my throat.

If he'd said anything like *I didn't ask you to come here*, or *you made those vows on purpose*, I really could have hated him, even though those would have been true things to say. Instead, he just pressed his cheek to the top of my head and murmured, "I know, I know."

It didn't sound like a lie, but how could he possibly understand?

He carried me inside and set me down on his cot, where the bedclothes were still warm from his body. After a moment, I heard the door close.

He went somewhere else to sleep; I didn't see him again for two days.

12

THE FIRST GIFT Taran ever gave me was a single perfect snowflake in a tin cup. Winter had come early that year, and he'd been monitoring the clouds with growing excitement for days, like he'd never seen snow before. He shook the frame of my tent just after dawn.

Look, nightingale, it's snowing!

When I blearily stuck my head out, he presented the cup to me with a flourish, only to find that the snowflake had melted in the transferred heat of his hands. He ran off shouting that he'd catch me another one, returned ten minutes later with a selection.

I'd only known him for four months then, and I'd already fallen in love with him.

When Taran finally came back to Wesha's palace, he brought me more gifts. As promised, he found me a set of bedroom furniture and arranged it in the solar for my use. A bed—better than the cot where he slept—and a trunk for my clothes, plus a small desk with a polished bronze mirror. He brought me new clothes. Two silver combs and a glass bottle of rosewater. A kithara with ten strings and a lyre with ivory inlay. Small and beautiful objects he readily admitted to pilfering from the other Stoneborn.

I wasn't familiar with how Taran might go about courting someone, as every gesture I'd recognized as romantic had come after we were already betrothed, but it felt as though he was not so much wooing me as attempting to tame me, the way a small boy might try to lure a wild creature inside his house with patience and a handful of grain.

"I'm your prisoner, not your priestess. I don't need any of this," I told him, dumping the latest pile of expensive baubles on his bedroom floor.

"Prisoners *hate* presents," he agreed with syrupy sarcasm before flouncing off to another of Genna's endless calendar of ceremonial parties.

When he reappeared to ply me with plates of prepared food and other obvious bribes, he was unforthcoming about the intentions of the Stoneborn. While Genna's plan for a cold peace was prevailing by default, he admitted that every immortal could feel the silence that had replaced the words of devotion formerly lofted across the divide from the mortal world. Sacrifices no longer arrived in the storerooms, and the residents of the City were growing anxious as the gods' power slowly dwindled. Not Taran though—I would think, if I hadn't seen him with my knife in his hand only a few nights ago, that he was perfectly content.

I thought often about leaving tacks in his bed.

Weeks into our standoff, I woke a couple of hours after dawn to Taran shouting my name and banging a silver serving platter against my door.

I glared at him over my thick feather coverlet; he'd never previously disturbed my privacy, although he made no secret of his scorn for the hours I was keeping.

"Finally. You'd think I had you making bricks all day, the amount you sleep," Taran said.

"I know a blessing that will stop the blood flow to every extremity below your heart. You know the ones," I mumbled at him.

"Brilliant. Would love to learn it. But right now you need to get up and pack. We're leaving."

"I'm not going anywhere with you." I rolled back over.

Undeterred, Taran threw open the shutters to let the sourceless morning light in, then snatched the coverlet off of me. I balled up around a pillow, but he grabbed one ankle and dragged me to the edge of the mattress while I groaned in protest.

"I know you're very busy feeling sorry for yourself," he said, still cheerful, "but I didn't actually ask. We're going, and you can walk wearing clothes you picked out for yourself, or you can go in a nightgown, thrown over my shoulder."

I begrudgingly got up and shoved some clothes into a pack as he hovered, nearly bouncing on the balls of his feet. I'd cut up the terrible carnelian-encrusted frock to make a hood, and when I was dressed, Awi hopped into the space between the fabric and my hair, uninvited but apparently determined to keep an eye on me.

Taran shot me an unaffected look of glee when we reached a wide stable yard on the City's outskirts, and I saw the reason for his good mood. There was a chariot constructed of half an enormous, iridescent clam shell yoked to a team of four silver-dappled horses, and not even Marit's position as driver could entirely dampen my awed reaction to the gorgeous creatures. Marit's horses were famous—enormous and unearthly, with hooves that did not quite touch the ground they pawed. Legend said they could run across the crests of the ocean waves, though it would have been centuries since Wesha let anyone test that myth. As Taran was watching me closely out of the corner of his eye to see if I was impressed, I kept my face blank.

"Where are we going?"

"To the estate of Lixnea, the Moon. Marit is going to renew his bonds of friendship with the other Stoneborn on a grand tour of the Summerlands," Taran said in a voice that carried. When I frowned at that, he said in a lower voice, "And Genna would like to know where the other Stoneborn stand now on the question of what to do about our delinquent mortal worshippers."

He looked at me like he was waiting for something, which I realized was a *thank you, Taran, for bringing me along.*

"Has anyone seen Death?" I asked instead.

Taran gave an airy wave of his hand, like this was of no importance. "Perhaps we'll hear news somewhere."

Marit was attended by two nervous immortal horse-masters and delighted with himself when he got his team to trot a neat circle.

As he pulled to a halt in front of us and hopped down, Awi shot out of my hood, fluttering to the roof of the stables to put some distance between herself and the mercurial god of the ocean.

"Oh dear," said Marit, watching her go. He looked between the bird and me, face creased with uncertainty. He seemed more cogent than the other evening, but I knew that could change, so I was braced to flee.

"Have we met?" he asked me yet again.

"Yes, this is Iona, my priestess," Taran patiently answered for me.

"Do I owe her an apology?"

"I'm sure she thinks so."

"I'm always apologizing, and I can never remember why," Marit said unhappily. But then he brightened and smiled beneath soft gray eyes. "I do think I'm getting very good at it though! I'm sorry, Iona, for whatever I did—I'll probably do it again, but I'll be sorry then too. Do you like my horses?"

It was probably unsafe to reject this sincere expression of feeling, and I *did* like his horses, so I extended my hand and he smacked a kiss to the back of it, grinning. There was no guarantee he wouldn't try to kill me again, but as I still didn't know whether that had been Taran's plan when he asked me to marry him, I was less inclined to hold it against Marit.

At the urging of Taran's hand on my lower back, I approached one of the horses and held out my palm for the animal to sniff. His huff at my mortal scent was somewhat skeptical, but so was I, with one daring hand on the velvet of a perfect equine nose.

"We're supposed to ride in that chariot?" I whispered to Taran.

He looked down at my bad foot. "Can you stand in one? I've been meaning to have a peace-priest come look at your foot."

I shook my head. Hiwa had looked at my foot, but there was nothing a peace-priest could do once the bones had begun to knit in the wrong places. It needed surgery, and the last maiden-priest could hardly operate on herself.

"I guess I can't go," I said sweetly.

Taran smiled even more beautifully.

"Don't worry, I asked them to bring my horse."

What was brought, after a short wait in which Marit made me nervous by driving his team in bored circles around the yard, was an enormous white mare whose eyes glowed like heat lightning and whose hooves had the insubstantial outlines of cloud banks. She wore a bridle and reins, but no saddle.

"I'm not riding that," I said, but Taran just patted the creature's neck with loving affection.

"Isn't that your father's horse?" Marit asked, slowing down to look at her.

"Diopater would wash your mouth out if he heard you accuse him of my paternity," Taran said, catching me around the waist when I tried to run. "And he doesn't ride her enough."

"Who was your father, then?" Marit asked, confused.

"Oh, who even knows. My mother hates that question," Taran replied, not really answering his friend.

Despite my flailing, he effortlessly deposited me on the horse's back, where there was only a small blanket for padding. Kicking him in the ribs hurt my foot and made him laugh before he used one hand to vault up behind me, muscular thighs framing mine. The mare turned her head to look at us, sharing my outrage about the situation.

"I'm not a good rider," I said in a panic—that I'd fall, that I *wouldn't*, wrapped in Taran's embrace like a lover, with Taran's arm curled around my waist and his palm splayed over my hip. My blood raced up in my veins to match his heartbeat at my back, traitorous body nothing but exultant to be in his arms again.

Taran chuckled, warm breath tickling my ear.

"I am though."

He tightened his legs and the horse leapt forward as though shot by a bow. Her dark gray mane evaporated in my fingers like fog, so I had nothing at all to hold on to, not even the reins, which Taran kept in his free hand. I would have fallen off within seconds, but Taran held me tightly as the mare gained speed.

I yelled when we approached the stone wall around the stable yard, and Taran must have considered that to be encouragement, because he gave a loud whoop and leaned us over the horse's neck to make an impossible leap over the wall. Part of me thought I was still dreaming, one of those dreams where I could fly. I even didn't feel the mare land.

"Open your eyes," Taran said breathlessly.

As soon as I did, I laughed, the sound reedy and unfamiliar to my own ears. I instinctively clapped a hand over my mouth to stop it, but Taran took his own off the reins to pry my fingers away and scold me. "*My* priests are allowed to laugh."

Wesha's priests had been discouraged from the practice, trained against it from childhood in deference to our imprisoned goddess's sorrow.

But why shouldn't I laugh? Who did I owe my grief or humility or even dignity to? Not to Wesha, who hadn't even wanted them.

I'd come here hoping for joy instead, and I was starving for it.

The world whipped by at fantastic speed, an exhilarating green-and-blue blur that resolved into forests where bluebells and lilacs and daylilies all bloomed at the same time under a perfect canopy of trees in summer foliage.

Marit called out encouragement as he was forced to detour to the road while Taran dove straight ahead, trusting the horse to leap over every obstacle as the buildings fell away. The sea god gained on us with his team of four, but he had to keep to the path while we flew on as though the white mare had actual wings.

I was glad that I was allowed to laugh now.

I was on a fast horse with Taran's body warm and solid behind me, and in this moment I was alive and unafraid. I got this moment of joy when it had felt like there would never be another one, off-balance and uncertain and breathless too as Taran and Marit competed for the lead, wind stealing the words from their lips. I lifted my hands from the mare's neck, marveled at how the air spun around my fingers, and tilted my head back against Taran's shoulder to look up at the sunless blue of the sky.

Anything else Taran offered me, I'd take it, I decided. Because I did want this moment, and a hundred more like it.

13

W E REACHED THE house of the Moon shortly before sunset. All day we'd ridden steadily upward, the verdant park of Genna's lands fading into wilder territory as we climbed, oaks exchanged for mountain pine and birch trees arranged like marble pillars to line the road.

The Mountain's shadow at dusk lay over a precisely circular crater lake. A thin waterfall sliced the Mountain's conical side like a sash and fed the pool, where a palace was built on stone pilings that seemed to not just reflect but emit the fading daylight.

For the past half hour our path had been traced by small gray owls, the first birds I'd seen in the Summerlands besides Awi—little night spirits, who carried secrets to the Moon and inspiration to her poets and dreamers—but I was still surprised to find that our arrival had been anticipated.

In the center of the stone causeway that led to the palace stood a goddess with a hooded black robe nearly concealing her body and white face.

Lixnea had come to greet us herself.

Taran dismounted and helped me down, and Marit slowed his chariot to a halt as the Moon approached.

"What are you doing here?" The goddess's voice was husky

and not at all pleased to see us. She had the appearance of an ancient crone: thin, wrinkled skin draped over fine bones that hinted at former beauty, but her posture was confident and upright.

Marit blinked, taken aback, but Taran did not let his smile falter.

"Is that how the cult of the Moon greets her guests?"

"The last time you were here, I chased you out with a broom. This greeting is kinder than you deserve. Again—what are you doing here, Taran ab Genna?"

"I thought all were welcome to celebrate the darkest night here," Taran countered. "And that the Moon would not turn away an envoy of the Peace-Queen or her old friend, the sea."

Lixnea sighed and put her palms on her hips, considering the three of us. After a moment, she approached Marit and cupped his face between her two wrinkled hands, turning it back and forth. The sea god was startled but bore her inspection with good humor, batting stormy eyes at the old goddess as though attempting to project a lack of threat.

Maybe he'd looked different before Taran killed him.

"Don't make innocent eyes at me, Marit," Lixnea said with one lifted eyebrow. "We used to lure ships to their doom together, you know. I do welcome Marit Waverider to my home, even though it is small and fragile."

His smile was guileless and pleased, but he immediately lost his focus when a splash below the causeway drew his attention away. I hadn't noticed them when we arrived, but there were shapes moving under the still water of the lake: water nymphs, watching the scene from below the surface. Marit wandered to the lakeshore but carefully stopped before the water's edge to see the immortals swim, hands folded behind his back.

"Will I regret inviting him in?" Lixnea asked Taran in a lower voice, watching the unsteady sea god.

"I'll keep an eye on him," Taran promised.

The Moon scoffed. "I did not invite *you* in yet. I didn't think you were still running the Peace-Queen's errands, *Stoneborn*."

Taran blanked his face. "Would it matter if I were here on Genna's behalf instead of my own? I'm equally delightful, either way."

"I'm familiar with what you consider delightful," Lixnea grumbled. "You strong-arm me into acceding to the Peace-Queen's demands, then make off with my blessings, steal my treasures, and debauch my priestesses."

Lixnea wasn't watching Taran's face as she delivered this judgment, but I was. A pained moment of surprise flitted across his features, quickly smoothed away.

How strange it had to be for him, to be informed of who he was. Did he really not know?

But Taran recovered and put his prettiest smile on.

"Forget Genna's demands. What if I were just here to enjoy a lovely evening with a lovelier lady? Would you welcome me back?"

"Are you flirting with me now? I was the midwife at your birth."

"It would be very unfair to forbid flirting with anyone older than me, as that's everyone. But if you prefer, I could brood soulfully instead."

I would have folded in Lixnea's position, but she was made of stronger stuff than me.

"I meant it before, Taran ab Genna. You've worn out your welcome here."

I jolted when Taran turned to put a hand on my lower back.

"I'd be on my best behavior. I have no need to debauch your priestesses, as I've brought my own along."

"*Your* priestess?" Lixnea said, eyebrows climbing.

I tried to smile, but I probably made a face like I'd just bitten into an unripe persimmon. Lixnea looked me up and down, now studying me with a gaze that seemed to slip beneath my skin to peer at my mind and soul.

"Yours, I suppose, yes," she said to Taran after a moment. "Very well. Come in. Don't cause trouble, or I'll do worse than the broom."

There was a muffled cheer from beneath the causeway as the goddess relented and gestured for us all to follow her—the other immortals of Lixnea's domain were either glad for the excitement of company regardless of the perils, or they hadn't minded Taran's debauchery on his previous visits.

"What did you do the last time you were here?" I whispered to Taran as we crossed the causeway.

He gave a small, stiff shrug. "If you find out, please let me know." But he couldn't have been that concerned about it, because he spread his arms and walked a few steps toward the water, and two immortals with long hair like corded glass climbed onto the shore and threw silver-blue arms around his neck with squeals of excitement.

I turned to Lixnea, because I did not want to see someone else stick her tongue into Taran's mouth. She was staring out at the trees, eyes searching the branches until they landed on Awi, an incongruous songbird hanging back amid all the watchful owls.

"You can come in too. You're always welcome here," Lixnea called in a gentler voice, but Awi didn't answer, disappearing alone into the darkening forest before everyone else was done kissing Taran hello.

WHEN I ONCE imagined what awaited the fortunate priests called to cross the Gates of Dawn and serve the gods in person, this was what I'd pictured. As soon as it was fully dark, the Moon's priests sang gentle lights into hundreds of dangling gilt lanterns that reflected like stars in the water surrounding the palace. It came alive in the early evening with a rising murmur of voices and music from the residents of the palace and the lake below. The white stone and pale wood of the palace subtly gleamed around us, archways draped with soft gray curtains and floors warmed by tufted carpets, a dream of luxury and ease.

On most nights, Lixnea rode her silver chariot across the skies to listen to the secret wishes of dreamers and inspire them in turn, but on moonless nights, she rested with her court and rejoiced in the dark evening's beauty.

All the immortals sat at long, low tables flanked by couches and cushions, and their priests took turns sitting among them and attending to the dinner. The Moon was the patron of the creative arts—poets, actors, musicians—so we were treated to their performances while dinner was served. The atmosphere was celebratory as everyone moved smoothly through a service they knew well but still enjoyed after decades.

This was an eternity worth living in—if I'd been a little prettier or more talented at composition, perhaps I would have been taken in by the Moon's cult instead of the Maiden's. I couldn't regret giving my life to the sick or to the rebellion, but part of me did wish my future had ever looked like infinite nights of wine and poetry. I could have wanted this, I thought with a wistful throb.

I was served a large river fish steamed whole in clay and plated with tender asparagus spears and tiny peas, which was easily one of the better things I'd ever eaten. I bolted it down like I had every meal in the past few years before remembering that I'd once possessed the manners not to lick my knife clean.

"You should ask Lixnea's priests to give you some tips," Taran murmured into my ear. "For example, you're supposed to be pouring my wine for me."

He seemed to expect a smart rejoinder—*I'll ask if they can toss you in the lake while you sleep, Taran*—but I'd actually been trying to think of a way to thank him, so I just sipped my own wine and kept my eyes on the stage. Lixnea had kept the dinner conversation light, but she recognized and named each of her priests who came to the head of the table to bow and perform their most recent works in what seemed to be a deliberate example for Taran.

"Iona's very talented on the kithara," Taran told the Moon goddess after the next rotation. "Perhaps she'd be willing to take a turn later."

Lixnea inclined her head, but Taran didn't smile until I gravely nodded my agreement, and then it went straight to his eyes, making them sparkle like the lanterns that brought the stars inside. He topped off my wine, then leaned against the cushions with an arm propped behind my shoulders.

There had been an undercurrent of tension behind his frivolous attitude in the City, but here his happiness seemed genuine, if tempered by equally genuine concern for me. He'd never understand why this scene of beauty filled me with regret.

If this was what he'd wanted, he could have asked for it. If he'd only appeared to us as Genna's son and insisted that we continue to worship the gods through the war, we would have done it. We thought the gods had abandoned us; we would have welcomed a little divine intervention. If the price for freedom from Death's rule had been an eternity of service, well, I would have given much more than this. This wasn't even hard. I would have poured his wine and sung for his guests and even pressed his damn clothes if that was what he'd wanted.

I wouldn't have broken my heart expecting a god to love me back.

Priests moved the tables and chairs, rearranging the furniture to face the stage. When the plates were all cleared, musicians gathered at one end of the room and began to play popular dances.

Despite my efforts to covertly swap his wine for juice during dinner, Marit was by now happily drunk, and he lifted his head at the change in music.

Lixnea stood and clapped her hands in a shower of silver sparks to mark the next stage of the evening, but as she passed Marit, she ran tender fingers across his forehead and his eyes half closed in response. He put his head back down on his forearms, looking abruptly sleepy.

Taran and I watched Lixnea withdraw from the main hall toward a balcony over the water.

"Did she say anything to you about the other Stoneborn?" I asked.

"No. She keeps her secrets close, that one. But if you want to ask her about Death, now's your chance. Her chariot flies over the mortal world and the Summerlands both—she'd know if anyone does."

"You want me to ask her? What about you?"

"Oh, I promised several people I'd dance. I don't remember their names, but that didn't seem to matter," he said, straightening his tunic and smiling at a group of moon-priests who'd raised graceful arms into the air when the drummers began to hit a quick three-count.

Taran looked at me as though waiting for an objection, but when I didn't voice one, he backed away until his arms were seized by members of the growing crowd of revelers, and he was pulled away into the lines of the dance.

My stomach ached, because I remembered dancing with Taran on more than one night. Hiwa playing reed pipes, Drutalos slapping his lap desk like a drum. Stepping on Taran's feet before he wrapped my legs around his waist and spun me till I was dizzy. Kissing him until he was breathless too.

For three years I had thought that Death would probably kill me someday. But that didn't mean that there hadn't been moments full of complete and pristine joy.

"Do *you* want to dance?" Marit asked, startling me out of my memories. "I'll dance with you."

He was surprisingly coherent for his flushed cheeks and glassy eyes.

"Thank you, but I can't dance anymore," I said, touched by the offer despite my caution. "I hurt my foot."

"You can't dance ever again?" When his eyes widened in dismay and began to well up with dangerous tears, I hurried to reassure him before the floods could begin.

"But I could play some music later if you want to dance."

"I'd like that," he mumbled, face softening. He put his head down on his arms. "I think I like music. I'd like to hear you play sometime."

I patted him on the shoulder, then followed the Moon outside.

So close to the Mountain, the air was a cool touch on my skin and sweet from the lake below us. Lixnea stood by the rail, looking into the water. Her white face was reflected back like the heavenly body we saw in the mortal world, and I had a sudden pang of homesickness for my own sky, of all things.

I'd picked up a discarded kithara as I went, thinking that I could pretend to be offering that performance if she was offended at my approach, but she turned around when she heard the door.

"What, Taran is going to fob off Genna's dirty work on his priestess?" she said by way of greeting, face creasing in wry amusement. "Not very much like one of the Stoneborn, after all."

"I'm not here for Genna," I said cautiously, hearing several things in that statement I wanted to know more about.

Lixnea smiled without teeth, like she'd expected that response.

"No, I didn't think you were, Iona ter *Wesha*. The Maiden and the Peace-Queen never did get on well."

I froze, only just realizing what the Moon might have seen during her flights over the mortal world in the last three years.

She beckoned me closer.

"Don't fear, child. I never speak of what I see during my voyages across the night sea, and I dearly miss my lost little dawn star. We might have a few words later about the state of my temples, but I'm not about to harm Wesha's last priest."

"Thank you," I breathed. "Though I'm not one, not really."

"Aren't you?" the Moon said gently. "You remind me a bit of her—though not her priests, who were very stuffy. The little Fallen girl I raised."

"You raised Wesha? Not Genna?"

Lixnea flicked her eyes toward the ballroom.

"Wesha's father was a moon-priest. That was no secret, even if it was a shame. Do you not tell this story?" When I shook my head, she ducked hers in fond remembrance. "Her father was Carantos ab Lixnea. He was so handsome, and so talented, that I brought him across the sea before he took his vows. Ah, that boy! When he sang, even the birds gathered to listen, and the Stoneborn too. I lost him to Genna—the personal attention of the Peace-Queen must have turned his head. Poor child had more in the way of looks than common sense. Of course, Skyfather then scattered his body across the width of the Summerlands when he found out Genna had strayed, which made me rather cross, but Wesha's arrival a few months later made for some small recompense." Lixnea sighed at the memory, looking up into the sky at those luminous, too-near stars. One seemed to wave at her. "I love my children, but I had them when the world was young, and they've been out of my arms for a long time. I was glad to have another baby to hold when Genna dropped Wesha here. I should have raised Taran too. I would have done a better job of it than Genna."

I swallowed hard. Part of me wanted to know the entire story, and part of me hated everything I'd never known about Taran. But ignoring the truth didn't change it, and if I was ever going to escape this tangle between Taran and the Maiden, I wanted to know where it began.

"Is there more?" I asked Lixnea. "I only know the Maiden's story from the moment she walked down the Mountain to marry Death."

"Ah," Lixnea said with growing interest. "Perhaps you'd like to see her garden?"

I nodded, and the Moon goddess waved me away from the railing and led me around the side of her palace. She moved slowly, either due to her age or because she noticed my limp, and I had time to gather myself before we reached a damp, green garden that flanked the waterfall feeding the lake. It was one of those gardens that looked wild until I found the patterns, saw the harmony in the arrangement of night-blooming datura and faintly glowing mosses.

Lixnea arranged her black skirts on a stone bench and gestured for me to take the seat next to her. Wesha was the Dawn goddess, and this garden faced east. I imagined the girl I'd met as a child, seated on this same bench, watching the sunrise.

"Poor Wesha. The changeable heart of a mortal, not to mention her father's attraction to power. I think that was the root of her tragedy."

I made a small noise, and Lixnea renewed her focus on me. I would have swallowed it, but the shrewd gaze of the goddess made me speak.

"You disagree," she said, narrowing her eyes.

"Why do you say it was her mortality that made her heart changeable?"

"We may be deceitful, cruel, stonehearted—but never inconstant," the goddess told me, but I still shook my head.

"Immortals can forget all they loved. Like Marit forgot the ocean," I said, even though I was thinking of Taran.

Lixnea shrugged. "We are always what we are. We may *be* changed, as Marit was changed by his ordeal, but only a mortal could imagine trifling with a god, the way Wesha did with Napeth. For a god, to love something is to grow around the shape of it. She knew he loved her, which meant he had to have her or forever feel the lack. But she didn't feel the same—she couldn't."

At the mention of Death, I sat up straighter. "Before the Great War? Or after it?"

"That story is no secret either, though I regret to speak of my own part in it. Death loved her from the moment he set eyes on her, with her father's voice and her mother's grace. I didn't discourage him—I thought she might meet a worse fate than being adored by the youngest of the Stoneborn. But Wesha was like an infant reaching out for a candle flame, only thinking it was lovely and bright. She soon learned that fire burns as well as it warms," Lixnea said, voice dropping into a hypnotic register as she recited a story she had to have told before. "For a fire, having is consuming, and it scared her. She tried to run away, but he pursued her, and eventually the entire world was aflame. Yes, he went to war for her."

"And Wesha sacrificed herself to end it," I murmured. Genna negotiated peace at the price of Wesha's hand in marriage, with Wesha to remain forever at the Painted Tower, holding the Gates shut against the souls Death would command in the Underworld. "We learned that song first, in Wesha's temple."

Lixnea nodded. "It's lovely, isn't it? Though Taran couldn't stand it. He recalled the events rather differently."

I'd been lulled by the evening and the sound of the waterfall, but when my mind belatedly processed those words, it was like plunging into the cold lake. I had a moment where I lost my bearings.

"What?" I cried ungracefully. The events that *founded* my temple?

She had been watching me carefully, and she was keen for my reaction. The Moon was the goddess of secrets and dreams, and not all secrets were good secrets, nor all dreams. She might be one of the gentler members of the pantheon, but she was still enjoying my shock.

"He was still a child then, and Wesha rarely gave him a kind word, but he cried and cried when she was imprisoned in the Painted Tower. I thought she might finally take some interest in him then, but alas, it was mostly self-interest."

"That was three hundred years ago," I said, my voice soft and fuzzy.

The Moon goddess nodded. "Taran went to his grandmother, the Allmother, and asked her to give him the power to strike down Death and free Wesha. But the Allmother will not abide violence among her children, and she refused him."

Lixnea grimaced in the direction of the noisy great hall. "So Taran made himself his typical charming presence in her court until he got what he wanted anyway. He stole stone blades from the Mountain for Wesha, who promptly forced her new husband across the sea at the point of a knife. And that was nearly the end of Taran."

I held very still as Lixnea concluded her tale. "The Stoneborn were horrified that their weakness was exposed, and most of them wanted Taran buried at the bottom of a pit where he was unlikely to be found, with one of his new knives through his heart. Genna and I were against it, but I'm hardly a power to contend with, and Genna was angry too. In the end, Genna made him swear to obey her until she was satisfied that he'd learned to act in a manner befitting one of the Stoneborn."

"Three hundred years ago," I repeated, still reeling at the idea.

I didn't doubt that it was true. It sounded like Taran, or at least the person he used to be.

"Yes. I would have told him to run instead of making that promise. He has enough red in his blood that he might have made a life for himself in the mortal world, and Wesha surely owed him the passage. But he didn't think Genna's service would be so long, or so hard, I suppose."

"You mean—you mean Genna forced him to put down the mortal rebellion?" I asked, heart leaping in my throat.

With a trace of pity, Lixnea shook her head. "No, he agreed to go. After hundreds of years where Genna spent him like coin for all he could purchase her. It was difficult for me to forgive her for Wesha—I still haven't forgiven her for Taran."

Seeing my dismay, the Moon goddess stood up and inclined her head at the party. The music was louder, spilling out over the dark water of the lake.

Now I knew so much more than I had when I stumbled into the Summerlands, but not the few things I'd followed Lixnea outside for. I had a sudden hunch that she'd done this on purpose, distracted me with this sad story from long ago, instead of telling me what the Stoneborn might do next.

"Wait. I was going to ask you about Death. You must have seen what he did to the mortal world after his exile. Do you know where he is now?"

The Moon goddess's face fell back into shadow as she stepped to the edge of Wesha's garden. "I'm afraid I can't part with any of my secrets about Death—it would be entirely contrary to my nature. But you might ask Taran, who still knows more about Death and the Maiden than anyone else." She gave me another smile, half malice and half compassion. "Before he asks you what *you* know, Iona Night-Singer."

14

I SNAGGED A GLASS of sweet wine the color of the harvest moon from a black-robed priest with kind eyes and drained it immediately. He smiled and offered me a refill, and I took that too. I thought getting as drunk as Marit sounded like a good idea—and unlike him, I was less dangerous when emotional and intoxicated.

How old are you? I asked Taran when I'd known him for a month. He was cagey about his background, and I had come to suspect he didn't have an honest claim to his name. A runaway acolyte couldn't profess to be the "son of Genna," the way all priests were called sons and daughters of their patrons, and anyone with his talent should have been ordained before his apparent age, which I estimated at a little older than my eighteen.

Guess, he replied, grinning broadly. I had not yet noticed that his smiles warmed me like sun on bare skin, but I smiled back. This was the only fun I had, most days. A few moments with Taran while everyone else was asleep.

Twenty.

Taran had smirked and pointed one finger toward the ceiling of the abandoned cowshed we were sheltering in for the night. Older than twenty.

Twenty-two.

Someone older than twenty-two would have been married and a father already, especially someone handsome and strong like Taran. Even with no family or trade, some farmer's daughter would have caught him and brought him home.

Taran laughed and pointed up again. Older than twenty-two. I gulped.

Twenty-five?

Taran laughed harder. He didn't look twenty-five. He didn't have sun damage around his eyes or scars on his hands. But he laughed at my wide-eyed dismay, finger still pointed at the ceiling.

I opened my mouth to guess *thirty*, but I closed it again. For reasons I didn't care to examine, I did not want to know that Taran was thirty, when I was only eighteen.

Twenty-seven, I decided but didn't guess out loud.

I'd lost count of the days, but I was fairly certain I was twenty-two as I made my way across the dance floor on the buoying float of the wine. Several of the revelers tried to pull me into the whirling, ever-changing knots of dancers, but one moon-priest with long black braids put an arm around my waist and warm lips to mine before spinning me on my good foot and pointing me toward the performers. My head spun too, but I welcomed the opportunity to join the other musicians and feel like I knew what I was doing.

The moon-priests cleared a space at the front of the stage and passed me a lute. I was prepared for a challenge—an obscure hymn of Lixnea's, or a composition that would tax my rusty skill with the instrument—but instead the flutist trilled the opening notes to a simple ballad, a hundred years old but perfectly suited to my range. I smiled with gratitude and prepared to send my voice to the rafters.

How healing, to find myself the right tool for a task. So much easier to sing than to lead an army—or love someone complicated.

I wore one of the dresses Taran had stolen for me. The soft

fabric clung to my body in a green so dark it was nearly black, with sleeves that fitted down to my fingers and a fluted hem that swished around my ankles. I felt almost pretty in it: not overwhelmed by the symbolism of Wesha's thick white wool or overshadowed by the gems on her castoffs. From the corner of my eye, I caught the gleam of Taran's gaze where he watched me from a knot of his admirers. Locked on me like the point of a compass needle.

Were there hollows in his soul where our vows once tied us together? Was there something in the shape of him that remembered me, the way the Moon claimed that Death yearned for his bride?

At the end of the set, when the flutist yielded his spot to a piper, I excused myself and wove back to a padded bench at a table in the corner of the room, planning to sit and enjoy the music for the rest of the evening. Still, I wasn't surprised when Taran peeled away from the crowd a few moments later and claimed the seat at my side.

"I overheard at least two brewing plots among Lixnea's people to steal you away from me," he announced, pride on my behalf only outweighed by his self-satisfaction.

"You still don't have me," I said, smiling anyway.

"A distressing thought." He gave me a melting look through his dark eyelashes, an expression no less effective for being practiced. "I didn't know you played the lute too. I'll get you one."

Three hundred years of punishment did not seem to have made any impact on Taran's respect for the property of others, because he was obviously planning another theft soon. I hoped he didn't steal from our hostess.

"What about you? Just the kithara?"

"I don't know. Nobody's mentioned it," he said, expression dimming a little.

Before he could get lost in that thought, I took his left hand and wrapped it around my wrist at the approximate position he'd press the strings on a lute.

"Listen. Everyone knows this song. See if your hands know the music."

Lixnea's priests were playing one of my favorites. It wasn't some great epic, just a sweet and silly song about an actor who prayed to the Moon for the ability to change his appearance onstage but forgot his own face afterwards. He came home with his landlord's eyebrows, his baker's nose, and his neighbor's beard, but his wife knew him anyway.

I waited for Taran to press the shapes of the chords onto my skin, but after a moment, his fingers slipped down to my hand. I gave him a startled glance when he gently traced the scar a ragged plectrum had left with the tip of his thumb, but he was intent on his study.

I had a maiden-priest's hands. Slender and strong, but scrubbed ruthlessly clean and flecked all over from encounters with snapped strings, stray cinders, and broken mortal bones. Taran held the one with his ring on it—I knew I should take it off, but I couldn't quite make myself do it.

"Do you remember anything? Anything at all?" I asked softly. Several times he'd already said he didn't, but I still hoped that wasn't true.

"Before I died? No." He didn't look up as the warm pad of his thumb dipped up and down across my knuckles. He let his fingers rest in the hollows between my own, marking their size against my smaller hand. The weight of his hand resting in mine made my stomach tighten with yearning.

"But there are a few things I just . . . know," he added after a moment.

I didn't want to put as much hope into that statement as my

heart urged me to, but if Marit could still feel the well water around him, why couldn't Taran feel his hand in mine? He didn't elaborate, leaving me to dream that some part of him found this familiar.

He pulled his fingers from mine to rest on my wrist, thumb brushing the fragile skin over my pulse, which quickened at the tiny intimacy. When I didn't squirm away, he lifted my palm to rest against his upper arm, and we sat back like that. As delicately as I'd replace a baby bird in the nest, he shifted so that my head fell onto his shoulder.

I let the wine and the music slide through me, and my eyelids grew heavy as the night stretched on. Nobody sought us out, though Taran drew some speculative glances from the dancers who passed by. Moments of peace had not been so common in my past few years that I needed anything more than the comfort of Taran's warm, solid form next to me and the beauty of the music to feel content, but his energy was more restless.

He let go of my hand to sit up and refill both our glasses from one of the open carafes on the table. I took mine but didn't drink— I was feeling a little fuzzy already.

"If you're not going to sing again, do you want to go back to my room?" Taran asked with his voice nearly obscured in his cup.

"Why?" I asked with complete innocence.

I didn't catch his meaning until he gave me a wide, slow smile, eyes brightening with delight at my naive response.

"I need your help reaching something on a low shelf," he drawled, trying to pull my hand onto his arm when I turned my shoulders to frown at him. I did know what people left parties to do in bedrooms, at least in theory; I just hadn't expected him to ask when he never had before.

I would have been very easy to seduce—from the beginning, even. It had been my first time out of the strictures of Wesha's temples, I was terrified and alone with the burden of leadership, and

Taran had been everything I could have wanted. I used to lie awake cataloging the times he'd smiled at me that day.

And once we were betrothed—well, he could have had me by crooking the least little finger. I loved him to distraction. It wouldn't have taken words. It could have been a look, a hand pulling me toward his bed. I would have gone. I had been waiting for our wedding night not to keep Wesha's favor but because he'd seemed to expect I would prefer to wait, and I didn't want to disappoint his idea of me.

Well, there was nobody but me to care what I did now.

What had felt like respect for the vows I nearly made to Wesha now felt like another mistake. Why had I never pulled him away from the firelight and asked him to demonstrate some of that eternal devotion he was always professing? Was he actually indifferent to me, or would it have felt too dishonest to cross that line? I didn't think I'd feel any more betrayed than I did now if I'd left the three years I loved him with a better idea of what two people did when they left a party hand in hand.

There was a little power in having these particular regrets in this situation though. I crossed my arms, let my glass sit loosely in my hand, and considered him with lowered eyelids.

"Why?" I asked again. "No, really—tell me."

If this was just another priestly duty he expected me to attend to, I'd dump my entire glass of wine in his lap and leave, but Taran was rarely direct about what he wanted, so the casual way he'd asked made me think there was more to it.

If anything, he seemed flustered by my challenge. He tilted his head, gaze hanging on my lips when I took another sip from my glass.

"I'd like to see what your hair looks like when it's down and loose," he said after a moment, voice a shade raspy.

I waited for more. Surely, after three hundred years, he could manage better. I knew I wasn't beautiful, but I had to have a few charms worth listing.

When I quirked one eyebrow at this lack of effort, his cheeks colored, but he didn't amend his response, which made me wonder if he'd neglected to lie out of sheer surprise that I hadn't stormed off.

So I shrugged. "Alright," I said, and set my cup down so that I could pull the pins out of my hair. For the party I'd done a more complicated style, arranged like a double crown on the top of my head, and it took a few minutes to get enough pins out so that my braids fell over my chest. His eyes widened but held mine when I took out the ties and carded my fingers all the way to the roots. When it was all loose, I bent my head and shook the dark red strands out so they fell around my shoulders. Even crimped from the braids, my hair brushed my thighs, shining in the lantern light. There.

Taran had a small, puzzled frown on his face, like I'd done something inexplicable, even though many women wore their hair loose every day. He picked up one lock and wound it through his fingers, but it was just hair—there was no magical seductive power in it, or I wouldn't be the sole frustrated virgin at this party.

When he didn't say anything, I put my hands behind my neck to coil it up again, but he kept his grip and concentrated on the lock he held. I cleared my throat, and he finally recognized my quizzical expression and blinked, seeming to come back to himself.

"I meant I'd like to see it spread across my pillow," he said belatedly.

At my nearly audible eye-roll, he pulled my resistant body toward him, almost into his lap.

"It's true. Everyone who heard you sing is imagining the exact same thing, except they're afraid I might be concealing a stone knife and a jealous streak," he said in a more conversational tone, wrapping one arm around my shoulders with his fingers still woven into my hair. The tug on my scalp made a spark catch low in my belly, a small curl of desire I might still decide to fan into flame.

"Really?"

"Yes. Unfortunately for you, they're right."

It had never occurred to me that anyone but Taran would be interested in me, and I scanned the crowd as though I might somehow be able to confirm it. People had been watching us, openly and covertly, but I had assumed that was about Taran's beauty.

"Then why would I choose you? No one else has tried to trap me into ironing his clothes forever," I said, still not convinced this was about his straightforward interest.

"Oh, I've heard it's a remarkable experience, if you'll accept the recommendation of people who knew me while I was serving Genna. I don't remember, of course."

There was an edge in the flippant words that made me sure there was something more he wasn't telling me. I continued thinking out loud. "Why ask me though? Because you think I won't tell anyone if you've completely forgotten what to do . . . ?"

"I have *not*," Taran said, looking like he would have liked to haul me out of the performance hall before someone overheard us. Unfortunately for him, I was in the corner, which meant I couldn't escape but also he couldn't easily make me be quiet.

"Is that it? Then what if you've chosen poorly? Maybe I'm terribly indiscreet. Maybe I'd get up tomorrow and gossip to Lixnea's court that Taran ab Genna is all elbows and knees in bed, and he snores too."

I'd missed teasing him, even if I never would have dared on this subject, and I grinned until he pulled up one corner of his mouth in a reluctant smirk.

"Again, I do *not*," he said, tightening his grip on my hair until he held it in his fist. "If I disappoint in any way, you have my permission to ruin my flawless reputation."

My chiding look bounced right off his determined face. He didn't let go.

"So?"

"So? This doesn't sound like it has anything to do with me."

I wanted to hear him say he was overcome with desire for me—and more than that, say something to make me think he always had been.

"Of course it's to do with you," he insisted, but he turned his face toward the wall behind us. It took him several reluctant breaths to speak again, voice low when he finally continued. "Fine. I've heard a lot of things about myself tonight, and it's not pleasant to be the most ignorant person in the room on that subject, but I'm trying to catch up. So I was just . . . thinking. While watching you on the stage. About the light on your hair, and your hands on the lute, and your lips while you sing—anyway, I was thinking how much I wanted to take you to bed, and that seemed like a good reason to ask you, but it occurred to me that I don't know if that ever was a good enough reason before. I don't know if that was ever even one of my reasons before, or if it was always for Genna's power."

My smile faded, and after a moment, Taran reluctantly let go of my hair.

"That's awful," I said quietly, which made him scowl and shift in his seat.

"I don't know if it was or wasn't. All I know is if there was ever anyone I wanted for myself, they weren't waiting for me when I got home." He ran one careful knuckle along the curve of my shoulder. "But you—I'd know."

He exhaled and finally met my eyes, honest and piercingly lovely in the lantern glow. I twisted my hands together in my lap, caught between regret and desire. I wanted to smooth the hard edge of his mouth with my thumb, kiss the line of his jaw to softness, tell him that I'd never doubted he could be good to someone in every way one person could be to another.

I held myself back.

"I'm not sure that wanting to prove something to yourself is a good enough reason to go to bed with someone."

"Not just that. I said—"

I sighed. "Yes, even with my hair, and my voice, and everything else that you can see right here."

"What is a good reason, then?" he asked, sounding curious.

"You're asking a maiden-priest?"

"You were going to be married. Surely you at least *thought* about it."

Now it was my turn to look away. "I thought about it."

I wished I knew.

There was a lot in my short, declarative sentence, and after Taran had digested it, he said simply *oh*. Not in a pitying way, just thoughtful.

Perhaps sensing that my resolve was not rock-solid, he took my hand again and traced a fingertip along the edge. Followed it slowly down the line of my arm and let it fall to my thigh, where he spread his palm to smooth my dress over my leg and let me feel the heat of his hand. A small show of finesse: this was how he'd touch me. Gently and intentionally.

I wished that he'd ever asked when I could have been unconflicted about my answer. But there was probably a reason he never had. I let the moment pass.

"Taran, it's a bad idea. I'd be all elbows and knees. Tears, too."

He blinked, taken aback. "Tears? Why would you cry? I wouldn't do anything to make you cry."

It was the first thing I'd said that made him sound honestly wounded.

I'm sorry, Taran, I'd be thinking about my betrothed, who is dead, and is also you, and I find that very confusing sometimes.

I ducked my head as I looked for a way to deflect his question, so I was startled when I felt his hand cup my cheek.

He moved slowly enough that I could have turned my face away, but I found that I desperately wanted to know how Taran kissed someone he wanted to go to bed with, and I held very still as he leaned toward me.

The kiss was gentle and coaxing, his lips lingering at the corner of my mouth to warm me with his breath until I lifted my chin and turned into him. He took me in small sips, just a sweet give and take that drew on the hidden reservoir of heat in my center and urged it to spread through my body. When I opened to him, his thumb swept down my jaw, but only the tip of his tongue brushed my own. Making me the one to pursue him, the one to chase sensation and feeling.

He was being oh so careful, saying without words that if I left with him, he'd take very good care of me.

That ember of desire flared and brightened in my core, a feeling that for years I'd put aside for later. But this time I fed it, leaning in and pressing the backs of my hands against the hot skin of Taran's throat, just below where his hand cupped my face. My forearms rested against the taut muscles of his chest. This had been the place I felt safest. Loved.

Our first kiss wasn't like this. It had been about a minute after he asked me to marry him, or a minute after I realized he was serious. I hadn't known what to do with my nose or my hands or my *breathing* because it had been not just our first kiss but my first kiss ever, and Taran had been more concerned with getting an answer out of me than with showing me what to do.

Is that a yes? Please say yes, nightingale.

After I did get that single, joyous word out, Taran had run outside to tell everyone, and then a full day's march and our inescapable responsibilities had meant it wasn't until late that evening that we had another moment alone. I spent some hours of reflection that day—the ones not spent selecting flowers for our wedding or naming our future children—on the thought that I had certainly not been *Taran's* first kiss. Acolytes of Genna had considerably more freedom than acolytes of Wesha, after all, and a reputation for . . . freedom.

When Taran finally did pull me aside late that night and lifted my face to his with two confident fingertips beneath my chin, I apologized earnestly.

I'm sorry, I'm probably terrible at this. But I'll try to get better.

Taran was rarely serious, and he wasn't then. He ground the tip of his nose into my cheek until I squealed and collapsed against him.

No, you're perfect. But you are welcome to practice on me as much as you'd like.

And I did. As hard as I'd ever worked at singing the Maiden's blessings with perfect pitch and diction, I worked on kissing him. I kissed him until our lips were swollen and his pupils were blown, until his hands flexed convulsively on my hips and his breathing ran ragged.

For all he'd imagined some stone-solid line he couldn't cross with me, I couldn't believe there was anyone who was as expert at kissing Taran ab Genna as I was—even in three hundred years, there couldn't have been anyone as motivated as me to learn.

The kiss was deeper now, intent in a way it had never been before, with one hand tangled in my hair and the other pulling me hard against his body. I took his tongue fully into my mouth as my body lit with three years of carefully banked need. The kiss was no longer careful; it was hungry and desperate.

He was the one to break it, pulling back with a noise of surprise from deep in his chest.

Taran's face had lit with the same gratified astonishment as the night I sang to Marit, softened by what looked painfully like tenderness.

I'd hoped to learn something about him. Instead, he was obviously wondering why I kissed him not like a woman trying to decide whether she wanted to take a man home from a party but like his sweetheart, who'd missed him terribly. Who loved him.

"Say yes, Iona," he breathed, and my given name in his mouth was like a splash of cold water.

I wasn't his sweetheart. He wasn't a runaway acolyte who'd died on the cliffs half a year ago. If this new man wanted to celebrate his freedom, he could start by offering me my own.

"Take me to the Painted Tower," I said, forcing myself back to the present.

"What?" Taran jerked away, whipsawed by my change of subject.

I shook my head, mind grasping for clarity. Trying to hold on to the things I now knew about him.

"Are you . . . trying to bargain with me?" He was not just stunned but angry, but I needed to remember to stay angry too.

"Yes. If you'll take me to the Painted Tower, you can have whatever you want from me."

His lips parted in shock.

"You *still* want to go? You think, what, Wesha will really give you your betrothed back?"

I didn't know. Wesha didn't have the power to change Taran's heart, did she? She'd promised me Taran exactly as he was—as willing as he'd ever been to weave his life to mine, I supposed, so he might not go home with me.

But at least I'd have a choice about how to spend my life.

"Yes, I do."

"And what would your husband-to-be think of you buying his life with that bargain?" Taran retorted with silky fury.

"I think under the circumstances, he'd be understanding," I drawled.

The joke didn't land, of course. Taran's jaw tensed, emerald eyes going hard and resistant as he gave his answer.

"No. Don't ask me again."

Some part of me was relieved that he didn't offer anything else, but I shoved at his arm anyway until he slid down the bench so that I could get up.

His expression was still stung when he was on his feet. "So that's it, then? That's all you want?"

I nearly laughed, because I didn't want so very much—only the things he'd chosen to promise me. I hadn't asked for anything!

But yes, I still wanted all of it.

"I want what I came here for," I said to his beautiful and wary face. "I was going to be married. To someone who was . . . the best man I'd ever met. A hero. Who promised to build me a stone house with a plum tree by the front window. And love me forever, until the stars fell out of the sky. We were going to be together for the rest of my life, Taran. That's what I want! Explain it to me—why would I ever accept less from you?"

I knew he couldn't actually have an answer for that, so I excused myself quickly, fighting the part of me that wanted to soothe away every hurt on his face, even the ones I had inflicted.

15

A CRATER LAKE FED by a mountain waterfall should have been too frigid to swim in at any hour of the day, but here in the Summerlands, it was only bracingly cold if I went in just after dawn. I braved this breath-stealing plunge every morning, because Taran insisted that I wake when he did, and this was the only hour when I could go in and be confident that none of Lixnea's very friendly priests would try to strike up a conversation while clad in nothing but a look of serenity.

I still wasn't graceful in the water, but the lake was glass-smooth and clear down to its shallow stone bottom, so I found that if I spread my arms and legs in the shape of Wesha's star, I could float on my back and look up into a pastel sky that mirrored the one at home. With the water filling my ears and the scent of reeds in my nose, I achieved something like calm, with memory and duty falling away like gravity did.

Taran never followed me out here, which I was silly to find disappointing. I must have been a passing fancy, because he never mentioned his question on the night of the new moon again. I got polite distance instead, leaving me with daydreams where he waded into the water and confessed that he'd never learned how to swim, which would make at least one thing he'd told me true.

That's alright, we'll learn together, I'd say, and I'd take his hand, and we'd begin anew.

The daydream felt close to solidifying into an intention, but several weeks after we'd arrived at the house of the Moon, I hadn't yet acted on it. I was lulled by the simplicity of life here. It felt like I had time to think.

Nonetheless, my tranquility was interrupted on this morning by an enormous black cormorant, whose webbed feet struck my diaphragm with great force and no warning.

"Having a nice time? All relaxed and entertained?" Awi hissed viciously as I rolled and choked on lake water and contemplated a bit of drowning.

That had *hurt*.

I hadn't seen the bird goddess since our arrival, and I couldn't say I'd missed her.

The bottom of the lake was too deep here for my toes, so I treaded water with difficulty as I recovered from being hit in the stomach for no good reason.

I'd borrowed a short, black linen shift from a moon-priest as a bathing costume, and it puddled around my armpits when I was up-right, so my furious look at the bird wasn't very effective intimidation.

"I am, thank you," I snapped.

"Lazy girl! You're supposed to be finding me a way out of the Summerlands, not lolling around and listening to moon-priest po-etry," Awi insisted as she bobbed in the water.

"You didn't put a time limit on your vow, and Taran's not ex-actly in a hurry to get me to the Painted Tower," I reminded her, though I felt a stab of guilt for Drutalos, who by now was surely worried about whether I'd ever return.

Awi honked judgmentally, long neck swaying like a snake.

"You need to go *now*. Today. Make him take you—what are you waiting for?"

"Do you know something?"

The bird didn't immediately answer, as withholding as always. I resisted the urge to squeeze her feathered neck.

"Is it Death?" I pressed. "Have you seen him yet?"

"No! And that worries me. He spent three hundred years acting the demon, trying to get Wesha's attention, and he just gives up? No. He must be here, planning something."

"I need more than that if you expect me to make Taran do anything except compare wine-tasting notes with Marit," I said, still suspicious that she knew more than she was saying.

The bird heaved a sigh. "I did see something yesterday. On the Mountain, all the way to the east. Smenos Shipwright was cutting timbers, big ones. For the hull of a ship."

"The Shipwright is building ships? Sounds like him," I said, not following.

"Not since he helped trap poor Wesha in her tower! How does he think he's getting through the Gates? Wesha would never let him pass. He came and asked her last month, was a real jackass about it. She told him no, uh, *forcefully.* So what's changed?"

That was enough to make me frown. Smenos had to be one of the ones Genna was worried about, the Stoneborn who wanted to cross the Sea of Dreams and punish the disobedient mortals.

For all that I'd known this stay was temporary and I hadn't come here of my own volition, I was reluctant to climb out of the lake and ask Taran about what Awi had told me. I supposed that Awi might be right, and I was lazier than I'd thought—nobody expected anything of me here but that I'd take the occasional turn in the scullery or fill in if someone needed a mezzo-soprano to test their new musical composition.

Lixnea's people mostly kept late hours, but she and the other two Stoneborn were eating breakfast on the veranda after I'd dressed. I slid in on a bench next to Taran, and he made room and passed me a carafe of orange juice without pausing his conversation.

I had decided not to feel guilty about enjoying any simple pleasures of the Summerlands. And some of the pleasures of mornings at Lixnea's palace were simple: trays of sliced fruit and cheese pastries drizzled in honey, the experimental harmonies of the moonpriests' songs, the light on the calm surface of the lake. Others were more complex, like the warm solidity of Taran's thigh pressed against my own.

I didn't think for a moment that he'd ended his campaign to add me to his retinue in a permanent way. He introduced me to everyone we met as his priestess, like it would become true if he repeated it often enough. And I wouldn't give an inch on that. I'd meant what I said—I was never going to accept less from him than what he'd promised me. I'd never be his priestess after wanting to be his wife.

But sometimes he touched me without thinking about it. When his eyes were on the horizon or a group of actors performing a new play, his fingers would unconsciously seek to rest on my hip or my knee. And I wouldn't object. He'd look up, startled, after half an hour with his lips against my bound hair, and shoot me a suspicious glance, like I'd somehow snuck his arm around my waist.

That wasn't a simple pleasure. It was a complicated one: a single rented room in a home that was supposed to have been mine.

Marit didn't notice my arrival at the breakfast table: someone had mentioned a few days ago that he'd liked carving driftwood, so he'd obtained a knife and the raw materials, then taken to the hobby with gusto. He had already managed the recognizable shape of a sea serpent with sharp fins and spread jaws, and he'd promised it to Lixnea over her gentle attempts to demur.

"Who could Smenos be building ships for?" I asked Lixnea rather than Taran.

The Moon goddess raised a faint white eyebrow. "Who did you hear that from?"

"Awi. She said Smenos asked Wesha to open the Gates, and Wesha refused. But he's building ships anyway."

"I saw that too, and wondered myself," Lixnea said after a speculative look at Taran.

"Taran, was Smenos one of the Stoneborn that Genna was worried about?" I asked, afraid this really was the preparation for an invasion.

"No," Taran said, voice cautious. "He's angry that the mortals burned his temples, of course, but he has hundreds of priests here. There's no reason for him to cross the Sea of Dreams."

Lixnea didn't say anything, but I could tell she didn't quite agree. She saw the mortal world. She knew it wasn't just a matter of burned temples but of all craftsmen falling silent at the queen's command, when they would have once muttered prayers to Smenos while they worked.

"Well, *something* made him start building ships. He must plan for someone to board them, and the only place to go is through the Gates."

Nobody challenged this point, though I could tell that Taran wished I would drop it.

"It could be Death," I added, keeping my face straight and stern. "He'd want to recruit more priests, wouldn't he?" I had made a real dent in their population, after all.

Taran tossed his napkin on the table.

"Stop worrying about it," he growled. "If Death shows up on Wesha's beach, she'll chase him off again. And don't worry about Smenos either—the boat's probably for me. He built the one I took last time, and he can shove this one right back into the Mountain if he thinks I'll go again."

"Better you than Skyfather or one of the Stoneborn who wanted to wipe us out," I urged him. My heart leapt at the idea that I might lure Taran home.

"Not *you*, the rebels," Taran said smoothly and incorrectly. "And also *not me*, as in, never again. Darling, please recall that the last two Stoneborn to enter the mortal world were recently assassinated? Genna is right—let them sit in their mess until they come to their senses."

I balled up my fists beneath the table, unable to think of a way to correct him without exposing our own part in the *mess*.

"What do you want to do?" I asked Lixnea, who was watching me with a rapt smile on her face, like a cat who heard mice in the wall. Secrets. "About the divide from the mortal world."

"You're the first person to ask me," she said, with some humor and a chiding glance at the two immortals. "Not even Taran has asked—I do believe he's forgotten why he's supposed to be here. Well. I can see the Earth more clearly than the other Stoneborn. I see the mortals suffering for the lack of our touch and blessings, and it pains me. I also see how thin and small this place has grown without new prayers to fill it up. So, I have to say that I would prefer to return. If Smenos built ships, I would board them with my priests, and I would ask the mortals to worship as they used to."

This didn't seem to be a happy thought, and Lixnea folded her ancient hands together.

"But there is the question of Wesha's Gates. I sat out the Great War, you know. My people aren't warriors, and neither am I. Which is why I am so very old. I wouldn't raise a hand against Wesha or the mortals who've rejected us, even to restore my temples."

"And if someone else did? Death?"

I was pressing my luck with the ancient Stoneborn, and her expression cooled. "Napeth was once my beautiful youngest brother, who welcomed the dead to their peaceful rest in the Underworld. He wasn't always a monster. I can't help but blame Wesha for that."

This seemed to be a pretty way of saying that she wouldn't do anything. That shouldn't have surprised me, when she'd called her priests back like all the others, but it still made me angry how quick the Stoneborn were to forgive each other for the loss of mortal lives.

"A man doesn't become a monster just because a woman rejects him," I insisted. "Not if that wasn't in him already."

"Perhaps a man would not, but a god? One forever sundered from his soul's purpose? I suspect that it improves none of us to deny who we are." I expected her to stare me down, remind me that most gods would gladly end the life of Iona Night-Singer, who'd overseen the fall of Death's reign on Earth, but instead her attention was on Taran, who seemed abruptly fascinated with the distant landscape.

"Excellent advice from the goddess of secrets," he replied, pushing the bench back with a grating noise of metal on the whitewashed planks of the veranda. He stalked away, ending up at the far edge of the deck, apparently declaring the conversation over.

I followed him with a conciliatory nod at Lixnea.

It was midmorning now, and the moon-priests were waking up. I heard vocal warmups from one outbuilding, and smoke was rising from the kitchens. The quiet of the lake felt louder than it had before though. This was a small part of the Summerlands, an even smaller part of the world. I couldn't forget the rest of it.

"I suppose we should still go," I said in a voice that wouldn't carry. "We know where Lixnea stands now, but we can confirm what Smenos is planning."

I'd unthinkingly put my hand on his arm when I spoke, and Taran glared at it as though I was making an unsubtle attempt to manipulate him instead of genuinely asking what he wanted to do.

"Smenos and Wirrea's palace is not nearly so pleasant as this, and the two of them are very boring," he said, using the diffident voice I was not fond of. "I'm not inclined to visit."

"I thought we were here to get Genna some intelligence on what all the other Stoneborn were doing."

"We're here because I thought you would like it," Taran said gruffly. "I thought we might stay a few months."

I blinked at him in surprise. "What? But you said—"

"I lied," he said unrepentantly.

So this hadn't been a mission for Genna, after all. I leaned away, anger sparking at him. "Why do you even *bother* to lie to me? You know I can't leave."

"Because Lixnea's priests are happy! And you weren't."

"And that matters to you? I tell you every day what I want. Take me—"

"To the Painted Tower, yes." Taran's face shuttered with frustration. "Loyalty's a virtue, so I can't complain that you still feel you owe it to Wesha or . . . or anyone else. I just hope that you someday offer me one tenth of that loyalty after I've done ten times more for you than they ever did."

He met my eyes again, and the hurt I saw made my hands ache to reach for him. The jut of his jaw was challenging but his green stare was brittle, almost vulnerable.

"Actually, that's another lie. I want all of it," he amended his statement. "After what I hear was a very unpleasant three hundred years for me, I finally have something to look forward to. Genna ceded me a chunk of her lands in exchange for my little misadventure in the mortal world. If you're done with the moon-priests, let's go there instead. I could put in an entire plum *orchard* for you."

"Oh," I said, shoulders curving around my fist, pressed against my heart. Every time I thought he was fully absorbed in himself, I was reminded that he must have gotten very good at playing a certain role here, and I shouldn't be completely fooled by it when I'd seen him be someone good and true. Both had to be in him. "I could . . . never be happy while I'm afraid that one of the Stoneborn is going to force their way past the Gates and do worse to the mortal world than Death already did."

"Now we need to add the entire mortal world to the list of people who've somehow earned your loyalty? Ask for less, darling. I'm still stinging from the object lesson in minding my own business that I received the last time I meddled in the affairs of the other Stoneborn."

"Were you meddling? Or trying to help?" I asked softly. I couldn't imagine he'd left three hundred years of forced service to the Peace-Queen without some care for the suffering of other people.

His eyelashes brushed the austere lines of his cheekbones as he grimaced. "Well, it came to the same end, whichever it was. I failed."

"You didn't *fail* the mortals. They're—"

"Not my problem anymore," he said, and cut me off with a warning look.

I shuffled my feet, helplessness churning in my stomach. I'd never disagreed with him before on what we ought to do.

"If you won't take me to the Painted Tower, can't you at least ask what Smenos Shipwright plans to do?"

Taran stilled, and I knew he was waiting for me to lay out terms. That was how things worked here. Mortals sacrificed to the gods when they wanted something, and I suspected he still hadn't forgiven me for offering up myself in exchange for fulfilling Wesha's bargain.

When I didn't immediately bite, Taran turned from his view of the lake to examine my imploring position. He lifted one hand to the side of my neck and the other to tangle in my wet hair, both of them tilting my face up. His thumbs held me in position as he looked down, no pity in the hard, clean lines of his face.

His expression didn't alter when he pressed warm lips to the corner of my jaw, just a flicker of his eyelashes when he looked for my objection and didn't find it. Then another kiss, close enough for me to feel his breath on my lips but not the softness of his own.

"It's like you've never had to ask for a thing in your life," he murmured, quiet voice at odds with the tension in his words. "You're terrible at it. No wonder you never get anything you want."

So angry, even though he'd walked into my life all smiles and laughing deflection. I'd never seen him angry before; I'd always thought that deep down he was more sad than anything else.

Fine, Taran, stay angry. I will too. Just remember that I wasn't the one who used you.

I peeled his hand off my face but squeezed it instead of pushing it away, interlocking my fingers with his. I spoke to him the way I always had instead of growling at him.

"I'm not asking you to do it for me. Taran, you *live* here. I know you have to be worried about what's happening."

"*We* live here," he immediately replied, but from his non-plussed face, he didn't expect an appeal to his better nature. He had to have one: a heart that could open for Marit in the well or Wesha in her tower could never be completely closed.

I leaned my cheek against his hand for a moment, soaking in the play of emotions across the elegant lines of his features.

I knew he'd do it before he did.

He dramatically groaned and rolled his head back before stalking over to Marit, who was still peacefully bent over his toy serpent.

"Look alive," Taran said, tossing a grape at his friend. "Tell the grooms to tack up the horses, we're leaving today. We have to go all the way to the western slope of the Mountain. Smenos's workshops."

Marit stretched out his arms and loosened his neck muscles,

looking regretfully at the water nymphs, who were beginning to wake and play in the shallows of the lake.

"Smenos? Does he want to see us?" Marit asked.

Taran tightened his face unhappily. "Not at all. You used to smash his ships for fun, and I'm fairly certain I slept with his wife."

Both Marit and I absorbed this news, one of us with a great deal more equanimity than the other.

"Ah, well," Marit said. "At least we're bringing Iona. Who wouldn't be pleased to have a musician as a guest?"

I forced myself to smile at the sea god, but I very carefully didn't look at Taran as I went back to my room to pack, and I slid the knives he didn't know I had into the pack right next to my kithara. I wasn't sure which I might need to use, but I was prepared for either situation.

16

FOR ALL I'D wanted to go, and Taran had not, he was in a much better mood than I was once we rode out to the east. Where Genna's parklands had been lushly cultivated and the Moon's lands had been a pristine forest, we encountered a maze of rocky red hills after a week's travel toward Smenos's workshops. Straight, black ironwood trees crowded the tops of the cliffs, obscuring even the sourceless daylight. We saw a few other immortals traveling between the City and their estates, but these travelers dwindled and then vanished as multiple roads converged into a single path through a narrow canyon with severe, high walls.

I grew stiff and nervous as I rode in front of Taran, and he'd noticed it, though I couldn't explain myself.

This is not how we would have done this when we were leading the mortal rebellion, Taran.

We would never have ridden straight into a settlement of unknown allegiance during the war, let alone done so in broad daylight, via the only apparent evacuation route. We would have sent in a couple of scouts the night before to tell us what lay ahead. We would have put someone under a canvas tarp at the top of the canyon walls to watch who came and went for a few days and cover our retreat if the approach went badly. But I had the hard-won wisdom of surviving three years of war, and Taran no longer did.

He dropped a hand onto my thigh and chafed it through the thick fabric.

"I've got you," he said into my ear as quiet reassurance, and I wrapped myself tighter into his embrace without relaxing. He'd said that before.

It was my hypervigilance that caught sight of the first rock tumbling into the pass. I leaned back hard, which was enough to make Taran slow, but the rockfall nearly clipped us when half the cliff face gave way. I screamed a halt, and Marit pulled up on his team before the larger boulders crashed down, striking the walls of the canyon and ricocheting into deadly shards and choking dust.

I didn't freeze—still soldiers were easy targets, and I was a survivor. I tumbled off the horse, taking Taran with me and trusting that the horse was too well trained to kick or rear as I rolled on my shoulder to absorb the impact of the ground and return to my feet as quickly as possible.

Trap. Ambush.

Jagged fear spiked through my veins as Taran looked up at me with wide, astonished eyes, blinking away the dust instead of searching for the source of the threat, because he didn't remember living through this.

Seizing the front of his tunic, I hauled him toward the nearest cover: a pile of sharp-edged boulders that had barely come to rest. If someone had been waiting for the rockfall to trigger, they'd follow it with a volley of arrows to pin down any survivors and make time for the death-priests to move in with a curtain of fire.

The familiar nausea of combat roiled in my gut as I pushed Taran into the small shadow of the boulder, my mind desperately churning on what tactics our tiny group might respond with. Marit was still wrestling with his chariot, but perhaps he could wash out anyone who came up our rear flank? Could Taran do anything? Genna's blessings were of limited use in battle, and if he'd forgotten all the others he knew—

I whined in panic, dithering between calling Death's fire down preemptively and raising more of a defense to give Marit and Taran time to get their bearings. When Taran didn't go for his belt knife, I chose defense. I sang a cloak of darkness over us, a dome of night that enveloped the horses and the rockfall. It wouldn't obscure us at close range, but archers couldn't get a lock on us while we armed and regrouped. Which direction were they coming from though? From above? Behind? I bit off the final words of the chant—*oh, Moon, who hides in the Heavens, our lady of dark skies*—and listened for the snap of bowstrings or the vibration of booted feet striking the ground to tell me where the enemy was.

And listened.

Instead, all I heard was the ragged whistle of my own breath and the thud of my heartbeat where it pounded against Taran's chest. The pawing of Marit's chariot team, a little distance away. Awi, who'd trailed us all the way from Lixnea's estate, was chirping in confusion, high above. Everything else was still.

I'd tossed myself over Taran when I took shelter against the boulder, and now we were nearly nose to nose, with my body protectively splayed over his.

"Darling, I don't want to discourage you from throwing me to the ground whenever you happen to become stricken with desire," he said as I gathered myself and tentatively determined that we were not, in fact, under attack. His voice became a pointed whisper, though his face was just mildly quizzical. "But what are you doing?"

"I—" I listened again, hard. Nothing. What had caused the rockfall? I'd survived ambushes that began exactly like this. "I thought it was a trap."

Taran's sculpted lips pursed with consternation. I'd panicked, thrown myself on top of him, and launched a defense using the power of the Moon. Not a reasonable thing for me to do, from what he was supposed to know about me.

"Did you learn that blessing at Lixnea's villa?"

"I saw her priests use it during the scene changes in a dramatic opera," I said, true words to conceal a lie.

No. I learned it from scatterbrained, funny Windilla ter Lixnea, who didn't survive the mudslide in the second year of the war. Our best scout.

I carefully peeled myself away from Taran's body. Now that my fear was fading, I had half a dozen places where I'd likely be sporting bruises tomorrow and a rising blush that spread across my cheeks and neck.

At Taran's skeptical look, I added, "Why, what were you doing all this time?"

"Eating pastries and trying to seduce you." His tunic stretched over his chest as he sat up. It left me with my thighs spread over his lap, and our bodies aligned. My heart thumped a little faster even if there was no danger, and for entirely new reasons. Baser instincts declared that Taran's muscles were, as expected, very nice to press against.

"Well, then," I said unsteadily, fighting my fluster. I supposed that casually pursuing me was better than wondering whether I was part of that mortal rebellion he'd been tasked with stamping out, but only just. Taran gently brushed dust off my cheekbone and the tip of my nose.

"You wouldn't try to leave me for Lixnea, would you?" he asked, in that light tone that he'd always used to calm me when things were at their worst. "Because you know she makes her priests wash the dishes, and I'll let you toss them on Napeth's front lawn when they get dirty."

There were questions in his brilliant green eyes, but underneath them, real concern, and I impulsively hunched forward to bury my face against Taran's neck. The last of my fear came out in a muffled noise against his collarbone as I curled my hands into his tunic. I'd thought I was losing him again.

"You're fine, I've got you," he crooned, rubbing the gap between my shoulder blades until I unsteadily climbed off him. Marit had gotten the horses under control, and he rolled the chariot over to demonstrate only mild confusion at the situation.

"Why did we stop?" he asked Taran.

"Iona was concerned that we might be under attack, and she decided to protect us."

"Attacked? Who would attack us?"

I gestured at the rockfall. "Someone could have triggered that."

The sea god fixed me with a chiding expression. He was more present by the day, as though Taran and I were rubbing some sanity off on him.

"You didn't have to do anything," he said, tone grave. "The Allmother forbids us to harm each other, but even if someone tried, you shouldn't interfere. You're mortal, and we're not. We'll protect you."

I nodded slowly, because that made sense, but I'd yet to see these laws stop any of the Stoneborn from doing anything they really wanted to do.

Taran rested his elbow on my shoulder. "Speak for yourself, Marit. I was terrified. I think Iona should come straddle me in the dirt for a little longer, until I'm positive I've survived."

I rolled my eyes at him, reassured despite myself to hear him sound exactly as insincere as he used to.

"Are you alright?" Taran asked in a lower voice. "We can stop for a while. I'll clear the stones if you need a moment."

I rubbed my palms over my face, urging my heart to slow down.

"But what *did* cause the rockfall?" There was no wind, and our horses were at the base of the canyon, not the top, where the rock had sheered away. I still felt uneasy, and I didn't want to believe I was so damaged by three years of war that I fell to pieces at a loud noise.

Taran squinted at the canyon wall and put one hand out to press against it.

"You know that the Allmother lifted the Summerlands out of the sea and formed it from mortal prayers? If I had to guess, it's falling apart in the absence of those mortal prayers. We're less than what we were. It used to take a month to cross the Summerlands. Now it takes a week. It's all dwindling."

That was an unexpectedly sad thought, for as little as the gods had ever done for me, and all of us meditatively lingered on it.

"Or it just happened to fall," Taran added. "Come on, let's get inside by sunset."

I thought it would take days to clear a path, but Marit lifted a hand, and the rocks began to slide up the walls and slot themselves into place like pieces of a child's puzzle. For his part, Taran squatted at the edge of the rubble, squinted hard at it, and pushed a boulder to dissolve into the stone of the road.

At my startled noise, he looked back and gave a casual shrug, pleased at my reaction. "We inherit some of our ancestors' power, and we're all descended from the Allmother. A step removed, in my case."

It took me a moment to realize why Taran's hand on the stone had thrown me so much—it was the first time I'd seen him do something that a mortal, or even one of the Fallen, could not. No song, no other god's blessings. Just one small, shifting rock, moving at his will. The first proof I'd seen that he was really one of the Stoneborn.

He and Marit cleared the path, moving large boulders like they were sacks of grain, and soon we were mounted again and moving toward the citadel of Smenos Shipwright, though my sense of un-easiness didn't lift. Awi went back to hiding in my hood as we crossed a final switchback and the citadel came into sight.

"Something is wrong," she declared in her tiny piping voice as we surveyed the collection of buildings. "Where is everyone?"

From my position on the horse, I couldn't turn around to look at Taran for an answer, but I wondered that myself.

Smenos's palace was vast, a red stone structure carved directly into the Mountain behind it, but his workshops were bigger. They were a small city of three-storied white stucco and timber build-ings that filled the valley and crowded around a stream obstructed by several water mills. I saw dozens of open forges, kilns, and worktables—but they were all empty. There were no lamps lit in the windows, and the chimneys were cold and still. Not a single soul was visible.

Smenos was famous for calling back all his master artisans at the sunset of their years to cross the sea and preserve their knowl-edge for future generations. There should have been hundreds of priests here, not to mention the lesser immortals who supported the Shipwright in his work—gods of metal, patrons of the professions, spirits of old bridges and great monuments.

"Hello?" Marit called as we approached the central courtyard. "Is anyone home?"

No one immediately answered, but we dismounted and gazed at the forbidding stone face of the palace. It had been carved in stages, with some of the earliest pillars showing marks of mortal chisels, while the highest and newest decorations, far above our heads, were ornate scenes of battle from the Great War.

Some of it had crumbled. There was rubble in the courtyard and the smell of stone dust. The potted olive trees by the front stairs were withering from neglect, and their leaves had not been swept away.

"How long has it been like this?" I asked Taran, whose face was drawn as he surveyed the dark windows around us.

"It wasn't like this a few months ago," he said curtly.

"Should we knock on the front door?" Marit wondered out loud, but as he said it, the polished bronze gates of the palace spread open, and one immortal exited, while another, a smaller shadow, waited in the darkness inside.

There was a certain gravity I'd felt around Lixnea—the weight of her power, her age. I'd felt it even more strongly in Death's presence, like a deep vibration in the soles of my feet. I felt it a little around Marit, but from Taran only if I looked very hard. It was the same for Smenos, when I recognized him.

Every idol of Smenos depicted him with one of his tools in his hands—a hammer, a chisel, a protractor—yet today the god's arms hung empty and slack at his side as he descended the stairs. His skin was the flawless, cool black of wrought iron, and his build was powerful under the simple leather apron he wore, but no divine presence accompanied his arrival. Aside from the metallic glint in his eyes, he could simply have been a tall, strong man.

From Taran's expression, he recognized the void of Smenos's power immediately, and he couldn't explain it any more than I could. Smenos had died and been reborn, very recently.

The Shipwright didn't bother to greet us.

"Did Genna send you?" he asked in a quavering voice. "Go and tell her it's too late."

Marit shot Taran a wide-eyed look, as confused as I was. Smenos's reputation was as an exacting, stern master—and the being standing here had the same unsteady posture as Marit the night I met him.

"Too late for what?" Taran asked, sketching a short bow. "I'm afraid Genna didn't send me or even know that she ought to come."

The crafter god's mouth pulled back in a rictus of a smile.

"You have a reputation as a liar, Taran ab Genna. Was she afraid to come and see what's become of her peace? I'll go to the City tomorrow and show her. You should leave."

Taran didn't let his calm expression slip, though I saw his jaw tighten.

"I happen to be telling the truth. I heard a rumor that you were building ships again, and as a Stoneborn, I felt compelled to come ask why."

"A Stoneborn?" Smenos looked among our group. "Do I have two Stoneborn at my doorstep, or one Stoneborn and another jumped-up Fallen with pretensions of power?"

"Another?" Taran said. He frowned, then asked in a more gentle voice. "What happened to you, Smenos? I swear by all the gods that Genna didn't send me. What are you talking about?"

"If Genna doesn't know, perhaps you could ask your bitch sister," Smenos said bitterly.

"Wesha and I have not really been on speaking terms for the past few centuries," Taran replied, eyebrows coming together in confusion. It took him longer to ask the question than I wanted, and when he did, it was in a rougher, lower voice. "What did Wesha do? I heard that you argued."

Smenos's big shoulders bunched as he gestured around his desolate lands. "What did you expect? Aren't you the one who gave her the stone knives in the first place?"

"Not for this," Taran said, shaking his head with his face full of dawning dismay. "Smenos, nobody would have wanted this."

According to the Moon, he'd given his sister the stone daggers that could kill a god only to drive Death away from her prison. But it seemed that Wesha had turned them on another of the Stoneborn. I slowly, unobtrusively reached for my hood, planning to wring Awi's feathered neck—she must have known!—but the little bird climbed around the back of my hood, burrowing into my hair.

"Genna asked if I would go to Wesha and beg her to let one ship pass. Me. You. Anyone. We're shrinking by bits, starving slow and quiet. The mortals *have* to be reminded of what we owe to each other. I thought Wesha would listen to me—I never lifted a hand against that girl, not even when the Summerlands were aflame because she wouldn't choose a husband." Smenos turned and looked up the stairs, face grief-stricken. "My wife found me stumbling down the Mountain a month ago."

"Why would Wesha do that?" I cried, forgetting that I was only there as a priestess to someone Smenos had called a jumped-up Fallen.

If Smenos had died, thousands of years of knowledge had died with him. I couldn't even imagine a city without his brown-smocked priests presiding over half the shops and smithies.

And where *were* all his priests?

The crafter god's mouth trembled with anger. "Wesha doesn't care if the entire world cracks and falls into the sea, so long as she gets her freedom." He took a deep breath and gestured roughly at his palace. "You can come in, I suppose."

He turned abruptly and headed back up the stone stairs, ignoring the smaller figure who stood in the doorway. Wirrea, I assumed. She was a minor goddess, the Huntress.

Smenos and his wife were famously ill-suited. Perhaps their match had made sense at the dawn of time, when tools were made of leather and bone, but Smenos's cult had become one of the largest and the Huntress's followers had dwindled as our country turned toward cultivation. The crafter god was said to be an indifferent husband to his wild bride, who made scandals and distracted his priests.

I frowned at Taran's back as we approached Wirrea. That didn't excuse *him* for getting involved with her.

The Huntress had the long, narrow skull and slender limbs of a deer, with the dappled, white-spotted fall of brown hair over her shoulders to match, but her large, green-gold eyes were set in the front of her face, and the teeth cutting into her full lower lip were sharp. She was predator and prey both, sizing up Marit and Taran as they came to the doorway.

"Taran ab Genna, back so soon." She spoke in a low, dangerous purr, heedless of her husband's grief-stricken presence just a few feet inside. "Do you want something again? Or is it Genna this time? You're such a lovely guest when Genna wants something from us."

Taran's face was guarded as he stopped in front of her, but he stoically allowed Wirrea to press her hips against his and rub a pointed nose across his throat.

"You're in a remarkably good mood for someone whose husband just died, Huntress," Taran said with a curled lip. "But no, I came only because Marit wished to get reacquainted with the other Stoneborn."

In response, Wirrea smirked and pulled Taran into the palace after her, one clawed hand tight around his wrist.

"Are you staying for dinner, then? I'll have to arrange something grander than I'd planned. I thought we'd have only one guest at our table," she cooed.

"Who else is here?" Marit asked, trailing behind them and oblivious to the mood.

The Huntress glanced over her shoulder, her eyes sparkling with malevolence. "Another Stoneborn, one who knows a few things about Wesha's betrayals."

My stomach sank, because somehow I could feel the answer already.

"Death is our guest tonight," the goddess announced, and even Taran's step faltered for a moment as the unlit stone halls swallowed us up.

17

I WRAPPED THE THICK, silver cloak Taran had given me during my first full day in the Summerlands around my body, but I was still shivering. The high ceilings of the stone room swallowed up light and heat, and no amount of fur rugs or tacky murals of hunting scenes could soften it. Taran offered to kindle a fire in the enormous red granite hearth that dominated one wall of the room we'd been assigned, but when I flinched, he lit a single lamp and left me to dress for dinner.

Wirrea's decorating scheme drew heavily on the trophies of her kills, and the taxidermied heads of several fantastical creatures—one with two blunt horns on its head, the face of an antelope, and the long neck of a snake—gazed down on me in glass-eyed stupor. Even if we all survived dinner, there was no chance I would be able to sleep in this room. Actually, there were several reasons I would not be sleeping in this room. At the house of the Moon, I'd slept in the priests' barracks, but when I inquired as to sleeping arrangements here, the craggy old hunt-priest who'd led us in just pointed to the woven leather mat in front of the single, enormous bed.

In case Taran needed anything in the night, like a drink of water, or an orgasm.

I couldn't even distract myself with that idea, though I tried hard. My thoughts bounced and spun in my skull without escape.

Taran rapped the open door to announce himself.

"Are you ready?"

Taran had gone very quiet when Wirrea announced the presence of the reborn god of the Underworld, but I doubted that anyone who didn't know him as well as I had would have seen that he was rattled at all.

"Not yet," I said, one hand still holding my cloak shut at my neck. "When we came in, did you happen to see whether there are any other doors on the ground level besides the main gates?"

"I didn't notice. Are you wearing the dress I laid out for you?"

I hadn't noticed either, which was careless of me. I hadn't survived this long without being aware of the exits.

"You forgot to pack whatever goes under it," I said, briskly answering his question.

Taran's lips curled with amusement, but I couldn't spare any outrage upon confirming that nothing went under the filmy bodice of the dress except me.

There was only one narrow window in the room, and I opened the shutter and peered out into the courtyard, where the waning light had turned the red stone to the color of embers. The ornate face of the palace might offer enough purchase for hands and feet if we had to climb out, but we'd be totally exposed during our descent.

"Come see if your shoulders will even fit through here," I said, gesturing for Taran to try.

"My shoulders? Why am I climbing out the window?"

"Only if the main exit is blocked."

Instead of confirming the feasibility of an escape from the second floor, Taran crossed his arms and leaned against the wall, eyes narrowing.

"Are you scared?" he asked, sounding surprised.

"Yes, of course I'm scared." I was surprised to have to say it.

"What are you afraid of?"

I gave a small laugh. "I've been scared for the last three years straight, ever since every other maiden-priest was incinerated by Death. Why aren't *you* afraid?"

"It's just a dinner."

And it had just been the midsummer solstice rites. It had just been a stormy day in Ereban. It had just been a few remaining death-priests and their loyalists.

"I know," I said slowly, tapping the window frame. "Please, I'd feel better if I knew there was another exit."

Taran humored me by kneeling in front of the window. It was too narrow even when he turned to the side, which meant Marit probably couldn't fit through it either.

"Do you want to leave?" Taran asked when I bit into the side of my cheek in worry.

"Right now?"

"Sure. I'll have Marit get the horses." His face was utterly serious.

"We can't just leave. We don't know anything yet."

"We absolutely can. There's a benefit to having a reputation like mine—I'll explain that I forgot that I previously arranged a threesome back in the City, and we'll just go. Nobody will think anything of it."

When I forced a laugh, Taran got to his feet and covered my hand on the window frame with his own.

"I don't want you to be afraid," he said, voice intent. "You don't have to come tonight."

"I can't let being afraid stop me from doing anything, or I'll never do anything again. I just . . . want to be ready." I took a deep breath. "So, what's the plan?"

"The plan? We'll have what is sure to be an awkward dinner, during which you are likely to hear many unkind words about the Maiden, but you shall be your typical model of tact until we go home. That's the plan."

I snorted at that blithe assessment of the risks.

"Taran, the Shipwright was just *murdered* by the Maiden, and now he's brought the Lord of the Noonday Heat to his home, probably to help him plot revenge. Aren't you worried what they might do?"

"*No*," he said firmly. "Because we are not going to get between Death and the Maiden."

I closed my eyes, fighting back the memory of the roof collapsing over my head at Ereban. The blast that took Taran's life on the beach.

"The entire world is between the two of them."

Taran's hand lifted from mine, but I didn't open my eyes until he brushed a strand of hair away from my cheek.

He was uncharacteristically solemn, but if anything, he was calmer.

"Don't be afraid. You should realize that what happened to you was Wesha's fault. She locked her husband away from his family, his power, and his home for three hundred years, and all the mortals were trapped in there with him. But that's over now."

I didn't believe that. Not after what I'd seen. "I was at Ereban three years ago. About to take my vows when . . . the riots started." When I started the first riot. "The other maiden-priests weren't any threat to Death. He killed them out of spite. He just lifted one hand"—I waved mine, to show Taran the gesture that had forever changed my life—"and they were gone. In one second. Everyone I knew. There wasn't enough left of them after the fires burned out to fill a single funeral boat."

Taran leaned in, sympathetic but undeterred. "Wesha abandoned her priests, hung you out to answer for her sins. She practically fed you to Death. I would never do that to you."

I took a deep breath. That wasn't what I was worried about. But it made me feel better to hear it.

He didn't even know he was doing it, but it felt like Taran was still keeping his promises to me. He said he'd finish this.

I nodded tightly, and Taran wrapped his arms around me, over the cloak, to brush a kiss against my temple. I leaned into the warm solidity of his body, anchoring myself in his embrace and listening to his breathing until my heart slowed.

"Now, are you ready?" he asked again.

I put my hand on the ties of my cloak, hesitating to take it off.

"I understand the point of the dress, but I look ridiculous."

Long before we even left the City, I'd explained my feelings about appropriate clothing to Taran, and he'd nodded thoughtfully. The resulting dress had a wide, black band at the waist, one thick enough to conceal two sheathed knives. And while the skirt was slit all the way up to my hips, the opaque panels of black hammered silk overlapped enough to cover my legs. The problem was the bodice, which theoretically covered me from collarbones to wrist—with a gold mesh so thin and fragile that not only the shape but the *color* of my nipples was visible through the transparent fabric.

"The point of the dress?" Taran lifted one eyebrow.

"So that I don't look like a maiden-priest."

Bracing myself, I let the cloak fall to the floor and fought the urge to hide. In response, Taran took a step away so that he could look me up and down with a broadening smile on his face. It lit his face up, made the dimples in his cheeks pop and his green eyes sparkle with warmth.

He used to tell me I was beautiful. Not from the beginning. Later. After he'd already told me that I was brave and clever and good. After I'd promised to marry him and after he'd promised to love me past the end of the world. *You're beautiful because I love you* was what I'd heard.

His hands had never touched the places his eyes brushed now, but my body tingled all the same.

"No, that's a good idea. And I'm glad nobody will recognize you," Taran said, minutely shaking his head without looking away.

"But?"

"I just wanted to see you in that dress." If anything, his smile grew wider until he nearly shone with suppressed laughter. I would have swatted him and thrown him out of the room to put on something more concealing, but his grin was so conspiratorial that I wanted to soak in it.

He didn't have to say it. He was delighted with how I looked.

Taran opened drawers until he found a tray of cosmetics to offer me. I would have just rubbed on a little rose salve, but he wet his thumb in his mouth and stuck it in a jar of powdered gold dust. He delicately wiped a little over each of my eyelids, then ran his thumb over the center of my lower lip, pulling it down until the inside of it caught on the salt of his skin. I marked the contraction of his pupils where they hung on his thumb against my mouth.

"You look . . ." He shook his head again. "Like I imagined you would."

My heart beat faster—not from fear anymore, but from the heated promise in his eyes. A different kind of promise, one not about life and death but about bodies and heat, my lips and his hands.

Someday I'd let him keep that one.

"Are you ready?" he asked again, leaving a smear of gold against my mouth when he finally pulled his hand away.

I nodded and squared my shoulders. Although I might as well be wearing nothing, I didn't feel the chill anymore. I'd meet Death again, and this time Taran would be at my side. Perhaps everyone would survive this evening.

Taran paused just before we stepped into the hall and took in my resolute face.

"A hundred years from now, you won't be afraid anymore," he murmured. "I promise."

He was too much a Stoneborn to be making that kind of reckless vow, but as it wound through me, as comforting and solid as the cloak I'd left behind, I couldn't be anything but glad for it.

18

THE CRAFTER-PRIEST WHO served the dinner was dead, although I didn't see a body anywhere. He had the white beard of an old man and the brown smock and gold amulets of a master artisan, but his nearly transparent outline gave off the same foxfire glow as the dusk-souls I'd seen on Wesha's beach, reflecting on the copper-sheathed walls of the Shipwright's great hall. It was a fortune in metal, beautifully wrought with bas-reliefs of his great works, but all I could think as the dead priest pulled out chairs and poured wine was that it smelled like old, rotting blood.

The expression on the dusk-soul's features didn't vary from abject horror, but his hands were by turns smooth and scarred from a lifetime spent fashioning little treasures. These jeweler's hands trembled under Death's control, but the Shipwright, his patron in life, did not spare him a glance.

This spectacle, the enslavement of the dead—this was Death's oldest power, and only Taran looked even a little sickened by the display of it.

The souls of the dead rose from their bodies after three dawns, and if they were not laid in running water to journey to the Sea of Dreams, dusk-souls stalked single-mindedly toward the same destination. It was bad luck to even see one, and whatever they touched was cursed. Grass shriveled under their feet and animals fled from the sight of them. During the rebellion, we did our best to attend to the dead after every battle, but we always missed a few, and the distant flare of green figures walking to the sea haunted many of my night watches.

When the dead crafter-priest placed a stone bench for me a short distance behind Taran's chair, I tried to catch his eye.

What happened to you? I mouthed at him, but he didn't see me. All he could see was his task and his own death, and when the first course was set on the table, he left the empty banquet hall.

There were only four chairs around the single table for five gods, and Wirrea instead sprawled across Death's lap, her legs spread to offer Taran a view up her short, rabbit-fur tunic. She'd made a joke about the lack of seating—*by the end of dinner Marit Waverider will be under the table anyway, and Taran ab Genna bent over it*—and I was ready to leave then, but Taran had laughed and looked through her like what she said didn't matter.

It was Death he looked at, and he didn't let his smile slip when he was introduced to the god he'd killed. Seeing the two of them together, I had a dizzying moment of déjà vu. Some memory or understanding that my mind had flinched away from, hidden with Taran's death. My gut churned—this had been a mistake. I didn't want to be here. I didn't want Death to look at Taran and smile back.

Death was smaller than the two times I'd seen him before, no taller than Taran. There was no more golden armor or bronze lion mask, so I saw him plainly, but I could never have smiled at him. His form was a warped reflection of Taran's immortal beauty: very similar in the lines, nearly painful in its perfection, but obscuring the horror of the soul beneath.

My eyes couldn't quite focus on his bright hair and eyes—white and blue, like heated metal—but it was his stillness that unsettled me. He was still like a candle flame, still like a stone, and this was not the stillness of a living being.

Taran had barely passed for human, and none of the other Stoneborn would, but the way Death moved and spoke turned my stomach when even Marit's swirling irises and always-wet hair did not.

What had Wesha ever seen in him? His power? Wondering whether he was handsome was like wondering whether a house fire was handsome. He and Taran might both have admirable cheekbones, but I didn't see how someone could ever look at Death and see anything but a hungry monster whose appetites were as cold as his fires were hot. Still, Taran had rallied his effortless appeal and taken his seat with good manners intact.

I did appreciate the things Taran's winning smile had done for me over the years, but I thought it was the wrong weapon for the battle ahead.

Arbalests, Taran. Defensive earthworks. A couple of acolytes of Skyfather, ready with the lightning bolts. That is how we greet Death, not smiles and small talk.

It was still easy for me to speak to the Taran who existed only in my head, the one who would have helped me barricade the doors, and not the one who looked over his shoulder with a raised eyebrow, wordlessly instructing me to begin the night's entertainment.

Death paid me no notice when I started to play on the kithara, but I doubted he could hear over Smenos's wailing. It was rapidly apparent that the crafter god was just as unbalanced as Marit had been. He rose from his chair without warning, his empty hands clasping for nothing. When Marit put a glass of wine in his hand, he clutched it to his chest like a toy and pointed to the vacant hall, begging his guests to explain the grimy copper bas-reliefs of his past accomplishments.

"That marble bridge! I must have taught the mortals how to lay the keystone. And do you see, do you see the dome in the ceiling—there! Only my priests ever learned the formula for the arch. And now I've forgotten. I can't even think of it. I don't know it!"

As he ranted, bits of the ceiling began to rain down on us. Chunks of plaster, half a brick. When a flake of plaster landed in her glass, Wirrea dumped her wine on the floor and refilled it, and Taran brushed dust out of his dark hair.

I looked anxiously at the ceiling beams, which flexed with each of Smenos's shouts about his lost art. I'd already survived one building collapse, and it was an experience I wasn't eager to repeat, but Taran and Death seemed locked in a silent competition for who could pay the least attention to the crumbling hall around us or the growing puddle under Marit's chair as the sea god white-knuckled his chair arms.

I mentally begged him to turn around, so that I could indicate that I'd changed my mind.

Time to go, Taran. Make that excuse and get us out of here.

But he sat back and dangled his silver goblet from the tips of his fingers, smiling at the god of the Underworld and picking at the first course of quail livers on toast. Wirrea solicitously asked Taran for news from the City as the dead crafter-priest returned to heap live coals on the grill built into the center of the table for the meat course. The dusk-soul handled the coals and the raw steaks with his bare hands, and both sizzled from the contact, as did his tears when they hit the vibrating flagstones. Smenos nearly walked into the dusk-soul as he wove around his dining hall, only to recoil with a shriek as his wrist brushed the luminescent shoulder of his dead priest.

The other Stoneborn studiously ignored the noise, and Death complimented the wine.

"You always liked this one. It was served at your wedding," Wirrea replied.

When I saw a crack begin to snake through one of the pillars in the corner of the room, I decided I wasn't willing to die in defense of good manners.

There was a sappy, popular ballad written with the same time signature and key progressions as the blessing of Wesha that we used for light sedation—for tooth extractions and minor procedures. The coincidence was an in-joke among maiden-priests. When we were little children, the other acolytes of Wesha and I used to giggle about what love did to people, dramatically swooning and drooling through pretend declarations of devotion.

Did I dare? Would anyone at the table recognize either melody?

Feigning nonchalance but sweating into the waistband of my dress, I plucked out the notes of Wesha's blessing on my instrument and began to sing. I firmed my diaphragm and trilled the opening lines of the overwrought ballad about star-crossed lovers.

For just a moment, Taran's attention broke from the blue-white stare of the god he'd killed for me, but I didn't dare acknowledge that he'd caught on. I wasn't even sure I would be able to call Wesha's power without singing the words, no matter how precise I was with the melody, but seconds later, it answered.

I hoped to invoke only a drop of it, enough to settle Smenos and avoid a second roof collapsing over my head, but once I felt it begin to resonate with my voice and course through the room, I had to pour my entire concentration into the song or risk being found out.

Wesha was imprisoned on the other side of the Mountain, but her power was here, swirling around that of four other Stoneborn like the first rivulets of rain down a dry streambed. Stronger than I would have expected, when all her priests were dead.

I didn't dare stop after it took hold, or it would be obvious what I'd done, so I searched my memory for the other songs I would have performed at a concert for the brokenhearted and moved seamlessly into the next piece, hoping that any gods affected would chalk up their stupor to the force of the music. Slowly, over the next three songs, I released Wesha's blessing.

"You're a wonderful singer, Iona," Marit said dreamily. "I think I'm very fond of music."

Taran's reaction to my little experiment hadn't been a given either, but when the other gods broke into applause and Smenos absentmindedly took his chair again, still clapping, I saw him let out a long breath before shooting me a chiding look.

Thank you, nightingale, that was a close one, I imagined my love saying, because he would never have expected me to sit like a painted figurine while the ceiling came down.

"Breathtaking," Death agreed, tipping a goblet toward me in appreciation. "Where did you get her, son of Genna?"

Taran held out a hand and shifted to make room in his seat, so I was obliged, in my part as the dutiful priestess, to put down my instrument and slide in next to him, nearly propped over his knee. This put me mere feet away from Death, closer than I'd ever been. Candle-blue eyes dissected my face and figure without recognition.

I was palpably aware of the stone knives hidden in my waistband.

"Don't eat anything," Taran whispered under his breath before nipping my earlobe to cover his words. He straightened and gave a belated response to Death.

"A souvenir of my time in the mortal world." The caution in his voice was so strong that I forgot to be angry that I was being discussed like an imported wine.

"Another reminder of what Wesha keeps from us," Wirrea said from Death's lap. Her husband did not seem to notice that he'd misplaced his wife, and Taran was focused on the god behind her, but I very much wished she'd worn more underclothes.

At Wesha's name, Smenos scowled into his goblet.

"Did the Allmother tell you what happened at the Painted Tower?" Taran asked him.

The crafter god shook his head. "No. The death and rebirth of so many of her children in such short succession has tired her. She slept again before even announcing Wesha's punishment."

"Perhaps something like yours, Taran," Wirrea chimed in. "But longer, since she actually did murder a Stoneborn, rather than merely provide the means. What do you think, my love, would a thousand years of service by the Maiden suit you?"

Smenos grunted agreement, but Death's smooth face cracked for a moment, opening to the rage inside. He still said nothing.

"A thousand years of service from inside the Painted Tower would be of little use to anyone," Taran said, probing.

"Maybe it's time we knocked Wesha off her perch at the Gates," Smenos grumbled. "I will take my ships back to the mortal world and recover what I've lost. What we've all lost! She had no right to close the Gates for so long."

Taran pretended to consider that. "But how? All the Stoneborn together granted Wesha the power she uses to hold the Gates, then took her vow to seal the Underworld."

Silence met this point, but it was flavored differently. Sullen from Wirrea and Smenos, but far too still from Death. Taran let it draw out before looking around the table, meeting the eyes of each immortal in turn, and I felt his thigh tense next to me before he spoke.

"We are the youngest gods now. But our short memories might be an advantage as we imagine how we might resolve this impasse. There's no reason to mourn for what we can't even remember. Wesha holds the Gates closed because she wants her freedom. The other Stoneborn deny her that freedom because it guarantees Genna's peace. We could agree tonight to that peace. We could let go of all our claims, all our grudges—and release Wesha from her vows.

We could simply act according to our natures, then. Build your ships, Smenos. We and the mortals will come and go like we used to."

Marit, surprisingly, was the first to object to that. "But who would make the mortals obey? They killed you too."

Taran pressed his cheek against my temple, and my heart beat faster at the attention it drew to me. "My priestess was the last one to cross the Gates. I think I have a clearer picture than Wesha from her tower. The mortal world is in ruins, but those ruins could be your masterwork if you rebuilt them, Shipwright. Their forests are untended and overrun with wild beasts, Huntress. Their seas are empty and lifeless."

He picked up his wine and swirled it, concealing small signs of stress in the gesture. "And even you, Napeth—the mortal world is rich enough to satisfy even you, once the other Stoneborn cultivate it. We could take new vows for a new peace, one that does not doom either world to fall into dust."

It was so unexpected a speech that I froze, shocked by how little like a careless princeling and how much like my Taran he sounded.

Is that you?

He sounded like the same man who'd convinced the mortal queen not to salt the fields of the loyalist nobles who refused to surrender, the same one who urged forgiveness toward the ones who did. A man who met anger with patience and despair with understanding.

It was strange to feel proud of him for being like this today when I'd spent three years falling in love with him for being this person *every* day, but for once the shiver of recognition gave me more hope than wistfulness.

Marit's smile was tentative, and Smenos looked thoughtful, but it was Death I watched for an indication of whether we might avoid more conflict. Meeting the hot core of his blue eyes took effort—my body rebelled like I'd stuck my hand in the oven—but I searched him for some clue of his plans. He was a cipher.

Hope died when Death sat back and placed his goblet on the table. He slowly clapped, once, twice, again.

"I hear that it was as amusing to speak with Wesha as it was pleasant to hear her sing. A familial trait, I suppose? Some genius of the Peace-Queen's line? That was a lovely little speech, Taran ab Genna. I heard you were charming, and you did not disappoint."

Death's voice was soft and even, and his words weren't hostile, but they chilled me to my marrow. "I cannot remember any more than the rest of you, but I am told that I was once a friend to all the Stoneborn. My kinsmen would visit my citadel in the Underworld to marvel at my crystal gardens and rich hospitality. When I traveled across the Sea of Dreams, mortals generously thanked me for caring for their dead. And Wesha—I am told that my lovely bride went to me willingly." Now he smiled, and Taran shifted next to me, hand slipping from my knee.

"My question for you, son of Genna, is why I ought to be satisfied with what I have now? I had dominion over the Underworld, I had the Dawn-star as my wife, I had the respect of the Stoneborn, and I *want it all back*. Why would I bind myself with new vows when I won the last war? Why would I give up a single shred of my freedom? For Genna's peace? That is not *my* nature."

"We are not so simple," Taran said in a low, insistent voice. "You are not fire any more than Marit is the ocean. We can choose how to get what we want. Burning the world didn't work. It didn't win you the respect of the other Stoneborn or Wesha's love. Try something else this time."

At this, Death beamed at Taran, like I would at a talented child who'd performed his first ballad on the lyre without making any mistakes. It was just as unsettling as his stillness, wide enough to display the dimples in his cheeks.

"I can see why the Peace-Queen made you her envoy. Among all my regrets, I wish I could have known you when you were deploying your many talents on her behalf, as the Huntress has recounted to me with such . . . loving detail. But no, rest assured, I will be trying everything. War. Fire. Terror. Do not fear that I will run out of creativity. My powers are just as varied as your mother's."

"All those powers did not get you past the Gates of Dawn for three hundred years," Taran said pleasantly.

"That was from the other side. I can *see* the Painted Tower from the top of the Mountain behind us," Death observed.

"And the last time you approached it, the Maiden ran you off with a single knife."

Those unnatural eyes glittered as the god of the Underworld stared directly at Taran. "I shall take your advice, then. Employ new tactics. My own . . . *charm*. I also know how to choose the right tool for each task, son of Genna."

He pointedly sucked the tips of two fingers into his mouth and popped them out with a wet, obscene sound, leaving them slick with spit. My stomach turned as he examined his wet knuckles. "I look forward to it, even. I may not remember, but I hope Wesha inherited every talent you did."

It was a cheap attempt to provoke, and when Taran looked away with a small, tight smile on his face, I thought he wasn't going to fall for it.

The second when his muscles bunched was the only warning I got to dodge as Taran jumped straight up out of our chair. He landed in a crouch on the lip of the table, knocking it over as a lever to fuel his forward momentum and launch himself straight at the god of death. The two of them toppled to the floor, and for a moment my biggest worry was the spray of hot coals that Taran's maneuver had tossed across the hall.

My attention immediately shot back to the fight at the organic, meaty sound of Taran's fist striking Death's face, followed by the scrape of chairs on stone as everyone else shot to their feet.

Taran's arm jerked back for a second blow, then a third—but it didn't land. Death threw him off, sending him into a roll that terminated at Smenos's feet.

Wirrea was the first person to make a noise, a high-pitched, feral screech, because she'd been dislodged from Death's lap and toppled onto the ground. His wife's angry yowling sparked Smenos into action, and the crafter god reached for Taran, ready to yank him up by his throat. Taran moved first though, hammering an elbow to the side of Smenos's knee before leaping to his feet.

Death rose to his knees, expression incredulous at the trickle of golden ichor that dripped from his broken nose. He wiped it with his sleeve, smearing it across his chin and bared teeth, then snarled deep in his throat as his gaze locked on Taran.

Taran's broad shoulders straightened in readiness and red flooded his cheeks, posture as graceful as a stone statue of a warrior in a monument when he spun to block Smenos's bull rush.

It was faster than my eyes could track. None of them were hampered by mere mortal strength and agility, only by their surprise and incandescent rage. It wasn't a brawl—it was more like a rockslide, given the forces being applied. Taran fought like it was a bar brawl though, a dirty one, striking out at weak points, eyes and groins and kneecaps. But he was outnumbered and not as strong as the other two gods, his defeat inevitable even as they exchanged five blows, ten, the seconds twisting up and tighter like the air was being torn out of my lungs.

I shoved at Marit's shoulder, trying to push him into the fight, but he winced away with a reproachful expression.

"A guest should not fight with his host. But look—Taran's winning," he said.

And somehow Taran was—he had more experience taking hits, or perhaps in dealing them out, and Smenos was flagging quickly while Death couldn't aim past his black eye and swelling nose. Taran's lips were drawn back in fierce battle-joy, even though the skin on his knuckles had split and he was favoring his left leg. The way he moved was like a dancer as he hammered the side of his hand into Death's floating ribs before Smenos finally got a hold on him by the back of his skull to lift him into the air with his feet dangling. Taran made an impossible flex of his stomach muscles and swung his feet back to connect with the crafter god's diaphragm, but Smenos's grip didn't slacken.

That was when I felt the change. The taste of dust and decay on my tongue prickled into metal, swelling and heating in my nose. Divine power. This room had been empty of it before I called We-sha's here, and now some other god's power was sweeping in like one of Marit's waves. I saw nothing, heard nothing, but I recognized it, what I'd felt in the high temple of Ereban a moment before the fire fell from the rafters and turned dozens of maiden-priests into unwilling sacrifices.

Death. He'd stretched back his arm as though pulling something heavy out of the world, and his face was no longer that of the smiling young man who taunted Taran over wine, but the bright shape of the lord of the Underworld who scoured life from the Earth. He'd dropped the mask, gathered his power, and now he prepared to fling it at Taran.

Abruptly certain I was about to watch Taran die a second time, blasted into his component atoms by the raw force of Death's hatred, I screamed.

"Stop!"

In the second before Death launched his attack, the voice of a trained singer was enough to carry over the grunts of Taran and Smenos where they grappled hand-to-hand, the growling fury of

Death . . . and the outraged howl Wirrea made when she realized I had a knife pressed to her carotid artery.

I tangled one hand in her fawn-dappled hair, hard enough to bow her neck back and make it clear to Smenos that the knife I held was a stone one. I firmed my feet before I looked at the other gods, but my relief that Death had stayed his hand fell into pulse-skipping confusion.

Four gods stared at me in identical, horrified disbelief.

Even Taran.

I licked my lips and shot my eyes at Death, wordlessly indicating to Taran that he ought to take this momentary reprieve to get his own knife out and even the odds.

Instead, his voice was appalled when he spoke. "Put the knife down, Iona."

"What?"

I tried to understand what the play was. How were we getting out of this room? I glanced at Marit, wondering if a giant wave was going to deliver us from the standoff, but the sea god slowly shook his head, eyes beginning to fill up with fat, wobbling tears.

When I didn't move, Taran shook Smenos's grip off and slowly approached me. I didn't believe he was serious about it until he put his hand over mine and wrenched my fingers away from the knife. It clattered to the ground, and Wirrea burst free, running with a wail to her husband.

I turned to Taran full of confused horror, because why weren't we fighting our way out of the room? How had he thought we were getting out when he hauled off and slugged the god of death in the face?

Smenos briefly embraced the wife who'd been grinding her hips into Death's lap a few moments before, then stalked across the wreckage of dinner to me.

Even then, I had the impulse to align my shoulders with Taran.

I should have realized by then that he didn't see us as fighting this battle together, but it still took me by surprise when he let the crafter god scream into my face so loudly that spittle flecked my cheeks.

"A guest. A mortal. You attack my wife in *my house*?"

The last two words made the beams of the rafters creak and flex as though ready to bring the entire building down on top of us.

Which I might have survived. Smenos's rage looked worse.

The Shipwright wasn't known for his displays of emotion, and he stretched out both arms as though attempting to gather calm. The walls and ceilings flexed and vibrated but finally stilled as the panting of our breaths slowed.

Once he had recovered himself, Smenos slowly looked me up and down.

"I will remember this. I will turn your teeth into the decorative inlay for a lap harp," he told me conversationally. "And your sinews into its strings."

"Oh, please don't, that sounds dreadful," Marit moaned, the only defense I got, because Taran had gone absolutely still next to me.

What's the plan, Taran? How are we getting out of this one?

Death had pulled himself off the floor and put his urbane mask of civility back over his features, and now he dabbed at his bloody chin with a napkin soaked in spilled wine.

"That seems like a waste," he said in the tone of an idle observation.

"I'll tan her leather into hawking jesses. There won't be any waste," Wirrea snarled.

"Don't be hasty."

Once his face was clean, the god of fire straightened his clothes and came to stand between Smenos and Taran.

"If I don't like a wine, do I smash the goblet it came in? The girl's got an exquisite voice, and her form would serve. Willfulness is a flaw, but it requires a will to animate it. I don't allow it in *my* priests."

"You can't suggest I let this go unpunished," Smenos said, staring at my collarbones as though imagining the places where he might pry them apart.

"Not at all. But as your guest, I am suggesting that it might be appropriate to consider the insult to *me*."

Smenos roughly snorted. "I already paid for the insult to you. Genna's brat loosened three of my teeth, and I'll probably piss blood tonight. We're square."

"Not that," Death said easily. "The insult was watching a *mortal* hold the sacred stone of the Mountain in her hand after you'd offered me shelter under your roof."

While Smenos chewed on that, Death looked back at the fuming Huntress to give her a conspiratorial smile. "I'm saying I'll take the little redheaded she-cat for my troubles, and I promise that if she's ever seen in public again, her behavior will not disgrace the Stoneborn."

I began to edge backward, but Taran's hand came around my biceps like a vise, holding me in place. Betrayal made my throat close up.

Smenos tilted his head thoughtfully, considering whether I might rightfully be enslaved to the bright-eyed monster who'd burned the world twice over now.

When Taran said nothing for slow, oozing seconds of time, my eyes darted for my knife, discarded on the ground. Death wouldn't take me easy. He wouldn't take me *alive*. Wesha's mercy, what if that was his plan? What if I was to be turned into another gibbering, terrified puppet by his power? A dusk-soul, to serve forever? I subtly, unobtrusively shifted my shoulder as I prepared to reach for my last hidden blade.

Taran tightened his grip.

"Napeth is right," he said to Smenos.

I couldn't help a small noise of despairing outrage, which made Taran twist my arm behind my back and turn us both to face the crafter god.

"Then we're agreed?" Death asked, looking with interest at my nearly bare, heaving chest.

"No, I mean that she didn't know any better. We *are* disgraced, but the fault was mine. I am deeply shamed to see my priestess dishonor your hospitality, your trust. I brought her into your home. Let me make this right," Taran said to Smenos and Wirrea, as serious as I'd ever heard him. Actually, serious like I'd never heard him before.

Death raised his eyebrows, and the Shipwright crossed his arms, listening.

"Let me apologize to your wife," Taran said, voice vibrating with sincerity. "And I beg you not to shame me further by having a mortal take a punishment in my place. I'm not a child anymore. I'm one of the Stoneborn."

After a moment's thought, Smenos looked to Wirrea and her sullen pout. "The little bastard is the one who brought her in the first place. And you did ask for him, didn't you? Do you want him? Which would you prefer, dear wife?"

Taran turned the force of his beautiful, pleading eyes on the Huntress. "You know that I make a lovely apology," he said, adding a darker note to his voice, one that made my chest go tight and anxious even as I saw how this might not be a betrayal but only a very, very bad decision on Taran's part.

No. He couldn't. She was horrible.

He couldn't actually plan to go through with it. That had to be the play. While the Huntress put on whatever garments the gods donned to engage in open adultery, Taran and I would escape. I told myself this even as doubt brewed out of the pinched look on his face.

"I do enjoy your apologies," Wirrea acknowledged, eyes narrowing. When Taran didn't dispute this, she drew herself up to her full height, brushed her tunic down over her hips, and let her eyelids fall into slits. Her approach was measured, but the crack of her arm was like a strike of lighting.

She slapped Taran full across the face, hard enough to stagger him backwards and split his lip open. Before he could recover and wipe the spot of red-gold blood away, she lunged up to suck his mouth clean with a hungry noise, her narrow features curving wide with satisfaction when Taran didn't resist.

Death slowly smiled to see it, the expression more disgusting on his face than a rictus of fury would have been. "Well, then. Look how quickly we can all agree to peace when we decide to be reasonable in our requests. I've also heard about your apologies, Taran ab Genna. How skilled you are at giving them."

"After three hundred years, I ought to be," Taran said, but I couldn't understand why I was the person he turned to look at when he said it, anger carving deep into every line that love had ever softened.

The tension was too much for Marit; he collapsed to the floor and sobbed until my shoes were soaked with seawater.

TARAN BEGGED A moment to see me off Smenos's lands, then dragged me roughly into the hall.

My hope that it was a show for the other gods was flagging, but it was the only scrap of protection I had left. I clung hard to it, and as soon as we were alone, I bunched the muscles in my calves to run while Taran planted his feet and glared at me like I'd been the one to insult his sister instead of the one who'd saved him from being turned into a pile of charcoal.

"Are you so tired of eternal life that you want it to end this quickly?" His voice was a low hiss.

"He was going to kill you," I said, my shock at Taran's reaction finally shifting to my own anger. "He almost did! If I hadn't stopped him—"

"He can't kill me! I just showed you—he's no stronger than I am! I broke his damn nose! I beat him in front of an audience, and if you hadn't tried to take our hostess hostage, we could be on our way home right now."

"You have no idea what you're dealing with," I snapped. "You remember six months of sipping wine in the City. You don't know what Death can do!"

"And why do you know? Because Wesha sold you out for a fancy home and the power of a Stoneborn. Stop thinking like a maiden-priest—nothing would have happened to you if you'd let me handle this." He clenched his hands in front of my face instead of yelling, which he obviously longed to do.

"It's not that. Forget Wesha. Something is terribly wrong here," I said, trying to get myself under control and be persuasive, when what I really wanted to do was shake him. "Death's not like you or Marit, he's not powerless. He's hiding it somehow, but I could feel it, only for a moment . . . and something is wrong with the Shipwright too. Why is he alone? Where are his priests—the living ones?"

"His priests left him because his death released them from their vows. And because mortals are fickle. And ungrateful," Taran said, eyes still bright with what I was beginning to recognize as fear.

He was afraid of what the other gods wanted from him as an *apology*, and he was going to go anyway.

Don't accept it. Don't accept that they have the right to de-mand it. He would have agreed with me once.

"Then let's go right now, before they notice," I begged Taran, splaying my hands against his chest imploringly. "We'll figure it out later."

"Go? Where would we go? Really. Tell me. Where would we go, that this wouldn't follow us. Four people just saw my priestess put a stone blade to Wirrea's throat. Any of them could go to the Allmother, and any of the Stoneborn would hand me over to her justice."

As he spoke, my eyes landed on the serving station at the entrance to the dining hall: the unserved courses, the vegetables and roasts that had been sliced for the coals in the center of the table. The white bones that had been stripped clean for the meat course were too slender to be beef and too long to be pork. Their shapes were familiar to me from my first lessons in surgery.

No wonder the dead crafter-priest had wept.

I gagged and covered my mouth as my stomach convulsed.

"Do you see—" I squeaked, pointing to the butchered remains of the crafter-priest.

Taran had known. It was why he'd told me not to eat anything. Tears sprang to my eyes as a wave of dizziness swept through me.

"Yes," Taran gritted out without a trace of sympathy. "Wirrea has some disgusting habits, which is why I *didn't want to come in the first place.*"

I should have shoved that blade home in Wirrea's throat, but that regret didn't help us now. We needed to get as far away as possible.

"It's a straight line down that hall to the courtyard, and the stables are in the south wing. We could be gone before they notice," I urged him.

White lines of anger framed his mouth. "And then? What next."

"We—we could go east, up the Mountain. To the Painted Tower. And then we'll take one of the boats on the shore back to the mortal world—"

"Back!" Taran pressed a palm against his forehead, bending at the waist as though looking to the Heavens for assistance. When he wheeled on me, it was the angriest I'd ever seen him. "We are never going *back*. *We live here*." Each word was hurled at me like a weapon, punctuated by a jab of his finger at the floor, and I inhaled sharply at the viciousness of the tone.

With visible effort to regain his composure, he swallowed hard. "*I* am going to stay here and pay for your little outburst, on my fucking back if I'm *lucky*, and hope it doesn't take three hundred years this time to get free. *You* are going to wait until Marit is sober, and then he will take you to my rooms in the City, where you will stay and speak to not a single other immortal until I return, whether that is next week or next year. And then, we are going to have a lengthy, lengthy discussion of how I expect my priestess to behave."

"I'm not your priestess," I snarled, fists at my sides.

It was an even more bitter laugh that rasped out of his throat, and he loomed over me, close enough that I shrank a half step away.

"Careful, darling," he said in a dangerous undertone. "You keep saying that like you want me to believe it. And yet the only reason your pretty hide isn't forming a part of Wirrea's next decorating project is that *you are mine*. Think about *that* on your way home."

I went rigid in fury, but Taran must have taken my silence as acquiescence, because he raked his hands through his hair, trying to put himself back into order. He squared his cloak and made an effort to smooth his features. He used to be better at hiding how he felt. He still looked like he was headed for a battlefield, not a bed-chamber.

"I'll see you when I return to the City," he snapped and turned on his heel, stalking off to the dining hall without a backwards glance.

MY VISION WAS smeared with red as I limped to our rooms. Marit wasn't there yet, which gave me the opportunity to pick up an ornamental vase and hurl it at a wall without the fear that I'd spark a tsunami by acting out in front of the sea god.

The pottery fragments vibrated on the floor like they longed to rearrange themselves but didn't quite have the power to do it. I kicked them, just for good measure.

I shouldn't have listened to him. I shouldn't have *obeyed*.

What was I doing? Who was I with my breasts exposed in a gaudy dress and my face painted, perched on Taran's knee like a docile pet? Before I met him, they were calling me Iona Night-Singer. Before I met him, I had survived the disaster at Ereban. Before I met him, I had started a war against Death himself. I was angry, but most of all at myself. If he'd lived, Taran wouldn't even have recognized me.

Quickly, I stripped the dress off, tearing the fabric in the pro-cess, and wadded it in a corner. I put on my warmest clothes; I wasn't waiting for Marit, the damned coward. I was leaving tonight.

Perhaps by the time I made it back to the City, I'd no longer regret leaving Wirrea's circulatory system in one piece. Perhaps I'd think of a plan I liked more than rendering Taran unconscious by the most expedient means possible and dragging his limp body feet-first up the Mountain to Wesha.

If I wrapped my ankle well, I could walk for a couple of hours straight, then make my own camp. It was going to be days before I could bear to look at Taran again, and I could use the time and space to remember Iona Night-Singer instead of whatever I'd become.

Nobody stopped me as I stomped out the unattended front gate, and I even made it to the edge of the courtyard before my vows caught me. Just as it had the night I tried to run from Taran, the pain grabbed my throat and held me in place. The leash had no slack to give.

"That's not fair!" I cried as though Wesha might hear me over the Mountain and take pity on me. "He told me to go."

But when I tried to take another step out of Smenos's domain, the breath squeezed out of my chest and my vow lit my nerves to agony in warning.

"What are you afraid of—he'll smother between Wirrea's blessed thighs? Marit'll drown the lot of them out of shame? Let me go!"

I shouted defiance at the Maiden, but some part of me didn't really believe that Taran was safe. I didn't believe he'd survive to take me to the Painted Tower if I didn't turn around. I knew Death was dangerous, I knew something had happened to Smenos's priests, and I knew Marit wouldn't protect him if the situation turned again.

I fought the pain down, wishing I'd never made any vows at all. Part of me had realized it, that day at Ereban. That I could never be any god's priestess. It wasn't just Death—they were all complicit, from the Allmother down to Wesha. None of them could be trusted with our freedom. The Taran I'd loved must have realized that at some point.

If I ever wanted him to remember that, I needed to be the rebel he met three years ago, not this half-broken girl with the fully broken heart, crying by myself instead of avenging every life Death ever stole.

I turned around and stared up at the dark shape of the Mountain, the broken facade of the palace, considering what I could do. What would I have done back when I was Iona Night-Singer, not his protected darling?

I would have brought him home with me, and left everything else to burn.

I considered Smenos's vacant workshops, where his hundreds of priests should have been after crossing an ocean, trusting their god to give them life eternal. I thought of the dead crafter-priest whose fire-cursed feet had scorched the carpets he walked on.

I'd always fought Death's fire best with fire.

The Shipwright should have known better than to build everything out of stucco and timber—I sang Death's blessing in each of the corners of the valley, using the empty buildings as kindling, and soon pillars of flame stretched up so high I hoped Wesha could see them from her tower.

19

A WEEK AFTER DEATH massacred the maiden-priests at Ereban, I'd walked into his temple, singing. When everyone was asleep under Wesha's power, five of the queen's guard crept in after me, their ears sealed with wax, and slit the throats of every last death-priest there. When I fled to the countryside with the other acolytes, more riots erupting behind me, I had a new name. Iona Night-Singer.

That was who I was when Taran met me. A rebel, a survivor, a killer. He never asked me to be anything different.

I didn't sing Wesha's blessing of night when I slipped back inside the palace. After the alarm went up, I let the Huntress's few priests rush past me to the spreading fire, and I sang Lixnea's blessings instead. *Don't look at me, don't see me, I'm not here.* We'd slipped past enemy lines with this song, Taran and I, whenever we thought it was worth the risk to catch some clever death-priest or loyalist general unawares.

Smenos's palace was still as I shuffled through its enormous warren of halls cut deep into the red sandstone of the cliffs, uncountable rooms that had once housed crafter-priests now vacant and musty. It must have been welcoming when occupied, but now it felt like an empty beehive with the honey left to rot in the comb.

Something terrible had happened here—I saw signs of it in jewelers' glasses on a side table, a half-sharpened quill fallen to the floor with no one left to sweep the shavings. They wouldn't have just left when they felt their vows dissolve—not without their tools, surely?

I didn't have to think about how to find Taran, at least—I just followed the tug in my chest and kept a tight grip on my last knife as I went deeper into the complex.

I was prepared to yank him naked out of the Huntress's bed if necessary—then disinfect him and my eyes both with strong vinegar—but for a second time since landing in the Summerlands, I nearly collided with Taran. He was barefoot and stumbling in his unlaced trousers, one hand clasped around the neck of a pottery jug of wine, the other holding his ornate cloak shut over his bare chest. He registered my presence enough to stop, but without forward momentum, he lost his balance and slid halfway down the wall behind him, barely keeping to his feet.

I grimaced, assuming he was drunk. Not that I blamed him for wanting to drink off whatever he'd just done with the Huntress, but it wasn't going to make our exit any easier.

If we survived this, *I* would get drunk, and we'd never speak of this night again.

Taran lifted the jug and took a long swig despite his awkward half crouch against the wall, expression as furious as when I'd last seen him.

"You've had enough," I said, reaching for the wine.

At my movement, Taran wheeled away, trying to put his back to me.

"Get your own," he snapped.

Either his tone or the jerky way he'd moved made me take a second glance at him, and it was enough to wash away at least half my anger. His pupils were blown wide and shocky, and the hand that held his cloak shut didn't entirely conceal the raw burns on his throat.

There were drips of liquid on the floor behind him, and until I was close, I thought he'd spilled the wine. But no, Taran's blood gleamed like newly minted gold coins on the dirty inlaid wood of the floor.

"What did she do to you?" I whispered.

"Nothing. Get out of here." He convulsively licked his lips before trying again to lift the jug. This time I managed to snatch it out of his resistant fingers. If he was hurt, the last thing he needed was more wine.

Quickly scanning the hallway, I tried doors until one opened to an austere bedroom. The air was stale, but the single bunk and simple cedar furniture were clean and neat, ready for a crafter-priest who'd never returned for the shoes tucked under the bed.

"In here," I ordered him. I held out my hand, which he ignored to shuffle unsteadily to his feet.

"I told you to go home."

"I didn't listen. Get on the bed and let me see whatever injury you're hiding," I told him, fairly certain I would win this argument, as I had a lot more experience with stubborn patients than he did in commanding priests.

"Skyfather's done worse when he didn't like how I bid him good morning. It'll heal by tomorrow."

"No. We're both leaving *tonight*, even if I have to push you out in a wheelbarrow."

With an angry twist of his lips, Taran moved stiffly to the bed. I gave broad warning of my movement as I approached him, but he was still reluctant to release the white-knuckled grip on his cloak and let me peel it away from his skin.

I hissed as my mind automatically reconstructed what had been done to him.

The bruises were the oldest. On a mortal, I would have said they were a few days old, vivid and painful, all up and down the breadth of his chest, with only his unlaced trousers and the folds of his cloak concealing the extent of it. Bruises in different shapes, sizes—from fists, boots, belts, whatever objects had come to hand.

That had been done first, and his immortal constitution was already trying to heal the damage. What was more recent, what had me struggling to keep from crying, was the incision. It started at the vee of his collarbones and went down the length of his chest, all the way past his navel. Someone had neatly peeled through layers of skin and muscle, down to the *bone*, cut him open like a field-dressed buck to be aged until tender. Blood still welled along the edges, thin spiderwebs of red over bright gold—a mortal wound on an immortal body. The burned skin on his throat, puffy blisters in the shape of a handprint, told me how he'd been kept still long enough for the Huntress to do this.

"Oh, sweet Maiden, *Taran*, I need to suture this," I said wildly. A mortal wouldn't even be conscious by this point, let alone panting fury through clenched teeth.

"Leave it alone."

"The hell I will."

I fumbled with my pack for a needle and thread—how would I sterilize anything? Could Taran even get an infection?—then climbed onto the bed as Taran tried to bat me away.

"Don't bother. She used a steel knife, not stone. It won't kill me."

"*Why* would you let her?"

His lip curled. "You remember they were about to hand you over to Death, don't you, darling?"

I wouldn't have let him go if I'd known this was what she'd do. I should have dragged him out when I had the chance. "I thought she just wanted—" I couldn't get the words out through the choking deluge of guilt, because I'd been thinking about my own useless jealousy rather than the expression on his face when I first mentioned Smenos. He didn't want to come here, but I made him.

"You know, I would have preferred that," Taran said caustically, arms wrapped around himself. "It's harder to close your eyes and think of something else when your *liver's* being fondled. But no, she was called away by some alarm before she could turn to the romantic portion of our time together."

His teeth were bared like a fox with its leg caught in a trap, both of us snarling and angry because anger was easier than fear. Easier than my bottomless sadness that Taran had obviously endured this at her hands before.

I pressed my hands over my eyes, dashing tears away against my palms. My distress finally registered with Taran, who stopped trying to push me off the bed. He lay back, hands still protectively curled over his stomach.

"I'm sorry," I said, letting my anguish crack my voice. "Please let me help. I could suture this. Or do you—do you want me to try to heal it? I've never done it before, but I could try. Genna's blessing for closing an incision. It'll hurt."

I was reluctant to make the offer. His injuries didn't look internal, so it wouldn't kill him if I fumbled the intonation, but healing was exquisitely painful, which was why it was done in tandem with a maiden-priest who'd keep the patient asleep. That had been me and Taran, after every battle—standing together over the wounded, his hand under my elbow to hold me up while my voice faded to a whisper. I remembered it deep in my bones.

Taran had more confidence in my abilities than I did, because he looked down at the angry gash in his chest and exhaled before pushing his face into his shoulder to brace himself.

I put my hands on his body and sang his part. Just the way he would have done it.

After a few measures, the cut began to close, forming a red line and then fading thin and pale. It wasn't perfect, but after ten minutes of chanting, his insides were no longer visible from the outside. Once he was no longer bleeding, I could breathe again.

"Let me see the rest," I said, tugging at the waistband of Taran's trousers.

He really must have been in pain, because he didn't even make a crack about not being in the mood. He slipped off the rest of his clothes and lay facedown on the bed, so that I could sing each square of skin from livid purple back to smooth marble. It took nearly an hour, and it must have been agonizing, but he curled his fists over his head, making no sound.

As I sang, I rubbed his shoulders to break up the bruises, urging stiff muscles to soften under my fingers. Even once the blessing was over, I kept speaking, a stream of meaningless reassurance through tears. *You're alright, it's over, don't worry, you're safe.* He pushed himself up the bed enough to put his face in my lap, a wordless request to keep my hand moving in a circle between his shoulder blades. For me, it was a relief just to be able to hold and touch him as much as I'd wanted to.

Who had ever loved Taran over the course of his long life, except for me? Had anyone even been gentle with him?

When Taran rolled over and tugged me down beside him, I draped myself over his chest and stroked his face and hair with my hands, reassuring myself that every precious line of him was fixed. I nestled into the length of his body and matched my heartbeat to his. When he tilted his head back to kiss me, my nose rubbed into his cheek as our lips and tongues met, and it felt natural, despite the novel press of his naked body against my clothed one. I'd held him just like this before, because this was nothing but care to me. Gentle. Intimate.

I'd only pulled away to take a breath, not stop, when the expression on his face surprised me. It had harder edges than I'd expected, knowing and a little sad, even as he traced the curve of my mouth with a fingertip.

It bruised my own heart when I understood—he'd been trying to coax me back into his arms for weeks, and this was how he finally got me there.

"Oh, no, Taran. No. This isn't how you get this," I said, withdrawing far enough to frame his face with my hands. I couldn't let him think he could buy me with his hurt any more than I could be bought with gifts. "Don't ever do something like this again, do you understand me?" I tapped his collarbone, right where the Huntress had sliced into him. "I will call down Wesha's blessing of night, or I will help you fight our way out, or I will *just die*, but I will never want you hurt on my account."

I said that because I couldn't say *sometimes I think I still love you, you terrible lying bastard, please be more careful with yourself.*

The glittering wariness in his face held for three more heartbeats before dissolving in pained confusion. Taran sat up and pulled on his trousers in silence, then drew his stained cloak over his unbroken skin.

"You only get one mortal life," he eventually said. "And I'm one of the Stoneborn. What am I immortal for, if not for this? Don't think too much about it. Tomorrow it will be like it never even happened."

"Tomorrow it will still have happened," I said, recovering a bit of my anger. "You should have let me kill her."

Taran huffed out a small laugh. "It is really interesting to me that you thought that was an option, but let me remind you that killing the Stoneborn is strictly not allowed."

"Says who? The Allmother? She didn't do anything when you died, when Death died, when Smenos was murdered! If there are no consequences for doing something, then it *is* allowed."

The Allmother's laws protected men as well as immortals, and I'd yet to see anyone ask the Stoneborn to answer for a single dead priest. Laws that were never enforced were no laws at all, as far as I was concerned.

"Believe me, there would have been consequences if my priestess killed the Huntress in her own house."

"Only if anyone found out we did it," I said, giving Taran a serious look.

Taran shook his head in amazement. "Were all maiden-priests this bloodthirsty?"

I shrugged, managing to find the humor in my proposal to eliminate any witnesses when Taran pulled out one corner of his mouth in a crooked smile. "Surgeons, you know . . ."

Taran laughed and reached for me, and this time he kissed me more deeply. Possessive, with an intentional graze of teeth against my lower lip. "I probably shouldn't find that so attractive," he said, knocking a knuckle against my chin. "Seems likely to get me into trouble."

Always did, I thought, but this time it made me smile too.

Taran looked ready to settle in the bed and rest for a while, but I cocked my head at the door apologetically.

"While we're on that subject, I set fire to Smenos's workshops before I came in here looking for you. We should probably leave before they put it out."

Blinking, Taran tipped his head back in dismay. "Remind me not to leave you to your own devices ever again."

I nodded. That would be fine with me.

He got to his feet, experimentally stretching his arms and checking his range of motion. When he found it all satisfactory, he shot me a sidelong glance. "If you're trying to convince me I should let you go, you're not doing a very good job at it. You're making yourself both dangerous and precious to me."

"The point is not to get away from you. You should come with me. The mortal world, the rebellion . . . you'd understand what happened if you came back."

"It would be a little crowded on the ship, don't you think? You, me, your mortal lover, fresh from Wesha's clutches?"

If I thought that question had anything to do with our next destination and not his claim on my loyalty, I would have told him everything. Or almost everything.

Good news, Taran! If you'll give up this nonsense about eternal service, I'll stop looking for my betrothed and row you to Lubridium myself. You may hear a few surprising things about me once we get there, but please remember that I was very understanding, all things considered, when you tried to make me worship you. In five years we'll laugh about this.

I winced and tucked my hands into my chest, because Taran was probably not in the mood to see the irony at this exact moment.

"Come anyway? We were betrothed for almost two years, but we never married, and after all that's happened, I wonder if there was a reason for that," I confessed, giving voice to my secret fear. He probably hadn't thought we would both live when he proposed.

"You mean after you've sailed the Sea of Dreams, bargained with Wesha, and upended *my* life, you're not sure this dead idiot would want to marry you?"

I nodded unhappily.

"Then you're well rid of him, plum tree or no," said Taran, looking pleased with the theory.

Through great effort, I kept my face straight at that announcement. I drew breath to chant the opening notes of Lixnea's shroud as I headed for the door, only to feel another twinge of disquiet in my stomach, the opening salvo of one of my vows. Which one? I had Taran, and I had not abandoned my efforts to get him to the Painted Tower.

"We'll get Marit, and we'll leave before the others find us," I said, trying to reassure myself, but it didn't work.

I turned, following the pull in my chest. Not toward Taran.

"Awi," I realized. "Have you seen Awi?"

"The bird? Not since we arrived."

I hadn't seen any lesser immortals in the entire complex, even though Smenos and Wirrea should have had retainers and children filling up the palace. They would have had no reason to desert the Shipwright upon his death, unlike the priests he let his wife prey upon.

Had the little bird gone looking for them?

My vow dug its claws into my stomach like a cat kneading bare skin.

"I can't leave without her," I said, breath still coming fast. "I need to find her before we leave." There was some relief in forming the intention, but the twist in my chest still thought there was some risk that my vow to bring her to the mortal world would go unfulfilled.

"Perhaps we need to consider ways of getting you out of your vow to the bird goddess before we work on your obligations to We-sha," Taran said, eyes darkening, but he reluctantly followed me out of the room, and together we began to sweep the empty halls for any sign of life.

20

FINDING AWI WAS not as simple as finding Taran. The tug in my chest seemed to be pointing to the center of the Mountain, not any one spot in the anthill of the palace. And the layout was confusing the deeper we went: organic rather than carved from the rock, curving and doubling back and sometimes expanding into vast caverns.

The entire wealth of kingdoms was kept here in metal ingots and rare woods and other treasures: the tithes of generations of craftsmen, dimly illuminated by the single lantern we dared carry.

After half an hour of wandering, I stopped to rub the cramps out of my foot, and Taran took the opportunity to rummage through a felt-lined jewelry box, forgotten for the past hundred years if the dust was any measure.

When he lifted a gold chain set with chips of lapis into the air as though picturing how it would look on me, I automatically opened my mouth to scold him—Taran's inclination toward casual theft needed curbing—and stopped to laugh. In light of my recent crimes, Taran might as well enjoy himself.

"It's been a trying day," he said, smiling when he saw I wouldn't object and spinning the chain on a finger. "We deserve this, don't you think?"

I played along, batting my eyelashes at him. "Oh, thank you, yes, I agree this day merits jewelry, but I actually prefer emeralds."

Taran peered into the coffer. "You can have emeralds." He rustled thoughtfully through a tangle of jewels until he pulled out a heavy torque set with green stones. "This one comes with a matching diadem."

"Of course I need the matching diadem," I said, giggling as I imagined us sneaking out of the palace, wrapped in Lixnea's blessings and weighed down by enough jewelry to buy a farm. It was worth it to see some of the care lift off Taran's face as he came over to arrange it over my bound hair.

When I turned to let him fasten the torque around my neck, I spotted a small flutter of movement down the next dark hall. A plain brown house sparrow, hopping just ahead of us.

"Awi!" I hissed, as loud as I dared. "What are you doing? We need to get out of here."

In response, she flew away from us, farther down into the Mountain.

"Should have brought a net," Taran muttered, giving chase.

We pursued her deeper and down, the ceiling dropping and the walls pressing closer together, until we came to an iron-barred door at the end of a narrow hall. Everything in this part of the palace was covered with months of dust, but the boards of the door seemed new, and the iron locks that held it shut still had faint ridges from their recent manufacture, not yet worn smooth by use.

There was a small open panel where Awi flew to rest. The air that passed through the window tasted dry and warmer.

As I approached, ready to snatch up the bird goddess in my hands, I realized she was making a little creaking noise. Crying.

"What happened?" I asked, now hesitating to reach for her, though she didn't appear injured.

"Napeth! Did you see him? He's totally cracked. Off his stool."

"Yes, I know," I said, annoyed if nothing in particular had happened to Awi. "He's so terrible, we had to fight a war about it. Two! And also why we need to go right now—"

"No, not like he was before. He's worse, he came back worse. He would never have done this before." She was still crying, sobbing if a bird could sob.

"What's he done now?" I asked, but Awi abruptly flew at Taran's face.

"You did this to him. This is your fault!" she cried, tiny feet almost scoring his cheek before he swatted her away, his face creasing in confusion.

"Mine? How is it my fault? I met him for the first time today. Wesha was the one who decided to exile her husband for three hundred years."

"He was just supposed to stop being such a brute, and he could have come home. I never thought he'd go this far. Nobody would have." Her voice was a hoarse screech, and she darted through the window before I could stop her.

"Damn it!" Taran spun on his bare feet. "A net *and* a birdcage."

I tried the door and found it locked—not only locked, but bolted in three places.

There was no furniture nearby that might conceal the key, but though the tugging of my vow had disappeared with Awi's flight, I still wondered where it led. What she'd seen.

"Where does this go?"

"Deeper into the Mountain, I guess," Taran said reluctantly, examining the bolts.

I gnawed the inside of my cheek, then did my best to paste a look of nonchalance across my face as I sang the short blessing to open the lock, hoping Taran wouldn't notice.

His head whipped toward me in surprise.

"What did you just do?" he demanded.

"This blessing opens locks," I said, fingers crossed that he'd let it go.

"But where did you learn it? Not from Wesha. Or Lixnea," he said with new wariness on his handsome face.

I hesitated on how to dissemble when I'd never heard anyone but Taran use it.

"I heard the man I was going to marry use it a few times," I said, pulling the latches apart with my best expression of distant grief. This did not discourage him from inquiring further.

"Did he belong to a temple? Who was his patron god?"

I shrugged, not daring to look at him as my vow of truthfulness prickled my throat.

"Which god was his patron?" he pressed.

I hauled the creaking door open. "I'm not sure. Genna, maybe?"

"It never came up?" he asked skeptically.

I grimaced, because this was not the best moment for Taran to get curious about how I'd spent the rebellion.

"I'm coming to realize there were a *lot* of things we never talked about, but should have."

"I understand," he agreed after a moment, and I relaxed when he gestured for me to proceed into the tunnel behind the door.

There was only one way to go, so we descended, pace quickening to what my limp would allow. The slope was still gently downward, but now precise and straight as it went farther into the Mountain.

After a few minutes, I began to worry about the distance. How was it possible someone had cut this far down?

"It must have taken ages to cut through this. Even for one of the Stoneborn," I said.

Taran swiped his fingers across the wall, expression blanking when he saw the black soot it left on his fingertips.

"It wasn't cut. Someone burned through the rock."

My steps faltered. "Death?"

"This would take . . . an incredible amount of power," Taran said slowly. "How many priests did he have left, when you came here?"

"No more than a handful," I said, mind grappling for an explanation. "The mortal queen outlawed all sacrifice and worship. He couldn't have managed this when he died."

I resisted the urge to say *I told you so.* If he could melt through bare rock now, he could have obliterated Taran in the banquet hall. But Taran's face was paler than realizing how close he'd come to nonexistence would account for. He'd put something together, either from what Awi said or what I had.

There was a breeze from underground, sharp and gritty, and it stung my throat with every breath. We'd been walking steadily downward for almost half an hour before I spotted a red glow ahead of us. The rising heat was nearly intolerable, and when we reached the first open space since passing through the door, the source proved to be a pool of lava as big as a cistern, bubbling up from within the stone.

I'd heard stories of lava deep inside Mount Degom, the mortal twin to the Mountain, where the Allmother had formed the Stoneborn at the beginning of time. There used to be annual pilgrimages there, to light Death's sacred flames for each temple. I would have gone after being ordained, and I still felt a little religious awe to see the pool of it, but the lava wasn't what seized my attention.

Death's temples all had a sameness to them beyond the chosen ornaments and idols of any other Stoneborn. I'd been in most of them to personally oversee their destruction during the rebellion. The angles were all born out of the same immortal mind and repeated from the western shore to the northeastern mountains. I would have known that this cavern was a temple of Death even without the bronze lion or wing ornaments capping the peak of the altar behind the lava pool. But that wasn't what knocked out my breath.

Instead of stone, the entire thing was constructed of bone. Hundreds of bones. *Thousands.* Lashed together with leather and sinew, femurs and tibias and shoulder blades and a pebbled layer of skullcaps, all of it resting on a thick bed of tanned hides and thick furs. Some divine genius had been warped to the challenge of constructing an altar using only the parts of living things.

Some of the bones might have been those of cows and goats and sheep. Most were not.

"Smenos's priests," I whispered, throat closing up from horror. The surface of the altar was caked black from frequent and vicious use. This was what had happened to Smenos's priests. This was the sacrifice that had fueled Death's power so quick after his death. This was what had made even the heartless little bird goddess weep. "Why would he give Death his priests?"

"Because they weren't his priests anymore, after he died," Taran said, voice low and tight. "But that's not why he made an altar of bone. It wasn't made to sacrifice mortals."

My entire being rejected any closer inspection of the grotesque structure, but I forced one squinting eye to focus on the cracks in the skulls that formed the base. And beyond the black of dried blood there were dried rivulets of gold in the crevices, places where the lifeblood of lesser immortals had gathered.

"What does he need this much power for?" I whispered.

Taran looked around the cavern, face drawn with disgust. There were a dozen branching passageways, both natural and constructed. Some of them were sealed with thick, crude doors of stone, while others led farther down.

"Wesha. It's always about Wesha. Reaching her in her tower. Being stronger than her. And then going through the Gates, for Smenos. That must have been the bargain."

"Can Death *do* that?"

"With the sacrifice of a thousand mortals and some of the All-mother's lesser children? He could crack the Summerlands in two."

Clenching my teeth against this nightmare, I drifted toward one of the stone doors. It was locked, but my numb lips managed the blessing to open it. Beyond it was a hallway, with dozens more stone doors set at regular intervals along the rock wall. All of it fit together as though the stone had just grown into the shape.

There were small holes at the top—not large enough to be windows, but perhaps big enough for air. When I put my eye against one I saw nothing but darkness, but it wasn't quite silent within. The door had no lock or handle. I pushed to no avail, then tried to get a grip on the stone. It didn't budge.

"Taran, help me. I think there are people in here."

He came just to the start of the hall with his hands curling against the sides of his neck in horror.

"We need to go," he said from the doorway, voice cool. "When the Allmother finds out about this, we shouldn't be here."

"Didn't you hear me? This is some kind of prison. They haven't sacrificed everyone yet."

The remaining priests were being stored here the way a spider caches a fly in a corner of its web to consume at its leisure. I was certain of it—the pens that would have held goats and sheep in Death's temples were full of Smenos's priests and retainers.

"If Death finds out we've seen this, he can't afford to let us live. We've already been down here too long."

"We can't just leave them," I said, whirling reproachfully on Taran.

"There could be hundreds of doors in here. We don't have

time. Someone will notice we're missing, Death will come down here to finish the work, and then we'll be two more bloodstains on that altar."

He wasn't saying he couldn't do it. He was saying he wouldn't.

"You wouldn't leave Smenos's priests down here to die. To be— to be *fuel* for Death. This is worse than what caused the rebellion! That was one child!"

I said he wouldn't because I wanted to be right about Taran, not because I was certain I was.

"They're not *my* priests," Taran said, eyes going hard. "Don't make me carry you out of here."

"You won't. You wouldn't," I said, desperate to believe that.

Taran's response was to grab my arm and bend his legs as though ready to toss me over his shoulder.

I let my knees give out, falling on them despite his attempt to hold me up.

"Please," I whispered. "Please don't leave them. Don't be someone who would leave them."

Taran made a despairing noise, but he let me go and turned back to the first door. He put his hands on it and concentrated until his fingers sank into the stone like bread dough. Then he braced his legs and pulled.

Sweat beaded on his neck from effort as it slid open, just a crack. As soon as the stone was unsealed, a terrible wave of cries wafted out. Dozens of voices, mortal and immortal, a chorus of hopelessness. Fingers and claws waved frantically through the crack without the power to slide the door open farther.

Taran stopped, no doubt realizing that so many people could never escape through Smenos's palace unnoticed. His expression went haunted and trapped, and he looked again at the exit.

"I can't do it," he said, voice ragged. "I'm sorry. I'll tell everyone what we saw—Genna, Diopater—"

They wouldn't help. The most Genna had done was send Taran, even when it was all the gods' power at risk.

"Please help them," I begged again. I only had one card to play. "I'll do—I'll do whatever you want. What do you want? I'll be your priestess. Take whatever vows you want. I'll obey you."

Anything would be better than leaving Smenos's priests to die down here in the dark.

Taran's jaw, if anything, went more taut. "You can't offer me that! After what you saw tonight? You *know* what I could make you do if you promised to obey me."

I hit the stone floor with the sides of my fists. "These are innocent priests, people just like me. They're being used for *meat*. What do you want? I'll do it."

"I could have you chained naked in my bed for the next three hundred years. Or I could parcel your body and soul out to the other Stoneborn. Humiliate you in ways you can't even imagine yet," he shouted, some echo of forgotten torture bleeding into his voice.

"Is that what you're asking for when you keep asking me to be your priestess?" My heart was so brittle it felt as though it would crack and stop.

His face pulled into a stiff mask of hurt at my words. "What have I ever done to you, except keep you safe and offer you everything I have? Why do you treat me like a monster?"

Because I don't want you to be one, even if the rest of them are.

I didn't answer out loud. I grabbed Taran's tunic and held on to it, because there wasn't a single blessing I knew that could help us now. He had to do it.

He trembled as though wavering on the edge of a pit, but finally ducked his head and rubbed his pale cheeks.

"Fine," he said softly. "I'll do what I can to get them out. And we'll discuss later what you owe me, if we survive. Get ready to run."

Taran snatched my knife off my belt and knelt down. Before I could ask questions, he cut a swift line across his palm, just enough to make blood well up in a line of red-streaked gold, then pressed his bloody hand to the stone floor.

We waited a minute together with my breath still whistling loudly from grief, but nothing happened.

Taran sighed in frustration and sat back on his heels. With an unhappy twist to his lips, he considered the wound in his palm, which was already starting to scab. "Damn you, Wesha," he said softly. Then he closed his eyes, took a deep breath, and lifted the knife again.

This time he slit his wrist.

I cried out and dove for him, trying to close my fingers over the vein he'd sliced open. All my training said that was a fatal wound. His lifeblood was scorching against my hand as I stumbled into the first lines of Genna's blessing to heal it.

Taran jerked back as though surprised that I cared, but his expression softened for only a heartbeat.

"Don't think you'll be rid of me so quickly. This shouldn't take *all* my blood."

When I reluctantly released him, he lowered his wrist to the floor and shook it to let blood drip onto the stone in a pool. This time, in only seconds, there was a response. A faraway rumble.

Taran stood up, his other hand clutching at his wrist while I tried to locate the source of the noise.

"Get out of here. Run. I'll make sure the bird makes it."

I wasn't leaving him *either*, and I spread my feet to balance as the floors and walls began to vibrate and creak.

A few moments later, from far down the hallway, a large lump appeared in the stone floor, for all the world like a cat trapped under the bedcovers. It spun back and forth, searching, lifting the stone floor as easily as cotton gauze.

When it was near the spot where Taran's blood had spilled, the stones split and re-formed. Slowly, they shaped themselves into features. A nose jutting out of granite. An eye with a rim of stalactites and an onyx pupil. Enormous lips made of rose quartz geodes, the entire face the size of a horse cart. Taran clenched his jaw as the face solidified.

"Who?" A creaky, inhuman voice issued from between the stone lips. "Who hurt my babies?"

Taran frantically gestured at me to go, but I hesitated a few feet behind him.

"Good evening, Grandmother. Several of the Stoneborn have broken your laws and sacrificed your children," he announced, muscles coiling in anticipation.

"Grandmother . . . ?" the stone lips muttered. The tone was distant, sleepy, as though the stone giant had just woken from a very deep slumber.

Incrementally, the face turned so that the roiling eye could focus on Taran. The great black pupil constricted as it found him, and the stone lips spread into a rictus of anger, one which opened in a dark, ragged tunnel down to the center of the earth. Abruptly, the mouth began to shriek.

"You! How dare you call me *grandmother*, you murderous little shit."

Taran winced and took a few unsteady paces back as the stone face continued to scream invective at him.

"You're the worst thing my children ever brought into this world! Oh, they should have let me punish you. They should have let me eat you up!"

Much faster than the face had drifted up the hall, a wave of stone flew toward Taran, forming out of nothing but moving with enough force to splatter him against the side of the tunnel.

Taran dodged to the side, but his movements were sluggish

from blood loss, and he crashed into the opposite wall and bounced off with a painful thud. I ran to pull him upright as the ground shook hard enough to rattle my bones.

"Run," he gasped again, and I dearly wanted to, but I gripped his arm to get him steady on his feet.

The shrieking continued, because it seemed that the Allmother was still holding a grudge, three hundred years later, over Taran's theft of the stone blades that could kill immortals.

Or she knew more about the circumstances of Death's last defeat than Taran did now.

"I should have known it would be you," the Mountain's voice moaned and burbled. "What have you done now?"

"I haven't done anything this time," Taran called, grabbing my wrist and scrambling backwards, toward the large cavern. "Come here and see what Napeth has done to your children."

"Get my poor son's name from your mouth," the Allmother sobbed, eye searching again for Taran as the ground violently wobbled. "I don't claim you. Thief! Liar! Murderer!"

"You're still my grandmother," he yelled, pulling me away from her blindly snapping mouth. "So at least you should see where immortal blood was spilled!"

We stumbled together back into the large cavern, where the lava pool was now bubbling over and beginning to spread. Sweat dripped into my eyes, nearly obscuring my vision as the form of a giant woman rose from the middle of the pool.

She was made of stone mortared together with lines of solid gold, but her shape was maternal and terrible. Wide hips and strong arms, skin patched in granite and basalt and ore, body taller than Wesha had been in her tower. The Allmother, the first of the gods, the Mountain. The ultimate ancestor of every immortal being. Her stone features glared at Taran like she planned to break him into pieces, but her attention was inexorably drawn by the fetid stink of the altar. She took one step toward it, two, the ground vibrating as she moved. When she reached it, she pressed her barrel-sized hands to the altar of bones, fingers digging for the gold blood trapped there, then sampling it with senses I lacked.

Recklessly, she pulled the altar apart, snapping femurs like blades of grass until her hands were spread on the gold that had pooled at the very base, prevented from falling onto the stone by the thick leather hides spread beneath it.

"*Who?*" she hissed again. "Who killed them? Was it you again, you viper?"

"Death," Taran said, edging backward with me. "With the Shipwright and the Huntress. He sacrificed your children here, just for more power. Mortals, immortals, some still trapped here, inside your stone—"

She didn't care to listen to the rest of the explanation. The Allmother dug her jagged fingers into the altar, then tipped her head back as though gathering breath for a scream.

"Time to go," Taran breathed again, pushing at me as the stone goddess's form pulsed.

I blinked dust from my vision as the Allmother's temporary form dissolved, flowing into the ground. A mouth formed again in the ground, five times larger than before, and the Mountain keened.

The scream echoed through my skull, pounding against my eardrums. My teeth vibrated in my clenched jaw, almost hard enough to chip. I couldn't think through the noise, couldn't even breathe through it. I was only distantly aware of the howls of the imprisoned sacrifices joining the din as their cell doors popped open, and of Taran grabbing my wrist to pull me toward the tunnel to the surface.

21

THE STONE OF the cavern roiled like the gut of a living creature, making every step unsteady. My foot was in agony within a few moments, but I was afraid that if I stopped, I'd fall, and if I fell I'd never get up again. There was the roar of the Allmother, the thunderous noise of rock shifting, and the screams of the captives disorienting me, but there was also Taran's grip on my arm as my lodestar. He was flagging as badly as I was, immortal strength failing after all he'd suffered today, and he was running on bare feet across the hot, jagged rock of the tunnel, but he somehow kept us up and moving.

Immortals began to pass us in their desperate escape. Abandoning all pretense of human form, they crowded around us and sped upward on wings, hooves, and clawed feet, adding to the noise as the Mountain convulsed in the Allmother's fury. I knew what panic could do to the gentlest soul, so I expected no aid from anyone else fleeing the altar of bone if we stumbled during the long, treacherous climb.

We reached the mouth of the tunnel under an unexpected beam of light from the rooms ahead of us. As we followed the fleeing crowd, I tipped my head back and saw the night sky where there should have been the ornate, coffered ceilings we'd passed on the way in.

The Allmother had lifted the entire top of the Mountain off Smenos's palace, and now she rummaged within, looking for her disobedient children.

I pulled on Taran's arm when he would have plunged ahead.

"We should climb out!" I yelled over the din, pointing behind us. Everywhere things were crashing to the floor—shelves, cupboards, the *walls*.

"I have to find Marit," he insisted, face drawn. "He won't understand what's going on."

I would have said that Marit was better able to take care of himself than the two of us, but as I was the one who'd gotten us into this disaster, I nodded and ducked my head as we pushed on. The former crafter-priests and immortal retainers knew the layout of the palace and were taking the most direct way out, but caution made me tug Taran into a side passageway of the confusing warren.

While we were navigating a series of trophy rooms filled with dusty, ancient beasts, I heard distant chanting that would have made me sit up and pay attention if I'd been in a months-long coma.

"Death-priests," I hissed, jerking Taran into an alcove long enough to weave Lixnea's darkness around us. I should have cleared the other guest rooms before looking for Taran; Death would never have come here without an entourage, and now he'd ordered his priests to dispatch the beings he'd meant to sacrifice. The final notes of the prayer for a curtain of fire were met with howls of pain ripped from countless throats, echoing through the wrecked halls.

"He can't possibly think he'll be able to stop news of this from getting out."

Taran was still wild-eyed with surprise, but none of this had felt the least bit surprising to me from the moment I'd heard Death was here. This was what Death did.

"He killed every last maiden-priest," I said, lifting Taran's knife off his belt and pushing it against his slack palm. Death was entirely capable of eliminating every witness to this outrage, and I didn't doubt that was what he intended.

Soon more screams ricocheted through the building as death-priests found the first line of crafter-priests and tried to prevent them from escaping by conjuring the fire god's flame. The shouts widened, spread, as combat was joined throughout the palace, and the tempo of the shaking overhead quickened in response.

Despite everything, or perhaps because of everything, a deep clarity had settled over me, stopped my hand from shaking where it held my own knife. It made me quick to act, almost happy to do it, even though Taran was showing signs of shock from the trauma. Part of me was back in Ereban two years ago, and the muddy hillside was collapsing around the city, but Taran and I had survived that day and *we were going to survive this one.*

Wrapped in Lixnea's darkness, we wove back to the guest wing, obscured from the hunt-priests and death-priests who were assembling barricades while the much more numerous crafter-priests and lesser immortals battered them down with the sheer weight and force of their bodies. Despite the holes in the roof, smoke was beginning to fill the corridors—we had only minutes left to make it out before it would overwhelm us.

But I knew what to do in a fire. I knew to stay low and follow the smoke out. I knew how to kill death-priests under the choking darkness they'd created. I knew Taran's shape at my side. I knew how to do this better than anything else I'd done since following Taran to the Summerlands.

We found Marit passed out in a pool of mingled wine and seawater, insensible to the wreckage already strewing his room and the thunder of the battle outside.

"Come on, wake up." Taran patted Marit's cheeks frantically, then lifted the other god's arm as though preparing to drape him across his back.

I looked around for something we could use as a sledge—I wasn't certain Taran could carry the other man in his state—but the sea god jolted awake in midair.

"What is—is it time to go?" Marit yawned, making a face like a sleepy kitten.

"Yes, right now. We've worn out our welcome," Taran informed him while I peered out the narrow slit of the window.

The courtyard was full of rubble and flame, but the guest wing was mostly intact, and so were the stables. Unfortunately, between us and the mouth of the valley were the workshops, where my own fire had spread among the wreckage caused by the Allmother's battering arms on top of the Mountain.

When I craned my neck in the other direction, I spotted the Huntress and a trio of hunt-priests, who'd taken a position on the roof of one of the intact buildings so as to pick off people fleeing down the front steps. Her arrows must have been tipped in gleaming stone, because in the few moments I watched, I saw a slender being whose body was covered in segmented copper plates fall with a bolt in their throat and dissolve like a drop of honey in wine, leaving only a puddle of gold ichor on the stone.

Some people were making it past the Huntress though. She couldn't catch everyone.

"When we come out of the front entrance, we need to hug the wall on the left and head straight for the stables," I told Taran urgently. "I can cover us on the way there, but when we ride out, we'll be totally exposed."

Taran nodded gravely, and my heart twisted to see him that serious. The last time he looked at me like that, he'd died.

"It is not very polite to leave without saying farewell to our hosts, and . . ." Marit began to say, but he stopped and turned in the direction of the Mountain, hearing something in the din that my mortal ears couldn't discern. His eyes widened. "Mother?"

"Yes, she's here, and she's still not happy with me either," Taran muttered, yanking on Marit's arm to pull him out of the room after us.

Despite what I'd said, I paused as soon as we were outside, Lixnea's shroud on my lips, just to gape at the smoke and rubble that had replaced the Shipwright's domain. The earth was convulsing and shaking with an endless earthquake, and above us—

I nearly died as a boulder fell from the sky and crashed against the spot where I'd been standing before Taran tackled me to the side.

"Keep moving!" he yelled, hauling me back to my feet before the shards of rock had finished vibrating on the ground. Under the cover of the Moon's darkness, the three of us sprinted toward the stable, and this last bit of effort was what made my foot give up for the day. I collapsed in the open door by the hayloft, then twisted on the floor to stare up at the battle above Smenos's palace.

The Mountain behind us was alive. I couldn't separate the Allmother's shape from the jagged peaks anymore. Her angry, grasping arms reached out as columns of rock, smashing the Shipwright's holdings into smaller, smoking pieces.

"*Napeth! Napeth, I'm here. Where are you?*" she howled in a voice like a hurricane, blindly patting through the rubble in search of her youngest son. As I watched, one arm snatched up a deathpriest squirming in his red robes and dragged him beneath the ground. When her stone hand reemerged, he was gone without a trace.

But Napeth had not acquiesced to her punishment, nor had the Shipwright and his wife. They fought back in the rubble in their primeval forms, dwarfed by the size of the Mountain but still enormous and deadly.

We of the Maiden's cult rarely sang the songs that described the oldest shapes of our gods, and we might have said that the language these songs were composed in was now archaic and difficult to understand. The truth was that we did not like to remember that our gods only sometimes took the shapes of men. More and more often as centuries passed and as more of the world was cultivated and turned to man's will did our gods reflect our own nature, but there was still much of the world that did not bow to our hands, and that history was flesh in the nightmares that brawled in the flames.

The Huntress's shining green-golden eyes were lanterns in the smoke as she brought down her targets with stone-tipped arrows. The Shipwright was a hulking machine of iron and timber, tossing boulders at the lesser immortals who scattered before him. And Death—

All my life, I had seen depictions of the winged lion in the stonework of his altars. Artists had made the creature beautiful when they rendered him in gold leaf and carnelian. His form used to decorate the backs of coins, a symbol of strength before the war.

The reality was worse. The lion's mane was fire, and his mouth was grotesquely wide, big enough to swallow horses whole. Big enough to eat the sun, in the oldest story. More than large enough to swoop from the sky and bite a crafter-priest in two.

The Allmother was trying to defend her children, but she couldn't see her targets, and when she reached toward the Stoneborn who'd broken her laws, she just as often swatted down the little gods who were attempting to flee. Bodies were strewn everywhere, death-priests and crafter-priests alike, and gold blood spread on the stone where immortals fell too.

"Why are they fighting her? She's our mother," said Marit, voice puzzled and sad.

I was dimly aware of Taran behind me, trying to coax Marit's reluctant horses out of their stalls and toward the inferno before the stables were struck from above, but Marit drifted into the doorway where I was still sprawled on the ground.

His reaction to the great violence of the scene was unexpectedly muted. I would have worried he'd respond with one of his fits, but his pearly pink lips were pursed with nothing more than sadness as he took in the nearly impassable road out of the valley between the fires and the rubble.

"Smenos let Napeth sacrifice his priests and retainers to rebuild his power," I said, trying to at least roll to my knees. "They tried to hide it from the Allmother."

Marit's face brimmed with grief. "They shouldn't have done that. Our mother warned us not to hurt each other. That was the *first* thing she told me."

He turned and saw Taran bridling Skyfather's horse. I lifted my arms for Taran to put me on the creature's back, but Marit shook his head.

"Take one of mine," he told Taran. "I'll go behind you."

A wordless understanding seemed to pass between the two men, and Taran nodded. As soon as we were both seated on the bare back of one of Marit's gray chariot horses, Marit swatted its hindquarters, then lifted his arms in the gesture I now recognized as a Stoneborn gathering power.

From the rear of the stable, from nowhere, seawater rushed in. Marit's horses did not startle, even though I did, especially once the water lifted their feet off the floor as though the surface was glass instead of brine. Marit also rose with the tide, feet planted in the cresting wave that swept us forward into the courtyard.

More water flooded into the valley, extinguishing flames even as it slowed the fleeing crafter-priests. It rose faster than any storm could have filled the space, and within seconds I could no longer see the earth under the whitecaps.

With another casual toss of Marit's hand, a wave knocked the

Huntress and her archers off their feet, and Taran leaned us forward, urging the horse into a canter in the direction of the winding canyon that fed into this valley. We sped past Wirrea's position and now had only ruins between us and the road back to the City.

Marit had cleared a corridor for us to escape, though we were the only ones who could use it.

"Marit, the priests!" I yelled, twisting around despite the clamp of Taran's arms to point at the mortals who'd fallen beneath the waves.

This was all for nothing if they drowned within sight of safety.

Marit was only a few feet behind us, keeping pace with his horse despite planting his feet in the surging floodwaters. He blinked his swirling eyes at me with mild affront, then made a cupping gesture with both hands.

"I know, I know. I won't let them drown. I wouldn't!"

Like leaves in a stream, the crafter-priests quickly began to bob to the surface, faces terrified but alive as the sea god's power lifted them up and carried them in his waters. All of us were borne forward, past the ruins of Smenos's workshop and away from the battle.

I started to laugh when the surge flowed high enough to bring us to the top of the canyon and the hooves of Marit's horse struck stone instead of water. Not today, Death! Not by fire or by water! Death had been punched in the face by his upstart brother-in-law and then reprimanded by his own mother, yet somehow we'd lived to thwart him again.

Taran pulled up the horse to watch as Marit floated the mass of crafter-priests past a concealing bend of the canyon, then allowed the waves to recede.

I beamed at the sea god, ready to chant every prayer of thanks I'd ever heard. Sing sea shanties all the way back to the City. Pour his wine myself, even if I ended up swimming home.

Marit nodded with satisfaction when the last crafter-priest was back on dry land, then turned toward the inferno, face alert to his mother's angry cries.

Taran realized what Marit was about to do a moment before I did. He lunged fast enough to topple himself off the back of the horse, and he managed to seize a handful of Marit's tunic but not to quite land on his feet.

They struggled awkwardly, Marit trying to shrug off Taran's grip without letting him fall and Taran attempting to drag the sea god back from the lip of the canyon. A wave already hung suspended in midair, poised to carry Marit to the Allmother and her battle with the other Stoneborn.

"Don't do it, you idiot! They don't care about the Allmother's laws, and she doesn't even know you're here."

"Let *go*," Marit yelled.

Taran grunted in pain when Marit landed an elbow in his gut, and the scuffle ended with Taran staggering back, dazed.

"Marit, no," I gasped. Napeth was as fat as a tick with the power gained from all those sacrifices, and Marit had no priests left. Even the waves had to have taxed his strength. The other Stoneborn would kill him.

But Marit drew himself up to his full height and glared down at Taran. His soft, childish features shifted, turning hard and inhuman.

"You can't talk to me like that," he thundered in a voice whose echoes lifted the hair on the back of my neck. "I am the god of the *sea*, and my mother made my bones centuries before Genna even knew the word for peace. *I* keep the laws, even if no one else will."

At Taran's stricken expression, Marit sighed and turned his back on us. His voice still carried. "You're my friend, Taran, but really, you're just a Fallen, aren't you? You wouldn't understand."

I couldn't recognize the emotion in Marit's voice, though I

knew the grief in Taran's when he called again for Marit to come back. But Marit didn't flinch—he stepped onto the crest of the wave and let it carry him away from the canyon, past the flooded valley and to the chaos on the Mountain.

He didn't say goodbye, but what reasons were there for goodbyes between immortals?

The smoke made it hard to see Marit's change, but it wasn't so much a matter of a man's shape growing into a monster's as a shift in what my mortal eyes were allowed to see.

There had always been a jeweled serpent as well as the odd, wounded man I'd met that first night in the Summerlands—I just hadn't noticed. Now the great sea wyrm of legend that sometimes wrecked ships and sometimes led sailors to shore spread delicate fins and waded into the melee. His scales were all the colors that his eyes could shift between, chalcedony to onyx, and his long, strange shape was familiar. He'd carved it from driftwood last week at Lixnea's palace—beautiful and deadly in the water but vulnerable to the fire and rubble flying through the air.

As more priests and immortals crawled out from beneath Smenos's palace and reached the safety of the water, little waves carried them away from the Huntress's arrows and the Shipwright's boulders. Marit was saving who he could, all the stragglers who'd fallen behind after weeks underground, but Marit wasn't safe himself. The Allmother's grasping arms had not yet pinned Death, and the winged lion was leaping closer and closer to Marit, whose long, trailing tail and stubby legs made him ill-suited for battle on land.

Taran ran to the edge and teetered at the precipice like he wanted to leap after the sea god, but the sheer rock drop wouldn't even let him climb down.

"Can you do anything like that?" I demanded, pointing at Marit's scaled form. Anything to even the odds, anything that would save Marit from what I knew was coming.

Taran's fists bunched helplessly at his sides. "If I could, don't you think I would?"

His angry stare made the question real, and I was instantly sorry that I'd asked. He would have saved his friend if he could have.

And I then knew, just as strongly, that he hadn't held back before. He would have lived through his own battle with Death if he could have, but it had been him or me, and he'd chosen me.

"Come on," he said, voice still dripping with fury as he climbed up behind me on Marit's horse and reached for the reins.

"No, wait," I begged, striving to keep Marit's jewel-like scales in view as Taran turned the horse to follow the thin lip of the canyon. There had to be something I could do. Sing Wesha's blessings or Skyfather's. Take my tiny stone knife back from Taran—

"Will it help him to watch?"

Again, Taran's question was real, and I knew the answer from bitter experience. Marit wouldn't want us to stay and watch, any more than Taran had wanted me to run after him on my broken foot.

But I couldn't help but look back through eyes blurred with tears. I looked over Taran's shoulder as he urged the horse to run in the opposite direction of its master.

I saw the moment the winged lion pounced on the sea dragon and began to tear golden rents in his sides, but that was my choice, and I wished I could spare Taran the sound of Marit's strangled roar when Death bit viciously into the side of his neck. The delicate fins were shredded in moments, and his vestigial legs could find no purchase. Marit's coils looped uselessly around the body of the larger god as his waves began to recede, but teeth and claws alone were not enough to kill an immortal. All the time, he continued to scream as he struggled in Death's grasp.

The Allmother had commanded the Stoneborn not to fight, but Taran had worked out how they could kill each other—their mother's stone. So it was the Allmother who ended it; she heard her son's anguish and shrieked in answer. The Mountain erupted, turning the sky black and the smoky air to dust. Her stone arms had become pillars of lava, bright enough to leave flowing afterimages on my retinas when I blinked tears away.

It was Marit's cries that finally let the Allmother locate her disobedient youngest son, teeth still caught in his brother's neck as water turned to steam and earth to flame. The Allmother's fire-flowing hands grasped for her children, seized them, and, in a final flash of light, dragged them all down beneath the stone.

TARAN RODE ON long after the cliffs turned to forest. It was almost dawn before he stopped, at a shabby stone structure by a small pond, as humble as any building I'd seen in the Summerlands. Little curricles were stacked outside. Some immortals enjoyed fishing, I supposed. I couldn't be sure, but I thought we'd made it out of Smenos's lands. The night smelled like wet grass and fresh dew, though smoke still clung to our clothes.

Taran didn't speak a word as he lifted me off of Marit's horse, though when my foot still couldn't bear my weight, he scooped me back up to carry me inside.

There were no beds in the single room, but there was a thickly woven rush mat in front of a cooking hearth, and I gratefully slumped to the floor there. My breath emerged in shaky spurts as I tried to calm muscles that were releasing days' worth of fear. Instincts from three years of war compelled me to rest at the first moment of safety, because safety never lasted long.

Innocent of that experience, Taran puttered around the room first, opening drawers and rattling window shutters before his feet dragged closer to me. He lay down on his side, facing me, studying my silent collapse.

"Are you hurt?" he asked.

I shook my head, and Taran scooted closer on the mat.

After picking a few loose strands of hair away from my face, he rolled on top of me.

He'd never done that before, but the heaviness of all that muscle felt wonderful, and after a second of surprise, I welcomed his weight and wrapped my arms tight around his waist. I'd thought he was still angry at me, but he'd just had what was surely the worst day of his new life—of course he wanted comfort. So did I. I tucked my face against his shoulder, the warm scent of his skin registering beyond the smoke and blood.

We lived today. He'd saved me, then saved every person who made it out of the underground prison. I felt more than in any moment since I reached the Summerlands that I had him back, the same person I'd lost. Maybe I'd never have to let him go again.

Taran shifted his weight after a lengthy inhale, gathering my hands into one of his and tangling my legs with his own. Even then, I didn't recognize that he wasn't holding me but pinning me down until I felt the edge of my own knife prickle against my neck.

"Alright, darling," he said softly. "I'm ready to collect on that debt you owe me. Let's start with some answers."

22

TARAN HAD SO many reasons to be angry about my short but eventful tenure in his immortal life that I had to wait for him to explain which of my sins we were going to discuss first. His tangled hair nearly brushed my face, and I deliriously wondered whether he'd be open to having this conversation in a different position, because I was too tired to fight back and his eyelashes were distracting.

"You've been remarkably untruthful for someone who can't lie to me," Taran said in a low, furious rumble.

At this accurate but somewhat irrelevant accusation, I exhaled, letting my head tip back and my gaze drift to the ceiling in pure wonder. With my unparalleled talent for disaster, I'd managed to get Taran tortured, his only friend killed, and a second great war in the Summerlands started—just today! Gods were dead! He was barefoot and bleeding in the wilderness. But no, what he was really exercised about was that *I* had kept things from *him*.

I teetered on the edge of breaking into hysterical giggles. I'd lived under the axe of my secrets and the prospect of it falling felt like relief. Was that all? A few lies of omission?

Sorry, Taran, sometimes the people you love will disappoint you. Life is complicated.

"You lie all the time," I pointed out. "And I try not to hold it against you."

His eyes widened in outrage. "I am not a mortal dependent on the gods' mercy."

"I'm a mortal you've basically kidnapped and attempted to force into eternal servitude," I said, giddy at the opportunity to speak my mind.

"You—" He made an incoherent noise of frustration and shook his head. "We are going to address the things *you've* done. Your little blessing that opens locks. Where did you learn it? Tell the full truth this time."

"I already told you," I said peacefully. "I learned it from the man I was going to marry, and I don't know which god it invokes."

Taran put the knife down, out of my reach, and tapped his chest. "I'm the god it invokes, *darling.*"

I blinked in mild surprise while Taran carefully watched my reaction.

"Oh, interesting," I said, because he seemed to want my feedback, but my mind was so unmoored that I couldn't make my thoughts travel in a straight line.

I had wondered whether he had any area of patronage, and this one made sense in light of his very casual relationship with property ownership. "Well, it's hardly as dramatic as hurling lightning bolts, but I suppose it comes in handy more frequently?" I suggested when Taran kept waiting for a response.

"Yes, please do spare my ego now, of all things. Think a little harder."

I tried to understand what he was saying. "It makes you the god of thieves?"

"If I had a little less mortal blood, I would be," he said, face still tight and expectant. "Or had any worshippers. Which I don't. Because before I left for the mortal world, everyone thought I was nothing but one of the Fallen. I never taught anyone a blessing to invoke my power—at least not here."

"So, that's why you were surprised," I said, realizing where he was going with this line of inquiry. I was ready to get there. I'd hear his plan to lie, charm, and seduce his way into the mortal rebellion. I'd finally get some answers too. What he'd really wanted with me.

"That betrothed of yours," Taran said, and my pulse began to race in anticipation. "The one who taught you my blessing."

"Yes," I said eagerly.

"Someone willing to turn the blessings of the gods to his own purposes. Someone who didn't hesitate to steal a priestess away from the Maiden. Someone you sailed all the way to the Painted Tower for."

"Yes," I said again, allowing myself to adore the elegant lines of his face. Beautiful, even in a rage. Taran's full mouth tilted with grim satisfaction at having put the clues together at last. Here it was—the true story of the two of us.

"Your betrothed joined the mortal rebellion, didn't he? That's how I knew him."

His conclusion was so inadequate that I felt like I'd missed a stair step. A laugh rattled up through my throat, then another. I wheezed. It convulsed in the back of my throat. I couldn't breathe.

"Do you not realize we are discussing whether I ought to execute you for blasphemy right now?" Taran demanded, face going outraged. "You were almost a maiden-priest, and you were going to *marry* someone in active rebellion against the gods?"

I laughed harder, tears beginning to leak out of the corners of my eyes. Everything was right there, but he still couldn't see me through this ridiculous image he had of me on my knees, Wesha's devoted priestess.

I pulled one of my hands out of his grip and put it against his cheek, replacing it despite his snarl and attempt to move away.

"Taran, my love, my heart, my beloved two-faced lying bastard, I *led* the mortal rebellion."

If he'd been paying attention, he could have figured that out by now. I didn't have a lot of practice in deceit, and I'd covered my tracks poorly.

"*You?*"

That was enough to make him fully release me and sit back in appalled dismay. He stared at me as though I'd just transformed like a Stoneborn in battle.

"Yes! What did you think I did after Death murdered the rest of my temple?" I asked, fatigue making me snippy. "Cry alone while my country burned down? No. I took my kithara and my knife and I started killing death-priests. I started the rebellion. I led it. You knew *me*."

"*You* led an army against the gods," he said, horror and amazement warring on his features.

I didn't think at this point that he mistook my reasons but merely doubted my capability. Which was insulting.

"I've told you enough to explain what happened. All the priests had fled, the gods were silent, and the queen wanted revenge for her sacrificed child. I organized the acolytes who were left behind and started fighting back against Death. In the end, he died and we won."

Taran's chest heaved, and the bare muscles of his arms tightened as he considered the knife on the floor. His expression was stricken with the same betrayal I'd felt on the day I discovered who he really was.

"Was it you?" he asked, voice dull.

"Me what?"

"Is that why you were so surprised to see me alive? Did you kill us both? Me and Napeth?"

Oh, that made my heart ache, despite everything.

"Me? Maiden's mercy, Taran, no. Death killed you. You killed him. That's how the war ended."

"You're lying," Taran said, appalled. "How are you lying? Why would I attack Death, when I was sent to put down the mortal rebellion?"

"You expect me to know? You never told me! You strolled into our camp a month after the rebellion started and offered to *help* me. I thought you were mortal! The last I saw of you before Wesha dropped me here was when you went to confront Death with my knife in your hand, because the queen's army was trapped against a line of his fires. You didn't put down the mortal rebellion, you fought in it."

Taran wildly shook his head. "No. That's not possible." Face darkening, he snatched my knife back up, looming over me. "Killing Death would just return him to the Summerlands, *where I live*. Turning the mortals against the gods would destroy both worlds. I wouldn't do that!"

"You're that certain? That you would never care about what had been done to us? Even if you could see us starving, dying, chased by death-priests. You don't think there's any chance you just . . . changed your mind?"

"If I'd changed my mind, it would *be* changed. And I know I wouldn't do that."

"You never did a single thing to stop me from putting every death-priest in the country to the sword, nor the queen from tearing down the temples. What did you possibly want, if not to help us? You cared about us. I know you did."

I'd raised my head to talk to him, but Taran prowled over to me, on his hands and knees, knife still caught in his fist.

"Even if you're lying, if anyone here thought there was a chance you were telling the truth, I would be . . . buried alive, probably. Entombed in stone forever. For encouraging rebellion against the gods. For spilling the blood of another Stoneborn."

"You killed Marit," I pointed out, trying to scoot away.

"Which everyone *wanted* me to do, and Skyfather still hung me by my wrists at the entrance of the grand arena for a *week* to pacify the Allmother. You saw what she did to Napeth just now. For this, nobody would forgive me. Ever. Putting down the mortal rebellion was my chance to be free of what I did when I stole the knives. Killing Death would be—" His eyes were hard and glittering. "You are going to vow to never speak of this again. You are going to vow to forget this vendetta against Death entirely."

I firmed my mouth. "No."

"I don't think you understand. If you want to live until dawn, you are going to make that vow."

I curled my hands into fists and pushed up on my elbows until we were nearly nose to nose. "I'm not making any more vows to you."

"A few hours ago you were willing to spend a thousand years naked and feeding me grapes just to get a bunch of wretched crafter-priests and immortals you've never met out of Smenos's dungeon," Taran said incredulously. "Now you won't make a vow that will save both our lives?"

"You aren't even offering me anything in exchange." He'd had three years to kill me; if he couldn't bring himself to do it then, he wouldn't do it now.

"You're trying to extract something for yourself? Do you have a death wish?"

"Honestly? Maybe?" I was fizzy and intoxicated from the relief of being able to talk about it with him. "That would explain a lot, wouldn't it?"

The laugh that came out of his nose sounded like it hurt.

"If you launched a campaign of deicide, tortured my secrets out of me, put a stone knife in Death's heart, and then rowed across the ocean to torment me further, I could almost admire your single-minded devotion to our ruin, but tell me how I am supposed to make it stop. It needs to stop, Iona. What am I supposed to do with you if I don't kill you?"

"I keep suggesting you take me to Wesha so that I can go home."

"With your mortal lover, off to plot more inventive methods of our downfall? Why would I allow that?"

"I've never done anything to hurt you," I said, finding a little more rebellion when I needed it. "I built your funeral barge myself. I bandaged your body. I sent you past the Gates with my scarf wrapped around your hands. Who did you think did that?"

Was it so hard for him to imagine, after today, that he'd cared enough about us to sacrifice his life?

"It's hard for me to appreciate all your *help*, because I *died* in your war," Taran said, green eyes blazing.

"Try harder then, because you are *still* in my war, and I'm the only one who wants to save you."

Taran's eyelids lowered, his expression becoming even more dangerous. The blade on my neck was pressing against my skin hard enough that I felt the burn of a first drop of blood welling up.

His voice was soft. "You know, I thought you were my reward. Sent by Wesha, the Allmother . . . fate, maybe. And I'd be yours. For surviving everything Wesha did to us both. But now I wonder if she sent you here to destroy me. You're a wildfire. I'm dying in the flames."

It felt like a compliment, or at least reassurance that he'd really seen me. I wasn't a redheaded ornament to play pretty music for him. He knew me.

I was glad we'd finally had a halfway honest conversation, even if this was the last one. This was healing.

"My love, you should see what I can do when I really try to destroy someone," I said, taking the opportunity to appreciate how his eyes sparkled when his face was lit up with anger. Taran being beautiful had seemed contrary to the point of him when I first knew him, impolite for me to notice.

Were you trying to be good, Taran? I was. If I'd known you were such a liar though, I might have allowed myself a little more of you.

I tilted my neck to the side, not trying to avoid the blade, just getting enough freedom of movement to stretch out my legs and enjoy the weight of his body. I supposed I would never know whether he'd wanted me, but I didn't have any illusions about my own desires. He was being terrible, and I was still shallow enough to be thinking about the way his every exhale pressed his chest against mine.

Every thought I had went directly to my face, so I wasn't surprised when Taran's eyebrows dipped in a knowing way, or when he bent his face to mine. When his teeth deliberately closed around my lower lip, I was surprised, but more from the bolt of heat it sent through my stomach than by the pain of it. He held the bite for a second, then soothed it with a wet swipe of his tongue. The noise I made was swallowed by his mouth covering mine in a kiss that was less hungry than punishing. I gave in to it, even though he tasted like copper and stone dust, even though the sharp points of his teeth and his knife were very present dangers as I sucked his tongue into my mouth.

My body was so light and unmoored from fatigue that his weight felt like the only thing keeping me from floating to the ceiling. I pulled up a knee to tip him farther into the cradle of my thighs, and the friction of his hips against my core made us inhale in unison as anger flashed into desire. Fear, anger, want—those emotions were all closer to each other than I'd ever let myself admit. I should have shown this part of myself to Taran while I still had the chance to be truly openhearted with him.

He shifted onto an elbow, hand raking down my side to fumble with my clothes in a quest to get his palm against my skin. I didn't help him at all, twining my hands into his filthy hair instead and pulling hard enough to make him curse. If he wanted to get my clothes off, he needed to commit to putting the knife away, and he still had it in his other fist.

His next movement brought the hard length of his thigh between mine, and it felt purposeful. It was permission to chase the thread of tension curling in my stomach, even though I didn't know this route and had never reached this destination. The scrape of Taran's stubble against my chin as he looked down to examine how the catches of my clothing were tied was the only encouragement I needed to roll against him and follow that thread a little further.

Pressure flashed into pleasure, with even the drag of fabric across the hard points of my breasts suddenly exciting and new. I twisted against him, discovering a rhythm that made my body sing. Just like this, I thought, this would be enough, more than enough—

I was never not listening for an ambush, even with Taran's tongue in my mouth and his fingers curling into the waistband of my trousers, so I heard the fluttering of wings outside even before the pull of the latch of the door. It didn't sound like an attempt at stealth, so I didn't embarrass Taran by taking the knife away from him, just pulled my mouth from his as the door creaked open to admit a very bedraggled black swan.

"Genna's rosy tits," she swore at the sight of us, hiding her face under a dust-streaked wing.

Taran jolted in surprise but didn't roll off of me until I jabbed him with two fingers in a sensitive spot below his rib cage, and even then, he only scooted to put me between him and the bird goddess.

"Is this some kind of sex thing, or are you trying to kill her?" Awi demanded of Taran, her beaked face somehow horrified. When my disappointed grimace suggested that both were true answers, she violently rattled her feathers. "Never mind. I don't even want to know. Just stop!"

Taran wiped his mouth on his forearm and propped himself up.

"Don't think that I was looking for you in Smenos's palace because I care what happens to you," he warned Awi. "My priestess and I were in the middle of an important discussion. Scram."

Discussion, ha. I'd been prepared to disregard all of Taran's past lies and present threats of violence just because I was thirty seconds away from finding completion with all our clothes still on.

"I've said all I want to say until you've calmed down," I retorted. And taken a bath. And firmly committed to no executions for blasphemy. Probably other things I'd think of when my head was clearer too.

"Did you finally tell him?" Awi exclaimed.

"Tell me—"

"Yes. He joined the mortal rebellion and killed Death."

I wasn't inclined to tell him what he'd been to me—at least not unless he accepted that I'd been right to rebel and he'd been right to help me. He'd never be able to tell me whether he'd meant what he said, and if he hadn't, I didn't want to give him any brilliant ideas on how I might be best manipulated.

If you promise to love me forever, I won't ask any more questions.

He made a strangled groan and scraped himself to his knees, glaring first at me, then at Awi.

"How many people have you told?"

"About two dozen people saw you head up the cliffs to confront Death, and most of them survived," I said, putting my clothing to rights with what I hoped was more serenity than I felt. "Why hide the fact that Taran ab Genna heroically sacrificed himself to destroy our tormentor?"

"How many *immortals* know," Taran said, eyes narrowing.

"I forget we have a different definition of *people*. Just Awi, then. Oh, and Wesha."

"Wonderful," Taran said, eyes closing in dismay. "Just the god-damn bird and the goddess who's willing to kill and blackmail her way to everything she wants. The one responsible for this entire fucking situation, you mean."

That did seem like he'd accepted the truth of what I'd said, at least, which was encouraging.

"Do we need to move again?" I asked Awi, trying to turn back to the situation at hand. Instincts from my time in command. "Did you see which direction the survivors went in? And was there any pursuit? What's the Mountain doing?"

As I peppered her with questions, Taran got to his feet, grim determination in the lines of his body.

"I'll go look at the Mountain. We'll leave for the City when you've rested."

"I'll go with you," I said immediately, but Taran waved me off.

"No, you're going to stay here until I'm convinced that murder-ing the bird and then deflowering you on the floor of this filthy hut is a bad idea."

I blinked but was cheered by the news that murdering me seemed to be off the table, even if parts of me didn't think the rest sounded like a *bad* idea, exactly.

He fixed me with a stern look. "You are going to want to be asleep when I get back."

"And then what are we going to do tomorrow?" I asked, feeling daring.

Taran sighed and put my knife away on his belt.

"That's what I am going to think about while I'm out walking. Because you're right that I'm still stuck in your war, but I'm telling you right now that I'm not dying in it again."

"Good," I said firmly, and this was the second thing I said to-night that seemed to really surprise him.

23

THE MOUNTAIN WAS still on fire the next morning. Orange flames were occasionally visible through the black smoke, and the wind brought cinders that clung to the inside of my nose and throat. Taran said all the Stoneborn were vanished beneath the rock, but he could hear Death's cries below the surface. We had until the Allmother was satisfied with his contrition to prepare for his return.

"It could be a thousand years. It could be a week. The Allmother loves her evil stoat of a baby boy," Awi mused.

"Ah, maternal devotion," Taran said sourly. "I've heard stories about that."

Little immortals had been disappearing for months, Awi eventually told us, the forgotten gods of dried-up springs and abandoned hilltops. The Stoneborn had taken no notice, fully absorbed by their own dwindling storerooms and the silence where mortal prayers had once been.

No wonder Awi had been so desperate to escape when I met her. I found a little sympathy for the bird at last, although her presence in the knot of my hair prevented any continuation of my conversation with Taran, clothed or otherwise. His stormy face said he'd come to no conclusions anyway. It only took three days to get to the City even at the pace of one lame horse and two riders, the weird logic of the Summerlands prevailing over my understanding of its geography. Taran went into the baths as soon as we arrived, stripping without a word of warning—or bothering to close the door. I yelped and scuttled off to the little room he used as a kitchen when he bared the dimples at the base of his spine, mumbling flimsy excuses about finding us something to eat.

He quickly reappeared with his wet hair combed back from his forehead and his skin scrubbed raw and pink. As soon as he was dressed, he headed for the door again.

"Bird," he addressed Awi. "Do you want to come tell Genna what you saw?"

"Better not mention that I was there at all. Genna doesn't like me," she said, shrinking back to her old hiding spot on top of the wardrobe.

"I don't like you either," he said pitilessly, then scrubbed his face with a palm. "Not that you've committed half the capital crimes I apparently did."

"What are you going to tell Genna?" I asked.

"I'm sure you'll be shocked to hear this, but not everything."

"Should I come?" I asked, though I was still filthy, since I was not exactly up to joint bathing with Taran.

"No. I don't want you anywhere nearby when the Peace-Queen starts thinking of what she can throw at Death to pacify him this time. Stay here and don't unlock the door for anyone until I return. Even Marit. *Especially* Marit, if the Allmother has already brought him back."

"But—" I began to argue, not liking the idea of Taran going out unarmed and exhausted when we knew that Death had been snatching immortals off the street to sacrifice.

"Do I need to lock you up again, or can you stay out of trouble for one hour while I find out if we're the first ones back with a story about what happened?" Taran thundered, eyes beginning to crackle with anger.

"I'll just go clean up, then," I said, looking down at my feet with what I hoped was an appropriately contrite expression on my face.

I kept my posture demure until Taran had slammed the door shut and locked it behind him. Then I did exactly what he should have expected I'd do.

I bathed and washed all the ash and soot out of my hair. I put on the least revealing of the green dresses Taran had stolen for me before we left the City. I took two stone knives out of Taran's hidden stash and fastened them to my belt.

And then I sang the door open and headed toward Genna's palace.

TARAN'S VAGUE REFERENCES to cooking and cleaning for him had led me to believe there were domestic facilities underlying the visible buildings in the City, but I wasn't prepared for the maze I found beneath Genna's dormitories. For as empty as the surface of the City seemed, the less-decorated rooms underground were packed and busy with saffron-garbed mortals hard at work.

Nobody challenged my right to walk through the rooms where priests labored for their goddess, silently taking a census of the number of mortals who might be residents in the City. Perhaps a few thousand if the other Stoneborn were supported by as many priests as Genna.

A tiny number, compared to those at risk in the mortal world if Death could force his way through the Gates, but vulnerable sooner.

"Excuse me," I finally asked an elderly peace-priest with peppercorn hair in one of the kitchens. "Do you know where I might find the high priestess?"

He did not release the raw duck whose backbone he was laboriously extracting with a cleaver, but he spared me a kindly glance.

"You must be new. Several of us were high priest before we were
called here," he said, with a trace of wry irony.

"I see," I murmured. This dignified man, whose face had the
sweet appeal of all of Genna's chosen, had once advised our kings
and queens before crossing the sea to spend eternity doing kitchen
chores.

I didn't know what Genna's priests were told before their ordination, but the service I'd anticipated prior to taking my vows was service to my people—and it hadn't involved spatchcocking any poultry.

"Who are you, then? Oh—Taran's girl," the priest said, thinking back only a few weeks.

"Yes," I agreed after a moment, because if I wasn't going to lie,
I couldn't come up with a much better descriptor for what I was
doing in the Summerlands. "Do you know where I'd find Teuta ter
Genna?"

I was directed farther downstairs, to the laundry facilities. It
was humid and warmer the deeper I went, the stone on the walls a
little damp and smelling strongly of lavender and cleaning solvents.
I'd seen a few immortals near the kitchens, coming in for food, but
down below, it was all mortals.

Teuta was in a small room with piles of mending. We'd met the
day I started my surgical training—I was fourteen, years younger
than typical, and very anxious about it. Teuta had come to assist
our temple with removing the diseased half of a teenage girl's co-
lon. She'd healed the incisions so neatly there wasn't even a scar,
and the patient had woken up well enough to walk home with her
parents.

Afterwards, I'd bowed to Teuta and smiled nervously as my
accomplishments were recited by my mentor, and Teuta had promised to assist on my first surgery, after I was ordained. That hadn't

happened, since I didn't take my vows and she fled with the other priests.

Instead, my first surgery had been a month after Ereban, when I tried to fix a shoddy battlefield amputation. There had been no older maiden-priests to advise me, and I'd muttered apologies to Wesha and my patient for my incompetence while thirteen-year-old Hiwa ter Genna assisted, doing her best just to stop the bleeding. After a terrible hour, Taran had strolled in and corrected Hiwa when she stumbled with her blessing, and that was how the rest of my life began.

Today, Teuta's strong, clever fingers were engaged in repairing a line of feathered trim on a decorative cushion, and I felt another sullen burn in my stomach at the use the gods had put us to.

"Iona!" When she noticed me, she did look pleased, at least, though she didn't stop working. "I wondered how you were adjusting. Well, I hope?"

That was a complicated question, and I'd let her draw her own conclusions.

"Teuta, would it be possible to get all of Genna's priests together somewhere? Quickly? The ones who don't know about . . . Ereban. And what's happening now. I need to tell them."

The former high priestess looked down at her mending, smile fading. "Even if I was certain that was a good idea, I'm working right now, and so is everyone else in the building."

"When are you free?" I asked impatiently.

"Next week."

"What about—dinnertime, then," I said, confused. The priests didn't seem ill-kept, just busy.

"We have meals in the dormitory upstairs," Teuta said. "Genna bid us stick to a schedule."

"This is important though. I'm sure she'd understand. Taran's talking to her right now."

"Have him get permission from Genna and come back," Teuta said. When my face said that I still didn't understand, Teuta sighed and put the pillow aside. "He hasn't asked you for any vows, then? That's good."

I paused until I finally understood. Genna's priests had been told to do this work, and their vows of obedience wouldn't permit them to deviate from the schedule even for a good reason.

I hadn't ever thought of myself in rebellion against the gods, plural, no matter what the mortal queen had said. The other gods were known to us chiefly by what they'd left behind. The Shipwright's architectural marvels, the secrets of agriculture and weaving and music that we called gifts from our departed deities. And their blessings, of course, the power we saw wielded by mortal priests who gave as much as they took for the gods in offerings. I'd agreed with Taran that we ought to rebuild the temples at the end of the war, pray for the priests to return and finish training our lost generation of surviving acolytes.

It skittered across the surface of my mind though, as Teuta patiently took her mending back up, that perhaps the queen had been right, and we were better off without the gods. Wesha had given me the blessings I used to win the war and save countless lives, but had she ever deserved the whole of mine in exchange? It wasn't a fair bargain, and I hadn't even understood that I'd been about to make it.

"Is there somewhere down here that's big enough to gather in?"

"The laundry?" Teuta said reluctantly when she saw that I wouldn't abandon the idea. "I could try to convince people to eat their dinner in there."

In the end, she was able to gather only a couple dozen priests in the steam-filled room where large copper cauldrons boiled the linens for Genna's court, an enormous furnace at one end supplying hot water to the laundry and the hypocaust underlying her baths.

A couple of priests were stripped to the waist, shoveling coal to fuel it and paying me no attention when I stood at the cooler end of the room with sweat sticking my hair to my neck.

"I'm Iona," I told them when it was clear I wouldn't be able to draw a larger crowd. "A couple of you knew me when I was called Iona ter Wesha. I was in the high temple at Ereban on the day Death destroyed it."

I didn't lie to them at all, even if I didn't tell the full truth. I described the rebellion without my own part in it. I told them I'd followed Taran to the Summerlands, even if I was vague on the details of timing. But I was very exact when I described what I'd seen at the Shipwright's palace: mortal priests, sacrificed to restore the power of the youngest Stoneborn.

The day after the massacre at Ereban, I'd given a report to the queen. I'd only ever seen her from a distance before, and I was probably still in shock at the time, because I didn't recall being afraid of her. She already knew her daughter was dead, but she hadn't known the exact details, and I'd recited them the way I would have accounted for the facts of a failed surgery.

She went willingly; I tried to stop them; everyone is dead.

These priests of Genna were familiar with my mode of recounting, and they grimly absorbed my words without question until I was done, just as the queen had. But while the queen had risen from her throne to call for someone to bring her a sword, the priests shuffled their feet and waited for me to say more after I said that Death would see them all dead in his bid to rule the world again.

"Does the Peace-Queen know?" Teuta finally asked me when our stare-off lasted more than a few seconds.

"Yes, Taran is telling her right now," I said impatiently. But Genna hadn't done anything to stop Death from making a wreckage of the mortal world. "What are *you* going to do? I don't know how long we have before Death is free again."

"What can we do?" another priest asked skeptically.

I looked around the crowd at a loss. I'd expected a little more initiative from priests who'd once led Genna's cult in the mortal world.

"Does nobody here remember the Great War? What the mortal priests did to survive back then?"

"In Lixnea's cult, maybe," said Teuta, shaking her head. "Nobody here is that old. After Taran was born and Genna wouldn't name his father, Skyfather expelled all her priests in retribution."

I pinched the bridge of my nose. One terrible god's evil at a time, but perhaps all of them, one day.

"We'll start planning a defense, then. With Skyfather's priests too. Anyone else in the City."

It should have been easier to imagine it with dozens of fully trained priests than the handful of scared, injured children I'd started off with after Ereban, but the lost acolytes that had formed the core of our army had been a lot more eager to do what I told them than this group seemed to be.

"Iona," Teuta said, voice firm. "You know that we take a vow of nonviolence as well as obedience. We're not fighters. It'll be up to the Stoneborn to protect us."

I saw movement from the stairwell at the room's entrance. Taran, slipping in the back. I froze, wondering how deep I was in trouble with him, and Teuta's face asked the same question, but all he did was lean against the wall and cross his arms over his chest to watch.

"So, what will you do when Death comes looking for more lives to put on his altar? Just die?" I asked the peace-priests again.

I was sympathetic to their divided loyalties, to the shackles of their immortal vows, but there was always space, within those, to decide who to be and what to do.

"What are *you* going to do?" Teuta tossed it back to me with a nervous, sidelong glance at Taran.

I firmed up my mouth.

"The same thing I did last time," I warned them both. I took a step back, wiped my palms together, and sang the chant:

Hail Death, who kindles flame.

Fire dropped from my hands to the stone floor without incident, but Genna's priests buzzed with muffled protests at my casual violation of the ancient taboo against invoking the blessings of a god who was not my patron.

Genna's vows required them to do no violence, but if they could help a maiden-priest remove a diseased organ, they could light a backfire to deny Death fuel in his war. If they wanted to survive, they would.

"And that's enough for tonight," Taran announced, marching through the crowd to cut the chatter. "Teuta. Always a pleasure. Glad you're looking well." He hooked one arm around the back of my neck and began to drag me toward the exit.

"Practice that blessing. I'll come back tomorrow," I tried to tell Teuta, but I wasn't certain she heard me before Taran muscled me into the stairwell.

24

"YOU COULDN'T WAIT until after dinner before engaging in some light sedition?" Taran asked once the wet evening air was between us and Genna's priests. He didn't sound too angry at me, so rather than answer directly—*if you think that was light sedition, wait until I really get going*—I ignored the second part of the sentence and asked, more hopefully, "There's dinner?"

He hadn't taken his arm off my shoulders, though it was as much companionable as punitive as he steered us back toward Wesha's old quarters.

"Yes, I have acquired our dinner, at great risk to myself, because *my* priestess doesn't cook."

It was hard to parse his mood. A little punch-drunk, maybe, like I'd been the night before. He was often the least serious when he felt most under threat.

"Both of us could cook, actually, and I'd be happy to remind you how. So that you won't have to steal every dinner."

"Where's the fun in that? Skyfather's priests know how to cook but not how to secure their kitchens, and that's good enough for me. Besides, of all your hidden talents, I don't think cooking is the most relevant one, hm? Didn't I ask you once which blessings you knew?"

"And I did offer to set you on fire," I replied, realizing that I felt comfortable strolling toward Taran's rooms with his arm around me. "You used to know more than I did. Certainly Death's first blessing."

"Not anymore. Though I'm certain I was more circumspect about calling other gods' blessings than you just were."

"You taught me that one. It wasn't like we had a death-priest handy."

His stride barely slowed. "But you had at least one acolyte of Genna, to teach you her blessing of healing? I suppose your betrothed wasn't as devoted to nonviolence as those priests back there were."

"Not very, no," I said with a snort. "Did you know that if you sing a rest instead of a triplet in every fourth measure of the blessing that repairs a leaky mitral valve, you'll stop the heart instead of healing it?"

"I still think you'd have more luck with Skyfather's priests. The ones who know how to call lightning."

I absently rubbed my hands together. "Lightning takes at least five minutes of chanting, and the clouds have to be there already or it takes even longer. Genna's blessings are faster, but I'd forgotten the vow of nonviolence. I'll have to think about that."

Taran quietly laughed.

"What?" I asked.

"You. Thinking about your next war." It was dark, but his face was rueful and almost tender, his eyes crinkling at the corners when he looked at me.

"Aren't you thinking about it?" Was *not* thinking about it an option?

"I told Genna and Diopater what happened. Most of what happened. I tried to keep you out of it, though one of the priests back there will probably inform on you forthwith."

I didn't stop walking.

"And?" I asked. I didn't have high expectations, but I did hope they'd look out for their own priests, if nothing else. They had to remember that they hadn't defeated Death in the Great War, only bought the Summerlands a ceasefire with Wesha's hand in marriage.

Taran stroked his neck with his palm. "And nothing. I don't think they believed me."

I closed my eyes and kept walking, borrowing a little of his gallows humor for a moment that needed it.

"Why? Are you considered an untrustworthy person?" I asked sweetly.

"By the Allmother, you're such a brat. No wonder Wesha foisted you off on me," Taran said in his most loving voice, squeezing my shoulders until I squeaked. "No, we didn't actually *see* Napeth sacrifice any immortals on that altar. If he did, the Allmother will handle it herself. And I could just be making up wild stories to cover for Wesha or Marit's deranged attacks on the more respectable Stoneborn, which are things I have done before. I wouldn't take a vow that I was telling the truth."

"No?" I said, struggling a little to keep up the light tone of the conversation with the accusations that had been flung at Taran.

"As you are the primary beneficiary of my ability to lie to Skyfather, my darling little rebel, let's not second-guess that one," he said.

"So they're not going to do anything?" I asked, discovering that I was still able to be disappointed by my gods after everything.

"Well, Skyfather reargued his plan to invade the mortal world and demand sufficient sacrifices to restore order in the Summerlands, which he thought might appease Death as well. Genna wants to wait and confer with the Allmother, once she's calmed down and let loose the children she just dragged into the Mountain. Perhaps one more party will do it."

"You told them one of the Stoneborn was murdered, and a second one wants to launch a war to conquer the world, and there's not a single thing they'll change about what they've been doing?" I repeated, appalled.

"I suppose I could probably convince Diopater's daughters, the Winds, to go to the Mountain and investigate. They were alarmed at my story, and they despise me a bit less than everyone else in his court," Taran said.

There was something in the way he said *convince* that made me look at him sharply.

"Convince them how?" I asked.

Taran pursed his lips and looked away as though I'd asked an indelicate question.

I elbowed him in the stomach.

"How about you come up with a strategy where you keep your clothes on this time," I said, fighting a burst of jealousy.

"I'd be happy to, if *you* come up with a strategy where you don't set anything on fire," he retorted, grabbing my arm and wrapping his securely around it.

"No deal," I said. We walked on. The night was beautiful and silent and empty, but all this empty loveliness was fragile, ready to crack. I didn't know whether it was true that the Allmother had built the Summerlands out of mortal dreams, but those mortals had limited foresight. This was all too flammable.

"And you?"

"What about me?"

"What are you going to do?" I asked.

Taran spared me a curious look. "Well, I bowed and headed out through Skyfather's kitchens, as I mentioned, to get our dinner. And when I realized that my single, solitary priestess had wandered off to preach insurrection, I went to collect her . . . what do you want me to do next?"

"We need to get ready. Evacuate all the people who can't fight across the Sea of Dreams, organize the ones who can to fight back. If there are any of his Fallen or death-priests still in the City, we need to eliminate them so that Death doesn't have the power to sacrifice even one more person on his altar," I said, not abandoning my joking tone, even though it wasn't a joke.

Taran halted, which forced me to stop too. Half my mind had already moved to what he'd brought for dinner. He looked down with a long-suffering expression, even though he wouldn't remember suffering more than a few weeks of my direct approach to difficult questions.

"Is that all?" he asked faintly.

"I have some more concrete ideas, but let's eat before we do anything else," I said, craning my neck toward Wesha's former palace.

"I mean . . . Iona. My darling. That is not a fair request."

My heart squeezed at the real concern behind his tight smile. I'd seen that look before, and I'd always thought it was because he loved me and was afraid where the war would take us.

"I didn't think it had to be fair. You asked what I wanted you to do."

He laughed, another pained noise. "Mortals are fickle. Can't you want something else? Ask me again to dump you at Wesha's doorstep. Better yet, ask me for something I can give you. Jewelry? The head of someone who's offended you?"

"You can do this. We did it before," I pointed out.

"Which is something I am finding . . . difficult to believe."

I gestured at myself in the dark. "Why is it hard for you to believe?"

"You are a single mortal girl, and I'm the youngest of the Stoneborn, one with the unknown and unheralded ability to open locks."

"We also had a couple dozen teenage acolytes and some of the queen's guard." What we didn't have, that I really missed, was Taran's three hundred-odd years of painful survival in this place and the quiet empathy it had sparked in him for other people who had suffered.

"And your betrothed, who caused heart attacks instead of healing them."

"I can do that, if it's necessary," I reassured him, trying to guide the conversation away from any pointed questions about the third person between us, who didn't exist.

"I'm working on one right now," Taran muttered. "What I'm trying to ask is why we, of all people, are the ones who ought to deal with what I'll admit is the rather daunting problem that Death presents. Genna did eventually end the Great War, after all."

I didn't like Genna's solution. I didn't like any of the gods' plans, the ones that always asked for someone else to make the sacrifices.

"I never thought I was the best person to lead the mortal rebellion." I limped faster toward Wesha's palace. My stomach was making audible noises and felt ready to bite out the knobs of my spine if I didn't feed it soon. "I was only eighteen. All I'd ever wanted was to be a priestess of Wesha—to sing at children's ceremonies and treat patients. I didn't want to be in charge."

"Why were you, then?"

"I didn't think that nobody else *could* lead the fight against Death. I thought that nobody else *would* if I didn't," I said, voicing a thought that I'd wrestled with many times, whenever I'd felt scared and stuck. It wasn't like I was totally selfless. I'd wondered more than once what would happen if Taran and I just . . . left. Fled abroad, like most of the nobles. But I had also thought that Death might not stop at the border when there was nothing left to burn.

We reached the dawn-colored palace. Taran didn't say anything else until he'd closed the door to his sitting room. My attention was immediately drawn to the roast pheasant laid out on a sideboard, as well as the endearing image of Taran smuggling it out of Skyfather's kitchens whole, but before I could display my bad table manners again and rip off a wing with my bare hands, I realized Taran was still staring at me, his face thoughtful.

"What?"

He shook his head and went to pull out his mismatched and undoubtedly stolen silver cutlery. "Just imagining you. What you must have been like when I met you."

I took the offered knife to carve off the wing I'd been eyeing, then sighed in satisfaction at the first bite of cold roast poultry. "Same as now," I said, gesturing at myself with the bone. "Just younger. A little more self-righteous, maybe."

"*More* self-righteous?" he said, and I let that fly, because he had brought dinner. "No, I can picture it. The little priestess of Wesha with your white dress and red hair, ordering the entire world to reshape its very foundations just to suit your ideals."

"When you put it that way, I sound obnoxious," I said, mouth full of bird.

"Not at all. I have to think I was dazzled." The crooked line of his mouth made my chest squeeze tight and painful.

I forced myself to chuckle. "I doubt it." It had been a year before he'd said anything. We'd grown close, not started that way— not least because *he'd* been dazzling, and that had made me shy.

I liked holding on to the possibility that he'd fallen in love with the fact of me. I'd never been beautiful, and I woke up grumpy and didn't improve much throughout the day, but I had tried very hard to be good. I'd never lied or broken a promise before Wesha sent me here. The things I thought were worth loving about myself were things he could have only learned over time.

"What, did we not get along?"

"No, we did," I admitted.

He gave me that direct stare under his eyelashes again, like he was trying to peer into my mind. But the things I still held back were the things most precious to me. He'd told me that he loved me more than every beat of his heart. I didn't want to find out that hadn't been true. I didn't want to hear him speculate about what he'd thought of me.

I tried to play it off casually and sat down next to him to eat. I thought I'd managed to move the conversation away to the likely allegiances of the other gods when Death returned from the Mountain, but Taran wasn't easily sidetracked.

"What color was your scarf?" he asked once he'd put the dinner dishes outside his door, where for all I knew they'd vanish the way all clutter seemed to. "The one you said you sent with me."

"Green," I said after a beat, wondering where he was going with it. "You still don't believe me?"

"I don't think you're lying, because you can't," he said, the same pensive expression on his face. "But there has to be more to it. That first day—waking up on Wesha's beach, it's a bit of a blur. I felt terrible. But I do remember the scarf."

"Do you still have it?"

"Somewhere," he said vaguely. "But why your scarf?"

"Your hand was very badly burned," I muttered, tiptoeing along the wound in my soul and miming how Taran must have ended Death's last life with a thrust of my stone knife. "I wrapped it for your funeral."

Taran didn't look away. "But why *your* scarf?"

He was uncomfortably close to asking for the answers I didn't want him to have.

They had to drag me away from your body. It was all I could send with you if I couldn't go too.

"You gave it to me a few weeks before you died. Said it would look nice with my hair," I mumbled, and that true statement was so close to a lie that it burned in my throat.

"I think you stole it," I added, my cheeks heating from the effort of holding back the truth.

"Sounds like me," he said softly.

It could have been my vow punishing me, or maybe it was the lonely note in his voice, but I grabbed his hand hard, the same one that had been scorched almost down to the bone, and wove my fingers with his. That felt like relief, even if part of me demanded more—to weep and kiss his face and tell him I'd cried so hard at his funeral I'd made myself ill.

"If you came back with me, everyone would be . . . so happy to see you. Even our friend Drutalos, who still owes you money."

Taran looked down at our clasped hands, visibly struggling to keep up the same light tone. "I suspect your rebels would be slightly less happy to see me once they realized I wasn't mortal, or there to save you from Death's flames."

I couldn't argue with that, especially with how I'd reacted.

"Maybe, if you could explain it," I said, my voice trailing off.

"If I could explain it," he softly agreed.

I wondered what he pictured when he thought about his funeral. What he was capable of imagining of the mortal world, when the only mortals he knew were me and the priests of the Stoneborn. The idea of it shouldn't make him feel lonely. He'd been loved, and not just by me. If the Allmother really did rebuild the Stoneborn in the shapes they'd died in, he should feel it somehow that he wasn't lonely for the last three years of his last life.

Before I could talk myself out of it, I climbed into his lap and curled his arms around me again. I pressed myself against his chest like I was demanding admittance into my home in his heart after months away. It was what I'd wanted to do the night Wesha sent me here, and my body quivered in relief that I'd finally allowed it.

Taran was surprised, and when he turned to look at his bedroom door, it was obvious that his first idea was that I'd made an untimely and inelegant request to be carried off there.

But I rubbed my forehead against the pulse in his neck until he wrapped me tighter in his embrace.

"Taran, you're alive," I whispered.

There was a little hitch in his breath before he responded.

"I couldn't blame you for having some mixed feelings about that, given everything."

I pulled away just enough to let him see my wide eyes. "No. Not at all. Not even for a single second."

His body finally relaxed at that, and I put my head back on his shoulder so he could stroke my hair for long, quiet minutes. No matter what else happened, I got this. I would still have crossed the sea just for this much of him. This much was a miracle by itself.

Taran recognized my sigh when I slid out of his lap as *good night*, but he held up a hand before I could go.

"Show me Death's blessing again."

I was tired, but I nodded and we rolled the rugs to the side of the stone floor to clear a big enough area.

"Hail Death, who kindles flame," I sang, and we both watched the fire sputter out on the ground.

"Hail Death, who kindles flame," Taran sang, but he didn't make the first two syllables ring like he should have, and nothing happened.

"It's better to copy my intonation exactly until you understand the logic of it," I said, which was what Taran had said when he taught it to me.

He frowned in frustration, but the next time he sang it back in almost my voice, and flame fell from his hands as it had from mine. He watched the embers dissipate between his boots, and by the time they were all gone, he was smiling again.

25

THREE WEEKS LATER, the Mountain still belched smoke and flame into the sky. Death's palaces in the City were quiet and apparently empty, but Taran would not let me go in to check.

Or to make them empty, if they weren't.

"Did I really let you just murder people?" he asked, though the answer should have been obvious by now.

"Oh, Taran, some of our very best times together were killing death-priests," I said, concealed below the hedge that marked the border between Wesha's lawn and Death's.

"Then explain why your boundless sympathy for mortals who made poor choices in their vows runs out with Death's people," Taran whispered with a cautioning grip on the back of my neck, like he expected me to make a berserker run across the lawn to the palace where I'd first landed in the Summerlands.

I turned my head to smile at him. I'd treasured Taran's gentleness, the way it tempered my anger, even if I didn't always agree. "You do care."

"No, I just think this will be a more pleasant place to live if nobody's priests are indiscriminately slaughtered."

Did he still think, after what we'd seen, that there was any living with Death? There hadn't been peace in three hundred years; Death's campaign to destroy the world had just been slower and farther away from the Summerlands before now.

"Death's Fallen, then. There were more in the temple besides the two you buried alive." They would be even more of a threat than death-priests once Death was released by the Mountain. Even more adept with their father's blessings than death-priests, and harder to kill.

"As a former priestess of Wesha, you might be expected to believe that the children of the Stoneborn shouldn't suffer for the sins of their parents. Let's not murder any immortals just for the misfortune of having Death as a father."

I slapped the dirt, frustrated. "Well, what are you going to *let* me do? You know what he plans to do as soon as he gets free."

"I let you do quite a bit, darling," Taran said smoothly.

It irked me because it was true, but it wasn't enough. I was trying to build a firebreak by myself, with one garden trowel.

Once Smenos's people began to stagger into the City, half-broken in mind and body, Genna's priests had been happy to care for them. There were healers who'd gone decades without patients, and when I told them to set up field hospitals, they did what I asked.

When I requested things—maps to plan an evacuation, buckets and sand to fight the fires, food, bandages—they were brought to where I wanted them put, with at most a questioning glance toward Taran, who lurked a step behind me as I limped through the City. Either they were familiar with him from his time as the Peace-Queen's envoy and thought this was all Genna's will, or they were so used to obedience that they'd follow anyone's orders.

What nobody would do was plan with me for a war that would soon return.

The Summerlands were eternal and inflexible. If I dragged a wheelbarrow through a lawn, the rut was gone by the next morning.

If I cut back branches hanging too close to flammable roofs, the trees were just as verdant within a few days. The food didn't rot, the dishes were never dirty, and the City rejected barricades the way it did potholes and broken floor tiles.

It did something to the people who lived here too. Gave mortals immortal life, but made them a part of the fixed idea of the place—the Allmother's plan, I supposed. No one could imagine that anything could change; no one tried to change anything.

A doe-eyed ghost in Genna's golden vestments convinced me that it was no use pressing Genna's *priests* to act.

"Elantia?" I gasped when she shyly presented herself one evening at the laundry.

I'd last seen the queen's daughter bent backwards over Death's altar, that terrible day at Ereban. Her body burnt like an offering, then vanished.

"Teuta said you were here," she said, head bent and hands clasped. "I had to come see for myself."

She had been four years younger than me when she died, but she looked even younger now, her heart-shaped face soft and childish. I'd only known her a little: a vocate in Wesha's temple not because of her abilities or inclinations but because the daughters of the nobility got a reputation for chastity by sheer proximity to maiden-priests.

"How are you alive?" I asked, grabbing her by the shoulders to feel her solidity.

The girl gave me a forced smile. "I don't really know. I remember being called to the front of the temple at midsummer, the fire—not much else, really."

"Is anyone else—the others who died at Ereban, Wesha's priests? Are they here too?" My heart began to pound.

Elantia gently shook her head. "No, just me. I didn't even know what happened until the other priests came from over the sea. I just woke up here, in Death's temple."

Hope died hard for being only a few moments old. Of course not. She had been sacrificed, like Wesha sacrificed me, while all the others at Ereban had simply died. I'd overseen their funerals, sent their bodies out to sea.

But my mind still raced at the possibilities.

"Nobody knows what happened to you. I mean, they all know what happened at Ereban. But nobody came back—oh, Maiden. We have to get word to your mother somehow. We need to get you *home*."

She was the heir to the throne and the reason the queen's anger at the gods had never been quenched. If she came back . . .

Elantia fitfully smoothed her dress, face still lowered. "I'm a priestess of Genna now."

I made a noise of startled dismay. A royal daughter might take Skyfather's vows, or even Death's, but not the Peace-Queen's. Genna's priests could marry, but mostly wed other peace-priests—the demands of Genna's service left little of a life to spare for other causes.

"Nobody knew what to do with me. A mortal sacrifice. It hadn't happened in hundreds of years. Some death-priests said I ought to belong to them, like I was a goat someone had brought as an offering." Her mouth twisted. "Genna said I could choose whose vows I'd take, but I had to take someone's."

Genna's kindness looked a lot like greed to me. My hands curled into fists.

"You know that your mother . . . that the queen—" It was on the tip of my tongue to tell her how the queen had pulled down all the temple walls and destroyed the sacrificial altars to every god in vengeance for her slaughtered child. It was becoming harder and harder for me to say she'd been wrong to do it.

The princess squirmed. "Is my mother well?"

"Yes," I said, trying to be gentle. "Though she still grieves for you. I last saw her a few weeks before I came here. She's rebuilding the port at Lubridium as the new capital."

"I'm glad to hear it," Elantia whispered. She gave me another forced smile. "I'd be happy to help with whatever you're doing here, even though I'm not a very good singer. I never could get any of Wesha's blessings, and I'm not much better with Genna's."

I put my hands on my cheeks. It shouldn't be up to this girl to defend the City from Death. Where was Skyfather with a quiver full of lightning bolts? Where was Lixnea in her silver chariot?

Genna couldn't buy an end to every war with one of her children.

"If anything happens, you just run. In the opposite direction of any danger," I told Elantia.

She nodded weakly, and I directed her to one of the groups that was packing supplies into smaller bundles.

Taran had decided that I could be trusted to go to Genna's laundry on my own, or more likely decided that Genna's priests could be trusted not to report my attempts to foment insurrection, so I had to stomp back across the City to find him.

He was out on the lawn in front of Wesha's palace, stripped to the waist and skin faintly glistening in the fading light of sunset, practicing with a jeweled dagger. He'd spent hours a day at this since our return, the rest of them practicing the blessings of the other Stoneborn as fast as I could teach them.

Taran was getting ready for war, at least. He moved with more grace, more power than any mortal could, and there was joy in the lines of his body as he discovered it again. Two steps to the side, turning faster than my eye could track to meet one imaginary blow, ducking and spinning again to catch a second. His beauty still caught me by surprise sometimes, even after years of it, still took the breath from my lungs and made me freeze to capture the image in my mind.

There was a solid chance he was showing off, but I was a performer too, and I did like a show.

When he stopped the exercise and stuck the dagger in the earth, I clapped like I would for a brilliant aria. He swaggered over with a self-assured grin.

"I know that face. You want something," he said, rubbing his sweaty forehead against my cheek to make me squeak and laugh as I pushed him away.

"I do," I admitted, keeping him at arm's length with a palm on his chest . . . and fighting the urge to sweep that hand down his stomach and explore how the rest of it felt against my palm.

"Let me guess. You want to go sit with me on the northern terrace, where the first stars of the evening will appear over the tops of the cypress trees at dusk," he said in a grandiose voice.

I tipped my head back and smiled at his good mood.

"Now that you mention it, sure, yes."

"And you want to play something beautiful on the kithara for me, because it's been days since I heard you sing and I've already stolen dinner for us."

"That too," I agreed.

"But that's not all. You want to pull back your lovely hair with a new rope of pearls to match your blue linen gown, because Marit will never miss them," he said, casting a disparaging eye over the nondescript wool smock I had on.

"No sign of Marit, then?" I asked, imagining that was the real reason Taran had gone looting in the sea god's vacant palace.

"Not yet. I suppose the Allmother's busy," Taran said, glancing at the smoking Mountain with a little chill. He shook himself. "What did you really want, or should I keep guessing?"

I almost didn't want to ask him now. I wanted to have that dinner with him and flirt and pretend that nothing would change here, except perhaps what he felt about me.

"Would you take someone—someone who wasn't me—to the Painted Tower?" I asked instead of doing what I wanted.

Taran took a step back, letting my hand slide off his chest. He paused, not because he was considering it, but just to indicate politeness.

"No," he said, without asking *who*.

I firmed my jaw. I hadn't really expected otherwise, but it had been worth checking. I changed my request.

"Then I want to talk to Genna."

"Also *no*, but out of morbid curiosity, why?"

"I need to get as many of Genna's priests away from here as possible before Death returns. I can't make them take the threat seriously."

Taran scoffed. "I don't even steal food from the Peace-Queen, and you want me to steal her priests?"

"She doesn't need all those priests. They only came when the war started—she can send them home."

"Somehow I managed without you around for all these years, but perhaps Genna's grown attached to her priests too."

"Taran!" I kept trying, even though he was impossible when he was in a mood like this. "Genna has the heir to the mortal throne *serving* her."

He looked unimpressed. "You'll recall that until recently, she had *me* serving her. It's survivable."

"But Genna forced her to take vows after she was sacrificed. You, of all people, ought to sympathize."

"What does my sympathy do for her?" Taran asked stiffly.

"Let me ask Genna to let her go. If Genna wants mortal worship restored, returning the queen's daughter would go a long way toward convincing the queen to lift the ban."

More importantly, it would get more priests out of harm's way, once Death and his allies were free again. They were defenseless here.

"And how am I supposed to explain why you know that?" Taran said, rolling his eyes.

I nearly said, *you figure that out, you're good at lying,* but he really hadn't done much of that recently, so I sighed and waited. I just had to push him. I had to remind him. He wasn't the person Genna had tried to make him into.

"You think you can gaze up at me with big brown eyes and I'll do whatever you want again?" he asked scornfully. "My memory is short but it isn't that short."

"No," I said. "I think you'll do it because you're a good man, and you *do* care what happens to people, and you always did."

The noise he made wasn't an agreement, but he didn't dismiss the idea out of hand either. It wasn't until he'd stalked away, all ideas of dinner and a beautiful evening put to the side, that I realized with a little glow of excitement he hadn't tried to ask for something in exchange for any of it.

I NEARLY RAISED the question of Elantia and the other peace-priests again, because Taran didn't say anything for days, but one evening he handed me a pile of white fabric and told me to dress myself like a maiden-priest. We were both expected at Genna's court.

"I know that as my priestess, you think of nothing but how to best secure my comfort," he said, worry making him flippant. "So as you consider what you want to say to Genna, please remember that I would find it *very unpleasant* to watch her liquify your bones because you shared your positive opinion of the mortal rebellion."

Even though I'd asked him to set up the audience, I took a cue from his edginess and stiffened in instant apprehension about speaking with the Peace-Queen.

"What have you told her about me?" I asked as I put on the wool dress and bleached linen apron for the first time in months. It felt strange to dress as a maiden-priest now; I'd never felt the Maiden's presence in my life less.

"Don't worry about that. If she asks you a question, don't lie to her. I told her you served Wesha until Death destroyed your temple, and then you came here for me. She has no reason to object to that. But also remember that Genna will liquefy *my* favorite body parts if she thinks I was complicit in any of your more unfortunate life choices," he called from the other room.

Wonderful. Cowbirds were better parents. They at least didn't attack their own young.

"So what do you want me to say?" I asked, coiling my hair up tightly, the way I had every day that I'd worn these clothes. I barely recognized myself in the mirror as the acolyte who'd walked into the temple at Ereban years ago.

"I don't want you to say anything! But if you could support the idea that I have been diligently attempting to keep both the mortal world and this one from tumbling into chaos"—with this he came into my room, scowled at my bound hair, and began pulling the pins out—"perhaps we might both make it home tonight in one piece?"

"So she knows . . ." My voice trailed off as his hands brushed out the waves of my hair, his heat palpable against my back. We were framed in the mirror, me in the plain white dress, him behind me with a jeweled pin on his horrible golden cloak. One of us was still in disguise, but which one had changed?

The maiden-priest and the Peace-Queen's son. He looked more the part than I did.

"What?" he asked when he saw me watching his reflection in the mirror.

I looked away. "Just thinking that you must have stolen some poor farmer's clothes and then *rolled* in the dirt before I met you."

"Was I really convincing as a mortal?"

"Well, you convinced me."

"Did I have an exciting backstory?" His fingers rested on my hair as he appeared interested in the idea for the first time. I was reluctant to say more, but I couldn't think of a good reason to refuse.

"No, you didn't ever say where you'd come from."

"You must have thought *something*."

I sighed, wishing I hadn't brought it up at all. "You knew all the blessings of Genna, but you were too old not to be ordained. I thought you might have left her temple because you wanted a home and family."

This answer seemed to satisfy him, and he got up to return with the silver combs he'd attempted to give me during my first week here.

He toyed with my hair under the guise of putting the combs in, and I closed my eyes at the pleasure of his fingertips on my scalp. Nobody but Taran had ever cared if I looked nice, so long as I was clean and neat, and I'd missed his knuckles stroking along the side of my neck.

Look at this scarf I got you, nightingale.

You found it! The only color in the whole world that goes with my hair.

Do you want a dress to match for our wedding?

"Did you ever want that, or was it strictly '*justice or death*' from the start?" Taran jarred me from the memory, raising a half-mocking fist in salute.

"Justice or death?"

"Just wondering if you always planned to go out in a blaze of glory to escape your fate. You can't possibly have wanted to spend your life diagnosing colic in farmers' screaming infants in the event you lived through the rebellion. I should have offered you a third option."

"No, you've got it wrong," I heatedly responded, still startled. "I was going to be married. I was going to have my own home. I was—"

"With a plum tree, yes, I do remember. But that was what someone else promised you, not your idea."

"Doesn't mean I didn't want it," I said, squirming when he held me in place with his hands on my shoulders. His voice had been gentle, but his expression was more dangerous than usual.

I *had* wanted it; it had been the beautiful dream that sustained me through the worst nights of the campaign. I would lie awake, watching the embers of the campfire dwindle, and think about what I'd plant in our garden and what color I'd paint our front door.

"Do you still though? You'd like to go home with your beloved, have some simple mortal life together?"

There wasn't an easy answer to that.

"I don't—it doesn't matter. Death is going to get free at some point, and that's more important than what I want."

Taran's raised eyebrow said he didn't believe me.

"It seems to me that the priests of your temple died, your lover died, *I* died, and then you promptly threw yourself into the sea in the last of a series of very thinly considered ventures with the likely side effect of a heroic death. I can't imagine that little mortal life was ever big enough for you to want to live for."

I pressed my lips together in protest. He was wrong. He didn't know better—and couldn't remember. It only sounded horrible to him because he couldn't remember enough of the mortal world to imagine it.

Maybe Genna's immortal son was never going to learn stonemasonry and build me a little house by a creek and help me fill it with fat babies. He *was*, if I could manage it by sheer force of will, going to end the war like he promised. He was going to realize that he was, in his real soul, unselfish and loving.

My dreams were not getting any smaller, at least.

Taran ran his hands lightly down my arms, finally linking them loosely around my body when I shivered at the sensation. He propped his chin on top of my head and considered our embrace in the mirror.

"That's alright, darling. That's what you have me for. Wanting to live." He examined my appearance one more time. The concealing white fabric, the tumbling hair. The defiant expression.

"You should take this off," he said, and I didn't realize he had a finger and thumb on my ring until he was already sliding it from my hand.

I cried out and tried to put a protective hand over it, but it was too late. He already had the ring in his palm, examining it with the critical eye of a habitual thief.

"That's mine," I said loudly, trying to snatch it back.

"I'll give it back," he said in a soothing voice. "I don't want Genna getting sidetracked and wondering who the little priestess I brought here from the mortal world thinks she's going to marry."

This explanation didn't calm me down, barely made sense.

"I'll wear gloves," I said, reaching for it again. I'd never taken the ring off from the moment he'd put it on, and my heart was already twisting at its absence.

"In the summer?"

I made another distressed noise and turned around.

"I'll wear it on a different finger."

Taran was beginning to look annoyed. "It's not even very nice. The finish is uneven. Your betrothed should have been embarrassed to propose with that ring."

"Our friend Drutalos ab Smenos *made* that ring," I said, nearly stomping my good foot when Taran held it out of my reach. "Hiwa gave him her earrings, and Dousonna ter Diopater gave him the silver pin from her cloak. Drutalos stayed up all night working on it so that we could take our vows the very next day."

This failed to impress. "And where was I, as everyone else covered for your penniless suitor?"

I paused, realizing that I was close to dangerous territory.

"You were there," I said, cheeks heating. I stopped grabbing for the ring in his hand.

The side of Taran's mouth quirked in dark humor. "But I didn't contribute anything? I must have looked incredibly petty. Did I not approve?"

I was not immune to the irony of Taran imagining that he'd been jealous, but bursting into nervous laughter was not going to get me out of his line of questions.

Truthful words wouldn't help either.

You seemed really happy about it, in fact.

Taran had been proud and beaming for our vows, then uncharacteristically wine-drunk after a few dozen toasts, enough to let his hands roam in a way that younger me had found very thrilling. I'd spun his ring on my finger and smiled until my cheeks hurt.

Taran took my silence as agreement.

"So I didn't approve," he decided with some satisfaction. "I'm sure I didn't think he was good enough for you."

"And you should have found me someone better?" I curled my lower lip over my teeth to hide a smirk, because if I didn't get to enjoy this small joke at his expense, I really didn't have enough to live for.

Taran hummed thoughtfully, then tucked my ring into his belt pouch.

"I should have gotten you a nicer ring, at least," he said, holding out his arm to escort me from the room.

26

THE PALACE WHERE Genna lived was the largest in the City, visible from any point within it, but I'd never been inside. The forest of gilded columns that held up the green slate roof stretched high above our heads and as Taran and I slowly approached, I could finally appreciate its true size.

This late in the day I was limping badly, but that only gave me more time to gawk at the curtains of blossoms that hung down from a ceiling that vanished in the growing shadows. Flowering plants had been trained to climb over every surface, and even the tiled floors were spread with a springy moss that wafted green musk with each step. The only illumination came from blown-glass lamps set in iridescent clusters on the floor, and the under-lighting turned faces into masks.

Music and conversation spilled out into the evening from every direction; there were no walls to the palace, only pierced wooden screens that trellised more flowering plants, and alcoves created by drapes of golden fabric that twisted around the columns without any beginning or end. Most places in the City felt empty, or at least under-full, but Genna's palace was crowded and alive.

As soon as we stepped under the roof, Taran reached across his body to cover my face with his free hand, fingers spread to leave me only a tiny crack of vision.

"Eyes forward," he said.

I thought he was making a joke about the scene. It sounded like a large party was going on, a wilder one than Lixnea had hosted for the dark night of the Moon, because there was a rowdier edge to the laughter and a harder beat to the music that swirled around us. The air smelled like floral perfume and warm bodies, but it wasn't wholly unfamiliar to me.

"Stop it," I complained, tossing my head to dislodge his palm. "I have been in temples of Genna before, you know."

As the chief fertility goddess of the pantheon, her temples had murals that ranged from merely suggestive to quite explicit, and her rites could span the same spectrum. Young acolytes of the Maiden had been advised not to look too closely at what was going on if Wesha's service took us there. We just delivered the babies; we didn't need to know where they came from.

I'd looked anyway. So I was prepared.

"And you must have been so brave about it, my darling, but I'm sure you don't want to see this."

I made a noise of frustration. I was going to trip and get grass stains on my dress. "I'm a virgin because I was in a celibate order, not because I'm a prude."

"You are all those things, and there's nothing wrong with that; in fact, it gives me something to think about at night. But trust me on this, don't look."

I yanked at his wrist until Taran gave a shrug as though to say it was my funeral and took his hand off my eyes. After a moment, I wished he hadn't.

The statues and mosaics visible through the moss were what I'd expected, and maybe some of the embraces I could just make out in shadowed corners. I'd known it was a party, with performers and drinking and dancing. I'd known that Genna's followers were un-inhibited.

But for every golden goblet of wine that brushed lips, for every hand that bent to strings or drums in music, there were lips that touched bare skin instead. Hands that clutched at shoulders or thighs. Heads bent not in conversation but in ecstasy. Everywhere. In twos and threes and more, in shapes I recognized and some my mind reeled at. As casually as an ordinary guest might accept a drink or attend to a singer's performance.

I could still have pretended to be unfazed, even for the sheer scale of it . . . but for the number of entangled bodies that were dressed or half-dressed in Genna's saffron livery. Mortal priests caught in immortal arms. Not just pouring the wine or making the music, as I'd expected, but pressed against vine-wrapped columns or into beds of loose cushions and flower petals.

"Oh," I said, and the sadness in my voice made Taran look at me sharply.

I was tempted to hide my face in his shoulder, but if the peace-priests could bear this in their eternal service, I could stand to look. The immortals, for their part, probably wanted to be looked at if they were doing this in public.

We walked farther inside in mutual silence, though I was examining the faces of the priests for signs that they were fighting against their vows, and Taran's attention was locked on mine.

"I did warn you," Taran said after a few minutes.

"You . . . did."

This is an orgy would have been a more helpful warning. But I did appreciate the effort.

Taran needlessly bent down to adjust my hand on his arm, although he was used to helping me balance at this point.

"Genna's power isn't as obvious as Diopater's," he said in a low pitch. "But this is why she's queen of the Stoneborn—they all come to her and set aside their little squabbles and rivalries while they're here. And she wins them over, makes them see things her way. She's the real ruler in the Summerlands."

I made a faint noise of unamused understanding. What was a lightning bolt compared to the allure of a really good party? If eternity ever stretched too long, there would still be the novelty of some new embrace in a corner of Genna's palace. Maybe everything else fell into routine.

"You sound like you approve," I whispered.

"It's better than Diopater's method of solving problems, don't you think?"

I didn't answer, instead considering a knot of revelers who stumbled almost naked toward a woman who was giving a giggling toast to a small crowd while wearing only a lopsided wreath of orange blossoms.

Didn't these people—and most of them were immortals, minor herding gods and flower spirits, but still people—know there was going to be a war? Couldn't they see the smoke on the Mountain? Didn't they see the empty spaces in the City, feel the ground thinning and the Summerlands shrinking? This wasn't real peace, this was pretending. They ought to put their clothes on and find the weapons they put down after the last time Death attacked.

But that wasn't what I found painful about the scene.

This wasn't what Genna's cult was supposed to be for. Hiwa ter Genna had expected to spend her life judging inheritance disputes and matchmaking for merchants' daughters. If anyone had ever suggested she'd keep the peace naked, on her knees, she might have questioned those principles of nonviolence.

Hiwa came and told me the first time she'd kissed a boy—also the first time she'd kissed a girl. She'd looked happier than anyone here tonight.

"I'm sure they'd rather do this than the laundry or the cooking," Taran added, nodding at a peace-priest who was teasingly braiding a violet into the beard of a green-skinned immortal. The man didn't look unwilling, but if Genna had commanded him to be here and entertain her guests, he probably wasn't allowed to frown.

"Are you? Sure?"

It wasn't an accusation, but Taran still fell silent.

He wasn't sure.

"Genna's priests have to obey her," I said softly. "Even if she asks them if they want this—how free are they to say no?"

If I thought about it that way, what was going on here was just as monstrous as what had been done to Smenos's priests. Smenos had used his priests' bodies once, for sacrifice. Genna used them over and over.

After another moment of stormy reflection, Taran tilted his face down to me, dark eyebrows lowered. "Do you want me to quit asking you, then?"

That hadn't been the point I was making, and he looked so concerned that I answered quickly.

"No, I don't mind."

That was a less-than-full-hearted endorsement, less than the full truth, and my vows twisted uneasily until I amended my words. "No, I mean . . . I don't want you to stop asking me."

There was nothing stopping me from saying no to Taran. And I still wanted, someday, to be able to say *yes*.

He relaxed at my reassurance, began to nod at people he knew, but the further my mind traveled down this road, the worse it got.

"Did anyone ever ask you?" I said when he noticed that my face was still grim. I couldn't look at these beautiful, ageless creatures without imagining a small, raven-haired boy living in this palace with no other children. Later bound to Genna's will just as much as her priests. Lixnea had called Genna's service hard—I had a good idea of how he'd spent it.

"I don't remember."

Certainly true, but not the real answer. He didn't know.

He sighed and tossed his head back when my expression hardened. "Please, *please*, Iona, do not start something tonight. No fires, no rebellions, no accusations. I don't need you to feel sorry for me, much less defend me three hundred years after the fact."

"I would have though. Defended you. Someone should have."

The look Taran gave me in response was equal parts dismayed and tender, but when I stuck my chin out stubbornly, he ran a featherlight touch over my hand where it rested on his arm, his fingertips lingering on the empty spot where his ring used to be.

"I know," he said, and I couldn't help but hear an echo in that of all the times he'd ever said he loved me.

THE CENTER OF the palace was lower than the rest of the structure and open to the night sky above. From the oculus, a curtain of water fell from rooftop cisterns and created an audience chamber whose walls were made of mist, the droplets and sound separating us from the crowd of revelers.

I smelled standing water before my feet found it, the carpet of moss giving way to a thick layer of water lilies in pink and white. It soaked the hem of my dress and slowed our approach, but gave me time to assess the reclining figure on an island of woven reeds, surrounded by a half circle of kneeling peace-priests.

Everything about her was lushly rounded, from the perfect oval of her face to her curved body, obscured more by chains of gemstones and sprays of blossom than the wrap of raw gold silk over her breasts. Flower vines grew up through the reeds like supplicating hands, and they twined slowly around her thighs as though offering a lover's caress. From time to time, Genna would reach down and stroke one of the blooming flowers, then pluck it and toss it aside. Something about the gesture made my stomach hurt.

Genna's idols portrayed her variously, depending more on the carver's idea of beauty than any canon of her appearance. A halo of black curls to one, burnished copper skin to another. Perhaps everyone saw something different. For myself, I couldn't see a pinnacle of feminine beauty but only the immortal power of the Stoneborn. A woman with golden hair—not gold like a very fair-skinned woman might have, but the gold of metal and stone—and violet eyes like gemstones. For all of her peaceful surroundings, I reminded myself that Genna was born from the stone of the Mountain no less than Death, and she was just as dangerous.

It was hard to see any of her in Taran or in my memory of We-sha. She didn't look old enough to be their mother, for one thing, or perhaps it was that the lush sweetness of her pouting mouth and little folded hands wasn't reflected in the lines of her two youngest children. Taran was beautiful too, but his beauty was made up of the many hard, sharp edges to his face and shoulders, and the dark, shadowed sweep of his eyelashes owed nothing to Genna's indulgent smile as we came to stand before her.

When we were a few feet away, Taran halted and bowed precisely at his waist. At first I copied him, but at Genna's expectant stillness, I fell painfully onto my knees in the water and bent my head.

Genna wanted her petitioners low and *wet*, it seemed.

"My priestess, Iona, as you requested, Peace-Queen," Taran said, pitching his voice very soft, perhaps hoping that nobody beyond Genna would hear him.

"Come a little closer, mortal girl, let me see you," Genna said after a moment.

I wasn't certain what the protocol was, but I wasn't willing to crawl, so I got to my feet and walked to the edge of the dais of reeds, which put my head on the same level as Genna's.

Her expression was contemplative but not very impressed as she looked me over. Both Genna's and Wesha's cults recruited among the spare children of poor peasants, but I'd been told more than once that I lacked either the looks or the sweet nature to have been taken in by Genna's temple, and I wondered if the goddess was coming to a similar conclusion.

"My son tells me you sing," she said, and I jerked a little to hear her describe Taran that way. It shouldn't have been surprising, but Taran rarely referred to the other Stoneborn by their familial relationships.

"I do," I said after a beat.

"Beautifully," Taran added from behind me.

Genna looked again at my hands and face, then she nodded with a little frown of dismissal. I took that as leave to back up, not stopping until I felt Taran's fingers spread protectively against my waist.

I kept my expression neutral as Genna raised two fingers and beckoned at one of the priests to refill her goblet—made of iridescent stone, the same as Taran's stolen knives.

I had a sudden rush of anger against her, for Taran's sake and mine. Even if the other Stoneborn had emerged fully formed from the Mountain, Taran had been young once, like a mortal child. He'd deserved better, just as her priests did, as even Wesha had.

I would never have gotten on with my mother-in-law, Taran. No wonder there was no mention of inviting her to the wedding.

"Where were you trained?" she asked, drinking from her cup before pressing it directly back into her priest's hands.

"At Wesha's temple, goddess," I said, not daring to look at Taran before answering. He'd told me not to lie; I hoped he knew what he was doing.

"Why didn't you take your vows to her?"

"Death killed her priests. There was nobody left to administer my vows."

"But he didn't kill you?"

It took all my effort not to lick my lips. I was walking a very fine line. "Taran found me first. He protected some of the remaining acolytes of the other Stoneborn after your priests left."

"My softhearted child," Genna said of Taran, nodding slowly at my incomplete truth. "And so now you are his. I suppose there's a little symmetry in that. Wesha's last priest, his first."

"Peace-Queen," Taran said, clearing his throat. "You wanted to talk to her about whether your priests ought to return."

Genna did not like being prompted, but she pursed her mouth only momentarily before continuing.

"I believe you are the last one to make the crossing. The last one who remembers it, anyway. Tell me of the state of the mortal world. Are they doing very poorly?"

"Yes, goddess," I said, swallowing past my dry mouth. "When I left, we expected a famine soon. The rains did not come. The sailors' nets were coming up empty. The herds had yet to recover from our sacrifices to Death."

A few other immortals had begun to creep closer, shamelessly eavesdropping on my conversation with Genna. The goddess nodded again, hands still folded primly together.

"But if the mortals long for our blessings, why do they not sacrifice to us and beg our mercy?" she asked, softly concerned. "I hear only whispered prayers on the wind that brings the dust from their barren fields."

"I—I think that many believe the gods have abandoned them," I said slowly. "They prayed for peace and prosperity, but Death gave them only fire and destruction. Then your priests left and never returned. If they could see some sign of your care—"

I wasn't certain when it was supposed to be my opportunity to plead my case, but I didn't sense that Genna's attention span was very long.

"My care is evident in the very existence of mortals on their soil," Genna said, voice a little sharper.

Taran's hand was stiff on my lower back. He was poised to excuse us if I said anything more, but if this was my only chance, I had to make it count.

"Why not try telling them?" I asked, attempting to sound meek. "Send your priests, send the mortal queen's daughter home, and let them spread the message that the gods will still answer mortal prayers. That you still have the power to heal their world with your blessings."

"I sent Taran to tell them," Genna said, eyes narrowing at him.

"Sent me with a slightly different message," he replied in a somewhat less deferential voice.

Genna frowned and rubbed her dainty fingers along the stem of a bloodred anemone, looking between the two of us.

"It has been a long, long time since the mortals have seen any god but Death," Taran added. "They only knew you through your priests, who are now gone. Even their memories of your blessings diminish with every year."

I didn't dare give him a look of gratitude.

"I did my best to calm Diopater's anger," Genna said after a thoughtful pause. "I did not believe the mortals had turned away from us out of spite, but out of a lack of understanding—I believed that they did not know how much they depend upon us for their lives. But I hear you say that time alone will not be enough to mend this divide. If they have forgotten us, we must remind them."

My breath caught with the hope that she would agree to send back her priests. The mortal queen would not be pleased to see a challenge to her power land on her shores, but if she got her child back because of it—

If it wasn't too late to prevent a famine—

If I could get the mortal priests out of the Summerlands before Death turned his sights on the City—

I was so absorbed with the prospect that for once, someone had seen reason, that I nearly missed Genna's next words.

"We will go to the house of the Moon and discuss what is to be done about Wesha's blockade," Genna announced, standing up. "This division has benefitted neither group. Both the Stoneborn and the mortals have forgotten the Allmother's laws, and I will tolerate it no longer. I will instruct both Wesha and the mortals, as needed, until I have restored peace across the entirety of the world. Wesha must open the Gates, and I must cross the Sea of Dreams again. The world must be as it once was."

"I'm not sure that you need to go that far," I tried to say, but my words were lost in the applause of the other immortals standing nearby.

"Don't argue, she's made up her mind," Taran muttered into my ear while the noise covered his words.

Flower vines slithered up Genna's body to obscure her bare skin, then trailed behind her like a cloak as she stepped down into the water and delicately approached Taran to cup his cheek.

He pasted a worshipful smile on his face, one he had to have practiced in a mirror.

"Perhaps I expected too much of you, asking you to fix what Wesha had done all on your own. But only because we both had such high hopes for you," Genna told him fondly. "And it brings me joy to see you prosper. Mortal devotion has grown so rare, when it is all that makes the long years tolerable. I am glad you have a priest now, even if it leaves Wesha without a single one to her name."

I frowned at Genna as Taran wrapped his arm more closely around me, no doubt feeling a little possessive in light of Genna's description of my devotion as a thing that could be acquired like a horse or a cloak.

"Would you like to speak with Wesha before I do?" Genna offered.

"No, Peace-Queen." His tone was icy, and a hint of honest sadness crossed Genna's face in response.

"I suppose I can't blame you. Wesha was a sweet little girl—I don't know how she could have turned so cruel. After all the favor I gave her too."

Taran stiffened as Genna continued her musings.

"Do you think, after the Allmother has reminded Napeth of the strength of her laws, that you ought to try speaking with him before he does something dramatic again? I sometimes wonder if I wronged him, all those years ago."

How had *Genna* possibly wronged Death? Was she supposed to deliver a happy, grateful bride in exchange for the end of Death's campaign of conquest? Punish Taran even harder for delivering the means for Wesha to defend herself?

The set of his features did not alter with Genna's words, but I knew the lines of Taran's body, and it was fury that further hardened them. He replied very carefully.

"No, Peace-Queen. If you really thought there was anything Death wanted to hear from me, I assume you would have commanded me to say it to him, all those years ago."

She wouldn't find any impertinence in his words, but Genna recognized the shift in Taran's mood just as I did. I found myself holding my breath, hoping that she wouldn't take offense. Her power filled the room, clogging my nose like the scent of her blooming palace.

She smiled and let the moment dissipate.

"You're right, of course."

Genna ran a last finger across Taran's cheekbone in farewell, perilously close to his eye, and nodded that we could depart.

THE PROLONGED SOAK in the cold water of Genna's audience chamber meant that I was all but hopping one-legged by the time Taran and I emerged from the forest of columns. As soon as we were outside, he whooped, swept me off my aching foot, and tossed me over his shoulder, jogging a few steps in what I supposed was pure relief that he'd gotten me out before I told Genna that she ought to be locked in a pit for abusing the trust of her son and her priests.

I pounded on his back with my fists until he pulled me forward into the easy sling of his arms.

"I don't think that could have gone better," he announced. "Nobody is dead, nothing is on fire—I even think she liked you. How should we celebrate? Wine? Song? I know—I'll steal one of those roast pheasants you like, and you can sit on my knee while we eat it."

When I curled my hands under my chin instead of teasing him back the way he clearly wanted, it wasn't because I didn't like the way he laughed while afraid. I'd always loved him for that, just as I'd loved him for trying, despite what must have been his own misgivings, to help us.

But I couldn't move past the image of the Stoneborn walking mortal shores again. Reclaiming temples that had been turned to palaces, demanding tribute that had been promised to mortal rulers instead.

"What if I just made things worse?" I mumbled into Taran's warm throat.

He readjusted his hold on me before answering, careful not to pull my hair as he braced for the long walk back to the palace he'd stolen from Wesha.

"Oh, darling, you can't think like that."

His tone was still light and affectionate, and it reassured me.

"Do you mean it will be a good thing if Genna returns to the mortal world? Or do you think Wesha will still hold the Gates shut no matter what Genna does next?"

"I have no idea. I just meant that it's no use wondering after the fact whether you made things worse—perhaps you might try thinking about it *before* you attempt to dramatically alter the course of the world?"

And that stung, but he wasn't wrong. He could have told me that several times over the last three years, probably should have. It made me clutch him tighter.

Hearing uncomfortable truths might not be as familiar as his strong arms keeping me safe, but it gave me some hope as he carried me home that it meant we'd both live this time.

27

BY THE TIME Skyfather and the Peace-Queen departed for the Moon's domain, I'd managed to convince myself that it would be for the good if Genna led her priests back to the mortal world before Death could attempt worse. That morning, I'd been shaken awake before dawn by a tremor strong enough to crack the ceiling plaster and spill dust onto my face. I followed the sound of Taran's footsteps outside and found him barefoot and shirtless in the dew, watching the plume of smoke out of the Mountain. It was closer than it had been when I arrived—not just a distant smudge on the horizon, but a defined cloud of smoke that flared and contracted. The Summerlands were shrinking, day by day.

"It's fine," he said to a question I hadn't asked. "Go finish packing."

It was reassuring to see the ceremony of the Stoneborn's procession: the rows of priests in saffron and purple singing hymns in complex harmony, immortals carrying silk banners and playing pipes, and Skyfather's solid gold chariot pulled by a team of eight enormous horses. Genna made anemones bloom beneath her priests' feet, and the scent of the crushed petals covered the bitter tang of the breeze. Even the sunlight was brighter in their presence.

If the oldest gods landed on the barren, mortal shores promising the return of rain and growing things, it was surely not so far past the days when they ruled on Earth that we could not be reconciled. Paying tribute to the gods was no different than paying tribute to a queen—I didn't delude myself by thinking that I would have had anyone standing behind me as I faced Death if people hadn't been starving. If Genna's message when she arrived was anything but vengeance, mortals would answer it. Her cruelty landed on those closest to her—ordinary mortals would only know her through her beauty and her blessings.

I was content to ride in the back of a supply wagon and think more about it. The sunlight on my face and the pretty picture of the immortal host had almost quieted my underlying churn of worry about the inevitable conflict with Death.

There was a stir of activity as Taran pulled up his chariot to fall back to my position, matching the high-stepping pace of the two horses he controlled to the plodding one of the team of red-spotted oxen that pulled my cart. My heart lifted, and not just because he looked like a child's story of a magical prince with his hands on the reins and the wind snapping his hair around his cheekbones.

I wasn't alone in this.

"What's happening?" I asked when I heard a horn from the front of the procession. We'd been on the move for only a few hours and needed to keep up the pace if we expected to reach Lixnea's palace by nightfall.

"Breaking for lunch, I think," Taran said, scanning the other wagons and riders and then glancing at the Mountain and its reassuring seep of black smoke. "Do you think you could stand in the chariot with me for a little while, if I helped hold you up?"

To consider it, I flexed my feet, clad in doeskin sandals that tied with brass clasps in the shape of daisies. They'd appeared in my room this morning with a new sleeveless gown of beaded celadon silk to match, but I knew better than to ask Taran questions about where things had come from by now. If I saw a naked, barefoot goddess limping along behind Genna, I would plead ignorance.

"I could. But why?" If it was just to be shown off on our approach, I'd have to twit him for vanity before I agreed.

Taran gave me a slow grin. "I'm sure we'll be stopped for a while, and I'd like to take you by my villa."

I cautiously nodded, and he held out a hand to help me down from the cart and into the chariot. With an arm around his back and my hip against his, I was able to brace myself well enough when he snapped the team into motion again. I worried that we'd fall too far behind when Taran circled his chariot around and doubled back toward the City, but the speed of the horses once we left the procession put it out of my mind. Before we reached the farthest walls, Taran turned west, following a barely visible path through the trees.

"Whose villa is it, really?" I asked, the wind catching the words in my mouth.

"It's *really* mine."

The glee with which he'd answered made me laugh. "You really have a villa?"

"Of course I do, I'm one of the Stoneborn. Did you think I was some landless peasant?"

I was fairly certain that if he had a villa, he wouldn't have been squatting in Wesha's palace since returning to the Summerlands, but I knew I'd get nothing else out of him.

We cut through a forest of white oak and pine for hours, aiming at the Mountain's face south and west of the City. The ground sloped into gentle hills, with the woods finally opening to a pond fed by a little stream on one side of a clearing and a flat, clear valley on the other. In the middle, at the terminus of the path, was a rectangular felt tent, as big as most houses, with a peaked top and all the sides tied down.

"Behold," Taran said, pulling up his team. "My villa."

My arm was still around him from the ride, so it was easy to tilt my face up and give him a skeptical pout.

"This is a tent," I pointed out, one thumb pressing into my lower lip. I didn't see any permanent structures, and the trail was just a horse path.

Taran hopped down and caught me around my waist, spinning me so that I ended up pressed against him with a breath-halting moment of friction between his hips and mine.

"You don't see it yet?" he asked with feigned incredulity. "The fountains, the colonnades, the grand entrance? I'll show you."

I giggled at his grandiose tone as Taran took my hand and led me toward the tent. It was hard to resist him when he tried to be sweet like this, when I naturally wanted to feel his joy with him. This had to be the land Genna had promised him if he went to the mortal world, and his pride was palpable.

He got the front flaps open and tied back to let light into the interior, which was large enough that I didn't have to duck to follow him in. The inside was crowded with a bandit's hoard of stolen treasures: dozens of ornamented wooden chests, mismatched divans and tables, fat feather cushions, rich carpets in careless stacks, and a small pallet of layered fur cloaks that appeared to have been slept on. Tools too: axes and lathes and shovels, some new, some well used.

At the farthest end, there was a full set of armor on a stand, the first I'd seen in the Summerlands. I didn't know with what weapons the Great War had been waged, because no immortals carried any, deferring to the Allmother's command against fighting each other. It was unlike anything else stored here, and set carefully aside.

Taran flicked the breastplate with a thumbnail to make it ring before opening a cedar chest that contained bladed weapons wrapped in canvas. We'd lived with the queen's army for most of the time I'd known Taran, but I'd never seen him in armor, rarely even armed, and I was surprised he'd bothered to steal swords when he used to be able to drop an entire cavalry charge with Wesha's blessings.

I took a closer look at the armor's breastplate and its embossed patterns of flame in gold filigree. Then at the helmet, with a golden plume over the face of a snarling lion.

"Taran, did you steal this armor from *Death*?" I asked, appalled.

He looked over his shoulder without concern. Put a sword on the table, continued rummaging. "Well, unlikely he gave it to me as a present. But who's to say now? Neither of us would remember."

"Does it even fit you?" I asked, running a finger along the sharp edges of the faceplate. The teeth of the lion were tipped with rubies, and if Taran wore it, he'd look like he'd been swallowed whole. I pulled the helmet off the stand, uneasy at holding something that had belonged to Death. I didn't want to imagine Taran in it.

Taran smirked at me, then tossed another sheathed weapon onto the floor. "It does. I look fantastic in it, in fact. But look at these." He made a throaty noise of pleasure as he unearthed a set of vellum scrolls bound with scraps of ribbon.

"My villa. Or at least the plans," he said, beckoning me back outside with a bounce of excitement in his step.

The wind smelled good here, ripe with grass and the scent of the stand of chestnut trees by the stream that formed one border of the cleared field. We walked to the precise center, where Taran spread the scrolls on the ground and weighted them open with stones.

"Did you draw these yourself?" I asked after a moment, attempting to decipher the plans' architectural symbols and lines. Someone had thought long and hard about these buildings, spent years imagining the tiny details, down to the willow-tree pattern on the tiles in the entryway of the guest quarters.

"I'm not sure. That's my handwriting, but I can't make sense of a lot of the drawings now."

In the next pause, I considered that I'd never seen his handwriting: an angular, masculine scrawl instead of the precise lines of a temple scribe. Another piece of the full person he'd been when I met him.

"Genna told me about this place when I came home. In light of my abject failure to return the mortals to their proper state of obedience, she was tempted to take it back. But since I couldn't say what had happened, and those wily mortals had managed to murder Death too, she decided to be generous." Taran took a deep breath, expression faintly self-mocking. "So I rode here and found all this . . . stuff. I must have thought I'd come back and start laying the foundation. The grading is finished at the southern end, and there's a section of retaining wall started near the pond. See, the main building will go right . . . here."

Taran walked into the field to pace the footprint of the courtyard. When he opened the next scroll and began to ramble about the comparative virtues of marble flooring and terra-cotta, I went into the tent and retrieved a quilted cotton blanket to spread over the future site of the kitchen gardens.

I let his explanation of the stables and baths wash over me as I lay down and rolled the hem of my dress up over my knees. Maybe it was the thick sunlight, but there was an air of unreality to this place. I was surprised by every sensation—grass under my fingertips, wisps of hair sticking to my neck—that reminded me that I was not dreaming. It had been winter when I left, and I closed my eyes and spread my arms, soaking the eternal summer heat into my bare limbs.

I heard Taran carefully sit down next to me after he described the outdoor theater.

"I can show you where we could put your plum orchard, but it looks like our first crop is going to be freckles," he said, brushing a fingertip across the bridge of my nose.

"You're telling me I have freckles?" I said, pretending to be shocked. I didn't have as many as some redheads—my hair was closer to brown than blonde—but if I didn't go inside soon, tomorrow I'd be as spotted as a jungle cat and as pink as a primrose.

"Just a few."

I smiled without opening my eyes when I felt his lips carefully close over a spot on my right cheekbone. "One right here." When Taran wanted to be sweet, there was nothing better in the whole world. His lips moved to my temple. "A second here."

I tipped my head back expectantly, waiting for him to kiss my mouth next, but instead he pressed another warm kiss to the tip of my nose. "Three." He carefully closed his lips around my chin. "Four."

It turned out that I had twenty-seven freckles on my face, and my mouth buzzed with energy at being the only place not kissed by the time he was done counting. But instead of covering my lips with his at last, I felt his shadow dip before he laid an open-mouthed kiss halfway down my neck. "Twenty-eight." His breath ran over my collarbone. "Twenty-nine."

My body started to heat from within, rather than from the sunlight, when he pushed the strap of my dress aside to kiss a freckle hidden on my right shoulder. I didn't have many freckles on my legs, but he found one on the arch of my foot and one on the top of my knee. His lips trailed down each arm as my breathing quickened and my hands trembled from the effort of not reaching for him. Each kiss was butterfly-wing light.

He'd counted to sixty-one when he identified the last freckle not covered by the silk of my gown, on the bend of my right index finger. He sucked the fingertip into his mouth, holding it there with a satisfied, devilish sparkle in his eyes. The pull of his mouth on such an innocent location was erotic beyond what I'd thought was possible.

When he paused, it was to let his eyes drop to my breasts and thighs, still covered by my dress. My breath quickened at the implied question and the image of his lips tracing down my cleavage. *Yes. Please.*

I had to swallow hard before speaking. "I think I might have a few more?"

Taran's smile around my finger slowly widened, a cat in the cream, but then his gaze flicked up to the sky, and his expression dimmed.

"You're getting sunburned," he said roughly, pulling my dress down over my legs. He helped me up and toward the small pool of shade created by a grove of chestnut trees.

"Oh, I—probably?" I said belatedly, taken aback that he was so concerned.

Had I not been direct enough? Or too direct? I was going to die a virgin.

His attitude was slightly apologetic but no less determined when we regrouped at the edge of the valley. He took a deep breath and seemed to gather himself, smile firmly back in place.

"Anyway, what do you think of it?" he asked, gesturing to his grassy future palace.

I shook my head ruefully. I knew a lot about a lot of things, but this was beyond me. My own little stone house had seemed like an extraordinary promise at the time.

"Who's going to build it?"

"Me," he said with resolution. "The Allmother built the rest of the City, but as you saw, she's unlikely to do me any favors."

"Won't this take you an eternity if you plan to do it all yourself? Do you even know how?"

"Happily, I have time to figure it out. You can sit right here"—he pointed to our feet—"with your kithara and a glass of wine and watch me."

I laughed softly at the idea of Taran turning his considerable energy to learning stonemasonry from first principles. It had to be a joke, but he was keen for my reaction.

"I'm just going to drink wine and watch you haul stone for three hundred years? I sound very lazy."

"I don't know why I didn't ask you before. Did you have better plans?"

I smiled away from him, imagining the evenings where we'd slept under muddy hedgerows as the rain beat our faces through winter branches. *Oh, nightingale, this is unpleasant. Would you rather go to my villa for a few centuries?*

"I thought you were mortal. A big estate in the Summerlands would have been hard to explain."

"You would have been impressed though," he said, the corners of his mouth now curling up but not matching the intensity in his eyes. "If I told you I had a villa."

"I *am* impressed," I said, hand over my heart, trying to lighten the mood. "*Five* fountains, Taran? How extravagant."

That made the smile fade and the intensity grow, and he pressed a hand over the back of mine. My heart thumped faster, because every time Taran had looked at me like this, my life had shifted course.

"I did it for you, you know."

"Did what?"

He tilted his head at the land. "I can't imagine caring enough about a bunch of blaspheming mortals to give this up. Certainly not enough to die for. But I can imagine caring about you. I must have done it for you."

It was too close to the real heart of things for comfort. I didn't want him to have done it for me, because I wanted him to have been the kind of person who would have done it anyway.

"No. No." I shook my head, and Taran took it as rejection and started to pull his hand away, but I grabbed and held it. "I mean that you *did* care. I know you did."

"Because I did every dangerous, exhausting task you set me to in your endless campaign against the fundamental forces of the world? That would not look much different from right now."

I gave him a pained look. "It wasn't for me. You could have had *me*, if that's all you wanted." I could have loved him for less than half of the kindness and decency he'd shown. I would have wanted him just for being handsome and gentle when everyone else had treated me like an idea, not a person.

"Really?" He didn't look content with that answer, but he was intrigued. "Even though you were going to be married?"

I looked down at my sandals, struggling for a way to answer that wasn't a lie. "That wasn't until later."

"So I just missed my opportunity? I must have hoped your lover would catch an arrow in the back."

"It wasn't like that. I didn't make you help. I didn't even *ask* you."

"You constantly ask me. You ask me by everything you do! I can't look at you without seeing the two dozen things you think I ought to do to be a better man. But I couldn't have been then, if I'm not now," Taran said, pushing with his palm until I had to firm my feet to hold my place.

Questioning whether he was a good person wasn't evidence to the contrary. It proved that he cared about the answer. I gathered up his hands and brushed his knuckles gently with my lips

"I'm sorry, my love, you are just going to have to live with the knowledge that you were once a tireless, unselfish hero."

The corners of his eyes crinkled as he tried to put a smirk back on his face. "Setting that aside, as hard as it is for me to believe I'd give this up rather than execute a few insurrectionists and go home, it's harder for me to believe that I didn't always want you."

My pulse quickened out of both hope and fear. "Maybe you did. We'll never know for sure."

Why would he now, if he didn't then? But if he did then, why wouldn't he have told me everything?

Taran took a slow half step closer to me, then bent his head so that our foreheads nearly brushed to consider our clasped hands. When he exhaled, I could feel it against my lips again.

"You never thought about it?"

I couldn't lie, especially not when I still thought about it every day. Imagining a world where we somehow fit together, Genna's son and the woman who started the riots.

He was asking me to share his life here, I finally realized. Like he'd once asked me to marry him and live in a little stone house with a plum tree by the front window. Were these different questions or the same one, repeated? The size of the house wouldn't have mattered, or the ring on my finger. It was that he *loved* me.

My breath trembled in my chest. "I wish you'd told me why you were there. I might have understood."

"If you might have understood then, try *now*. You know now. I wanted you so badly that I'd betray the other Stoneborn and break the Allmother's laws, if that's what it took to bring you here and keep you with me."

The tugging on my heart was more insistent. "You think this is what you wanted to happen when you ran off to confront Death alone?"

"I must have thought you were worth it."

"But you died. You don't even remember me—you'd have known that you wouldn't know me."

"Death doesn't remember Wesha. And yet as soon as he woke up, he started looking for her. I think I was looking for you, even when I didn't know you existed. I think I died wanting you, and now I live wanting you."

His voice was soft, but it still rattled me. When I let go of his hand and tried to step away, clear my head, Taran seized me by my arms, forcing me to stay facing him. "So what do you want?"

"I've done nothing but tell you from the day I came here," I said, tense against his hold. "I want you to come home and be the person you were. And then, then, if you still wanted me—"

"*Please* want something else. You're a mortal, you can change your mind." He spun me around so that we both faced the empty clearing.

"Just look at it. Take ten minutes, take ten years, until you can see it. This whole world was built of mortal dreams. Can't you have just one about staying here with me?"

When he didn't slacken his grip, I tried.

The midday glow was bright and golden, so I had to slit my eyes to look past the meadow and the distant creek. I imagined a palace with cool marble floors on my bare feet and the sounds of running water on the summer breeze. It was more solid than the stone house had ever been in my mind, easier to picture, but the warm rise and fall of Taran's breathing against my back distracted me. That was more precious than any building could have been.

Taran pressed his cheek against my neck, and I wished I had those ten years to memorize the difference between the rough texture of his jaw and the silk of his lips, because *that* had been my dream. I turned my head to catch his mouth, but his kiss was brief.

"Keep looking," he said, lifting one hand to my chin and pointing my face at the vacant square of earth. "Do you see it yet?"

I imagined morning light pouring through the window in a stone room, lying on a bed with Taran, tangling my fingers in his sun-warmed hair. It was an old daydream, but if I unfocused my eyes, I could place it here. Quiet days with him, both of us free from every purpose we'd been put to that ran counter to our natures. Our only task loving each other.

Taran's arm was wrapped around me, but he slid his palm across my stomach and brought it back to rest at my hip, then placed the other to match. He slowly rubbed them over the small curves of my body, hands catching against the beaded fabric of my dress. I had to swallow past a knot of yearning to answer him.

"I'm trying," I promised him.

"Can you imagine this?" he asked, voice lower. "Imagine that you want me the way I want you, and you let me touch you even when you remember who I am."

I did. I do.

His lips turned into the fragile skin of my neck again, but this time he opened his mouth to taste the salt of my skin and roll it over his teeth. I shivered, body tightening as his hand wandered up to cover my breast.

"I'm imagining it," I whispered, closing my eyes as he gently cupped me through the bodice of my dress, thumb circling a nipple until it stiffened to a tight peak. It wasn't the sun's warmth spreading through me anymore, it was that long-banked ember of desire in my center flaring bright and needy as the lid lifted on my own wants.

"Did you want this?" Taran asked into my skin. His other hand caressed the curve of my thigh, then fisted in the fabric. He spread his fingers to gather more, and the hem of my skirt crept an inch up my shin. He spread them again, and the beaded hem climbed higher. My breath swirled in a heady round in my chest as he bared me inch by inch, walking his two smallest fingers along my hip.

"I—yes." The silk trickled up the entire length of my leg, from my ankle to the apex of my thighs.

I'd clasped my hands together in front of me, needing something to push against, but Taran prized them apart and put the wadded fabric of my skirt into one hand. "Can you hold on to this for me, darling?"

It didn't occur to me not to comply, because it freed his hand to sweep over the bare skin of my thigh, his fingertips pressing in and releasing. His mouth and nose rubbed hard into my neck in tandem, rough enough to leave a mark. It was an agonizing contrast to his hands, which were carefully light on my body. I pulled my shoulders back to press my breast into his hand; I shifted my thighs against each other, silently asking for something I didn't have words for.

"This is how I'd touch you," he murmured. "If you wanted me to. If you lived here with me."

"Just like this?" I asked, uncertain of what the flare of desire in my belly demanded, except more.

"Whatever you can imagine."

I imagined falling back into the soft grass and spreading my arms and legs wide, a real sun overhead until I felt warmed through forever. I imagined enough time to hold a sip of wine in my mouth so that the sweetness would pour down my throat and cover the memory of ashes. I imagined Taran's mouth on my body, my hands, my feet, kisses enough to erase every pain I'd felt. Everything beyond that was too vague for me to picture. It was sensations I craved: the weight of his body, some deeper pressure, a tighter embrace.

"You're going to have to show me," I whispered, cheeks heating at the admission.

Anything he could have said in response to that risked embarrassing me to death, so I was glad he didn't speak. He just slid his hand from my thigh to my stomach, tenderly stroked his thumb across the delicate skin, then ducked his fingertips under the wrap of linen that was all I wore under my dress. The only pressure I felt was from the heel of his palm as it slid down to the curls between my thighs, even though that left his fingertips covering the most intimate places in my body.

I drew in a deep, shuddering breath, not sure what to expect, only for that breath to drift out my lips in hitching half steps as Taran stayed precisely still behind me, only the tip of his nose moving along my neck.

It felt like ages, eons, glacial time we didn't have before two callused fingertips curled minutely against me. They delicately explored me while I shifted my weight, seeking to understand the resolution of this movement. The tiny circles, just the pads of his fingers. The motion didn't change, but I did. My body was turning into cables of gold that wound tighter with every pass.

"It could just be this for the first ten years. Or always, if you liked. Do you like this?"

"Yes," I said again, though shakily, because I was starting to feel pleasantly dizzy, and the idea that this was all it took was a bit of a revelation. Like being able to fly simply by thinking about it hard enough. I understood the place that the twisting of desire in my core would take me, but I hadn't realized I could reach it with only this small, gentle touch. "I just thought you would do, ah, more—"

My voice broke when he changed the direction of his fingers and the edge of a nail brushed against me. I jumped, that coiled wire of sensation in me tightening.

"Oh, I'd do more," Taran said, a low chuckle. "But I didn't want to overwhelm you while you're still trying to imagine this. Are your eyes open, darling?"

I'd shut them, but opening them to look at the same innocent scene—or down, at Taran's hands on my body—felt more obscene than closing them.

"I'm not scared," I said, words slightly belied by the wobble in my voice.

"Of course you aren't. My brave girl isn't afraid of anything. Not me, not this, not what you want," he crooned into my ear as his fingers moved more quickly. I clutched the fabric of the dress with one hand and his arm with the other, breath coming faster in tandem with the movement of his fingertips.

"Do you want one more thing to think about?" he asked when my toes began to curl against the leather of my sandals, and I nodded, gulping for air in assent. He turned his wrist and pressed one finger inside me, the shock of penetration making me gasp, as much at the idea of it as the novel stretch. Nobody had ever touched me like this; I hadn't even touched myself like this. It felt like an erotic achievement. A mountain we'd climbed together, and now we were standing at the peak.

His breath was ragged in my ear as my body twisted against his hand like a drawn bow, but when the tension finally released, it wasn't with the snap I'd somehow expected. It was like more of the golden sunlight flowing through me, spreading like ripples from a pebble in a pond. I gasped, and he turned his head to capture the noise in his mouth, swallowing it down and holding me up when my balance failed under the deluge of sensations washing through me.

I hung reeling and suspended in his arms until I could put words to the relief I felt. Not just the physical kind—there had been a small fear in the back of my mind that I couldn't do this, be like this. But I could.

When my breath slowed and my vision finally focused again, I was hesitant to squirm around in his arms and look at his face. He might have been a little arch and smug, under the circumstances, and I wouldn't have blamed him, but I wouldn't have been able to keep my guard down. But all I saw on his face was soft approval, no different from any of the nights I'd sung him lullabies.

He must have had his reasons before. There had been good reasons to wait. I was young and still wearing Wesha's white, and he was just off centuries of serving as Genna's pawn—but now I could barely close my teeth against the truth of *oh, I wanted you so much, please give me everything, I want everything with you.*

So I tossed my arms around his neck and kissed him hard enough to make him stagger back instead, uncoordinated and giddy. Peppered his chin and jaw with kisses, everything I could reach.

And he looked so happy for it.

Unlike all the times he'd pulled away to smile at me from a respectful distance, Taran held on tight to me now. He gripped loose handfuls of my hair and opened his smiling lips to taste mine. Whatever we'd started, it wasn't over, even if I didn't know what happened next.

I wasn't entirely unfamiliar with Taran's body, or even the hard shape pressed against my stomach through our clothes, but I was resolved to learn it much better before this moment passed.

"I don't care if I get sunburned," I said breathlessly, because it was hard to speak with my heart squeezing out all the air in my chest.

Taran chuckled and, in lieu of agreement, just reached down to grip me under my thighs and hoist me into the air. I squealed, trying to lock my legs around his waist.

"That tent is very comfortable, I promise," he swore.

He walked quickly despite my weight, his lips catching the corners of my mouth as I laughed and clung to his shoulders, and I was so adrift in joy that I almost didn't see it before he ducked inside. The sky.

The smoke from the Mountain hadn't stopped since we fled Smenos's palace, and it was familiar by now. But this was different. A different color of smoke. From a different direction. I wasn't so disoriented that I couldn't reason out where it came from: the City.

"Taran, wait," I gasped. "Something's wrong."

I unlocked my legs and tried to turn when my feet touched the ground, but Taran stopped me before I could step away from him, wrapping his arms tightly around my waist.

I looked over my shoulder, confused by his reaction, and then even more by the lack of surprise on his face. Instead, there was faint guilt.

"You knew?"

Of course he'd known: he'd heard something, or smelled the smoke on the wind, immortal senses warning him long before my mortal ones.

His eyelids fell as he looked away from my accusation, but his grip on me didn't soften.

"The Mountain fell silent this morning. I can't hear the All-mother at all—something's happened, and Death is free. If he murdered his own mother, I do hope she had time to reconsider who was her favorite before she died."

"Then, in the City—"

"Death, I suppose. Perhaps the Shipwright and the Huntress too. Stealing a march before the other Stoneborn can find out what they did."

I took in a sharp breath, betrayal coursing through my gut in a sickening wave.

"That's why you brought me here," I said numbly. His arms had been a shelter, but now they caged me against him. "You weren't going to do anything to help?"

"I *did* do something to help. So did you. We both warned them. We told everyone."

"Weeks ago! And Genna and Skyfather are hours away—"

"Because they have been content to see our home slowly fall apart ever since you started your little insurrection. Since Wesha shut the Gates! Why would I save them from their own neglect?"

"Taran, please, there are hundreds of mortals left in the City, and Genna's priests can't even defend themselves."

"You can barely defend yourself, and I am defending *you*," Taran said with grim determination. I wasn't swaying him at all. He'd planned this. He'd thought this through—probably from the moment we returned to the City.

"You're just going to sit here while Death massacres them? Or worse, sacrifices them and becomes even more powerful?"

"*We* are going to stay here until the other Stoneborn who are responsible for this world go back and defend their own priests. Until Wesha confronts the monster she created!"

"You wouldn't," I insisted, tears welling as I jerked at the hands that held me in place. "You're not going to keep me here."

"When the fight is over, we'll go find out what happened," Taran said, slow and deliberate. "The Mountain knows I'd stand against Death himself to keep you safe, but you and I are *living through this*. Neither of us deserves to die for Wesha's pride."

"They can't even go outside if Genna's given them something else to do," I whispered, thinking of Teuta in the basement workroom. Elantia, who ought to be home with her mother.

If I'd been a little prettier, a little sweeter, it could have been me. Genna's priests didn't train as long as Wesha's. I was more like them than I was like the unknowable immortal who held me captive.

My knees sagged, and Taran must have thought I was admitting defeat, so he let me take a couple of wobbly steps away.

I covered my face with my hands, both to get myself under control and to muffle my next words. A song.

Taran was slow to act when he didn't recognize the tune. He'd recognize Wesha's gift of sleep, but that one took a little longer. This one was only six measures, key of E, three-quarter time.

Every muscle in Taran's body locked up when I finished singing the blessing to test a patient's nervous system.

Taran's worked.

The effect lasted only half a second, but he didn't expect it. He crashed to the ground, hard enough that I winced at the sound of his head cracking against the earth.

I got a few more paces toward the chariot, already singing a second blessing. The look of betrayal on his face would have been laughable if it hadn't pierced me to the very core. He'd lured me here under false pretenses, did his best to distract me while innocents died, and he was surprised?

He'd just gotten to his hands and knees when the second blessing caught him. He gasped as the lower half of his body went numb and useless, unresponsive to his commands. It was the same blessing I'd sung before running down the beach on my broken foot, trying to save his life.

"Stop," he called, panic making his voice tight. "Iona, don't. You don't have an army behind you this time, and Wesha's power has to be failing. Just *stop and think*."

"You didn't give me a choice," I snarled in the face of his rush of entreaties. "I don't know what I would have said if you'd ever given me one, but you didn't." I meant more than today—I meant this entire place, this idea he had of the two of us in the Summerlands, endless years far from the land of my birth. I didn't know if I could have loved the person he was, instead of the one he'd pretended to be. I couldn't know. He'd robbed me of that chance.

"And now you'll never know if I would have said yes," I told him, voice shaking.

Taran had nobody but himself to blame, and I saw in his face that he knew that. He never made it back to his feet before I chanted every note of the Maiden's blessing of sleep, and he collapsed in the sunlit field as I turned away.

28

TARAN PROBABLY WISHED he'd never taught me to ride a horse, because I took both of them. I unhitched the chariot and rode one while the other trailed behind us, unhappy to be racing toward smoke and noise instead of away from it, but too well trained to buck or stray. I didn't dare leave a horse for Taran. I didn't know how long Wesha's blessing would incapacitate him, and if he caught me before I made it to the City, I was certain he'd drag me off even if I fought back. I wasn't certain I had the heart to injure him, but if I did, I knew I wouldn't be able to forgive either of us. As it was, I was so angry at him that I could barely breathe.

It wasn't a battle, when I reached the City. It was a reaping. The buildings were aflame, and death-priests were methodically stalking through the City, calling their lord's fire on every other living being, mortal and immortal alike. The war Death had calmly predicted—the one the other Stoneborn refused to consider—had begun.

I'd spent the ride considering what I would do when I reached the battle, but I discarded all my plans. I'd thought that perhaps I would rally defenders at some wall where we might hold off long enough for Skyfather or the Peace-Queen to rescue their people, but there was no defense possible against an assault that had already spread in every direction. This had begun hours ago.

Still, I had to save *someone*, or I might as well have sat with Taran in the meadow and pretended not to see the smoke. I slapped the reins of the horse to propel me into the City as ringing filled my ears and metal flooded my mouth.

For the second time in my life, I ran straight at Death.

In the far distance, in Skyfather's sector, the winged lion was leaping from roof to roof, his maw belching fire as his claws scored through slate and tile to expose the interiors of palaces that held priests at their tasks. If the Allmother was dead, her last work had been to re-create her murderer in golden perfection. Where were the other Stoneborn? Genna? Diopater? Even Marit? The only one I saw was Death.

He was smaller than he'd been at Smenos's palace and less bright, nearly shrunken to the size of a mortal beast, but still deadly to any creature he encountered. He dug priests out of their homes like the roots of an unwanted vine, sapping the divine power of the other Stoneborn with each screaming mortal death. I sucked in a breath to prepare for singing vengeance.

When I reached the first blazing structures, a pair of red-robed death-priests turned their heads at my approach, raising their hands almost languidly to call flame. Gracefully, ceremonially. I sang faster. These two must have spent generations here in the City, counting the sacrifices that arrived in Death's storerooms and mingling with the other mortals they'd just turned on. Today their lord had commanded them to set the City on fire, and they'd obeyed.

If they'd been here as long as I suspected, these priests had probably never killed someone before today, but *I had*. They died surprised, with Death's blessing of fire abruptly cut off when the Maiden's power paralyzed the breath in their lungs. They fell clutching their throats, grasping uselessly at their chests while their lips turned blue and their bodies slowly failed for want of air.

Taran had never liked that song. He said it was cruel.

With my own chest heaving, I pulled up the horse to stare down at the still-twitching bodies of the death-priests, trying to recall when I might have used that blessing in surgery. Or even who taught it to me and for what original purpose. All I could remember was being a small child, when my mother led me by the hand into the vast painted halls of the temple at Ereban and left me there.

The Maiden loves your singing so much that you are going to live here with her priests. You'll wear beautiful white dresses and always have plenty to eat, and someday people will bring their babies for you to bless.

I swallowed bile and rode to the tents where we'd housed Smenos's former priests, only to find them collapsed and empty. Death had probably come here first, attacked those who had no patron who might arrive to defend them. The elderly craftsmen were vanished, and there were footprints in the thick, weedless lawn, flanked by scorch marks down to bare earth where the grass had died. Either they'd just been taken, or whatever had happened to the Allmother had affected the ability of the Summerlands to keep the City static and pristine. I followed the tracks, hoping for the former, but found only more flames as I went deeper into the City.

As I approached Genna's barracks, there were signs that some priests had tried to fight back—the roofs were damp and smoldering, and there were puddles of water on the tile. The priests of some other god might have made a stand here before the battle moved to their part of the City, might have tried to protect the helpless peace-priests.

But there were also bodies in the street. Wearing gold cloth. Wearing purple. A rainbow of clerical dresses blotted with blood or pulled up to cover the faces of mortals who'd strangled on smoke or died under sacrificial knives. Dozens of them.

Once again, I was too late. I'd come as fast as I could, but I was too late.

I slowed the horse and dismounted, walking numbly toward the first group of survivors I encountered. Peace-priests were pulling the wounded and dead out of the basement tunnels, singing to stanch wounds or soothe lungs filled with soot.

Amid the crowd of saffron-clad bodies, my heart lightened for a moment to recognize Elantia—half her hair scorched away from the side of her skull and blisters down one cheek, but alive—until I saw who she carried out.

Burns could quickly render victims unrecognizable, but it must have been smoke that killed Teuta ter Genna, because her lovely dark eyes were open and sightless in her untouched face.

Teuta had often gone to the royal palace before the rebellion, trusted to advise on everything from marriages to foreign trade. My stomach twisted as I imagined her arrival in the Summerlands with all the other peace-priests, the first familiar sight to a frightened young girl who remembered dying on Death's altar. Teuta would have been the only person to remember Elantia's life before she belonged to Genna, just like she had been the only person who remembered me before I belonged to the rebellion.

Being a high priestess still meant something to the people here, because Elantia had the help of the other high priest I'd met in Genna's kitchens. Together they laid Teuta down apart from the other dead. Elantia dropped to her knees, crying raggedly, and I stumbled to kneel next to her.

Teuta should have been on her way home. She should have been presiding over weddings, she should have been bouncing her first grandchild on her knee, she shouldn't even have *been here* in the first place.

"She tried to stop them from taking us. Tried to barricade the doors. But the dusk-souls came right through the wood, dragged people out anyway," Elantia sobbed.

Teuta's arms were burned—not just her palms, but wrists and

biceps, charred all the way through the skin. Injuries from a dusk-soul's touch. They must have scorched the grass too, by the crafter-priests' tents.

An army of the dead had nearly destroyed the world in the Great War, and Death was building it up again. How was I supposed to do this alone, when it had taken all the Stoneborn together and Wesha's sacrifice to stop him the last time? I could kill death-priests and Fallen, but how was I supposed to stop the dead?

"Where did the dusk-souls go?" I asked Elantia.

The girl loudly sniffled back tears. "I don't know. I ran and hid until the smoke got too bad."

The expression of horrified guilt on her face was far too familiar to me. She would start by asking why the other peace-priests had died, then end by wondering why she still lived.

I grabbed her uninjured shoulder hard and tried to reassure her, despite knowing that nothing I said would really matter. "No, you did the right thing. You did what I told you to do. None of you could fight back. It was Genna's responsibility to protect you."

And where all the gods had failed, there was still me.

I scanned the wreckage of the City. I hadn't seen any of the former crafter-priests among the dead. They had to have been taken by the dusk-souls too, all herded away to serve as sacrifices.

I still had one of Taran's knives, and I took it out to tremble in a fist that was already tired from clutching the reins—I wasn't good enough with Diopater's blessings to call rain or with Genna's to heal smoke inhalation, but I could still account for any Fallen or death-priests that I found while searching for the captives. I closed Teuta's eyes and stood, prepared to follow the trail of scorched earth to its source.

As though summoned by my intentions, a small shape fluttered down from the sky, nervous sparrow wings fluttering with agitation. I was so on edge that I nearly set her feathers on fire again.

"What are you doing?" Awi trilled reproachfully.

"What are *you* doing? Have you been here the whole time? Did you see where the priests were taken?"

I hadn't seen the little bird goddess since returning to the City, and she was no more helpful than ever. She ignored my questions to shriek insults instead.

"You idiot. Death's still here! He'll find you, he'll find *me*! Get out, then get me out of here."

"You are the *last* person I was worried about," I said, trying to snatch her as she dove at my head.

"You promised! To get me out of here! And you've had weeks to get to the Painted Tower. What are you doing here, you lazy drudge?"

"Did you not notice that the City is under attack?"

She whistled a shrill dismissal. "Yes! Wesha's barely holding the Gates closed, and this entire place is about to fall apart. You were supposed to get the boy and go. Where is he?"

I grimaced, feeling my breath hitch as if it would like to become a sob instead. An unworthy part of me wished I'd done just that and didn't know this was happening.

"Probably waking up alone right about now—he tried to stop me from coming to help."

"Of course he did. With the Allmother gone—"

"Did you see what happened? Is she really dead?"

The little bird postured with one beady eye like she wasn't going to answer, but she hopped between me and the trail of scorched earth.

"I heard the fight go on for weeks, Napeth and the Mountain. Today he cracked the ground open to escape, and the Mountain is quiet. She's either dead or asleep or . . . I don't know. It's never happened before. If she's not there to remake us, who even knows whether we're still immortal? We could die, really die!"

Awi certainly meant herself and Taran, not Death, but that was where my mind immediately went. If I took my little knife and went after the winged lion in the distance, might I end things for good this time if I got in one lucky blow?

Worth a try, my despairing fury crooned.

Anger could provide enough light and heat to keep a wounded soul alive. I knew that from experience. It wasn't hope or righteousness that had fueled me when I started the rebellion against Death. I'd relied on anger, and I welcomed it back into the furnace of my heart now.

"I'll go find out," I said, a tingling sense of resolve stilling the shake of my limbs. I almost smiled, but the bird goddess realized my plan and panicked.

"What! No, you stupid little polecat, you're just going to leave me, all these priests, that wretched boy you came all this way for?"

"Taran wouldn't come," I repeated bitterly.

"So you're just going to ditch him?" she shrieked. "You're just as unforgiving as he is—a hateful, stupid girl, the worst priest I've ever had."

"I'm *not* your priestess. I have one little vow to you, and if I happen to live past sticking a dagger into Death's black heart, it should be *very* easy to convince Wesha to let you through the Gates."

I could hardly rush after Death while being heckled by a sparrow, so I was forced to try to catch her.

"Stupid! Stupid!" she chanted, dodging my hands. "What do you think a priest *is*, anyway? It's just a vow, and every vow is a sacrifice. You're the only priestess I have left—or that Taran has."

I'd never put that together before. Every vow was a sacrifice of our freedom, and the vows of complete obedience that priests took gave up their entire lives. No wonder the Stoneborn were so greedy for priests: it was the same impulse as Death's lust for human sacrifice.

Maybe I could end it today. I didn't delude myself that my chances were very good, but if Taran had managed it once, perhaps I would succeed today—maybe Death's fight with the Allmother had weakened him, or I'd catch him by surprise.

"I guess you'd better hope I live, then," I said.

The bird must have seen the determination on my face, because she flew directly at my throat, tiny feet scrambling for a hold on my neckline.

"Stop! Wait, I'll tell you where they took the priests."

With another wrench of anger, I halted, plucking her from my collar and holding her at arm's length. Her little black eyes bugged out as she pleaded with me.

"If you're just going to get yourself killed, you might as well do it with a tiny chance of success. Go after your mortals instead—I saw Death's Fallen take them. There's a passage to the Underworld hidden in Wesha's palace. They'll sacrifice the mortals there, try to give Death enough power to bring down the Gates from the inside."

My immediate reaction was that the bird was lying to get me off the battlefield, but it was almost too fantastical to be pure invention. I'd been living there for weeks, Taran for months—how could he have missed *that*?

Though he did have Death's armor—perhaps that was how he'd stolen it.

If the passage was there, he probably wouldn't have told me. He didn't want any part in my war, after all.

"Why would there be a passage to the Underworld in Wesha's palace?" I demanded.

The little bird swung her tail angrily in my palm. "Because back when Wesha was just as young and stupid as you are, she used to sneak her sweetheart up to see her. Stop staring at me. If you want to catch them, you need to go now."

"Her sweetheart? *Death?*" The monstrous husband she despised, the one she reluctantly married only to stop the Great War? How long had she "trifled" with him, as Lixnea had put it?

At my vehemence, Awi took flight and fluttered back a few feet, afraid I would squeeze her to shake out more answers. Was even a single thing I'd ever been taught about Wesha true?

"She wouldn't be the last person to make terrible mistakes for love," Awi said defensively. "As if your reasons were any better."

With that stinging rebuke, the bird goddess took flight, leaving me to weigh my chances between getting my dagger in Death's heart and following his Fallen into the Underworld. Neither sounded very survivable.

Between my vows, the people I'd lost, and the people I'd left behind, there was little of my soul left for love. I wished love had been the reason for more of my terrible mistakes. They probably wouldn't weigh on me so heavily if I could say I'd made them all out of love.

Cursing every immortal in the Summerlands, I turned and ran for Wesha's palace.

THE ENTRANCE TO the Underworld was open to the sky in the same courtyard where I'd tripped over Taran during my first night in the Summerlands. The potted flowers were shriveled and dry—dusk-souls had passed through with the captives here. The paving stones had been pried up, exposing a neatly constructed tunnel with walls smoothed by a Stoneborn's power.

My descent was entirely in darkness. I followed the downward slope by touch, tripping over my feet in my flimsy sandals. I didn't dare call for light and instead chanted Lixnea's shroud in anticipation of the moment that I would encounter the dusk-souls and the stolen priests.

I spent an hour alone in the dark with my thoughts before I saw the first signs of any captives. They were visible before the turn of the tunnel from the green glow of the dead, but when I crept close enough to make out the group, I counted four incandescent dusk-souls, one Fallen in Death's red vestments, and nearly a dozen stumbling priests of Genna who clung to each other as they were herded toward the Underworld.

Wrapped in darkness, I snuck closer. I was limping and tired, but several of the priests were injured, and I gained on them without breaking into a run that would have risked my balance. The dusk-souls, when I got a better look, didn't appear to have been soldiers. Instead, when their forms momentarily solidified, they were dressed like farmers or peasant laborers, their young-old-ageless faces twisted in the same horror as the dead priest in the Shipwright's fortress. They didn't want to do this—Death's power had enslaved them. Still, they carried spears whose bronze tips were pitted by age, and they harried the priests to follow the Fallen into the abyss. I had no idea how I might stop them.

I got on well with most of the senior priests of Wesha during my childhood, perfect student that I was, but one old stick of a man had proved the exception. During his surgeries he made every single incision, even when he was supposed to be training more junior priests. *If you want something done right, you have to do it yourself*, he'd say, like he was imparting wisdom instead of just demonstrating his low opinion of everyone else. Of course, I'd thought back then that I *would* do everything perfectly when it was my turn, and now all I saw behind me were my mistakes.

I didn't care now if someone else could do it better than me—please, let someone else who would do it worse have a turn! If I thought anyone else would care about the fate of these priests, I would have gladly turned around, but I hadn't even convinced Taran to help me.

What do I do? Taran, what should we do?

Part of me was still surprised, at every moment, to find myself here without him. Part of me still expected him at my side, hand under my elbow, eyes on my target, heart beating in time with my own. From the day I met him until the day he died, I wasn't ever alone, and it still *felt* like he should be here.

The worst thing was, I was certain that part of him remembered that too. Needed it. He just couldn't remember why. He must feel as betrayed as I did today—and he might never forgive me for this, even if I did survive to return to the surface.

The Fallen leading the dusk-souls had maternal ancestors of barnyard stock, and his cloven hooves tapped the stone as he descended farther into the earth—an abomination that barely registered for me in light of the other atrocities Death had committed. Without a better plan, I crept after the creature, thinking that I needed to see where he was taking the captives before I acted. The tunnel had branches, and I might lose the other priests if I stopped to free this group.

As we descended, the tunnel widened and the ceiling rose, yet the light emitted by the dead was not lost in the greater space. There should have been nothing but featureless, packed dirt in every direction, but instead I began to see new shapes out of the corners of my eyes: trees with pink blossoms, a stand of cattails. Movement too. Shapes that flitted, a breeze through tall grass.

When I tried to focus my eyes on what I thought I'd seen, there was nothing but rock. No light or sound. The hair lifted on the back of my neck as I reassessed the source of my growing unease.

I had plenty of reason to despair, but I probably owed the queasy lurch of my stomach to my instinctual mortal fear of the Underworld. We'd crossed an invisible line, fallen beneath the Summerlands and into the land of the dead. I didn't belong here, and my living flesh and fearful heart rebelled against my mind's instruction to proceed.

The swell of sound and shapes, just out of focus, was as dark and hallucinatory as a fever dream. I thought I saw the hovel I was born in, though it had burned down before I went to Wesha's temple. I thought I smelled the ocean breeze for the first time since I arrived in the Summerlands. I thought I heard Taran's voice, very distant, but when I turned around, there was only darkness behind me. Whipsawed by the unreliability of all my senses, I didn't notice that we had stumbled out of the tunnel and into a vast open space until the group I'd been following halted.

If I looked hard with my mortal eyes, there was nothing but stone for miles: stone beneath me, stone overhead, and stone walls sweeping away past where they were lost to the dark. If I unfocused and lost myself in the wash of false sensations, I could see a distant fortress of sculpted white stone, with high walls that nearly concealed a silver-green forest within. Looking at that beautiful fortress made my soul vibrate in a painful way, as though my vows wanted to shred me for just laying eyes on Death's citadel. Between it and our group were the drifting forms of the dead, moving through their memories of life at an infinitely slow pace. Free dusk-souls at the terminus of their voyages across the sea, blissfully unaware that Death sought to return and force them into war with the living.

This wasn't a place for the living. If Wesha had sent me here to retrieve Taran, instead of to the Summerlands, I wasn't certain how I would have survived long enough to lure him back to the Painted Tower. My body had never felt more useless: a fragile bundle of blood and sinew, animated by a mind fogged by fear.

The cloven-hoofed Fallen did not seem to suffer any such effects and turned directly toward the white fortress that I could see better with my eyes closed. This creature was real and solid, at least, and it didn't make my head hurt to continue following him and his captives.

The next real thing I saw was the altar. Everything else in the Underworld seemed conjured out of memory, but the pile of stones and the bonfire behind it were sharp and coherent as soon as we drew close enough for my eyes to pick them out in the dim light. That was our destination.

Our group had to be one of the last, because there were already dozens of mortal priests in a huddle near the altar, wearing the colors of Smenos and Genna and a few other gods whose blessings didn't lend themselves to combat. Death had always struck at the weak, attacked children and the elderly, like outrage was the point of it.

More Fallen were building up the altar fire without much skill, poking at logs with their weapons and trying to coax them into the bed of coals necessary for a ritual sacrifice. I counted seven Fallen and nearly three dozen dusk-souls armed and standing by with terrified faces. That was almost the largest number of *mortals* that I'd ever managed to affect with Wesha's blessing of night, and my wobbling mind had trouble composing the words of the blessing I might use for these particular circumstances, let alone the meter and rhyme.

My vows had also begun to prick at me too. I'd ignored the slight pain during the descent, but this far from the tunnel I'd followed, surrounded by enemies, I was feeling my promises pull tighter at my limbs. I'd vowed to bring Taran to the Painted Tower, and I'd vowed to bring Awi past the Gates, but I was very far away from any path that took me back into sunlight.

I tried to shake those doubts away and focus on the priests. They'd been tied in a line, one long rope looping through individual knots around their wrists and feet. The goat-Fallen called out a greeting to his siblings, then moved to add my group of priests to the previously bound captives.

I had only one fragile stone knife, and even if they were freed, most of the captives couldn't help me fight back. I supposed that the best plan was to untie as many captives as I could while Lixnea's shroud concealed me, sing the blessing of night to disable the Fallen and death-priests, then finally sprint to safety with as many of the captives as I was able to free. I might not reach everyone, but if I turned around and went for help, I couldn't imagine any rescue reaching these priests in time to save them from the altar.

I shifted into a crouch and crawled to the priests. My knife wasn't the best tool to saw through rope, but it was wickedly sharp, and I got the first crafter-priest in the chain severed from his neighbor, and then, with more difficulty, the bonds around his feet undone.

The look of shock on his face when he turned to peer at me was my first clue that something had gone terribly wrong. He shouldn't have been able to see me at all.

"Run back the way we came in," I whispered, stomach sinking as the priests he'd been tied to looked up from their prayers and weeping.

I didn't want to acknowledge that Lixnea's shroud had completely dissipated until I heard one of the Fallen roar in outrage.

"What's that one doing? Why isn't it tied down?"

The Fallen who'd just hissed through the split upper lip of a mountain cat wheeled on the one I'd followed in. "You ass-licking son of a whore, make sure the sacrifices are secured."

I jerked my knife through another set of ropes and spent precious seconds on a warning. "Run," I snapped at the two priests I'd cut loose, then began to sing as the goat-footed Fallen swaggered toward me with irritation curling his animal muzzle.

Wesha's song of sleep. I already knew it worked on Fallen. I could only hope that the goddess who'd taken half of Death's power had gained some measure of his control over the dead too, because there were more dead spearmen than Fallen, and the priests would never outrun dusk-souls whose feet did not quite touch the ground beneath them. I sang loud and clear so that my song could reach the last ranks of dusk-souls near the altar, and every word was as precise as it had been during my first surgery. I didn't mumble or miss a single note—my voice never faltered, and my perfect pitch didn't fail me then.

Wesha did.

For the first time in my life, my prayers went unanswered. There was not even a whisper of divine power, not even the sense of attention I got when I was struggling for the words to properly direct the Maiden's blessings. Nothing happened. I might as well have been singing to myself.

"What was that?" the Fallen asked with a brutal laugh. "Was that a prayer to the Maiden? Here? She left three hundred years ago."

I licked my lips, panicking. I gestured again at the two priests to run, but they were frozen with fear, eyeing the Fallen while they slowly advanced on me. As I backed away, I tried the blessing of Lixnea again, hoping against the dawning realization of my reckless overconfidence that it might conceal me. But the Moon's power did not manifest any more than the Maiden's.

The Fallen chuckled again as he waded through the shrinking priests to my side. "A pretty song, but there is no god in the Underworld but my father. No prayers reach through stone, and even the Mountain fell against his power."

Fine, then. I took another step back, waited for him to clear the huddle of captive priests, and invoked the bastard who'd sired this monster. It was just spite, at this point; I only knew one blessing of

Death, and it would hardly protect me against this many of his followers. But I could do a lot with just spite.

Hail Death, who kindles flame, I chanted, and fire erupted from my hands. It would have killed a mortal, and it probably hurt this Fallen quite a bit, but this monster's father was the god of flame. When his body was engulfed, he fell to the floor and rolled. He shrieked in agony as the fire clung to his body, but the demonstration only drew the attention of every other enemy within hearing.

Death's flame charred the Fallen's red robes and exposed black-and-gold-webbed skin beneath his fur, but before I could run more than a few steps toward the tunnel mouth, he was back on his feet and furious.

"Maiden-priest *bitch*," he keened, turning to gesture at the horrified dusk-souls who stood by with their hands tight on their spears. "Put her on the altar *first*."

"*Run now*," I called to the priests who had not yet been secured and to the two I had freed. But the prospect of death in some hours' time was still better than the risk of death now if they ran, and nobody moved. The dusk-souls obeyed the Fallen though, sliding after me when I tried to flee.

I didn't run very fast. I was tired, and my foot collapsed under my every step. They caught me.

I expected my dress to burn from the press of their hands. My skin felt as though it blistered and sizzled when they grabbed me by my upper arms to drag me back to the altar, but the fabric didn't char and I couldn't smell any smoke. It hurt like a palm over a candle flame though, every nerve ending that intersected with the green flare of their touch burning without the relief of extinguishment. I screamed, and the dusk-souls winced at the noise but did not stop.

I tried to tell the dusk-souls it wasn't their fault, mostly because

I wanted to apologize to someone before I died. I'd always tried to do the right thing, but I'd made it *worse* at every step of the way. If I had said nothing when Death sacrificed Elantia, that day in Ereban might have ended with only one death. If I hadn't led a reprisal against Death's cult, the other priests might not have fled to the Summerlands. If I had let Taran evacuate the acolytes from the battle on the beach instead of trying to confront a *god*, Taran would have lived. And now I'd die down here without having saved even a single one of the captured priests.

Many people in my rebellion must have died in despair, but dying ashamed seemed like my inescapable fate.

Taran was going to be so angry at me, if he ever found out.

The thought made me struggle again. Even if there was no chance I'd escape, I'd make the Fallen remember me. Give one a nasty scar across an ugly face, maybe a wrist that ached when it rained. I sang fire that passed harmlessly through the dead but made Fallen jump back and curse me again. I kicked, screamed. The touch of the dead burned, but they weren't stronger than they'd been in life. They had to heave and yank on my arms to get me toward the stone altar. I fought for every inch, but eventually one of the Fallen bull-rushed through the gusts of fire I was calling and got me pressed against the stone.

The hallucinations, or perhaps memories, had started to crowd in brighter and clearer as I drew closer to my mortal end. I no longer saw a stone cavern around me but the whitewashed walls and ceilings of the small temples of Wesha, where I'd spent most of my short life. I heard the voices of the priests who raised me and measures of the Maiden's melodies. Smelled disinfectant and honey salve.

Maiden-priests spent too much time trying to save lives to think much about what happened afterward, but before the rebellion, Death's cult had promised that the Underworld was a reflection of how a person had lived—the comfort of home at the end of a long journey if you'd lived a worthy life, a torment if you had not.

I snarled as much at the phantoms conjured by my own mind as the Fallen who was trying to hold me in place long enough to sacrifice me; I didn't want to die as Iona ter Wesha. The maiden-priests weren't my home. That wasn't what my life had been about, if the measure was moments that had mattered rather than the number of days.

If I had to pick one moment to live in forever, it would have been one with Taran. The day we met. The first time he asked me to sing the calendar of flowers for him. *Say yes, nightingale.* Or even *I'll love you till the stars fall out of the sky.*

Lingering in those moments forever wouldn't feel like a punishment; forgetting them would be worse than the pain of these last seconds. Another Fallen climbed to the altar and seized my hair in his fist, exposing my throat for the blade.

There was another shout. My name, maybe.

I thought at first that I'd succeeded in summoning my memory of Taran to comfort me at the end, because it was impossible that he would actually be here: I'd taken both horses, then rushed after the priests by a route that left no trail on the stone. But the Fallen heard him too, and they paused their chanting of the sacrificial rite to confront a second intruder.

Taran skidded into the firelight, panting so hard that the cords of his neck pulled with every breath, sweat gluing his tunic to his chest and his filthy hair to his cheekbones. One hand clutched a bare sword and the other a stone knife, but he'd come alone and unarmored.

Oh, you idiot. You didn't think either of us would survive this— why did you follow me down here?

He didn't know a tenth of the blessings I did, and they wouldn't work anyway. Marit had said he was really just a Fallen, just the youngest bastard child of the Peace-Queen, and he was outnumbered more than seven to one.

He shouldn't have come. He knew better, and he should have spent the rest of his eternal life wondering what happened to me instead of coming here just to die too. I twisted enough to hit the goat-like Fallen in the chin with the back of my head, winning a few seconds to yell for Taran to run, because I didn't have time to say *I'm sorry* or *I love you*. Even from a distance, I caught the emerald gleam of his eyes as they locked on mine.

The Fallen raised his arm, knife in hand, not even bothering with the final words of the rite in his haste to dispatch me.

I thought the last thing I'd ever hear was Taran screaming *no*, but the wordless crash that swept through the cavern in the next second was louder than any voice, flooding the cavern with a flash of green light like a ball of lightning striking a tree. Reality wavered, vibrated, and then swept away the cloying press of memories. My eyes flooded and blurred, but the echoes of the shockwave reverberated in my soul more than in my ringing ears.

Whatever had just happened stunned the Fallen into stillness too, but for a moment, I couldn't discern any real effects. Taran slumped to his knees, chest heaving like his breath had been knocked out of him, but everyone else kept to their feet. What had he done?

Awkwardly, as though walking on unfamiliar limbs, one of the enslaved dead who had dragged me to the altar left her position by the bonfire and stumbled toward us, her form wavering between green and a peace-priest's saffron. Before the Fallen could recover from the flash of light and slit my throat, the little dusk-soul shouted a high-pitched curse and drove her spear through his gut.

29

THE WAY TARAN moved with a blade in his hand had been beautiful in the courtyard. When it was for show, he turned like a dancer. Here, in the hot, dripping seconds after the dead turned on their handlers, the arcs of his blade were ugly and effective. Short, rough motions that caught the Fallen at the joints of their arms and necks. Faster movements than my eye could follow, but I could see the clench of his jaw from the distance of the altar, because he might have known he could do this, but he didn't remember it, and he had to blindly trust that he knew how to block the grasping claws of Fallen whose lives depended on taking his first.

They might have succeeded, teeth and talons against one man with a sword, but for the assistance of the dusk-souls, who were inexpert with their spears but screaming with fury at their captors. Several had thrown down their weapons and fled, but most stayed, and they threw themselves at the Fallen. The Fallen had lost all control of the dead, and the dead were just as invulnerable to immortal struggle as mortal blows. Every half-immortal abomination went down in a pincushion of thrusts, spears carving through red robes. Gold and crimson blood splashed the bare stone of the

Underworld, thick enough to run into puddles, long after the Fallen quit moving.

Every ounce of fight had fled my body. I clung to the altar I'd nearly died on for balance, breath whistling raggedly through my teeth as I tracked Taran's blade. The carnage didn't end even after the last Fallen had dropped to the cavern floor; Taran strode among the bodies and methodically decapitated each one, his shoulders straining from the effort until he was splattered up to the waist with gore. It took a long time. Multiple blows. The violence of it pulled my mind to the breaking point.

I didn't react when Taran viciously kicked the head of the Fallen who had nearly slit my throat to the side, or even when he climbed the stairs to the altar to stand in front of me, face incandescent with rage and chest still heaving with exhaustion. He looked like he'd spent the time it had taken him to run here composing a few really devastating observations about my folly, but when I didn't move or lift my eyes above the level of his blood-spattered hands, his first question was almost gentle.

"Are you hurt?" he asked again.

If he'd yelled at me instead, I might have slipped deeper into shock, but his question was like permission for something I'd often longed to do and never indulged in. I threw my arms around his waist and fell apart. I gave up all self-control and sobbed into his neck, letting myself go completely limp against him. Nobody was depending on me now. It didn't matter if anyone saw through me to the bottomless fear inside. I cried out all the tears and terror I'd stifled for years, clinging to the safety of Taran's strength.

He was as surprised as I was by my reaction, but after one stiff second with my messy face pressed into his throat, he groaned and wrapped his arms around me until my bones creaked, anger warring with relief in his touch. His bloody hands caught in my hair and pulled as they tightened, and the small pain did more to reassure me that I was still alive than any words would have.

He kissed my temple, the part of my hair, whatever he could reach, and I cried harder.

"I'm sorry, I'm sorry," I panted through sobs, eyes scrunched shut against perceiving any reality that wasn't Taran, impossibly here.

He pushed me back far enough to grip my shoulders in his hands, but I hung my head, unable to face him.

"You're not sorry! Isn't this what you wanted? If you're sorry, why do you keep doing this to me?"

"They didn't have anyone else," I said, weakly defending myself.

"I don't have anyone else! Was the idea of a life with me so terrifying that you couldn't wait a single hour before throwing yours away?"

"I would have done the same thing for you—"

"I don't want you to do the same thing for me," he said, really yelling now. "Do *more* for me. *Live* for me. I would let the entire fucking City and everyone in it fall into the sea before I risked losing you. Do you understand?"

"I know," I sobbed.

"Do you? What did you think would happen if you died down here? Did you think I'd take over your war against Death? Did you think I'd stop the other Stoneborn from subduing the entire mortal world? I wouldn't. I don't care if anyone survives, if you don't."

I tried to rub thick tears off my face enough to see him, but the entire world was distorted. "You don't mean that," I said, voice shaking.

Taran leaned back in, fingers tense on my arms.

"Act like I do," he said, precise words as sharp as a vow and eyes as hard as emeralds.

When I reeled back from that, he took some pity on me and kissed my wet cheeks again before looking over my body for missed injuries. Once satisfied that I was only wounded in spirit, he turned to the huddle of chained, weeping priests and the souls of the dead, who were beginning to drift away into the Underworld.

The grimace on his face said that he blamed them for getting caught only a little less than he blamed the Fallen for catching them.

"What did you do?" I asked, thinking of the flash of light that cut through Death's control over the dead.

Taran's jaw tensed, and he answered reluctantly.

"Napeth's power over them is like a lock. I opened it."

"Did you know you could do that?"

He shrugged like that was unimportant, uncomfortable with the question. I would have pressed more, but one of the dusk-souls broke away from the cluster of glowing figures and slowly approached us. It was the same one who had driven her spear into the first Fallen, but it still took a long moment of looking through the green flame to recognize a short, slender girl with her dark hair cut into a sleek cap.

"I wondered if I might see you here," said Hiwa, oddly serene. "Though I didn't think it would be like this."

"Maiden's mercy," I whispered in horror. I reached out a tentative hand, but my fingers were singed when I tried to touch her. This day had been an avalanche of heartbreaks, but this one threatened to collapse the rest of my soul.

Taran took a step to put his body between us, crowding me back. "Who's this?"

"Don't you know me?" Hiwa asked in her soft voice. "It's me. I'm still me." She appeared to concentrate, and the green blur of her form momentarily solidified into that of an acolyte in Genna's saffron.

"It's our friend. Hiwa ter Genna," I said, voice cracking into fresh tears. I was unsteady on my feet, and Taran put an arm around my waist to pull me protectively against his side even as his face creased in dismay at this dead stranger who knew him.

Hiwa didn't seem to notice his distance or my grief. "And you're alive again! Oh, Taran, I'm so glad."

"I'm sorry," Taran said after a moment, at a loss for words. "We were in the rebellion together?"

"Of course," Hiwa said, brown eyes beaming up at him through a haze of flame. "I had such a crush on you. I think you knew. You were always very patient with me."

I hadn't known, but Taran had always been much more sensitive to that sort of thing than me. He made a soft noise of concern, because he couldn't remember now.

Hiwa flicked her eyes to me, almost playful. "I'm glad I never did anything silly about it, but it was terribly unfair that he didn't fall in love with me. I saw him first, after all."

"You did," I agreed softly.

"Iona was going to ask me to officiate at the wedding, which would have been a wonderfully tragic and romantic moment for the two of us," Hiwa confided in Taran, her voice still soft and sweet. "I was already working on my speech when you died. It would have made you cry. I'm sorry I won't be there now."

"Hiwa, how—" I tried to turn her to a different subject, but Taran held up one hand to quiet me, a line appearing between his eyebrows.

"I would have cried?" Taran asked.

"Yes," Hiwa said, rocking back on her heels.

"Because you thought I was in love with the bride," he guessed with half-lidded eyes.

Hiwa looked at me in muted confusion, then at Taran. "I knew before Iona did. Every morning when you woke up you'd look around for her, and you didn't smile until you found her."

Taran made a derisive noise in his throat, releasing me to stalk a few feet away as though embarrassed. I took his distance as a reprieve and reached for Hiwa's hand, even though it felt like clutching a pot straight from the oven. This might be my last chance to see her, and the fire didn't really burn here in the Underworld.

"What happened to you?"

I'd thought she'd be safe when I stole the boat to follow the dawn. She still had some family, and she should have returned to her hometown on the western coast when I left.

She smiled brightly. "I heard about a bad outbreak of the spotted sickness at Lubridium two weeks ago and went back to help."

That simple sentence told me so much. The spotted sickness usually struck during winter, when people were in close quarters, not spring, when farmers were out in their fields. When the spring rains didn't come, people must have gone to the new capital to beg for help.

"Why did you go?" I asked through the ache in my throat. Only Wesha's blessings could cleanse an infection. The most Hiwa would have been able to do was lend a little strength during a patient's recovery.

"I thought it was what you would have done," Hiwa said with a little half shrug, smile not dimming. "I did cure a couple of cases of pneumonia. Remember that I followed a very talented priestess of Wesha for several years? I learned a few things."

Taran returned to my side, now listening intently.

"One little boy died anyway. And his parents were angry that I couldn't save him. They called the guard."

"And the queen wouldn't accept someone singing the blessings of the gods, even to save her own people," I guessed numbly.

"She hung me in the central square," Hiwa said. She pointed at another group of dusk-souls that hadn't yet departed. "Also the boy's parents. And the neighbors. Because they'd asked for my help in the first place."

I pressed my hands to the sides of my head in horror. "All these people? Has she gone totally mad?"

Hiwa's form dimmed. I sensed that it was hard for her to think about things outside of her own memories. It was a struggle to imagine a future she wouldn't be a part of.

"Some of the nobles are saying that she's made the gods curse us. She's paranoid there will be another civil war. There was a food riot the week before I died, when a ship came into the harbor with oil to sell, but too expensive."

"Drutalos and the others . . . ?" I was almost afraid to ask.

"They went down south to wait for you. Drutalos was sure you'd come back and make the queen see reason before the growing season was over."

This was enough talk of my departure from the Summerlands to make Taran finally interject, slashing his arm between us for emphasis.

"Is there not a single other person in your little coven of rebels who can sing the blessing for rain? Or assassinate one mortal tyrant? Haven't you asked enough of her?"

In life, Hiwa would have blinked in surprise, but she was beyond that now.

"Won't you go too?"

"I cannot imagine a sufficient bribe to go a second time."

She barely frowned. "But Iona hasn't even peeled her own fruit in years. You wouldn't make her do it alone."

Taran's expression tightened. "You must have me confused with the poor dead fool she was going to marry."

"I don't think so," Hiwa said, still serene.

To break off that line of inquiry, I touched her shoulder again.

"Can you come with me? I don't want Death's people to catch you again. And maybe Wesha would—maybe she'd let me bring you back too—" My thoughts spun for some solution.

"How many favors do you think the Maiden owes you? It's alright, Iona. I won't get caught. And I don't even want to leave this place. It's lovely here."

She gently waved at the bare rock walls, seeing something that I couldn't. After a pause where she looked into the distance, head cocked as though listening, she turned to point at the faint light in the opposite direction of the illusion of the white citadel.

"Though I could take you to the beach first. That's where the Fallen caught me."

"No," Taran said before I could respond. "Absolutely not."

I hadn't expected him to suddenly change his mind, but it still made my stomach tense, his stark refusal to consider it.

"Should we send the crafter-priests back with her, at least?" I said, gesturing at the crowd. The few I'd cut loose were slowly going through and freeing the rest, but many of the peace-priests were still curled on the floor, insensible from the collision of their vows and today's attack.

"Darling, I don't care if you want to eat them for dinner," Taran said.

He didn't mean that—his eyes were tight with hurt. I pretended he hadn't said it.

"Is the mortal world safer, or the City? What should we do with them?"

"*Now* you're asking me what I think?" Taran asked, face still angry.

"I always did," I said helplessly.

The flat line of his mouth pulled hard at that.

"Because you knew how I felt about you."

I gave a pained laugh and looked at my feet. "I thought I knew, but when we met for the second time, you thought all the rebels deserved to die. I didn't think you'd believe you once loved one of us."

"Not 'one of us.' You."

"And that's why I couldn't say anything," I whispered. Because I wasn't any different from the rest of them.

That made his face even darker, and he turned to look at the huddled crowd of priests, glaring like they'd done something to him. But after a moment, he shook it off and strode into their midst.

I didn't know what he planned when he took a deep breath and stretched out one hand over their bodies, but then I felt it again. That pull on my soul, the sensation of light and heat without any discernible source. It made my hair stand on end and the background chorus of crying and prayers fall silent. The muscles in Taran's neck pulled taut, and my head started to ache the way it did when the pressure dropped in advance of a storm, but he didn't lower his arm as the feeling grew without release.

Eventually, he cursed and dropped his hand.

"I can't," he said raggedly. "There're too many of them, and their vows are too old."

I couldn't solve the puzzle of his words before he cast around and his gaze landed on a trio of trembling crafter-priests in tattered brown.

"Make a vow to me," he demanded. "All of you. Smenos's people—I got you out of the dungeons once already, you owe me."

I shivered, and so did they, but the first one he'd addressed moved stiffly to her knees. An older woman, gray hair in neat braids, wide shoulders from forge work.

"What vow?" she asked, voice shaded with fear.

That nearly stumped Taran, who grimaced as though offended.

"I don't know—I don't care. Any vow. You'll sing me a little song once a fortnight."

They were taken aback, but after a moment, the first priestess pressed her hands together and nodded. "I vow that I will say a prayer of gratitude to you every morning, Stoneborn, for freeing me twice."

At her words, and those of the next priest, and the next, as they all repeated the same vow, Taran closed his eyes and tipped his head back. There was more to it than just the words. I'd felt it before, at every sacrifice. At Ereban, before the riot. A vow was a sacrifice, and sacrifice was power. It crackled in the air and gilded the edge of Taran's profile as he absorbed it.

It still staggered me, every time I was reminded that he wasn't human. He didn't look it now, his features lit from within, and his voice echoed like he was speaking from a high place when he turned to Genna's priests.

"If I free you from your vows, will you swear to me instead? If you were mine, I wouldn't let you be herded into the Underworld like stray cattle. I'd keep you safe. I won't demand your obedience, just your loyalty—you can't ever speak of what I've done here."

"Yes," said one priestess immediately. I recognized her from my ineffective lessons in calling Death's blessing of fire. The others were slower to respond. A few whispered to each other, and many expressions were full of doubt. But eventually all of the priests got on their knees and began to recite vows to Taran ab Genna.

This time, when he stretched out his arm, I smelled ozone. The dark cavern brightened, and so did the shapes of the priests. It reminded me of watching a meteor shower, the flashes of light that passed between Taran and the kneeling priests. One by one, then all at once. Bright light and heat. It had to hurt—several priests cried out and clutched their chests, and one fell to the floor in shock. Whatever was happening was reshaping their souls, and it frightened me like Marit's deep waves or the pillars of stone the Allmother had created from the earth.

"You're free," Taran said, dropping his hand with a gesture like he was ripping something loose. Every mortal in the cavern inhaled in unison as the divine working reached a crescendo. "Go. Find boats on the shore, leave the Summerlands, never come back. I'll tell Genna you're dead."

Taran had never looked less mortal than when he turned back to me, surrounded by his new priests. The exhaustion had vanished from his posture, even the grime and blood from the sharp lines of his face. His presence vibrated against my skin, and the green of his eyes shone from within. No, it was all of him, like a candle in the dark.

Is this what I wanted?

How could I want anything other than Taran alive and strong, and all of these priests released from their vows? I would be a terrible, selfish person to want anything else.

"Oh," Hiwa said softly. I'd nearly forgotten her in the spectacle, and now her form was a blur next to me. She no longer had the capacity for new experiences, and this had shaken her. Even I could barely begin to reckon with what this meant. With what Taran was. He could have freed me from my vows at any time. He could free every priest in the Summerlands.

My throat was abruptly full of tears, because he was beyond me again. "Take care of yourself, Hiwa. And give my love to Windilla and the others, if you see them."

I walked through the crowd to Taran, and the other mortals respectfully parted to let me pass.

Taran must have seen my thoughts on my face, because his mouth tightened before I could speak. "Don't ask me today, Iona. Not today. Let's just find a way out."

I nodded and batted at my tears with my dusty knuckles. I sniffed the rest back, trying to get myself under control.

It was still him, underneath this glowing shell. Because this must have always been there too.

I put a hand on his chest—for balance, and to reassure myself that he still had a beating heart—then pushed myself up on my good foot to kiss his unsmiling mouth. There was a fine, well-hidden tremble to his lips when they met mine, and realizing how scared he was at once broke my heart and made me feel a tiny bit better, because *me too, Taran, me too.*

He exhaled and wrapped me in his embrace, a slow sway until the scent of lightning had faded and the Underworld fell back into darkness. I heard the priests begin to depart, seizing their lives back from the Stoneborn.

Taran didn't have to do that. I would never have known to ask. He was better than he was trying to teach himself to be.

"What else?" he asked when I didn't make a move to find the tunnel to the surface. "Is there a lost kitten down here? You want to besiege Death's citadel? Find your betrothed and kiss him hello while I watch?"

"I don't think I can walk back up. Can you carry me?"

Taran nodded in relief to hear a request he could grant, then dipped to gather my legs over one arm while I put mine around his neck. I turned my face into his chest, wishing I could return to the moment when he was carrying me down the cliffs ahead of the fires, the last moment when I'd been able to feel only one thing about him.

30

THE CITY WASN'T fixed two weeks later. Whatever power had kept its columns erect and gilded murals bright had failed, along with Genna's long peace. The Allmother's design was falling apart. The flower bushes still bloomed in the endless summer, but there were charred brown tracks through the lawn and trash in the City streets. The ground trembled from time to time, like a wrong step might open a crack in the earth and send us crashing into the sea below. Every moment felt as fragile as the skin of an overripe fruit, ready to split.

I was the only one walking alone down the street from Genna's sector to Wesha's; mortal priests hurried together in groups, and even immortals went armed. The Stoneborn were frightened as their world had proven breakable and their eternity limited.

Death, the coward, had retreated as soon as Genna and Diopater reached the City, but with so many of their priests dead, the Stoneborn knew they were diminished and vulnerable to another attack. They could hear the distant sounds of digging—it was only a matter of time before Death reached the Underworld and captive dusk-souls marched through the Summerlands again.

I had my wish fulfilled: the gods now prepared for war against Death.

My eyes were always scanning the horizon for smoke or the rose-streaked sky for wings, so I nearly careened into Marit for the second time. He moved aside to avoid my path, but surprise made me turn to stare at him, and he halted.

Marit had wandered back to the City the day after Death's attack, newly reborn and confused by all the commotion, but this was the first time I'd seen him myself.

My surprise also took in the two sea-priests who flanked him, middle-aged men with lines around their wary eyes and the baggy blue-striped trousers of their god's old vestments. Swearing vows anew to the latest incarnation of the mercurial sea god must have been a difficult choice, but I couldn't blame them for making it. This wasn't a mortal place, and we were all at the mercy of the gods' protection while we were here.

Marit himself appeared a little different from what I remembered. Younger, maybe. Even younger than me, with more fullness to his pink cheeks and his seaweed-like hair a mess around his shoulders. It made him look almost sweet.

His storm-gray eyes were calm when they took me in, but he couldn't place me in my nondescript linen gown.

"Pardon me if I've forgotten, but have we met?"

Taran had warned me off the sea god, but we were in the middle of a public street, so I didn't think I was in much danger.

"Not recently," I said, and I took his hands loosely in my own. "Hello, Marit. I'm Iona. I'm glad to see you again."

I decided to remember only that he'd once asked me to dance and that he'd died just as unfairly as all the sacrifices on the bone altar, rather than his life before that. If his priests could forgive him, so could I.

His face brightened when I told him my name. "Iona! I thought that's who you might be, with your pretty hair." He turned to his priests and hooked a thumb at me. "This is Taran's high priestess."

They immediately ducked their heads in respect, and I took a small step back.

"Oh, I'm . . . not. Please don't bow," I stammered.

Marit laughed. "He said that's what you'd say."

"Yes," I uneasily agreed. "Is Taran here too?"

I had barely seen him since we reached the surface again. He'd been at Lixnea's palace, against the empty, silent Mountain, conferring with the other Stoneborn. Of course I was glad that he'd convinced them to take Death's threats seriously, but part of me wondered if he was avoiding the opportunity for me to ask him about which vows he could dissolve.

"We rode back together," Marit said cheerfully. "He's lovely, isn't he? It was very confusing when I woke up on the Mountain alone, but Taran explained everything to me."

That had to be a wonderful experience, having things fully explained by Taran—I wished I could experience it for myself someday.

But I smiled politely at the sea god.

"You two have been friends for a long time."

"Yes. He's going to show me the way to the ocean! Though it still feels odd to think about how I might carry ships in my arms instead of wrecking them. Smenos used to be the one who made them, you know, but I suppose anything is a ship if I make it float."

"You're making ships?"

"Taran said it's time to go. We're like too many fighting fish in one bowl here. Too many gods, not enough priests. That's why everything is falling apart," Marit said, jerking his chin at a smoking outbuilding.

At my expression of distress, he frowned. "I didn't mean to worry you. Taran will keep you safe—he has those knives, after all. Would you like me to bring you something from the ocean? Would you like a starfish?"

"Thank you, but I don't have anywhere to put a starfish," I said, trying to focus on what Marit and Taran were planning. "Are you saying that you and the other Stoneborn are leaving?"

"Wesha's lost her grip on the Gates, if Death can lead dusk-souls into the Summerlands," Marit said, eyes drifting to the horizon. "The others think they can push through. So, yes. Soon, I hope."

"Do you even want to go to the mortal world?"

If the queen was hanging the people who'd fought on her side just for praying to the gods for aid, her first reaction to Marit's ersatz ships landing on her shore was likely to be a pike charge.

"Well, I'd like to have more priests," Marit said, voice trailing off as he glanced over his shoulder at the two he'd lured back into his service. He cleared his throat. "And I want to see the ocean, of course."

I lowered my voice and pulled Marit toward the side of the road. He followed trustingly, hands still gripping mine. "But did Taran explain the state of the mortal world? Not everyone will be happy to see even the priests return. What will the Stoneborn do to the people who don't want to worship them?"

At this, Marit's face clouded. A tremor ran through his arms. "What do you mean? Why wouldn't they worship me? I would be a good patron."

The younger of his priests pressed his lips together and put a cautioning hand on the sea god's elbow, but Marit shook it off.

"Do you think I won't?" Marit asked me, gray eyes darkening and beginning to swirl. "I gave my followers all the treasures of the sea. I taught them to make pottery and glass. I calmed the waters for the sailors who sacrificed to me. Why wouldn't they worship me again?"

Stop it, mouthed the other priest, making a frantic face at me behind Marit's back. I took a deep breath, catching the scent of brine and remembering that it was best not to provoke Marit by bringing up any charged topic while only fragile mortals were present. He wasn't the one I needed to convince, anyway.

I should have said something different to Genna. To the mortal queen. I still had to say something to Taran.

"No, I'm sure you'll be a good patron," I said with more hope than honesty, squeezing his hands. "People won't go hungry once you lead the fish to their nets again."

This mollified him, and he rolled his shoulders back in stern satisfaction.

"That's exactly what I'll do. And then they'll build me a new temple by the shore, where I can watch the ships come and go."

That might have been true before my rebellion. But the only god we'd known for centuries was Death, and too many of us had died fighting him. If the Stoneborn returned now, the mortal queen would raise her own army and tear the world apart even further.

I bowed to Marit, and his priests inclined their heads to me, and we all continued on our respective paths, though my feet dragged even more as I returned to Wesha's former palace.

With only half a thought, Taran had sealed up the tunnel to the Underworld upon our return. The rooms here had also changed in the past two weeks—Wesha's dawn-colored murals and pink drapery had vanished overnight, replaced by the greens and blues Taran favored. The world now reshaped itself to his will.

Taran opened locks. He released the dead from their bondage. And he broke divine oaths.

Perhaps those powers could all be reduced to blessings and invoked by mortals, though the idea of praying to Taran made me want to jump off a bridge.

I knew he would release me from my vows if I asked, because he wouldn't be avoiding me otherwise. I just didn't know whether he'd come with me, much less whether he could ever be both the merciful god every mortal desperately needed right now and the good man that I still wanted to love.

I took my hair down and changed into a nightgown, then took his kithara off its peg on the wall while I waited for him. I'd still never seen him play it, and now I painfully wanted to.

There was a sensation like warm fur against my skin when Taran opened the door an hour later. He didn't make any noise, but his power filled the space anyway, impossible to ignore. I stilled my hands on the strings, but before I could turn around, he said, "Please don't stop. I hope that's what I'll hear every time I come home."

I swallowed over the lump in my throat at the simple happiness of his tone and started again. When I closed my eyes, I was nearly able to see him through my eyelids, like the afterimage of looking at the sun.

I'd steeled myself to see the corona of power that had haloed Taran ever since the attack on the City, but I was still startled to find him in Death's gold-embossed armor. It fit him perfectly where it curved around the visible musculature of his arms and legs, suggesting that it had been made to fit him. He held the plumed helmet under his arm, and I was glad I didn't have to meet his green eyes through the snarling mouth of the lion-maw faceplate, at least.

He was impossibly beautiful and terrifyingly inhuman in it. I understood why someone might worship him, and I felt like a villain for wishing nobody would. I wanted to strip the armor off him and drag him out of here with me. Knock him out and pray that when he woke up, he forgot the past year too.

"Was there more fighting?" I asked through a dry mouth.

Taran glanced down at his spotless breastplate. "No, just thought I ought to look the part today."

"What part?"

He smiled at me. Only his lowered eyelashes suggested any

fatigue—the rest of his face was taut and strong. "If we're to re-form the armies of Heaven, the Stoneborn agreed we'd need a general. Of course it took them two weeks to agree on who."

My stomach lurched. "You?"

Taran nodded and raked a hand through his hair with the segmented gauntlet still on, leaving furrows in the dark waves. "Today they gave me their vows. On the battlefield, I can command any priest in the Summerlands. Speak with their patron's authority."

No wonder I could taste it on my tongue, the charge in the room. He held out his arm as though observing the way the light clung to his skin now.

He used to pick the onions out of his food. He once brought me a snowflake in a tin cup.

Look, nightingale, it's snowing.

When he spotted my expression, his smile faltered. "I thought you'd be pleased."

I bought myself time to respond by standing and putting his kithara away.

"What are you going to do with an army?" I asked cautiously.

"Whatever we did last time. I assumed you'll remind me—I should have brought you along, but I thought I wouldn't be able to pry you away from Genna's people before they were all healed."

"We didn't have an army. The queen had the army. We had a few dozen half-trained acolytes who hadn't been ordained yet."

That made him laugh. "Then I like our odds even better this time, darling, if we don't have to fight Death with a bunch of children."

He tracked my plummeting mood, began pulling off bits of his armor with a puzzled frown. The gauntlets, the bracers. I moved to help him with the buckles on his breastplate.

"I thought you'd want me to take control of the defense," he said in a quieter voice. "Death attacked the City itself, which he didn't even do in the Great War. It won't end now until he's sworn to peace again or Wesha takes him back. And of the two of them, believe it or not, he's the one who cares more about the interests of the other Stoneborn."

"No, I know," I said, avoiding his gaze until I could pull the breastplate off him. "I just don't like the idea of you leading an army of priests into battle."

"I'm not very keen on it either, but who else would you like to do it? Diopater and Marit both volunteered."

I cringed at the disaster either of those would be for the mortals still living here. Or worse, the mortals across the sea.

"Marit said he was going across the ocean," I tentatively said.

"You saw Marit? I told you not to go near him unless I was there."

"It was in the street, and he had a couple of his priests with him. He said he was planning to return to the mortal world, and the other Stoneborn, too."

"Not immediately," Taran said with a frown. "But Death's power grows with every priest he can kidnap and sacrifice, and ours diminishes. Can't you feel the earthquakes?"

"So you'll get more worshippers from the mortal world? Taran, if an army of priests and immortals arrives on the shore, it'll be a bloodbath."

"If an army arrives on the mortal shores, I'll be leading it. You really think I'd butcher the peasants just because they won't swear vows?"

"I think you'd defend yourself if you were attacked," I said, hands twisting against each other.

Taran exhaled, his frustration palpable. "And of course you'd be sympathetic to mortals who attacked the gods whose blessings they need to survive without any provocation."

"Someone should go warn people about Death and the other

gods returning soon. Contact the other acolytes and the loyalist nobles. Tell the queen that we need some kind of accord with the Stoneborn or we'll all starve or burn."

He laughed again, but this time there was no mirth in it. He pulled off the last piece of the gold-chased armor and kicked it into the corner.

"And let me guess who you have in mind for this assignment. No. You're not going. I can't believe you're even going to ask me."

"You don't have to go to Wesha, and neither do I. You can break my vows. The same way you broke the priests' vows," I said.

"I could, except that I don't want to. I imagine it was a daily challenge, keeping you alive during your last war, and you wouldn't last the week if I let you go now. Your body'll decorate a gibbet right next to your little friend, and the next time I see you, you'll be pointing a glowing spear in my face."

I felt as though I were standing in a deep hole, looking up at a surface that was so far away that it would be easier to dig through the center of the Earth to escape. I couldn't stay here and watch Taran become something I didn't recognize in a war he didn't want to fight, and my soul shuddered at the idea of how many people would die because I'd helped turn them against the gods when the Stoneborn returned to demand their due.

"Then come with me." I put my hands on Taran's arms, bared by his sleeveless tunic. His skin was as smooth as marble but warm like brass in sunlight. "We'll both go. We'll do it together again."

He looked at my hands and didn't move. "And what kind of welcome do you think we'd receive upon our return, after abandoning the Summerlands?"

I swallowed hard. "We could stay."

"So you can age for a few decades, then die of some pointless mortal ailment?"

"I've always been mortal. It's not frightening to me," I reminded him.

"Well, it's frightening to me!" Taran said, stripping off his tunic and turning toward the baths.

I glared at his stupidly muscled back.

"I'm only twenty-two. I've got a little time before gray hair and wrinkles set in."

Taran spun around and yanked me against his body. He was bright and close, warm and compelling.

"I am trying to give you *all of it*," he said, eyes earnest. "All the time I have, all the power I have. I'd share it all with you."

I knew he meant it—and maybe he had always meant to give me this. An endless summer where he could protect me from harm or want, cherish and coddle me. He'd suffered to gain that power, but his power wasn't what had led him to confront Death alone, wasn't what made him patient with Hiwa or gentle with me or the hundreds of other things that had made me love him. I didn't need his power, I just needed him to believe in me again.

"Some things are more important than us being safe. You used to know that," I said, begging now.

From his face, he simply didn't believe me, even though I couldn't lie to him. He disentangled himself from my arms and stalked to the baths.

"I'll tell them tomorrow I won't lead their army," he said, swinging the door open. "Maybe Wesha will bestir herself when she can smell the smoke from her tower." He slammed the door behind him, hard enough to shake the wall.

My eyes were gritty with repressed tears, but I was willing to give him a moment. When I heard the water run to fill a bath, I tried the door, found it locked, and banged on it with an ineffective fist.

"You know you can't keep me out of it forever," I shouted through the wood.

"I'm willing to try," he called.

I began to sing the lock open, but Taran announced that he was already naked, and I was left to fume outside the door.

"Taran?"

He didn't answer.

There was only one exit from that room, so if I was more stubborn than him, we could still finish this argument. I sat down on the floor, but long after Taran's toes must have shriveled to raisins, I heard nothing from within. Maybe immortal toes were unaffected by a long soak; in retrospect, I really should have noticed he never got so much as a mosquito bite, let alone a pimple or a hangnail. He could probably sit in the bath until I turned to dust.

My bare foot started to ache from contact with the cold floor, so I crossed my legs and rested my head against the door. I missed him so much. I wanted him back so badly.

"You know, Hiwa wasn't even the youngest acolyte fighting with us," I said after a minute. Even if he didn't respond, I knew he could hear me. He couldn't stop me telling him who he was. "That was Acco ab Diopater. I bet he was the first child you ever met. He'd only just started his training when the rebellion began, but he couldn't go home because both his parents had died in Ereban. Acco barely spoke at first, but when you showed up, he took to you. You let him sleep in your tent even though he still wet the bed." I wiped my eyes, remembering Taran dipping a shrieking Acco into a pond by his armpits in an attempt to wash him off.

There was no sound from the other side of the door, but I continued with my eyes shut.

"Anyway, on the first long march with the queen's army, neither of you could stand the field rations. He was from a noble family and you . . . well, I guess you were too. So the two of you convinced each other that you could raid this wild beehive with nothing but a smoking branch of green wood, and we'd all have honey in our porridge. Of course it didn't work—you didn't get any honey, but you *did* both get stung all over. I pulled out the stingers and you sang away the venom, but you felt so bad about it that you turned around and walked an hour back to the last farmhouse we'd passed. You traded your winter cloak to get Acco his jar of honey."

I laughed and brushed away more tears with my palms.

"Which was when I decided that I'd love you forever."

I took a deep, shaking breath and pressed my cheek to the wood. I would have sailed across the sea even if I knew it would take years to find him. I'd keep searching as long as it took.

"I know you're not the person you're trying to be. I know it better than you do."

Though I was prepared to sleep against the door if necessary, a few minutes later it cracked open and I scooted out of its way.

We were a ridiculous pair, Taran with his wet hair and me on the floor, but he only sighed and helped me stand on stiff, numb limbs. He was wary and sad and beautiful, and my heart clenched to see all of that on his face. He closed his eyes.

"Fine. I'll do it," he said.

31

TARAN TOOK MY hands in one of his and walked me backwards toward my room, shaking off my attempts at clarification. Fine, he'd break my vows? Fine, he'd come with me?

When I was seated on the edge of my bed, he knelt in front of me with my feet resting on his thighs. He didn't even have to sing to ease the swelling in my bad foot now, just stroke his thumb along the arch. A careless show of inherited power.

He frowned at my tense, worried expression and leaned forward until his chest was pressed up against my knees.

"If you think you're in a cage, you'll just batter yourself to death against the bars," he said, more to himself than to me. "So, fine. If you want to go, you can go. I'll break your vows if you ask." His eyes lifted to mine, and with his jaw clenched tight, he pulled his other hand from behind his back to offer me two different treasures, both stolen: my green scarf, tattered but clean and neatly folded, and my silver betrothal ring. The look in his eyes was urgent enough to still my next breath.

"But you were right. I do want to know if you would have said yes. I do want to know if you'd choose me. So, here's my last offer. I'll go to the Painted Tower to fulfill your vows to Wesha and the bird. I'll retrieve your poor dead betrothed from the Underworld and send him back across the sea. Wesha has to allow it if she promised it to you."

My hand lifted as if of its own accord and pressed over my wildly beating heart.

"He can go tend to your hapless rebels. Wreak havoc in the mortal world," Taran said with heated determination. "And you can choose me this time."

"You'd really go to the Painted Tower? Help me stop the next war?" I asked, even as my vow to him punished me for entertaining what I knew was an impossible idea. There was no third person who could do this for us—only the image of Taran I still held in my heart.

"I've tried offering you everything else I have. What else is there?"

He'd be so close if we went to the Painted Tower together. Just one small sea between us and the mortal world. If he'd go that far for me, surely he'd go a little farther.

"Because you want me to be your priestess?" I asked gently.

Taran looked up at me with soft eyes, searching my face. "I know you said no more vows. And marriage vows are stronger than anything I'd have asked you to swear as my priestess. But that's what you wanted before, isn't it, someone to love you till the stars fall out of the sky? I actually can, Iona. If I marry you, it is for forever. Isn't that what we should do?" He didn't know we'd done this before—him on his knees, my heart trembling in my chest. "Aren't we in love? Isn't that what this is?"

It was an echo of the first time he asked me.

Isn't that what people do when they're in love?

Say yes, nightingale.

"Yes. Yes, Taran, we're in love," I said, gasping for breath after I said it, and oh, it felt like the shard of obsidian that had been lodged in my own heart since he died loosened and let it fully beat again.

The light in the entire room brightened with his smile. "I was looking for you," Taran said, putting scarf and ring aside and wrapping his arms tightly around my calves, chin resting on my knee. "When I woke up, I couldn't remember anything, but I knew something was missing. Someone. I looked through all of the Summerlands, and I felt nothing. I went down to the Underworld and walked through Death's citadel, but it was empty, and nothing there called to me either. Smenos's price for a boat was too high, so I went to Marit. The night I found you, I was planning to ask him to take me across the sea in his chariot. And then I found you and it was like—finally I could breathe. I could rest. I could sleep. I had you again."

"You tried to make me do your laundry!" I objected, laughing when Taran stood up and pushed me down on the bed.

"I thought I needed a priest. Everyone else had them, and I had those plans set aside for my big villa that was supposed to be full of people. I thought that was what I'd been missing—but it was just you."

His big hands cupped my waist through my loose gown, gripping me with restrained need.

"Tell me you missed me too. Even if you didn't choose me the first time."

That was the moment I should have told him. There was no reason not to now, except for how much it would hurt him to know I'd held the full truth back. But I wished so much that what he imagined could be the truth. I wished there was someone else who would go and fight and die so that for once I could just *live*. If mortal dreams could build the Summerlands, if mortal devotion gave the gods their power, why couldn't I want so much to be with Taran that the world would reshape itself to permit it?

"I *loved* you," I said, wrapping my arms around his neck. "How could I not have?"

He grinned in amazement, then kissed me hard enough that I gasped for air when he broke away.

"Tell me it always should have been me," he said.

"It always should have been you." I grabbed the fabric of his shirt and pulled it free, struggling with it until he tossed it aside. I sighed in satisfaction when I got my palms splayed against the hot, bare skin of his chest. "It always should have been like this."

"You thought about it?" Taran asked, fingers stroking my jaw as I explored the swells and hollows of his body.

"From about ten minutes after I met you. Not that I ever said anything."

His smile was triumphant. "Even after you were betrothed?"

"*Especially* after I was betrothed. But I was trying to be the perfect priestess of Wesha, even as we were burning down the temples."

"What idiots we were," he said with a laugh. "You must have felt guilty."

"Very guilty." So needlessly. Too afraid of disappointing him to ever ask honestly for what I wanted—what he must have wanted too.

He wasn't afraid of asking now, dipping his head and kissing me more deeply. He caught one of my bare legs between his thighs and pulled me against him, close enough that I could feel his racing heartbeat.

"We wasted so much time," I said, desire beginning to make me dizzy. "I used to stare at you across the fire at night and imagine—it felt impossible, but I'd imagine you suddenly looking at me and saying that you'd die if you couldn't touch me that night. And I'd say I felt the same."

His hands slipped up farther, until his thumbs brushed the undersides of my breasts through the fabric of my nightgown. It was thin enough to carry the warmth of his hands to my skin, which blazed up under his touch, heated even when his hands moved on.

"What did you imagine? Let's do all of it. Tonight. I would have done anything you asked."

"Oh, I—" I blushed at the idea I was going to have to say anything out loud. "I imagined *everything*."

Taran chuckled softly and rubbed his lips along my earlobe. "I doubt the perfect priestess of Wesha imagined *everything*. Though I would be delighted if you did." His hands trailed back down to my waist, then farther, and this time he slipped his hands under the hem of the dress and repeated the same broad caress with his palms against my skin.

"So, when I was sixteen, I was seconded to the high temple of Genna to assist in the burn ward," I confessed, daring enough to drop my own hands to his stomach and trace the hard lines of his hipbones where they disappeared into the drawstring waist of his trousers. "And it turned out that there were some very, ah, educational scrolls in their library."

Taran's breath was hot on my neck as his hands continued their gentle exploration of my body. "Something inappropriate for acolytes of Wesha, I take it?"

"*Very* inappropriate. And mostly . . . diagrams," I said, cheeks heating when he caught the tip of one breast between a thumb and a knuckle and rolled it in his fingers. "About twenty of them."

Taran laughed harder at my confession. "Maybe you'll teach me something, then. I'm not sure I know twenty different things off the top of my head. Maybe ten or so that I've been thinking about."

When he put his hands on the bottom hem of my dress and prepared to pull it over my head though, I kept my arms down, not quite struggling.

"This part probably looked better in your imagination," I warned him. I looked better with my clothes on, where tailoring could suggest curves. Maybe I should keep them on.

Taran snorted and slid my fingers from my hem to ease it up, inch by inch. "I have a very accurate imagination." I closed my eyes when he pulled it off and settled back down next to me with a couple of fingertips trailing between my breasts and across my stomach. "And there is not a single inch of you that I didn't imagine touching."

His fingers hooked in the waistband of my underwear and pulled my last scrap of clothing down over my hips. Completely bared to him for the first time, I held my breath as he silently looked me over. I waited for him to touch me, cover my body with his, break the moment. People liked the idea of me best, followed by the sound of me, and I hoped very much that Taran would like the feel of me too, but the sight of me didn't have much to recommend it beyond my hair.

But Taran's knuckles traced tenderly along the lines of my breasts, my stomach, the dips of my hips. "If I thought the Allmother cared for me at all, I'd think she made every part of you just to please me," he said, voice dropping and roughening.

"I want to," I said, my voice shivering when his hand briefly slid across my thigh, a tingling line of heat that burned even when he lifted it to my waist again. "I'll try."

"Darling, you already do," he whispered. "You're perfect for me. Your mouth fits against mine like it was made for me."

He kissed me then, sweet and drugging, and for the first time neither of us was pulling away to deny ourselves. I let my hands explore the sharp, familiar contours of his face and the new, exhilarating ones of his body, the downy hair low on his stomach and the tight muscles of his chest while his hands pressed against the mattress and suspended his body over mine.

My skin was already tingling with the pleasure of touching him when Taran broke the kiss to lower his mouth to my neck.

"Your body was made for me too," he said, hand brushing exposed skin before his mouth followed it. "The little hollow in your throat that moves when you laugh. Your breasts. I wanted this."

He lowered his head to run lips and tongue against the places he'd only touched with his hands, and my breath stuttered at the sharp, unexpected delight of his mouth on my breasts. I made a small noise of surprise when his teeth grazed the peak, startling at the jolt it sent to my core, and he looked up only long enough to shoot me a devilish grin and begin again.

"I didn't know," I said, lip trembling over my lower teeth. If I'd known it felt like this, I would have been braver. Another cry caught in my throat as Taran moved his head to the side and the cool air of the room hit the wet, sensitive skin he'd left exposed.

His mouth felt like worship, something that awoke power. He coaxed more noises from me as his lips moved to the lower curves of my breasts and then trailed down farther, to my navel. He rolled his nose against the small mound of my stomach and made my breath catch when he gave me a melting, secretive look from his position nearly between my knees.

"I thought about this too," he said, leaning forward so that my thighs parted infinitesimally wider.

I nodded solemnly. I'd memorized twenty diagrams. I expected him to touch me again like he had outside his tent, lift his fingers from where they gripped my knees and stroke them between my thighs, but even if he didn't, my body was already buzzing with desire. I'd welcome him anyway.

He slowly pushed my knees apart. "I thought about putting my mouth on this rosebud. Imagined the noises you'd make."

Puzzling that sentence through took me past his next movement— my head was swimming and maiden-priests didn't deal in euphemism— but I got it just before he lifted one knee over his shoulder.

"You're sure?" I whispered when he lowered his head enough to drag his wet lower lip over my core.

"No diagrams of this?" he asked with an amused sparkle in his eyes. "That scroll sounds very outdated."

"Is this new, then?" I said, words almost a gasp as nervous anticipation twisted in my stomach.

"I can't remember, so maybe I just invented it for us," he said, laughing softly. He settled himself between my thighs, pressing a kiss to the inside of my knee before leaning back in to spread me with his thumbs for his hot, worshipful mouth.

My hips lifted off the mattress at the first pass of his tongue, and I instinctively laced my hands across my mouth to stifle a cry before I remembered what he'd said about hearing me. Cheeks blazing, I grabbed the coverlet instead as his lips worked little whimpers out of my throat.

I knew the course of every muscle and sinew in my body, the tracery of nerves that connected them, the path from my heart to my fingers and toes, but the sensation that spun through my body seemed to follow none of them. It was more like a fiery, winged creature had awoken in my body and found a new sky to soar in, leaving hot sparks behind as it spun high in my heart and low in my core. I felt too small to contain it, twisting and bowing my back as Taran's mouth stroked my most secret spaces.

"Good," he said when I moaned, and I hadn't been aware of doing anything at all, but when I glanced at a stomach that was beginning to bead with sweat, he was looking up at me with fierce appreciation. I swept his hair away from his forehead, mostly to feel the silky strands between my fingers instead of just against my trembling thighs. I loved that too, the contrast between his soft hair and his rough cheek and the hot, wet pressure of his mouth. Every sensation was new, every part of me felt new—and made for this, just like he'd said.

I writhed as the heated tension in my stomach caught and pulled. I felt suspended even as my hands reached for something to cling to. I must have said something, pleaded out loud, because when that tension finally broke and let me fall through my own body, free from all constraints, I found I was gripping Taran's hand like it was the only thing anchoring me to the world.

I panted like I'd run a long distance, my body gathering solidity where it had just felt light enough to float to the ceiling and dissolve like a soap bubble. And Taran kissed the curve of my inner thigh. He kissed the jut of my hip. He kissed the rise of my stomach and the valley between my breasts. It was so gentle and so sweet, and yet when I finally opened my eyes, the slow, careful press of his mouth was entirely contradicted by the need written across his face.

His lips were swollen and red in the lamplight, and I caught a flash of white as he rubbed his teeth across them as though feeling the change. I thought about how they'd gotten that way and had a flash of amazed self-consciousness. I couldn't believe we'd just done that.

"I imagined what you'd sound like. What you'd taste like. But it was even better," he said when I pulled him over me and tried to hide my face in his shoulder. "No, Iona, don't hide. You were obviously made for this too."

He sounded so full of masculine pride that I relented, tipping my head back so that he could see my pink cheeks and how they curved when I let out the shy grin I'd been holding in. His voice was conspiratorial, like we'd stolen some guarded treasure through cleverness and guile.

Though hadn't we? Wasn't this unlikely? The Allmother hadn't helped us—every god had hindered us! So many vows and oceans and deaths had nearly stood between us and this moment, where my bare body nestled against his, and his last layer of clothing did little to conceal his desire.

Taran hummed in appreciation when I cupped him through the material of his trousers and used my palm to boldly explore a shape I'd only caught the vaguest sense of before. A hard press against my stomach or thigh whenever I let my restraint slip and kissed him like I wanted to had been a precious reassurance that he felt the way I did. This time I didn't stop, didn't tell myself *later*.

"Like this?" I asked, running a hand from his base up to his waistband. I didn't know how hard to touch him. He'd been gentle with me, but his body was so much larger and firmer than mine.

"You can touch me however you want to," he said in a rumbling voice, lying back and folding his arms behind his head. The slits of his eyes and the tension in his stomach contradicted his casual invitation though, and I decided I would like to see a little of that control slip.

"Like this, then?" I asked, letting my hand drift up, onto his chest. I climbed into a kneeling position, letting my hair fall over one shoulder and partially obscure my breasts.

Taran eyed my bare chest, almost but not quite out of his reach.

"If you like," he said with feigned diffidence as my hand explored the planes of his chest and stomach but didn't follow back down past his waistband. He was hard muscle and soft skin down his sides, rough hair on his stomach and quick heartbeats over his pulse points. I reveled in the chance to explore him at my leisure, drink in the perfection of his features while they were glowing with desire. I bent to kiss the dip of his collarbones, and he lifted a hand, nearly unconsciously, to cup my breast.

"Just like this?" I asked again, laying an open-mouthed kiss at the base of his jaw and following it with the scrape of my teeth. My hand rested chastely over his heart.

He chuckled at how transparent I was being. "I like this," he said, his thumb circling around my nipple. "I'll never tell you to stop."

"Is there anything else you like?"

"At least nine more things, remember?" he said, eyes crinkling into a smile. "But you can take as much time as you want."

"That was only one thing?" I blurted out, surprised. It had felt like quite a lot of things.

Taran laughed harder, then pulled me down to a hard kiss. It was wet and thorough, and the thought of what that mouth had just been doing on me made me squirm in a shivery, dazed way. With Taran's tongue in my mouth, I was daring enough to drop my hand back to his waistband and undo the knot of his trouser laces. I couldn't have done it while he was looking at me, and I was glad for his hand cupping my jaw and the way I could feel it tighten when I finally gripped him.

His breath caught, and I savored the jerk of his body when I rolled my palm along the feel of silk over metal.

"Like this?" I asked against his mouth, opening my eyes just enough to take in his heavy-lidded nod.

"Exactly like that," he said, breath clipped.

I'd imagined this, though I wasn't brave enough to admit it. How he'd look. How his face would change—jaw taut, lips parted, eyes nearly closed. I had only the barest hints of what he'd be like under the grip of desire. On a few mornings when he'd come to wrap his bigger body around mine with all our blankets over us both—*I'm cold, Taran*—I'd pondered what he'd do if I'd pressed a finger to my lips and slipped a hand between us like I was doing now. Would he have let me love him? Could we have been quiet enough? Could I have learned then how his breathing changed when I tightened my hand and slid it toward me?

His hips moved unconsciously as I stroked him, reaching for a rhythm I longed to learn. I greedily absorbed every detail, the exact angle of his thick eyelashes over his cheeks, the color of the flush that stained his neck.

"What else?" I whispered, my voice sounding dry to my own ears. I hadn't realized how much *want* I could feel from this position on my knees, my hand around him, but I knew there was more.

I wanted more. I'd told him I wanted everything, but I sensed he was waiting for something. "Should I—" I moved to suggest curling over him, putting my mouth on him like he had on me, but he stopped me with one hand on my shoulder, the other covering mine where it was still wrapped around his length.

"Not if you don't want this to be over in the next thirty seconds," he said, voice tight.

"What, then?"

With slitted eyes, Taran pulled me down next to him. His hand swept in a long stroke down my body, curling under my backside to hitch my hip against his and pull my thigh over his leg. I unthinkingly let go of him when his fingertips ghosted over my core, and he took my hand with his own to bring it back.

"Please don't stop," he said, nipping my lower lip in rebuke. "I think I might actually die if you stop, and you'd feel guilty about that later."

He was hesitating for some reason, and I wasn't distracted even when his fingers began to rub slick patterns between my thighs.

"You said *everything*," I reminded him. "Did you change your mind?"

"Darling, I can't change my mind, I'm Stoneborn. And you are very naked and tempting and I'm trying hard to keep my head about this when all I want to do is fall on you like a ravenous beast." His breath came faster when my hand moved more quickly, a reaction my scientific mind treasured and wanted to explore more completely.

"I don't mind if you lose control," I said, daintily biting into the large muscle of his shoulder. I thought I'd like that, actually, seeing Taran with no masks or pretense. Knowing that I had done that to him.

"You have no idea whether you would mind," he said, body jerking when I bit down harder, and he pulled my legs apart enough to press one finger inside me, a frictionless glide that nearly had me forgetting my important goals again. I twisted against the exquisite curl of his hand in my body, trying not to lose myself in it. I could have more, and I wanted more. "Consider that it is very, very important to me that you like this, so that you want to do this again in a few hours, and again in the morning, and also every day for the rest of eternity."

"Why are you worried?" I asked, firmly pushing aside the question of whether I'd get him for eternity or even one more night out of my mind.

Taran cast a skeptical glance down his body, where I did not quite have my hand closed all the way around him. "This might hurt a little."

I had to stifle my giggle, because I didn't want him to take it the wrong way, but that concern had been the furthest from my mind. With everything that he'd seen me survive, he was worried that I couldn't muster the same courage any other woman would before her wedding night?

"I don't think it will," I told him honestly, because the only pain I'd felt so far was the ache of desire, and that was only growing for every moment that he didn't touch me like I wanted him to. "But if it does, I expect you to be very brave about it."

That made him laugh, and a smile that was nearly painful for its tenderness spread across his face. His green eyes were bright and loving as he finally rolled to kick off his trousers and cover my body with his own.

"We'll both be brave, then," he whispered into my ear before ducking his head to suck on the tender skin of my neck. His knees parted my thighs, and he shifted his weight to one forearm so that he could pull one of my legs over his hip. He lined himself up with me and held the position with taut muscles and his lip caught between his teeth until I wrapped my arms around his shoulders and lifted my hips to welcome him.

When we came together, I'd always imagined that there would be some moment of clear division. Before and after. Like the note of a lyre's plucked string where there'd been silence before. And not just a physical sensation, but an emotional one too—I thought I'd be forever changed, after all, off Wesha's path for good. But as Taran exhaled and slid forward, fraction by fraction, until our hips were flush against each other, I realized it wasn't the first note of a song, but the refrain in a melody we'd already been singing.

I'd wanted this for years. I'd started singing this song the first day Taran's fingers brushed mine. My heart had sung it the day I realized I was in love with him, the day he asked me to marry him, every evening I played his favorite ballad, every time he made an excuse to comb my hair, every hidden kiss, every longing look.

This hadn't changed me; I already was this person who clutched her lover's arms and urged him to make the bright sensation even sharper. There wasn't such a distance between having something and wanting it, after all.

"Alright?" Taran asked, kissing my eyelids, my cheeks, the tip of my nose. I could tell that he was trembling from the effort of holding himself back, a fine sheen of sweat standing out on his cheekbones and shoulders, but he didn't move.

"Perfect," I breathed. It was perfect even if it was overwhelming, even the stretch of my body was caught just on the sweet edge between pain and pleasure. I would stay in this moment forever, if I could, because there were infinite little details I wanted to capture and hold. I experimentally lifted my hips against Taran's to explore the sensation that budded in my core with every movement, and he hissed, dropping his forehead to mine as he struggled to hold still.

I moved again, finding my bearings, grounding myself in the raspy noise of Taran's breathing. He dipped his head to kiss me as though trying to distract me, but I sucked his lower lip into my mouth and gave a peremptory roll of my hips, moving past the faint ache toward glints of pleasure I could sense in the distance.

At last Taran moved, so carefully that my heart swelled in my chest at his painstaking gentleness. It was instinct to press my fingers into his shoulders, deep knowledge to squeeze his hips with my thighs and urge him on. This had been locked within me, waiting to be expressed, and it was nothing but relief to finally express it.

His breathing was more ragged than the slow rhythm he set, most of his attention locked on my face, vigilant for any sign of distress.

"My love, you're not going to break me," I said, trying to pull him in deeper with my heel against the back of his calf. I wanted to chase that thread of tension I'd found earlier, but more than that, I wanted to see that thread in him unravel. I wanted to see him undone.

"You are shockingly, terrifyingly breakable," Taran said before kissing me again and doing something clever with his hips to roll against a spot that made me gasp into his mouth. I tried to object to that statement, but he did it again, and I couldn't say much with his tongue in my mouth and my heart fluttering in my chest. Still, I could dig my fingernails into his arms, hard enough that a mortal man would have worn crescent moon marks in his skin to gloat over the next day.

I thought I wouldn't mind a few marks. A little burn when I walked. A violet constellation in the shape of his fingertips over my hips. I turned my face into Taran's neck and let him feel the edge of my teeth against his skin.

He laughed in a shaky rush. "You are such a little demon. Fine, you know what you get?"

I was excited for whatever it was that I got, but I was still surprised when he wrapped his arms under my back and carefully rolled us over so that I straddled his hips, our bodies still joined together. I blinked with disorientation as Taran sprawled out on his back, smirking up at me.

"Go ahead, do your worst," he said.

My laugh sent flutters of pleasure through the spread of my thighs, and while I wasn't certain what, exactly, he thought I was going to do, every tiny movement was infinitely rewarding. When I hesitated, Taran put his hands on my hips and pulled me toward him, a sweet, aching roll that made our breaths catch in unison. I did it again, his hands still guiding me, and it was deeper, better. I had it. This was the rhythm, this was the song. I knew this one.

I closed my eyes to focus on the building pressure that coiled tighter with every movement, but the tips of Taran's fingers brushed my chin, startling me.

"No, look at me," he said, voice strained. It took me a moment to get it—there was nothing better in the world to look at than beautiful, inhumanly perfect Taran with his cheeks flushed red and his neck corded with tension, but I didn't immediately realize why he sounded so insistent.

Did he think I could imagine anyone else? It never could have been anyone else but him, and it would always have been like this. Even if it had been some stolen evening away from the campfire or on our wedding night, it still would have been just like this. I wouldn't have loved him any more or less. And he loved me, I knew that for certain. He loved me then and he loved me at this moment, with his eyes bright and fixed on my face while his fingers pressed bruises into my thighs.

I held myself up with one palm over his hammering heart as the knots of sensation in my body twisted and spun, drawing tighter and tighter until I felt that the sensation was all there was to me. I was only dimly aware of the rasping noises I was making, little sounds drifting from my lips without effort. I was losing track of the rhythm, suspended mostly by Taran's hands and the primal momentum of my body. Keeping my eyes open was the only conscious effort I could manage, and I found that I was begging Taran for help again, certain that I was going to fall or fail or perhaps die under the pressure building inside me as he moved.

He pressed his thumb between us, his other hand gripping the loose hair falling down my back. Between these two points of tension, he drew me like a bow. With one final snap of his hips, that tension broke, and I was undone. Taken apart. Remade. I was too small to contain the wave of feeling and emotion that vibrated through me, washing from the points of my breasts to the tips of my toes with a force that felt sufficient to pull the walls down.

This part, I could never have imagined. I had asked my body to sing and to fight and to survive great disasters before, but I hadn't known how it could ring with feeling. It would have felt like too much to ask for, but Taran's rapt eyes on my shaking lips said eloquently that this was what he'd wanted.

I would have fallen—to the floor, or perhaps the ceiling—but Taran's hands kept me barely upright as his rhythm picked up for a handful of heartbeats before the line of his mouth tightened. A long, low noise was stifled in his throat as he reached to cup one breast, my hair tangled around his fingers. His hard green stare lost focus and was replaced by a softer expression, one that suffused his face with something like wonder as the muscles of his body went taut and still. There was an echo of his pleasure in my body, one last throb of sensation that lingered before my breathing slowed and my heartbeat began to match the heaviness in my limbs.

I savored every second of it, my eyes determinedly open to catch the way Taran's head fell back and his eyelids drooped in satisfaction. He let out a whistling sigh and brushed my hair off my shoulders before thinking better of it, gathering the longest strands to fall around his face like a curtain when I slumped forward onto his chest.

"I first imagined this about ten minutes after I met you," Taran murmured into my ear when I finally closed my eyes. "And it must have been the millionth time."

32

WE LAY NESTLED in each other's arms for a long time, but eventually Taran pulled against my hands. I had my face pressed into his bare chest so that he couldn't see my expression, and I made a wordless protest as he attempted to disentangle himself from me.

Tomorrow. I'd tell him tomorrow. Ask him to go a little further tomorrow. Just one more ocean, just one more disaster. I'd bargained with myself for this one night, and it wasn't over. I wanted this entire night in his arms. But he rubbed his nose and lips into my jaw hard enough to make me giggle, then rolled to the other side of the bed.

I reluctantly sat up too, only to discover a wet smear on my thighs that unexpectedly shimmered like molten gold. Startled, I stifled a small laugh.

I supposed that I now had another plausible explanation for why he'd been so content to wait years for our wedding night. Even a sheltered priestess of Wesha would have grown a little suspicious about his ancestry when confronted with the apparent consequence of lying down with one of the Stoneborn.

Nose wrinkled endearingly, Taran tugged a loose lock of my hair to pull my attention away.

"I'll be right back." He pulled a sheet over my naked legs without bothering to cover himself before padding nonchalantly from the room. Moments later, he returned bearing wine and a folded linen cloth. He offered me my choice of these two new and appropriate gifts, and I reluctantly acquiesced to time continuing, despite my best efforts to freeze it while Taran held me and loved me and was happy.

Collapsing back in bed, Taran caught my left hand and held it out to examine my bare fingers, satisfaction in his every line. "What kind of a ring do you want? Emeralds? I have a few with emeralds. I suppose I could have a new one made, but I don't really want to wait that long, do you?"

I shifted my wrist to twine my fingers with his instead, pulling our joined hands to my chest. I didn't want the next hour, the next day, or the next year. Just this moment. But he was waiting for my answer, so I spoke reluctantly.

"Any ring is fine. I just want to get married in front of our friends."

Taran propped himself up on some pillows and took a deep draught of the wine, and when he answered, his voice was still relaxed and unassuming.

"What friends? Do you mean Marit, or that girl Genna's holding on to? They can come."

I didn't answer, instead burrowing my face into his chest. Taran put a hand under my chin to tilt my face up to his, somehow catching on that my thoughts were not marching in the same direction as his.

"I didn't hurt you, did I?" he asked after considering my expression.

"No, of course not," I said, trying to wrap my hands around his so that I could duck my head again. I was afraid I'd hurt the both of us though. I still felt him studying me and I squirmed, cheeks heating from shame that had nothing to do with my state of undress.

He took another deep swallow of the wine, silent for long thoughtful minutes before he set the goblet aside. When he finally spoke again, all the warmth had vanished from his voice.

"You mean the friends I can't remember? The ones back in the mortal world, where you'd rather go than stay here with me?" He sighed and closed his eyes, pinching the bridge of his nose between two fingers as his body tensed. "I see. Well, go on, then," he said, voice leaden. "You've softened me up. Ask."

"That is not what I was doing," I said, turning to splay my hands on his chest, even as my heart fell. I should have told him. "This was because I love you."

"I'm sure. As this act means *so much* to you. I appreciate the demonstration of your affection. Even if you were tracking the minutes you had to wait before you next asked me to take you across the sea."

That was a challenge thrown down, his eyes begging me to deny it.

"I love you," I said again, wondering if he'd ever believe it now. "Taran, I love you! I meant everything I said. We still have to go."

"I told you that it doesn't have to be you," he said, pointing at my scarf and ring where they were discarded on the floor with our scattered clothes. "I asked you just once to choose me instead. Me instead of anything!"

"And you said you'd let me go if I asked," I said, voice wobbling. "You were willing to go to the Painted Tower. It's only a little farther, it could only be a few months, and then we could still come back—"

His mouth flattened into a hard line. "You couldn't have asked me an hour ago? What if you're pregnant?" he demanded.

I froze, then began counting days. Such prosaic concerns had been slow to occur to me, but the math was familiar from long ago.

"I won't be," I said when I was done, shoulders relaxing.

Taran scoffed. "How can you possibly know that?"

"Wesha's the patron of childbirth, and I—"

Another flash of hurt crossed his face. "And *I* come from a line of fertility goddesses. Do you think my mother wanted *me*?" he asked, nearly yelling now.

"*I* want you, Taran," I cried, reaching again for his hands, but his face darkened, sharpened as he stood up and began to pace. "I want you forever, I want to watch you build that big marble villa, I want to have ten grumpy redheaded babies that we will love even if they look like me instead of you. And we will still have that, if we can ever finish what we started."

Taran sucked in a short, pained breath.

"If you think I am unselfish enough to let you sail home to wage more years of war against the gods, you dramatically overestimate my character. In fact, I'm feeling a very mortal change of heart coming over me *right now*. I think I ought to test whether you can forget your pointless war with a few more months in my arms, or at any point before the Moon mistakes her course and falls into the sea. You certainly forgot your betrothed quickly enough."

I devoutly wished I'd never begun this charade. Every terrible decision I'd ever made was clear only in retrospect, which was not helpful at all in making better ones now. Was it a kindness to keep it from him now, or a betrayal? The shine of his eyes was hard and brittle. If I chose wrong, I knew I could shatter him.

I got to my feet and cupped his face with my hands, heart aching at the way he turned his cheek into my palm. I didn't have to tell him to convince him to let me leave—I knew he'd relent soon enough. He wanted me to stay because I loved him, not because I had no choice. All I could do now was give him a reason to come with me.

"I didn't forget," I said, framing his face with my fingers. "Not for a single minute. I won't ever change my mind about you. Because that was you too. It was you, Taran. You're the one I bargained with Wesha for."

It took him a long moment to understand. He held stock still, staring at me in confusion as he tried to match my words with everything else I'd said.

"What?" His voice was a rough bark.

"I came to bring you home. That's what I've been trying to do."

There was a tremor in the floor under my feet. The Summerlands trembling either for the absence of the Allmother, or the emotions running through Taran's immortal heart.

"There wasn't anyone else?"

"No. There was always only you," I said, releasing him and sitting back on the bed.

Part of me felt free and light. I'd never wanted to have secrets from him. And now he knew everything.

"You—you said we were in love. You wanted to marry me. But we took vows? Betrothal vows?" he asked, eyes widening as he worked through it. "That's my ring. All those things you said . . ."

The shift from shock to anger in his face when I nodded wasn't entirely unexpected, but it still hit me hard. Taran backed away from me.

"You have been trying to leave me since the moment we met," he accused me.

That was not what I'd expected him to be angry about.

"If I'd taken you to the Painted Tower the night I saved you from the Fallen, you would have left me here. You've tried to run away from me half a dozen times. When you'd already promised to be my wife? Did you ever mean it?" he demanded incredulously.

I blinked, jolted by the accusation. "Taran, you *died*. And I was so convinced that I couldn't live without you that I sailed across the Sea of Dreams to ask Wesha to give you back. I'm only here because I wanted to marry you."

"Well, here I am!" he cried, arms spread. "I've been here the entire time. You can have me, every possible way you can have someone, until the end of time. Past it! What were you waiting for? Why didn't you tell me?"

"Five minutes after I got here, I found out you were only in the mortal world to *kill* me. Put down the mortal rebellion. Make us worship the Stoneborn you hate!"

"Which I *did not do*, even though I could have. Instead, I did everything you wanted, up to and including dying for you. What would have been enough, Iona? Was there a single thing I didn't do?"

I gripped my hands so hard together they cramped. "I didn't think you were the same person I knew. If I'd even known you in the first place—you were a Stoneborn, instead of a runaway acolyte. You're immortal! You have priests! I didn't know what you could have possibly wanted with me."

"So the second you found out I wasn't exactly what you expected, you changed your mind about me," he said bitterly.

"I didn't change my mind," I insisted, grabbing the sheet and trying to wrap it around myself, even though Taran and I didn't seem to mind shouting at each other naked. "I've been trying to change *yours*. You were looking for me? I've been looking for you!"

"Then you'll keep your promises? Good. I always keep mine. Let's go find a peace-priest. We can get married tonight," he said, expression fierce.

I put a palm over my face, nearly laughing in dismay.

"You want to get married now? Right now?" I asked incredulously.

"I shouldn't have to *ask* now," he said, bending down and retrieving my ring from the floor where my scarf was threaded through it. "You already said yes. You agreed to marry me when you thought I was a nameless, penniless mortal. I could have died young and left you a widow, or fallen sick and made you nurse me. We might have been poor or barren or chased out of every town by religious loyalists, but you went ahead and promised me your entire life for the price of a stone house and a plum tree. Well, I can still provide those." He looked at me steadily. "Are you really saying you wouldn't have said yes if you'd known who I was?"

I looked at him helplessly, because who he was before he met me was the furthest thing from what was pulling us apart. "It wouldn't have changed anything. But Taran, it still doesn't. What do you think being married means? I'm yours. I'm yours forever. I'll love only you till the end of my life and past it, but you were going to marry Iona Night-Singer who led the mortal rebellion against the gods. You always knew that!"

He'd always known who *I* was. I had blood on my hands and a prayer for vengeance on my lips the day he met me. I wished he could explain what he'd thought we'd do when the war was over, but none of that would change what *I* needed to do.

Taran stared at my ring in his hand unblinking, as the ghost of the person I'd known haunted us both. Eventually, he knotted my scarf around it and handed it back to me.

"You don't even know the half of it. You want to go to the Painted Tower? You want to be free of your vows? Fine, I'll take you. Pack your things."

I shook my head, not trusting this mood, whatever he was thinking, but he grimaced and snatched more clothes off the ground.

"That's what you've been asking for, isn't it? You don't really want a ring, or a wedding. You want to stand between Death and the Maiden. But you don't even know how you ended up in the middle."

My lower lip trembled at the accusation. "That's not true. Why do you think I'm here? I always chose you first. I don't want to be free of you, I want you *back*."

He rubbed his fist over his forehead, knuckles white. "You should at least know what you're choosing. Go on. We're leaving tonight."

He batted away all other questions and any suggestion of waiting until morning, his mood so wild that I eyed the walls of the palace with worry as his power vibrated against it.

What could we do, anyway? Go to bed? Try to sleep? Taran threw a few clothes into a pack and waited impatiently as I collected my belongings. His face was stiff and impassive, but his shoulders jerked at what I packed and what I left. I was abruptly attached to all of the fancy trinkets he'd pilfered for me, even if I knew there was no chance I'd ever need them. It hurt to leave them behind and take only the things I'd arrived with. My white dresses. My ring.

I gritted my teeth and packed for him too. He was coming too. He was coming home with me, even though he turned away when I stuffed a winter cloak into a saddlebag.

The grass soaked my boots when we stepped into the silent evening. It was too dark to see the Mountain, even with Lixnea's silver chariot racing high in the evening sky, but Taran turned to mark a point on the horizon as though he could feel our destination. He inclined his head toward the stables. "Can you ride tonight?"

I wondered whether he planned to carry me all the way there if I said no. Probably so.

"Are you fishing for compliments?" I asked.

He looked back so sharply that I couldn't help but make a face at him. It was still Taran, after all, and he'd thrown me directly out of bed on this journey.

"It's not funny."

"It's a little bit funny." I said it with a hand over my heart. He should think it was funny, because Taran never stopped trying to make me laugh, even when we thought we were doomed.

His jaw clenched, and for just for a moment I saw the same well of grief and confusion I'd been swimming in for months reflected in his face. He smoothed it away and tried to turn, but I caught his arm.

"Taran," I said softly, sliding my hand up his shoulder until I cupped his cheek, warm skin and breath against my fingers. "Just tell me, whatever it is. I'll still love you."

He searched my face, deciding whether to believe me.

He'll forgive me, I told myself. Because I'd forgiven him. And whatever else he had to tell me, I'd forgive that too.

"Don't make any more promises you can't keep," he said stiffly, and he strode off toward the stables.

THE MOUNTAIN WAS all around the Summerlands. Every road led to the Mountain, and the Painted Tower lay on the other side, on every side. It was a hard two days' ride up and down a trail that few people had ever traveled, with Taran stopping only when I asked to rest. The Painted Tower was visible as soon as we crossed the rim, a stark white line against the dark sea on the horizon. The faint, glowing forms of dusk-souls were visible even at a distance when they disembarked on the shore, leaving their funeral boats behind.

Taran must have traveled this way before I met him, his freedom finally in sight after three hundred years subject to Genna's will. And yet the first thing he'd done was bind himself to me, choose me, over and over, through death and rebirth and beyond.

Please, just once more. If you ever believed in me, believe in me now. And even if you didn't, stay with me like you did then. Don't make me sail back alone.

There were the ruins of stables behind the Painted Tower, surrounded by ages of uncleared scrub that had overgrown the gardens where none of the Stoneborn saw it or cared. Taran tied our horses before looking up at the tower. The one window did not face the Mountain, but I was abruptly certain that Wesha knew we were coming. Light poured out of the open doorway, drawing us inside.

Taran paused at the threshold and extended his hand to me. I thought he was seeking reassurance, and I gladly wove my fingers with his, but as soon as he set foot on the floor tiles, I was clutching his arm to stay upright. My vow to Wesha was unraveling in my soul, the threads of it tearing away from my bones to leave me gasping for breath at the sudden hollows it left behind. The ringing in my ears was so loud I nearly didn't hear Taran's shout up the staircase.

"Mother," he called. "I'm back."

33

ESHA HAD GONE to some pains with dinner. There was nobody else in the tower but her, but when we reached the top of the stairs, we found her at the head of a banquet table dressed in rose linen, groaning under the weight of dishes sufficient for an extended family. A whole roast goose with crisped brown skin. A fleet of crayfish swimming in cream sauce. Five types of soft cheese on a sideboard, decorated with out-of-season raspberries. Three chairs.

"I didn't know you could cook," Taran said, tossing himself into the chair farthest from her and reaching for a jug of undiluted wine. Wesha pointedly handed him a goblet, which he ignored in favor of sticking out his legs and leaning back to uncork the jug with his teeth. His throat moved as he gulped down more than a full cup before glancing back for me.

I was stuck on the landing, breath coming too quickly. The floor wasn't moving here, but it felt uneven beneath my feet.

"Sit," the Maiden said, pointing toward the free chair with a graceful arm.

I had a moment of vertigo, looking between them. They looked alike. Of course they did, even though Wesha chose to appear a few years younger than Taran. They had the same dark hair and thick straight eyebrows, the same full mouths and long, tapered fingers. Taran had inherited those from his mother. Which meant Taran got his bright eyes and sharp-edged beauty from his other parent. Got that power to break bonds, even his hold over the dead—

That was from his father, Death.

"If I didn't cook, how did you think I ate? There's nobody else here," Wesha asked tartly as I stumbled to the chair, my mind reeling wildly between the faces of Taran and the god of the Underworld.

"I supposed you might be gnawing your offerings raw so that you'd have more opportunities each day to feel sorry for yourself," Taran said.

I took a cue from him and reached for the wine, mostly for the opportunity to hold something solid between my hands.

"I tried being sorry for you too, but you didn't believe me the last time I said it," Wesha said, taking a delicate sip from her own cup.

I wondered if I ought to give them a moment to catch up while I perhaps stuck my head under the ocean surface and yelled, but Taran hooked a thumb in my direction to bring me into the conversation.

"Your last surviving priest might also want some apologies. For the pack of lies she organized her entire life around. The story of the pure and beautiful Maiden who so loved humanity, the innocents, little children, that she sacrificed herself to keep Death from destroying the world. Iona here is very attached to that story, but we've been in a mode of rigorous honesty recently, and I think she'd appreciate the real one."

Wesha's expression toward me was dismissive, but I rallied enough to curl forward in my chair to face her, though my heart hammered.

She'd had a child with Death—not the monster she fought from the beginning, but the sweetheart she snuck into the City—and that child was Taran. Three hundred years later, he waded into the wreckage that affair had made of the world and helped kill his own father.

No wonder he'd looked so sad.

"Was any of it true?" I asked through a cracked throat.

"Some of it," Wesha said while Taran gave a harsh laugh. She frowned at her son. "Yes, some of it was, and I'd know better than you, since it started before you were born. My father was Carantos ab Lixnea, the mortal fool Diopater killed for cuckolding him, and my mother handed me off to Lixnea without a second thought."

"Yes, poor you, left to be raised by the gentlest of the gods amid a court of poets and dreamers," Taran said mockingly.

"I was a Fallen in a world the Allmother made for gods and their priests. And as soon as I was no longer a sweet baby to hold in her arms, even Lixnea had no patience with me. I grew up lonely." Taran fell begrudgingly silent, and Wesha turned to me, her young face proud and wounded. "When I was seventeen, Genna finally invited me to the City. Gave me that palace you've been staying in, took me into her court—and let it slip that she'd promised me to her own husband as a concubine. As an apology for my birth."

There had to be more to it, if Taran expected me to be unsympathetic. This part sounded perfectly like Genna, who always spent other people to buy her peace. His face was expectant.

"Needless to say, I wasn't willing. I decided I'd flee across the ocean, find my father's family and live as a mortal. But when I reached this shore and tried to cross the Sea of Dreams—I met Napeth instead. Right where this tower was built," Wesha said.

"And he wasn't a monster yet," I said, remembering what Lixnea had told me.

Wesha sighed. "He was beautiful and powerful and kind to me. When I told him what I was running from, he said he wasn't afraid of Skyfather, and that the Summerlands would be emptier if I left. I thought . . . then I thought I could stay."

"But you changed your mind," I said softly.

"No, not immediately. He gave me everything I asked for. When I told him I was afraid of Diopater, he promised to keep me safe. When I told him I'd been lonely, he promised to love me forever. And when I told him I felt powerless, he gave me half of his. Those blessings you sing—for sleep, for surgery, to end pain—those were his."

"Which somehow wasn't enough for you," Taran said into the wineglass.

"We were happy for a few months while I did my best to push off Diopater's interest. But then Napeth took me to his citadel in the Underworld, where he'd built me a walled garden full of crystal trees and a wedding bower of night-blooming flowers inside a locked castle. Which was when I discovered that he'd promised me his love and my safety, but not my freedom. He wanted me to be his little songbird, singing in the dark forever while he tended to the dead on their journey. And I realized that my soul was still as mortal as it had ever been." She looked out the window at the dark sea. "So I ran. I went back to the Moon's domain. I thought she'd protect me, let me be a child again, not a bride, not someone's concubine. But then—"

Taran finally met my eyes, expression shadowed as he finished her sentence. "—then, inconveniently, there was me."

Their tones made Taran's very existence sound like a tragedy, and my heart ached for how easily he seemed to accept that conclusion.

"You gave him to Genna? The person who tried to sell you to her own husband?" I guessed, my hands curling into fists. How many childbirths had I attended in Wesha's service? How many feverish babies had I sung back to health? It made a mockery of her entire cult. Wesha hadn't even cared for her own child, let alone mortal ones.

"Napeth and Diopater had started fighting over me," Wesha said, eyes downcast. "Lixnea was outraged at Genna's bargain, so Genna agreed to claim Taran as her own to make it up to her. I thought she might take a little more care with Taran, since he was nearly one of the Stoneborn."

"And yet you didn't think to offer me to my father," Taran said, face rigid with anger. "Who might have actually wanted me."

Wesha frowned. "The Stoneborn don't *love* the way people do. You would have been a hostage to use against me, the way he tried to use the entire world against me."

"The Great War," I said. "He started it over you."

"His priests hounded me wherever I went. And he became— horrible. Did things no Stoneborn had ever done before. Murdered and stole. Scorched the world. Genna asked me what I'd take to return to Napeth and make him stop."

"What was it?" I asked, because Taran's stony face suggested that there had been no real sacrifice on Wesha's part. No noble choice to spare the world the consequences of Death's wrath, like I'd always believed.

"Nothing," Wesha said bitterly. "I never agreed. I was tricked. She tricked me."

"You did agree," Taran said, eyes slitted. "You gave your vows to a dozen of the Stoneborn. That's why you're here in this tower, holding the Gates shut."

Wesha tilted her chin in a challenge. "Genna told me Diopater and Napeth would never give up while they could still win me. So I said I'd marry if she promised me a handsome husband to cherish me, a beautiful home that no one could enter against my will, and the full power of a Stoneborn. This tower was supposed to be a

home, not a prison, and that power was supposed to be my freedom, not a chain to the Gates."

"But Death was the bridegroom, not some handsome mortal
stranger," I guessed, feeling begrudging compassion for her.

"I'd given my vows, so I had to go through with it," Wesha said,
looking at Taran.

"You *immediately* tried to get out of it." Taran's voice was
dropping, angrier. "You asked *me* to get you out of it."

"But you were just a child, and you weren't strong enough," the
goddess said sadly. "So you stole the stone knives from the Allmother and told me to free myself."

I bunched my shoulders, thinking of a frightened boy caught by
the enormous living Mountain who'd snatched up the gods with
her stone hands. Taran had obviously loved Wesha the way children always loved their parents, no matter how bad at the job they
were, and he obviously still loved her to be as hurt as he was now,
centuries later.

Wesha saw herself as the victim in this story, and to a point, so
did I. She'd been betrayed by her mother and treated like a war
spoil by the other Stoneborn, had seen her former lover turn hateful and cruel. If she'd made mistakes, they were the same mistakes
mortals frequently made in love.

I could forgive her for all of them, except for what she'd done to
Taran.

"So you let your son suffer all the consequences alone? You
know what Genna did to him." I leaned in, accusing the goddess
whose name was chanted by women in labor. She'd been alone all
this time, but her choices were her own, and Taran didn't even get
that dignity.

"What was I supposed to do? I couldn't keep him in this tower
with me forever. He wouldn't escape to the mortal world."

"I was ten!" Taran finally raised his voice. "You did nothing to protect me—after I handed you the means to kill my own father."

Wesha's face grew soft and troubled, and she didn't deny it. "I didn't want him dead. I wanted him to let me go."

"Which is also the only reason you've spent the day roasting goose and decanting wine for *me*," Taran said, and Wesha didn't contradict him.

Three hundred years later, Wesha was still asking Taran to get her out of the trap she'd walked into willingly. To break her vows to the Stoneborn, the ones that had her sealing Death's power over the Underworld, and set her free.

The legs of Taran's chair made a piercing screech on the flagstones as he shoved it back from the table.

"Well, there you have it," he told me, gesturing at the goddess. "The entire sordid story. Three generations of lies and cruelty. I'm sure you can see all the worst traits I've inherited from them—I'm hard-hearted enough to kill my father and spiteful enough to keep my mother locked up for three centuries, with enough of the Peace-Queen's guile to keep you from knowing about any of it while you were dying in the fires *we* all lit. If I were you, I'd do my best to forget it all on the boat home."

"Taran," I began, then closed my mouth. I didn't want to comfort him in front of Wesha, whose beautiful dawn-sky eyes were focused imploringly on her son.

"Don't say that I've never tried to do anything for you. When you washed up dead on my shore, I was the one who gathered the mortal pieces of your soul and gave you your life back. Yes, that was me. Did you think it was the Allmother? Did you think you were really one of the Stoneborn? My father was mortal, and there's red blood in your veins too. *I* cried when I saw you burned almost beyond recognition, and *I* was the one who spent the power to heal you. And even though you swore at me and left as soon as I asked you for help, when your bride came looking for you, I sent her right to you!"

"Only because you want out of here," he said.

Wesha's mouth tightened. "I do."

The lines around Taran's mouth were white from anger and grief as he glared at his mother.

"Do you know that I've never once broken one of my own vows? I could have. I would have been strong enough by the end of my first decade of service to Genna, but I didn't. I can live with my promises. I don't know why nobody else can." He said this last part directly to me as his shoulders sank. Without another word, he turned on his heel and stalked back down the stairs. The room was darker when he was gone, empty despite all the lamps burning in their niches.

Wesha made as though to stand and follow him, but I shook my head.

"Give him some time," I advised her.

"He's going straight to the stables and leaving," she worried, long black hair falling around her face as she folded in on herself.

"He's not. He wouldn't leave without saying goodbye."

The goddess gave me an ironic look. "You think you know him better than me?"

I did think that, but it wasn't polite to say that to someone's mother, so I just looked down at my dinner. The food was tasteless in my mouth, but I forced myself to eat a few bites, since it was the last hot meal I might expect for the next week. Wesha began to look at me speculatively, so I folded my napkin in my lap and got ahead of any ideas she might have developed about how to deploy me against Taran.

"What would you do if you were free?" I asked.

"Whatever I want, just like anyone else," she said haughtily.

Points for honesty, but not much else, I thought, rolling my eyes. "You're not making a great case for yourself."

She snorted delicately. "Would you like me to try?"

Wesha had been born into a world determined to treat her unfairly, but she'd done nothing to make it better, despite considerable opportunity. When I shrugged, she gripped that dawn-streaked hair in her hands and pleaded with me.

"Would you believe me if I told you I've been alone with my regrets all these years, and I wish I could make amends? How could I even begin? There was peace and plenty when I was born, and now all the Stoneborn blame me for the smoking ruins I see from my window. Would Taran believe me if I told him I wished that I knew him now, despite all the love I denied him as a child? Would even Napeth believe me if I told him I wanted to find a way for us both to live in this world?"

"Well," I said skeptically, "do *you* believe any of that?"

She didn't answer my question. "The story you heard," she said after a moment. "The one my priests sang. I wish it was true that I sacrificed myself for peace. That three hundred years of loneliness meant something."

"It's not too late to make the story true," I said, leaning forward with interest. "Do you want to make it up to Taran? Death would make the same bargain he did before. It would end the next war before it started. Stop the Stoneborn from reconquering the mortal world. And I could stay with Taran and give him the love and peace he's never had in his entire life. That's what he wants."

Her face fell. "So you're going to tell Taran to leave me here?"

I shook my head. Even if I was callous enough to demand that Wesha bind herself to the horrific lord of the Underworld for eternity, I couldn't ask Taran to be the one who imprisoned her.

"I think you should choose. If you want to be the goddess of mercy, you should choose that. Stay here. Hold the Gates closed. Tell Death yourself that he can still decide to stop. But it's not a sacrifice if we make you do it."

For most of my life, I woke up and lay down praying to Wesha, goddess of mercy. There was no meaning in her true story—just wickedness and tragedy and the echoes they had spread across the entire world. That didn't make mercy meaningless though. If it was up to me, I'd show it to her even if she had none for us.

I excused myself from the table and left the Maiden with the dishes and her regrets.

TARAN HAD STORED my packs in the vacant priests' barracks, a pointed message that I pointedly ignored, and I tried doors on each floor until I found him. As in every other room but the top chamber, the window had long ago been crudely bricked up, but Taran had pushed a few blocks out to create a small porthole with a view of the night and sea, and he sat on the simple cot below it.

Taran held a kithara and pick, and he was trying to play a ballad, unsuccessfully. When he closed his eyes he could follow the melody a bit, but every time he opened them to look at his hands, he fumbled the notes. He'd forgotten how to play.

When he saw me, he tossed the instrument to the foot of the bed and flopped over to face the wall. He was already stripped to his waist, so I put out all the lamps except the one on the nightstand and crawled in with him. The linens were clean and crisp and new. Nobody had ever visited Wesha.

His body was stiff and unwelcoming until I wormed my arm under his elbow and pressed my cheek into the gap between his shoulder blades, and then I felt him unwind by fractions until he covered my hand with his own, right over his heart's reassuring thud.

He ran a few degrees hotter than other people, and I didn't know if that was a trait all immortals shared or something he'd inherited from his father. I'd thought of it as unique to Taran.

"What are you going to do?" I asked.

He pulled my arm more closely around him. "What do you want me to do?"

Even though I was fairly certain he knew how I'd answer, I responded anyway. "Let her go. Let me go." I paused, spoke with my lips directly against his skin. "Come with me."

He craned his head back, made a counteroffer. "Stay."

I didn't voice my refusal, just tightened my arms and closed my eyes, summoning every memory that told me who Taran really was, because he was mine more than he'd ever been anyone else's.

"Wesha is selfish, and that selfishness turned Napeth from a caretaker to a tyrant," he warned me. "She's only thinking of herself, no matter what she told you. She'll disappoint you."

"All children are selfish, and she never got a chance to be anything else. And you—you're not giving yourself a chance either."

At every turn, he'd sacrificed himself for others. Wesha. Marit. Me. If he was capable of it, so was Wesha. And even if she wasn't, it wasn't right to found Genna's peace on her daughter's unwilling sacrifice.

What the two of us had given up had been given freely. I had to believe that mattered.

Taran rubbed fingertips along the crest of my knuckles almost to the point of pain, his muscles still tense.

"Can you promise me that this is the last one? Say we convince your mortal queen not to throw her people against the ships of the Stoneborn when they arrive. Will that be enough? Can we go home then, if the other gods forgive me? Would you stay with me longer than the length of one mortal life, if I do this for you?"

"I don't have a single secret from you now. Do I have all of yours?" I murmured against his back.

"Yes," he said after a moment, and he sounded honest.

"I don't remember my father's name. My mother left me with the maiden-priests when I was six, and I never looked for her again. You're not your parents, Taran, and neither am I. We're our choices. I can't say what will happen tomorrow or when we reach the mortal shore, but I'll probably want to do exactly what you imagine I will. I will love you with every single heartbeat. I will never want to be apart from you for a single minute of my life. I will still have made every mistake I ever made—and I'll probably make a lot more. I can't promise more than that."

He exhaled, a long, painful sound in the near darkness. I could feel his power swirling through the room, clinging to my skin and battering the stone walls around us as he struggled with what I'd asked him to do.

"I don't want to go. This good person you thought I was, who was trying to help—I don't think I ever was that. I think I knew better than to join your rebellion, and I did it anyway. For you, Iona. And so if I go with you—that'll be the only reason."

He rolled over to face me, nearly nose to nose. There was a shine to his irises that hadn't been there before—a glow clinging to him even in this quiet moment—but I brushed my lips against the solemn line of his mouth until the tense set of his jaw dissolved.

"What do your reasons matter now? All that's left is what you did and what I remember. Why don't you just let that be the whole truth?"

Taran lifted his hands to my face, thumbs pressing against my cheekbones.

"Because I know you think I became a better person, but I wonder if I got worse. The list of things I wouldn't do to keep you gets shorter and shorter. That ought to scare you. It scares me, some-times."

"I'm not afraid of you," I whispered.

"I know," he said gently. "Which is why I wonder whether I ought to tell you to go alone and not come back until you're sure you'll stay forever. Because I thought about not letting you. I thought about locking you up until you changed your mind. I think about how . . . happy I would feel, if I knew nobody would ever take you from me. Even if you hated me for it."

I swallowed hard. "You're not your father, Taran."

"Not yet. But you haven't ever left me."

Most people never had the opportunity to be very good or very evil, but that was just luck. Taran hadn't always chosen to heal the wounded and free the suffering out of a sheer lack of opportunity to harm and control. What was a good person except someone who'd always chosen to do good when he had the chance?

"Well, if the only thing keeping you from committing atrocities is me, then it sounds like it's very, very important that we stay to-gether," I said.

He huffed out a pained laugh. "That is the point you would take away."

I kissed the corners of his mouth to make them tilt in the other direction, and when he captured the whole of my mouth with his own, I opened my lips and deepened the kiss. I lifted my arms to help him get my clothes off and parted my thighs to help him settle between them.

He wouldn't leave without saying goodbye. I barely knew this language, the one spoken with his mouth against the fragile skin of my neck and his fingers pressing bruises into my shoulders, but I didn't think he was saying goodbye. That wasn't what I was saying, anyway.

Come home with me, I said. And *I'll wear that green scarf at our wedding.* And *If all we get is a little stone house and one mortal lifetime, we'll be happy in it.* I said it with every swallowed breath and pull of my hands in his hair, as devoutly as I'd ever prayed for mercy.

I'll love you till the stars fall out of the sky, he whispered with his mouth against my skin.

It wasn't until he was asleep with his head pillowed on my stomach that I realized that he must have answered my question about what he was going to do at some point, because he'd promised to answer all my questions, but I hadn't recognized his answer when he gave it.

34

I WOKE UP WHEN something slashed my cheekbone hard enough to draw blood. I was up for hours after Taran fell asleep, carding the soft strands of his hair through my fingers and trying to quiet my rising fear that he'd be gone the next day, and I registered the cold hollow where he'd slept next to me even before the sharp pain on my face.

"Stupid, lazy slut," Awi chirped, launching her raven-self into the air as fast as I could clap a hand over the place her taloned feet had scratched me. There was an ache on that side of my scalp too, like she'd been pulling my hair for a while. "Wake up already! You need to get out."

It was very dark in the chamber without any of the lamps lit, and the only light came through the gap left by the bricks Taran had pulled from the window, but that was indirect and white, mid-morning or later.

"What's going on?" I mumbled, even as my heart seized to see Taran's pack missing from its spot next to mine.

"The tower is on fire," Awi announced, shifting to the form of a sparrow and hopping to the window.

"What? Why?" As soon as she said it, I could smell the oily, musty stink of a house fire, deadly familiar from the war. Smoke was coming up through the cracks in the floorboards, and I was perhaps five stories off the ground. I shot to my feet and began to fumble around for my clothes, discarded on the ground.

"Because I set it on fire," the bird said like I was being very slow.

"What?" I cried again, nearly dropping my shoes. "Why would you do that?"

"So that nobody can live here," Awi said, edging into the gap in the window, as though that made sense. She looked back at me with one black eye, briefly dipping her beak in an awkward show of reluctance. "Well, goodbye."

"Wait!" I ran to the window after her, but she launched into the air and spread her wings in the direction of the sea. The tiny sparrow blurred into an albatross and gained height in the morning light, vanishing from my sight within seconds.

The smell of smoke was stronger already. With shaking hands, I pulled my scarf from the front pocket of my pack and wrapped it around my face. I put my ring back on my finger and groped for the door handle. Warm, but there was nowhere else to go.

A wave of darkness enveloped me when I opened the door, but I plunged through, doing my best to recall the layout of the tower.

The first glimpses of orange flame were almost like homecoming. I'd almost died in flame so many times that fear fell away. Yes, of course this was how it ended. I dreamed this! I went farther down the stairs anyway. Step by step, keeping to the stone wall. I started to choke as the smoke made its way through the flimsy barrier of the silk around my face, but I kept moving, knowing that every second mattered.

I stumbled one floor down, two, how many had there been, exactly? Awi must have set a fire in each storeroom, not trusting the wooden beams inside the concrete pillars of the tower to carry the blaze all the way to the top. By the third, I started feeling dizzy and needed all my strength to grip the wall. The floors were hot enough that the soles of my boots began peeling away from the shafts, enough that the skin of my feet began to blister. I gagged on ash. Even if I made it out at this point, my lungs were probably too damaged unless a priest of Genna happened upon me in the next few minutes.

I stopped on what I thought was the third level, considering the flames erupting from the open storeroom. More than hot enough to dissolve bone. Hot enough to melt my ring, probably. There would be no trace of me. If I died here, I'd vanish.

What would Taran think, when the armies of Heaven crossed the sea and found nobody waiting for them? He might think I failed. Worse, he might think there was something he should have done to stop me. He might think he'd been wrong, and he should have locked me up somewhere safe, no matter what I said.

If he'd left me today, it had been because he saw no other way to give me a choice to go and a choice to come back. I couldn't let him think I hadn't chosen him.

I wouldn't have gone without you, Taran.

I should have told him that.

I was just going to have to live.

"Taran!" I yelled, thinking of all the times he'd heard me when I thought he wouldn't. I coughed smoke from my lungs. Marit, I'd sing Marit's blessing. We never used it for putting out fires, because the waves it called were just as likely to wash away rescuers as extinguish a blaze, but maybe Taran would look back from the Mountain and see the sea change.

My voice was thin and reedy as I stumbled a few more steps down the grand staircase. *Waverider, ocean lord, dancer on the waters*—was there a key change in the chorus? I couldn't think straight.

I slumped against the wall, feeling the hem of my dress begin to smolder. Nothing had happened. Maybe Marit didn't have enough priests yet, or maybe I wasn't singing it right. I was only trained to be a maiden-priest, after all, and Wesha had abandoned me, just like Taran had said she would. He'd set us both free, but we would both disappoint him, when he'd never failed anyone he loved in his entire life.

The stones of the tower vibrated under my feet, and it could have been the waves or it could have been the mortar melting. I fell to my knees, and my head swam too much to stand again.

I stopped praying to Marit and thought of Taran instead.

I'm sorry. I really did try to survive this time.

35

I WOKE WITH TARAN'S mouth on mine and his breath forcing its way into my lungs.

That first lurch of my diaphragm to push out the foreign air and the pounds and pounds of black soot in my throat hurt like an arrow to the chest. Worse, actually, than the time I'd taken an arrow to the chest. My throat cracked and tore as I rolled in the sand, body convulsing in an attempt to expel everything I'd breathed in. I gagged and hacked, desperately seeking control of my most basic functions. But I was alive, and Taran was holding me.

Surprised to be alive was a recurring realization, but it had never felt as sweet at this one.

Every inch of my body ached when Taran snatched me up to cradle my body against his—not just the parts of me that had been singed, but the ribs he'd broken when he'd restarted my heart and the bare skin that shivered under a steady downpour of rain. He tangled his hands in my hair, making a noise that was close to a sob as he clutched me closer to his pounding heart.

My eyes were too gummy to see more than the vaguest shapes around me, but there were flames farther down the beach, and the shadow of the tower loomed from only a few feet away.

"What happened?" I tried to croak, but my throat was too raw to force even a single word out.

"Don't try to talk," Taran said, wiping my face off with his sleeve. "It took ten choruses of *Peace-Queen, beauty and grace* just to get your heart beating again."

I let my body go limp again under the familiar weight of Taran's prayers. His voice wrapped around me like a velvet shawl while Genna's power dripped down my throat, soothing my burns and mending the cracked ribs. It was nearly painless—*nobody is better at this than Taran*, I thought deliriously.

When he was done, I nestled my head into the curve of his neck, savoring the tiny contact of my wet skin against his much warmer body.

"Awi set the boats on fire too?" I mumbled.

"Wesha didn't want anyone following her, I suppose." His tone was humorless and bleak.

"But why would Awi help Wesha escape?"

Wesha was the one who'd kept Awi trapped here for three hundred years!

Taran forced a dark chuckle through a chest that still sounded tight with fear for me. "Awi *is* Wesha. Another thing she never told her priests. Only her mortal form was trapped here while she held the Gates."

At that mention of the Gates, I instinctively looked for the entrance to the Underworld. There were a few phosphorescent green dusk-souls at the end of the beach, but instead of drifting toward the mouth of the cavern, they milled back and forth by the boats as though confused.

Taran followed my gaze.

"We've really done it this time, nightingale," he said with one hand pressed to his forehead, anger beginning to replace relief in his voice. "Wesha left the Gates wide open."

Open to the gods, open to Death, open to every dusk-soul in the entire Underworld? Did Wesha really hate us all that much, that she'd destroy the world as soon as she got her freedom? What happened to all that regret?

"But she told me—"

"She lied. They're all liars. I *told* you that." He was working himself into a well-deserved fury.

He'd been right that Wesha only cared about herself. I was afraid what else he might have been right about.

My thoughts, which had been spilling out in every direction, slowly came to rest inside my skull. I seized on just one.

"Wait," I said. "You called me nightingale."

I was lifted into the air against his chest, still too weak to do more than roll my head back and stare up at him. I'd never told him that. I was positive I'd never told him that.

The smile he gave me was hard and sad and very familiar.

"Yes, I remember now," he said. "I called you that the first time I heard you sing."

And with that he carefully got to his feet, turning to carry me back up the Mountain.

Acknowledgments

If you have just finished reading *The Younger Gods*, you may suspect that I was the kind of child who carted around a tattered copy of *D'Aulaire's Book of Greek Myths*. I had the version with the bright yellow cover, as well as dozens of other books of myths and fairy tales and fantasy both high and low. It's a dream come true to publish a book with heroes and villains and magic in it, and the first people I want to thank are the people who put books in the hands of children: booksellers, librarians, teachers, and parents. I could only write this book because I've read so many books that other people gave me. Thank you for the work that you do: the seeds you plant may flower decades later.

I'm also thankful to the people who put this book in your hands, dear reader: my editors, Cindy Hwang and Elizabeth Vinson; production editor Lynsey Griswold; copyeditor Carly Sommerstein; Elisha Katz in marketing and Katie Ferraro in publicity; cold reader Daisy Flynn; Yahaira Lawrence in production; managing editor Christine Legon; Alison Cnockaert in interior design; and cover artist Elena Masci and cover designer Tyriq Moore, who made this beautiful cover. It takes so many people to take a few wistful daydreams about a girl sailing to the Underworld to bring home her true love and turn them into a book you can pick up from the store and take home to read under the covers. The magic of it never ceases to amaze me.

Thank you to the friends who helped make the cranberry-sauce-can-shaped early drafts of this book fit for the table: Ashley Mackie, Celia Winter, Diana Gill, and Emma Beckdale.

Thank you to the authors who have made my life so much richer with their books and friendship: Jenna Levine, Rebecca Gardner, Ali Hazelwood, Sarah Hawley, Naina Kumar, Thea Guanzon, Elizabeth Davis, and all the Berkletes. This book marks five years straight of not throwing our laptops out the window and running into the woods naked, never to return—may this streak endure.

Thank you to my agent, Jess Watterson, who said, "I can sell that!" when I told her I wanted to write something completely different, and immediately did.

And thank you to my family: my husband, my kids, and our beloved kitties, Inky and Triscuit. I'm sorry, but none of you are old enough to read this book yet, because this book has . . . hmm, did you know that there are ice cream cones in the back freezer?

 Shep

Keep reading for a preview from

GOD OF THIEVES

TARAN

THE BROAD SILHOUETTE of a bearded vulture's wings lingered above the horizon during my slow descent down the Mountain, circling ominously while I sweated under the weight of the small boat I'd balanced over my shoulders. In the wet air that rose off the Sea of Dreams, the Maiden would have flown more comfortably in an albatross's feathers than a vulture's, but I'd never say the Maiden lacked a sense of humor.

Wesha was funny, and everyone forgot that.

That she watched me for hours rather than help me haul the little boat down the rocky cliffs to the shore—

Everyone who'd ever known her would have expected that.

If she'd known *me* at all, Wesha should have expected spite would have me launch from the farthest point on the pebbled beach from her Painted Tower, beyond the wreckage of funeral boats that crowded the path to the Underworld, but by the time I'd finished raising the mast and rigging the sail, I could nearly feel her anxious attention on me as she wondered whether I'd really go past without saying anything to her.

I left it till the last, making a big show of securing my provisions, but I turned and trudged down the beach when I was ready to go. I was fairly certain I could get past the Gates of Dawn without her permission, but I'd look ridiculous if I was wrong about that. Better to pay any toll now.

Wesha had changed from beak and feathers to her tattered wedding dress and stood in the darkened doorway of her tower as I approached. It was all theater—she could have walked out onto the beach, could have worn a different dress, could have flown down and spoken to me as a bird at any time in the past three hundred years—but that didn't mean it was ineffective. It made the sharp edges of my soul prickle beneath my lips and fingertips to see her look exactly the same as the last time I saw her, rattled me enough to leave me silent for long minutes while she recovered from seeing me in the shape of a grown man instead of a terrified child.

Sometimes Genna, the Peace-Queen, would have a maudlin mood and list all the ways I resembled Wesha, though really she'd be thinking of Carantos ab Lixnea, Genna's last mortal lover and Wesha's unfortunate sire. It used to annoy me to hear Genna credit a mortal foolish enough to cuckold the storm god as the source of the straight dark eyebrows and attractive singing voices that Wesha and I had both inherited, but I had to admit that it was convenient to my current venture to look almost human.

I looked more human than Wesha did now, despite being less. Wesha had bargained for the power that had turned her eyes into a starry expanse of sky and her long hair to a slash of dawn, but despite the bleak expression of regret painted across her delicate features, I'd never heard her wish she could give that part of her bargain up.

"Hello, Mother," I told Wesha as soon as I thought I could manage the appropriate tone of pleasant nonchalance.

She used to wince every time I called her that.

It was strange, how often I'd been thinking of my long-ago childhood recently. That decade somehow felt more accessible than the three centuries since. I could remember my last trip to this tower with perfect clarity—the stolen daggers weighing down my pack, my stupid confidence that Wesha and I would soon live together like pirates on the Sea of Dreams, feared and respected by all the other Stoneborn—while the things I'd done more recently were shadowed like half-forgotten dreams, albeit ones that sometimes had me waking up sweaty and nauseous.

Today Wesha didn't scold me for wanting her attention. Perhaps the past three centuries had toughened her up too.

"Hello, Taran. I wondered whether Genna would send you."

Of course that was what she wondered. Not how her only child was feeling this morning. Not why the mortal world was in such disrepair that most of the dusk-souls farther down the beach were arriving not in lovingly tended funeral boats but on piles of brush, or why thousands of mortal priests had recently fled up the Mountain to the Summerlands—no, Wesha had wondered only whether her blockade here at the Gates had finally caused sufficient trouble to end her imprisonment, one way or another.

"Genna didn't send me," I said, which wasn't quite true. The point was, she didn't make me come. She'd rather richly bribed me to sail past the Gates of Dawn and clean up the mess my parents had made of the world. I was here on the beach with my little boat because the reward was worth the trouble, not because Genna still had the power to compel my every breath and action.

Wesha's starry eyes widened. "You mean . . . she released you?"

"Two weeks ago."

Her response was grimly amusing for everything it wasn't: *Oh, Taran, I'm so glad you're free! I never thought she'd punish you so long! If I forgot to say so before, I'm sorry I got you caught up in this, how can I make it up to you?*

Wesha only sighed and turned her face toward the sea, knuckles brushing over her very mortal heart.

Without Genna's will wrapped around my soul, forcing me to obey, I felt almost . . . hollow. Like my body had grown larger than my thoughts or feelings could fill, now that I was no longer the Peace-Queen's puppet. Empty.

Right now though, it was easy enough to feel disappointed that my mother couldn't pretend to be happy I could make my own choices for the first time since I was ten years old, at least not when it was obvious I wasn't going to use my newfound freedom to deliver hers.

"I've gathered the mortals are in open revolt, your priests are dead, and Napeth's are dropping like flies. Genna asked if I might consider going over to sort things out," I prompted Wesha, thumbs hooked on my belt.

"It's worse than that," she said quickly. "Your father's become such a greedy monster. The sacrifices he's demanded! The waste of it all. At this rate, there won't be anyone left to light an altar soon."

"And this surprised you? *I* got an inkling he'd cracked up when I started to meet my half siblings with *fur* and *claws*. But who could have guessed he'd act out after you drove him across the sea, besides absolutely everyone?" My cheerful mask was beginning to fall apart in the face of Wesha's complaints about my father, the god of death.

Death and the Maiden—long ago, he went to war to marry her. But neither half his power nor my birth could convince her to stay with him, and the world had been torn in two ever since, with Death trapped in the mortal world, and all the other Stoneborn here in the Summerlands.

Wesha's lips pursed as she chose her words carefully. She probably sensed my patience was limited.

"All he had to do was let me go, and I would have let him come home. All anyone *else* had to do was let me go, and I would have let them pass. It shouldn't have to be you."

"No, it shouldn't." On that, my mother and I were in complete agreement. Whether she meant I shouldn't be the one to put down the rebellion caused by my father's misrule or that I shouldn't get her out of her bargain—or her marriage—I agreed.

"You could tell him that," she offered, face troubled.

I laughed. "You think he's going to take advice from *Genna's* bastard, who he knows only for trying to get him killed for no apparent reason?"

Wesha was not the only one with regrets—just the only one who'd never tried to pay for them.

"He'd believe you if you told him who you are. You . . . you do look a bit like him. And if you showed him you could break oaths, could set me free—"

"So am I appealing to his fatherly pride or threatening him? Both? The Moon was right about you. You do have a mortal's heart. Still! Even with all your power and after all this time. You want what you shouldn't have and not what you were made to be. Napeth is never going to just *stop* because you've made the cost too high. He was born to be the god of death and rule from the Underworld, and *you* made him your husband. He can't stop wanting to be that any more than a fire can stop itself from burning."

I'd spent the last several days telling myself I was not going to lose my temper with her, was not going to engage with her, was going to cheerfully think about how lovely the new villa Genna had promised me would be once it was finished.

Think about fountains, Taran. Grand colonnades. Decorative gardens surrounded by very high fences.

The Maiden put her hands on her hips and growled right back at me.

"Is that how Genna justifies herself? She says they don't have a choice but to be greedy bullies? The Allmother made the Stoneborn to answer mortal prayers, and I hear the mortals praying day and night for mercy. Napeth is *fighting* his nature by brutalizing his people, not living up to it."

My careful smile finally turned into a snarl. If Wesha thought she'd impress me with a lesson on divine compassion, she was forgetting that the Allmother still wanted me dead for my childhood attempt to free my mother from the trap she'd walked into, and only Genna's self-interest had saved me when Wesha would have let my bones be scattered across the Summerlands.

"If the mortals are still praying to *you* for mercy, I would think that tends to disprove your point," I snapped. "At least the other Stoneborn do what they say they will."

Wesha shook her head sorrowfully, which only wound me up even more.

"You'll see when you get there. The gap between what we're supposed to be and what we've become."

When she waved her arm and the block of ever-present fog that surrounded this beach parted in front of my boat, I took that as leave to depart.

Fine. Thank you for opening the Gates. Maybe I'll bring you something nice on my way home, like a couple of new priests to replace the ones you got murdered.

I'd turned on my heel and made it fifteen paces away before she called out to me again.

"Taran! I hope you don't come back."

It sounded so much like a curse that I spun around, incredulous. She ignored me for the first ten years of my life, nearly got me killed, spent the intervening three centuries driving the Summerlands into decline, and now she wished me into exile like my father?

She'd stepped out of the tower onto the beach, bare feet on the rocks, her deceptively young face intent.

"I should have taken you across the sea when I had the chance.

I should have—well, you know everything else I should have done for you. You're right about that. But even if you're right about the other Stoneborn too, you're not like them. You're better off away from them, before you become just as selfish and cruel as they are. So even if it means I don't see you again . . . I hope you don't come back."

If I didn't have holes in my soul where my vows to Genna had once lived, it probably would have stung quite a bit to hear my mother say she didn't care if we ever met again, but as it was, I shoved my boat into the sea with my mind fully occupied by the tile borders I intended to install around the fountains in my new villa, and the very pressing need to choose between marble and terracotta flooring. I'd build walls so high I couldn't even see the Mountain beyond them.

I'D NEVER GIVEN much thought to what the mortal world was like. Unlike the other Stoneborn, I'd been born in the Summerlands, and I only knew the mortal world through their increasingly distant memories of it. So, if I pictured it, I thought about it only as the source of the priests who served the gods and of the sacrifices that filled our storerooms and palaces. Vast fields of grain to be milled into flour for our bread, expansive vineyards cultivating grapes to ferment for our wine. Herds of fat cattle, flocks of birds, looms and forges and workshops. And mortals, of course, dutifully offering the sacrifices and prayers that crossed the Sea of Dreams in exchange for the largesse of the gods' blessings that created all their wealth.

Before I landed in the shadow of sacred Mount Degom, my top concern had been how big of a boat I'd need for the return trip—I'd planned to acquire the furnishings for my villa while I was here, perhaps my first few priests while I was at it. But as soon as I set foot in the capital city of Ereban, my most pervasive thought was how bad everything *stank*. The mortal world smelled, quite frequently, like literal shit. I had no idea where all the rich sacrifices were coming from, except not here.

There was nothing here I wanted. Nothing even worth stealing.

Parts of Ereban smelled like ashes: the high temple was rubble and cinders, and so too were the temples of Death and the Maiden. The royal palace was still smoldering, as were a few neighborhoods where the riots had not quite died down yet. But there were other stinks too: unwashed mortals too afraid to venture out to the public baths, rotting food that had nobody to distribute it, uncollected garbage in the streets, sizzling in the midsummer sun. Nobody seemed to be in charge: the temples were empty, all the surviving priests having fled to the Summerlands, and the mortal queen had marched on the more religious southern cities, where Death's followers were massing in opposition.

Everyone knew who was responsible though: as soon as I arrived, I heard stories of an *Iona Night-Singer*. Iona Night-Singer had fought Death in single combat at the high temple in revenge for his sacrifice of the queen's young daughter. Iona Night-Singer had personally slaughtered dozens of Death's priests and Fallen in revenge for their massacre of the maiden-priests. Iona Night-Singer had set fire to the keeps of loyalist nobles when they refused to join the queen's war against the temples, and she was headed south to destroy the rest.

Once I recovered from my shock at how bad the mortal world smelled, the solution to the chaos I'd discovered seemed to be simple. I wouldn't need to argue with my father or put out any fires or raise any armies—I just had to dispatch one apparently terrifying woman with a grudge against Death, and then the mortals could go back to growing our food and worshipping us. I didn't like killing people, but I didn't like doing many of the things Genna had caused me to do, and killing was at least quick and impersonal.

I stole a horse, stole some clothes, stole a reasonably sized knife, and went looking for Iona Night-Singer. That part wasn't hard either—I just followed the smoke.

I wasn't challenged as I rode into the shambolic rebel camp two days later. The sentries seemed to expect all opposition to be wearing a death-priest's red robes and bronze lion mask, and my engaging smile dealt with any suspicion of my motives, just as it did back in the Summerlands. Even without Genna's will animating me, I retained the habits of a long lifetime, ones that allowed me to lie, steal, and infiltrate without guilt or discovery.

Go bat your big green eyes at them and bring them back in line, won't you, sweet boy?

After poking through rows of hastily assembled tents full more of farmers armed with scythes and pitchforks than soldiers armed with pikes and swords, I was informed that I should go to the priests' camp if I was looking for Iona Night-Singer. As the gods had called all their priests across the sea, I was confused by this description until I located an even shoddier group of tents filled entirely by children.

I'd never met any children before. I was the youngest immortal in the Summerlands, and all the mortal priests there were adults who'd taken their final vows to the gods. These children must have been acolytes who'd been in training to become priests. None of them were any older than my apparent age, and many of them were much younger: mortals who barely reached my chest, with big cheeks, bigger eyes, and awkward knobby limbs. I halted in consternation to look around for who was taking care of them. The Stoneborn might have forgotten that their priests had been responsible for these children, but didn't they have . . . parents? Families?

Somewhere else to go? They were sure to get crushed or incinerated if left around underfoot when Death caught up with the rebels.

The only person acting with any sense of authority was an adolescent boy wearing the leather tool belt of the Shipwright over his unbleached acolyte's tunic. He had brown skin, the scanty beginnings of a mustache, and rangy muscles he'd not finished growing into, and he was distributing small sacks of dried peas to a crowd of other acolytes.

"Excuse me," I approached to ask with my most non-threatening smile. "Who's in charge here?"

"Me. Drutalos ab Smenos," the boy said, not pausing in his task. "Assuming you need lunch. If you need something to do, grab a shovel and help Dousonna dig the trench latrines."

I tried to keep my skepticism off my face. "I'm looking for Iona Night-Singer. Could you point me in her direction?"

"Iona told me to keep anyone from bothering her."

"I'm afraid it's very important," I said, turning up the charm, which was less effective on men than women, and apparently useless on this adolescent boy.

"And who are you?" Drutalos asked suspiciously, eyes raking over my farmer's clothes and then, with more concern, the breadth of my shoulders and looming height.

"Taran ab Genna," I said, not seeing a reason to lie.

"Ab Genna? Oh! I'm so sorry, you're right, she'll want to see you right away. She's in that field hospital over there with the other acolyte of the Peace-Queen."

Amused to have been mistaken for an acolyte of my grandmother, I followed the boy's pointed finger to a large, tunnel-shaped tent, where linen sheets had been draped over the entrances in a failed effort to keep the flies away from a collection of groaning, wounded mortal soldiers on rag pallets.

Inside, it was dim and hot and home to the worst smells I had yet encountered: old sweat and dried blood, musty urine and the sickly-sweet smell of rot.

I initially assumed I'd gotten bad directions, because all the wounded soldiers were men, and the only ones treating them were two young girls, both bent over an unconscious patient whose left leg terminated just below the knee with a discolored, oozing stump.

The first girl wore the short, saffron-trimmed dress of the Peace-Queen's cult, and her round, doll-like face was blotchy and tear-streaked as she attempted to sing the blessing to close incisions. It was the wrong blessing in the first place, because infection had obviously set into the soldier's wound, and the girl had also pitched her voice in the wrong register. With her throat swollen from crying, she couldn't hit the low notes in the bridge, so Genna's power wasn't flowing. No chance this was Iona Night-Singer.

The second girl had her back to me. All I could make out in the dim light was a thick mass of dark red hair pinned at her neck and a stone blade clutched in her fist, which she was wielding to gingerly cut dead flesh away from the solider's amputation. Recognizing the knives I'd stolen for Wesha all those years ago being put to an altogether unexpected purpose, I belatedly took in the little surgeon's long white dress and linen apron—a maiden-priest? Weren't they all supposed to be dead?

The rebel torching temples and battling gods couldn't be a maiden-priest, let alone a slender girl whose voice shook as she apologized to the unconscious patient for her incompetence. But she inhaled and visibly steeled herself when the acolyte of Genna gave a loud sob of disagreement.

"Hiwa, please concentrate. You need to get the bleeding stopped or I'll have to take his knee," the maiden-priest said through gritted teeth.

"I'm sorry, I'm trying, but I'd just learned that one, and—oh, it looks so bad. Should you amputate more anyway?" the first girl asked.

"*No*, I can fix it," said the redhead. "Look at his hands, he's a farmer. If I take his knee, he won't be able to walk without a crutch, let alone push a plow. Shit, it's gotten into the bone."

She set the knife aside to tighten the tourniquet just above the man's knee, and the saffron-clad girl smothered another sob on her forearm, eyes landing on me when she straightened. They flew open as her face suffused in a blush, which was the usual response I drew from younger women.

Seeing an opening, I cleared my throat politely. "Excuse me, I'm looking for Iona Night-Singer."

This made the second girl finally notice my presence.

With that glorious mass of red hair, I'd expected blue or green eyes, but when she briefly turned her head to look me over, I was surprised by dark brown ones, set in a very ordinary face that was older than her height or slender figure would have indicated. Her cool, assessing gaze raked me up and down before completely dismissing me.

This was not the response I ever got from women of *any* age.

"I'm busy," the redhead said, clenching her jaw to cut off the words. She bent to look again at the stump of the man's leg. "Hiwa, I'm going to purge the infection, but you need to regenerate the marrow at the same time, then close the bone. Can you do that?"

"I don't know," the younger girl sniffled. "I've never even sung that one before."

"It's actually quite urgent that I speak with Iona Night-Singer," I said, taken aback at having been dismissed. "Is that . . . you?"

While I supposed carrying out a summary execution for blasphemy wouldn't take me very long regardless, in the unlikely event this young woman had been responsible for murdering dozens of death-priests, burning down the temples of several other gods, and turning the masses of mortals away from their proper posture of reverence, perhaps I might just . . . tell her to stop?

Have you noticed that it is extremely unpleasant to die of gangrene in the woods? Yes? Why don't you go home and sacrifice a few cows to Skyfather so you don't all starve to death this winter, and I'll consider the matter closed.

The redhead ignored my question in favor of seizing me by the arm and pulling me closer to the wounded man.

"Grab his hands and help hold him down," she barked at me. "This'll probably wake him up, and I can only sing one blessing at a time. Hiwa, get ready."

Three hundred years of obedience to the Peace-Queen's will must have left me primed to follow orders, because I found myself complying. I took the injured man's hands in mine and bent over his torso as the redhead and the acolyte of Genna both began to sing.

The patient's body jerked and his breathing quickened as his pain fought against whatever anesthesia he'd been given before I arrived. I pressed my weight to his body when he would have convulsed. Healing was painful, and both girls were calling the gods' power to heal.

The little acolyte's voice was breathy and halting and barely effective. The maiden-priest's though . . .

Even devoted to a ritual chant, it soared up past the canvas roof, as lovely and natural as a nightingale's song.

Every temple taught its priests to sing, because each god had blessings entrusted to their followers. Not all blessings were equally complicated though, nor all singers equally talented; the Moon's priests were excellent composers, and the Peace-Queen's priests mastered the largest number of melodies, but the Maiden's priests had been selected for their musical ability alone, and this one was the best I'd ever heard.

It was probably for that reason that I joined in. The maiden-priest had a beautiful voice and the other girl couldn't match it, and I was in a hurry, and I wasn't going to get any answers, much less out of this dank and malodorous tent, until the surgery was done, and I didn't like being dismissed as useless except for brute force. So I sang the blessing of the Peace-Queen that the other acolyte should have used, because over the centuries I'd picked them all up, and I had a drop of the Peace-Queen's power running through my veins to bolster it.

The redhead didn't so much as twitch in surprise when I started to sing, but she took advantage of the flush of healing in the man's wound to carefully excise the remainder of the dead muscle with her stone knife. Her hand didn't shake as she trimmed useless ligament and evened out ragged bone.

She must have been accustomed to working in tandem with a peace-priest, because her voice wrapped around mine like we were singing a duet, effortlessly matching phrase and meter. I was exquisitely conscious of her breathing, the tempo of her movements—curious to see if she could improvise, delighted when she exceeded my own talents. It was the first enjoyable thing I'd done since arriving on this shore. I'd had less interesting sex.

At last, satisfied with what she'd done, she put the knife aside. I switched to the blessing that would close the bone and the skin over it, and she just as easily sang the man back into dreamless sleep. The Maiden's blessing of night, some called it—achingly beautiful in the maiden-priest's voice. I now had a guess as to how the little rebel had killed so many death-priests, as well as where her epithet had come from.

When the amputation was completely healed, the redhead took a woozy step back as the Peace-Queen's acolyte, who'd been holding her breath since I took over her role, burst into fresh tears.

Unexpectedly, I was pleased with myself. Problem solved with minimal effort, now we could talk, and wasn't I better at managing these young priests than the Maiden or the Peace-Queen had been? They didn't deserve them.

I waited to be acknowledged, thanked, and admired.

Then I'd say, *This is not appropriate behavior for priests. The war is over. Go pack your things, I'm taking you all home with me.*

"I think this man's spleen is torn but not fully ruptured—can you heal that, or do I need to remove it?" the redhead asked instead, pivoting to the next man's bedside.

I made a chiding noise in the back of my throat, more amused than deflated.

"Just hold on a minute. Please tell me what you've been doing before I send the rest of your soldiers out to rampage."

"They're not soldiers," she said, fingers already palpating the man's swollen abdomen.

"Well, obviously they're not good ones. But this *is* the army Iona Night-Singer is aiming at the gods, isn't it? And that's you?"

She lifted her gaze in a level stare, utterly unrepentant. "We got to Cirta three days after the loyalists did. They took *all* the animals in the village—down to the last scrawny chicken—for sacrifices. When these men went to the town hall to complain, the death-priests collapsed the building on them. We dug the survivors out this morning. They don't even know there's a war on."

The story made me blink in dismay. Napeth shouldn't be stupid enough to set his own house on fire while he was still living in it. If my father had gone beyond trying to get Wesha's attention to actively sabotaging the mortal world, I'd have to think of some way to dampen his rage back down to his typical dull roar of disappointment before I extricated the rest of the priests from this awful place.

"You know, the Stoneborn *do not like it* when mortals deny them the things they want," I warned her. She was lucky she hadn't gotten any of these children hurt already.

The maiden-priest nodded in solemn understanding.

"Yes. I killed all the death-priests in Cirta. They wouldn't stop. I think I'm going to have to kill them all."

I sighed as she expectantly watched for my reaction. There hadn't been even a shade of doubt in her voice. She sounded like the Allmother pronouncing the law.

"Alright. I will . . . put this man's spleen back where it's supposed to be. But then we need to talk about the killing, nightingale."

Her expression finally shifted. It wasn't really a smile—I got the sense she didn't smile very often. But those dark brown eyes softened as she focused on me. It wasn't the stark desire I often saw reflected on women's faces, or even the careful admiration I was used to from the more discreet or disinclined among them. From someone who'd just met me, respect was an unprecedented reaction.

"Thank you," she said. "I'm Iona ter Wesha. Or . . . I guess I'm just Iona now, since there's no one left to take my vows."

So no promises of obedience to my mother. Nor poverty nor celibacy.

"She's Iona *Night-Singer*," the other girl put in quickly. "And I'm Hiwa ter Genna."

"Taran ab Genna."

The minute curve of Iona's lips when she wrapped her small, bloody hands around my own was absurdly gratifying.

"You know, I prayed to Skyfather for vengeance, to the Maiden for mercy, and to the Peace-Queen for just one single peace-priest. It seems they are still answering prayers," Iona told me seriously, hands gripping mine.

I gave her my most charming grin, though I was abruptly unsteady and less certain of myself than when I'd first stepped into this reeking tent. "I'm not a peace-priest any more than you're a maiden-priest, but the Stoneborn did personally send me here."

The quirk of Iona's eyebrow said she thought I was joking, and she gave me a polite huff of a laugh before turning her attention to the next patient. Her gorgeous voice swept out to soothe his pain away.

Even though I now realized it was going to be *weeks* before I might expect to lure her out of this disaster, go home, and start working on my villa, that thought didn't cause me distress. Not because I was too empty to register a response. Instead, listening to Iona's voice, matching my own to hers . . .

For the first time since I was freed, my soul didn't feel like it had holes in it at all.

KATIE SHEPARD is, in no particular order, a fangirl, a gamer, a bankruptcy lawyer, and a romance author. Born and raised in Texas, she frequently escapes to Montana to commune with the trees and woodland creatures, resembling a Disney princess in all ways except age, appearance, and musical ability. When not writing or making white-collar criminals cry at their depositions, she enjoys playing video games in her soft pants and watching sci-fi shows with her husband, two children, and very devoted cats.

VISIT KATIE SHEPARD ONLINE

KatieShepard.com

🦋 KatieShepardBooks

📷 KatieShepardBooks